PENGUIN CLASSICS

# THE ODYSSEY

The Greeks believed that the *Odyssey* was composed by Homer. In our ignorance of the man, his life and his work, we are free to believe it or not. Received opinion dates him *c.* 750–700 BC and places him in Ionia, the Greek-inhabited coast and islands off central western Turkey. The Greeks believed the same man composed the *Iliad*.

E. V. RIEU, editor of the Penguin Classics from 1944 to 1964, was a scholar of St Paul's School and of Balliol College, Oxford. He joined Methuen in 1923 and was Managing Director from 1933 to 1936, and then Academic and Literary Adviser. He was President of the Virgil Society in 1951 and Vice-President of the Royal Society of Literature in 1958. He was awarded an honorary D.Litt. by Leeds University in 1949 and the CBE in 1953. Among his publications are *The Flattered Flying Fish and Other Poems*, and translations of the *Odyssey*, the *Iliad*, Virgil's *Pastoral Poems*, the *Voyage of Argo* by Apollonius of Rhodes and *The Four Gospels* in the Penguin Classics. He died in 1972.

D. C. H. RIEU, his son, read Classics and English at Queen's College, Oxford. He joined the West Yorkshire Regiment and was wounded at Cheren in 1941, and awarded the Military Cross. He was Headmaster of Simon Langton Grammar School, Canterbury, from 1955 to 1977. He translated the *Acts of the Apostles* in the Penguin Classics, and revised his father's *Odyssey*, in consultation with Dr Peter Jones, and with him has revised his father's translation of the *Iliad*. On retirement he worked for Cruse Bereavement Counselling and for the Samaritans. He has been in Subud for many years, and has written books and articles about it, beginning with *A Life Within a Life* in 1963.

A Cambridge graduate with a London doctorate on Homer, PETER JONES was a schoolteacher and senior lecturer in Classics at the University of Newcastle upon Tyne. He is now a writer, broadcaster and journalist. Appointed MBE in 1983, he is Spokesman for the national Co-ordinating Committee for Classics and founder with Jeannie Cohen of the charity *Friends of Classics*. He wrote the *QED* and *Eureka* series for the *Daily Telegraph*, both now published by Duckworth as *Learn Latin* and *Learn Ancient Greek*. Duckworth have also published his *Classics in Translation* (another *Telegraph* series) and *Ancient and Modern* (from his weekly column in the *Spectator*). He has co-authored the *Reading Greek* and *Reading Latin* series for Cambridge, and published books, articles and commentaries on Homer.

HOMER

# The Odyssey

*Translated by* E. V. RIEU
*Revised translation by* D. C. H. RIEU
*Introduction by* PETER JONES

PENGUIN BOOKS

PENGUIN BOOKS

Published by the Penguin Group
Penguin Books Ltd, 80 Strand, London WC2R 0RL, England
Penguin Putnam Inc., 375 Hudson Street, New York, New York 10014, USA
Penguin Books Australia Ltd, 250 Camberwell Road, Camberwell, Victoria 3124, Australia
Penguin Books Canada Ltd, 10 Alcorn Avenue, Toronto, Ontario, Canada M4V 3B2
Penguin Books India (P) Ltd, 11, Community Centre, Panchsheel Park, New Delhi – 110 017, India
Penguin Books (NZ) Ltd, Cnr Rosedale and Airborne Roads, Albany, Auckland, New Zealand
Penguin Books (South Africa) (Pty) Ltd, 24 Sturdee Avenue, Rosebank 2196, South Africa

Penguin Books Ltd, Registered Offices: 80 Strand, London WC2R 0RL, England

www.penguin.com

E. V. Rieu's translation first published 1946
Revised translation first published 1991
Reprinted with new Preface and updated Further Reading, 2003

053



Set in 10.25/12.25 pt PostScript Adobe Sabon
Typeset by Rowland Phototypesetting Ltd, Bury St Edmunds, Suffolk
Printed and bound in Great Britain by Clays Ltd, Elcograf S.p.A.



ISBN-13: 978–0–14–044911–2

www.greenpenguin.co.uk

# Contents

# Preface

My father E. V. Rieu's translation of the *Odyssey* was published in 1946, as the first of the Penguin Classics series which he founded with Sir Allen Lane. His vision was to make available to the ordinary reader, in good modern English, the great classics of every language. This vision, shadowy at first, came to him in the early days of the Second World War, when he used to sit in the drawing-room after supper with the *Odyssey* on his lap, translating aloud to his wife and daughters, while the bombs fell on London. When he retired as general editor of the series he had searched out the scholars and men of letters he wanted as translators and seen through to publication about 160 books.

What need was there for revision of his *Odyssey*? It has many virtues. It has *joie de vivre*. It does not read like a translation: there is no sign of a tortured struggle with the Greek. There are no echoes of the Authorized Version or other archaisms. It has been enjoyed by millions. But there were areas that I felt might be revised in order to ensure that the translation continued to be as accessible and useful to modern readers as it had been to EVR's first readers.

EVR sometimes elaborated Homer's poetry. Thus the simple Greek simply translated: 'As soon as Dawn appeared, fresh and rosy-fingered', is translated by EVR as 'No sooner had the tender Dawn shown her roses in the East'. And 'When the bright sun climbs the starry sky' becomes 'When the bright sun climbs the sky and puts the stars to flight'. Also some of EVR's modernisms seemed out of place: for example, 'Amphinomus carried the day and the meeting adjourned' (echoes of the boardroom). So do catch-phrases like 'I could fancy him' and 'It's the kind of thing that gives a girl a good name in the town.' Some of his racier colloquialisms, however, I have kept, provided they come in dialogue; the narrative passages call for a degree of formality. Poseidon, in his fury with Odysseus, says (literal translation): 'I mean to give him his fill of trouble yet.' EVR's 'bellyful of trouble' is much livelier – and typical of the irascible Poseidon. Again, Antinous, fuming, refers to Telemachus as 'that young puppy' (literally 'young boy'). Absolutely right, and I keep it.

EVR also introduced an element of courtesy into orders and requests alien to the Greeks, who gave their orders crisply and bluntly. EVR sometimes prefaced such orders with a 'Kindly' or 'Be good enough to'.

Homer often brings gods and goddesses into the story, but when he brings in an anonymous god, EVR always cut him. Thus 'a god put this into my mind' became 'it occurred to me', and 'supposing he were to turn up from somewhere, brought by some god' became 'supposing he were to blow in from somewhere'.

Finally there is the question of Homer's oft-repeated words, his 'formulae'. First, the formulaic adjectives – resourceful Odysseus, wise Penelope, thoughtful Telemachus. EVR frequently omits these altogether or turns them into adverbs or clauses – 'Telemachus replied thoughtfully' or 'Telemachus showed his judgement when he replied.' I kept these epithets: Homer used them to create an atmosphere of the heroic past. He regards the qualities described as inalienable, permanent attributes of his characters. Penelope is always wise even when she is being rather silly; Telemachus is basically thoughtful even when he is committing a brutal act. Secondly, there are the formulaic sentences, like the one about Dawn mentioned already, or 'The sun went down, and all the ways grew dark.' That is beautiful. These sentences come and go like familiar friends. The one formulaic sentence I did not keep, either in wording or positioning, is the standard formula introducing a speech: 'The patient good Odysseus answering him said: "Friends . . ."' That to me sounds archaic. I translate '"Friends," replied the patient good Odysseus . . .'

When Peter Jones and I set out to revise my father's translation in 1991 we determined to retain the *joie de vivre* of his version. Our alterations were in fact puny compared with his towering skill. We frequently used to marvel at his mastery of words and gape with admiration at the way he conveyed the subtle nuances of a complex passage. I was reminded of Keats's sonnet 'On First Looking into Chapman's Homer' and felt 'like stout Cortez, when with eagle eyes/He stared at the Pacific – and all his men/Looked at each other with a wild surmise'. My wife worked closely with me throughout in the search for the right words, and often came up with the perfect suggestion. My sister, Rosamund Whalley, also acted as a valuable scrutineer.

DCHR

*2002*

# Introduction

The *Odyssey* is the second work of Western literature (the *Iliad* is the first). The ancient world agreed almost unanimously that both epics were the work of Homer. The *Odyssey* – the return of Odysseus from Troy to reclaim his threatened home on Ithaca – is a superb *story*, rich in character, adventure and incident, reconciling reality with fantasy, the heroic with the humble, the intimate with the divine, and making the household (Greek *oikos*), rather than the battlefield, the centre of its world. The story – its structure, content and characters – occupies pp. xii–xxvii, xxxv–xxxviii, and xliii–xlv of this Introduction.

The *Odyssey* was composed probably towards the end of the eighth century BC somewhere along the Greek-occupied seaboard of western Turkey (Greek 'Ionia'). It was not written down to be read, but was composed either orally, or at least in an oral style, and recited to listening audiences. There is a debate about the extent to which an epic this size could have been orally *improvised* – do 'memorization' or 'recollection' come in here? – and how far writing may have played some part in its production. These issues – and the question of how to read such a poem – are discussed on pp. xxvii–xxxi, xxxviii–xl, and xli–xliii of the Introduction.

The *Odyssey*, like the *Iliad*, seems to tell of a heroic past quite unlike anything in existence in the iron-age eighth century BC. It is a world of powerful kings, like Agamemnon and Nestor, living in vast, wealthy palaces, like Mycenae and Pylos, and in charge of huge armies wielding *bronze*, not iron, weapons. Mycenae and Pylos have in fact been excavated, and it is clear that their power (and that of all similar palaces) collapsed some four hundred years prior to Homer, in the twelfth century BC (the end of the so-called Mycenaean age of Greece). This issue is discussed on pp. xxxi–xxxv of the Introduction.

# HOMER'S *ODYSSEY*: STRUCTURE, CONTENT AND CHARACTER

## The *Odyssey* in Temporal Sequence

The time-span of the *Odyssey* is very large. It refers, in fact, to the period from the youth of Odysseus' father Laertes to Odysseus' death (predicted by Teiresias at **11**.134–7[1]): a period of at least sixty, perhaps as much as eighty, years. But, as Aristotle tells us (*Poetics* 1459a), Homer is unique in comparison with other epic poets in that he concentrates on *one* moment only within a complete epic cycle. In the *Iliad*, for example, Homer concentrates on the wrath of Achilles, in the ninth year of the Trojan War. In the *Odyssey*, he concentrates on the moment of Odysseus' return, twenty years after he had left his wife Penelope and their newly born son Telemachus in Ithaca to go to fight at Troy. Since this decision of Homer lands him with considerable problems – most obviously, how do you describe everything that happened to Odysseus and to his palace on Ithaca during his twenty-year absence? – I begin by outlining the story of the *Odyssey* as Homer would have recited it had he decided to tell it *all* in its *temporal* sequence.

(Where complete books of the *Odyssey* are not being cited, I have split the story into subsections by Roman numerals (I, II, III).)

I. Laertes, King of Ithaca and married to Anticleia (**11**.85), a great fighter in his youth (**24**.375–82), purchases a slave-woman, Eurycleia (**1**.430–31).

1. References in bold numbers (e.g. **23**) are to books of the *Odyssey*. Numbers after the bold numbers, in ordinary type, are Greek line numbers, which are used throughout this edition.

II. Laertes and Anticleia have a son. He is named Odysseus by his grandfather Autolycus, and looked after by Eurycleia (19.409, 482–3). Odysseus is raised with his younger sister Ctimene and another family slave Eumaeus (15.361–70). Laertes trains Odysseus in husbandry (24.336–44). On a boar-hunt with Autolycus' sons, he is badly wounded in the thigh (19.413–66).

III. Odysseus loves hunting, especially with his dog Argus (17.291–317). When he is sent on a mission to Messene (21.13–41), he meets Iphitus, son of Eurytus, who gives him a special bow as a gift. Odysseus uses this in Ithaca but takes it nowhere else.

IV. Odysseus becomes the wise and gentle King of Ithaca (2.233–4), and marries Penelope, daughter of the Spartan King Icarius. He builds their bedroom and constructs a bed around the bole of an olive-tree (23.183–204).

V. Although not eager to join the expedition to Troy (24.115–19), Odysseus does so just after his son Telemachus is born (4.112). An omen accompanies his departure (2.161–76). As he leaves, he tells Penelope that, if he does not return, she is to remarry when Telemachus comes of age (18.257–70). He leaves Mentor (or Laertes?) in charge of the palace (2.226–7).

VI. Odysseus has various adventures in Troy (4.235–89, 8.75–82); other heroes are killed (3.103–12, e.g. Achilles, Ajax, Patroclus, Antilochus); Troy falls to Odysseus' wooden-horse trick (8.500–520, 11.523–32).

VII. The Greeks depart for home, and various adventures befall them (3.130 ff.). In particular, Nestor, King of Pylos, arrives home safely and soon (3.115–83); the lesser Ajax is drowned, presumably for his seizure/rape of Cassandra at Athene's shrine in Troy, though Homer never mentions it (4.496–511); Menelaus, husband of Helen, has adventures at sea for eight years especially in Egypt (4.81 ff., 351 ff.); Agamemnon, leader of the expedition, arrives home in Argos to be killed by Aegisthus, lover of his wife Clytaemnestra; his death is avenged by his son Orestes eight years later (1.35–43, 4.512–37, 11.405–26). Odysseus has one false start leaving Troy before he eventually sets off (3.162–4).

9. For three years he is blown around the Mediterranean, experiencing adventures with the Cicones, the Lotus-eaters, the Cyclops Polyphemus (son of Poseidon, whom he blinds),

10. Aeolus the wind-god, the giant Laestrygonians (who destroy all his ships but his own), and the witch Circe, who sends him to the Underworld.

11. In the Underworld Odysseus consults the seer Teiresias in order to find out how to return home. He meets the ghost of his mother Anticleia, various celebrated women, some dead companions from Troy (Agamemnon, Achilles and Ajax) and sees other heroes in torment.

12. When he leaves Circe, he listens to the song of the Sirens, escapes Scylla and Charybdis and finally arrives on Thrinacia, the island of the sun-god. There his men refuse to heed Odysseus' warning not to eat the sun-god's cattle. His last ship is destroyed in the subsequent storm at sea, and Odysseus alone survives, being swept away to Ogygia, the island of the demi-goddess Calypso, where he is marooned for seven more years.

VIII. During the period that Odysseus has been away, his mother Anticleia has died (11.197–203, 15.358–80); Ctimene has left to be married (15.316–17); Eumaeus has been sent out to a country estate (15.368–70); and his father Laertes has retired to the country in grief (15.353–71, 11.187–96). In the seventeenth year of his absence, 108 suitors from Ithaca and surrounding lands take up permanent residence in the palace by day in an effort to persuade Penelope to marry one of them (2.89). Odysseus' growing son Telemachus (V) is helpless in the face of their superior numbers and has to watch them consuming his inheritance. Penelope delays the suitors' advances by the shroud trick (2.85–110).

1. In the twentieth year of Odysseus' absence, the gods convene a meeting and, on Athene's pleas, decide to order Calypso (12) to release Odysseus. Athene seeks to put some spirit into Telemachus and, disguised as an old friend of Odysseus (Mentes), arrives in Ithaca. She succeeds in her mission, and advises Telemachus to confront the suitors in public. If they still insist on staying, he is to visit his father's old friends Nestor, King of Pylos, and Menelaus, King of Sparta, to seek news of Odysseus.

2. Telemachus tries to stir the men of Ithaca to action against the suitors, but to no avail. He sets off secretly on the journey proposed by Athene. Athene accompanies him, disguised as Mentor (V).

3. Telemachus visits Nestor. First, he hears stories of other Greeks' returns (VI, VII), but nothing of Odysseus. Accompanied now not by Athene but by Nestor's son Peisistratus, he moves on to Sparta.

4. At Menelaus' palace he hears from both Menelaus and his wife Helen more stories of the returns of Greeks and of his father's exploits at Troy (VI, VII), and that his father is alive. Back in Ithaca, the suitors plan to ambush him on his return. Penelope is grief-stricken to hear of his departure.

5. After a second council of the gods, Hermes sets off for Ogygia, and Calypso releases Odysseus. Odysseus sails off, but the sea-god Poseidon, enraged that Odysseus blinded his son the Cyclops (9), creates a tremendous storm, which nearly kills him. He is finally swept ashore on the peninsula called Scherie, where the Phaeacians live.

6. Athene arranges that Nausicaa, daughter of the King Alcinous, should rescue him.

7. Odysseus makes his way to the palace, where he is kindly received, well looked after, and enjoys full Phaeacian hospitality.

8. During the next day's festivities, the Phaeacian bard Demodocus sings some stories of Odysseus' past adventures (VI). Alcinous enquires who he is and why he weeps. Odysseus announces himself and tells the story of his journey from Troy to Calypso (see 9, 10, 11, 12 above).

13. The Phaeacians load Odysseus with gifts and send him home. On his arrival in Ithaca, Athene meets him, warns him of the suitors, disguises him as an old beggar, and instructs him to visit Eumaeus (II, VIII).

14. Odysseus is welcomed by Eumaeus (who does not recognize him) and hears about events in the palace (VIII).

15. Athene summons Telemachus back from Sparta. He meets a prophet Theoclymenus, on the run for killing a man, and gives him refuge on board ship. Telemachus arrives home, avoids the suitors' ambush (4), disbands his crew, puts Theoclymenus in the care of a friend, and sets off for Eumaeus' hut. The beggar-Odysseus hears more news of Ithaca (VIII).

16. Telemachus sends Eumaeus off to town to tell Penelope of his arrival home. In Eumaeus' absence, Odysseus' disguise is temporarily lifted and he is reunited with his son. They plan their action against the suitors.

17. Telemachus reaches the hut and goes on ahead to the palace, followed by Odysseus and Eumaeus. Odysseus is recognized by his old hunting-dog Argus (III). Odysseus begs in the palace, and is attacked and insulted, but Penelope asks Eumaeus to arrange for him to meet her.

18. Odysseus beats up another beggar Irus, but remains on the receiving end of abuse and attacks. Penelope announces that she will remarry (V).

19. The planned meeting between Penelope and Odysseus takes place (17). Odysseus persuades her that he has heard of 'Odysseus', and the grateful Penelope orders Eurycleia to wash him. Eurycleia recognizes him by his scar collected during the boar-hunt (II), and is sworn to secrecy. Penelope, still in ignorance of the beggar's identity, announces that she will next day set up the trial of the bow and the axes: whoever can string Odysseus' bow (III) and shoot an arrow through the twelve axes will win her hand in marriage.

20. Odysseus and Telemachus remove all the weapons from the hall. In the morning the suitors return to feast and revel. Further insults are directed against Odysseus. He is introduced by Eumaeus to a friendly oxherd, Philoetius. Theoclymenus (15), in a ghastly vision, foretells the suitors' impending doom.

21. Penelope fetches the axes and bow. Telemachus sets up the trial and nearly strings the bow himself. The suitors fail. Odysseus reveals himself to Eumaeus and Philoetius and tells Eurycleia to bar the doors. Penelope retires to bed. He persuades the suitors to let him try the bow, strings it and shoots through the axes.

22. Odysseus, Telemachus, Eumaeus and Philoetius, first with bow and arrows, then with arms – and helped by Athene disguised as Mentor – slaughter the suitors. The house is cleansed, the faithless servants are hanged, and the faithful greet their lord.

23. Eurycleia wakens Penelope. She cannot believe that the beggar is Odysseus, but by testing him about the construction of their marriage bed (IV), she proves to her satisfaction that it is he. They make preparations to repel the suitors' relatives, and go to bed.

24. The ghosts of the suitors arrive in Hades, where Agamemnon and Achilles hear of Odysseus' triumph: Agamemnon praises Penelope, contrasting her with Clytaemnestra.

Odysseus is reunited with his father Laertes (I, II, VIII). The suitors' relatives gather to take revenge. After a brief engagement, Zeus and Athene intervene, and peace is restored in Ithaca.

IX. Odysseus will travel inland carrying an oar, until someone mistakes it for a winnowing fan. There he will sacrifice to Poseidon. He will return home to die in peaceful old age (11.119–37).

## Retrieving the Past

What stands out from this way of telling the story is the brilliant ingenuity with which Homer has engineered situations in which accounts of Odysseus' adventures and of developments on Ithaca during his absence can be plausibly given – not merely the great flashback of 9–12, but a host of smaller, highly significant, moments. And the more one thinks about it, the more difficult it becomes to envisage an *Odyssey* which *did* follow a purely temporal sequence of the sort given above. Consider an *Odyssey* which started in 1 with Odysseus leaving Troy. First, the adventures which the poet has put into Odysseus' mouth as a flashback in 9–12 would have to be narrated as a third-person narrative. ('First Odysseus went to X and then he went to Y', etc.) Consequently they would lose much of their excitement as a personal reminiscence, and of their significance as an extended exercise in heroic self-revelation. Second, once the hero had returned, it would be impossible to give the intensive treatment to Penelope, Telemachus, the suitors, and the effect of Odysseus' prolonged absence on the household that the poet achieves in his chosen version. One would not know what the hero was returning *to*, and why his return was so urgently needed. We would lose the rich and subtle characterization of, and interaction between, the people in the Ithaca to which he returns. Most of all, it would have become 'one damn thing after another': a sequence of events of the sort which Aristotle, by implication, so deprecated.

Seen in this light, Homer's decision to target the epic on the moment of Odysseus' return is a master-stroke. Far from losing perspective on the previous twenty years, the reader is endowed with a far sharper and more telling focus on it, because the events of the intervening years are selected by, and told through the mouths of, the characters themselves. What those twenty years *mean to them* is of far greater significance to the plot than simply 'what happened during Odysseus' absence'.

This rich interaction of past and present is one of the great glories of the *Odyssey*, and is an important component of the narrative's power and pathos. Consider three critical moments when the past thrillingly interlocks with the present. First, in Book 18, Penelope announces that she has made her decision to remarry. At the moment when we know Odysseus has returned and the signs that events are moving to a climax have never been better, this looks like an act of supreme folly (or disloyalty). But nothing can be more moving than the reason Penelope gives: when Odysseus left for Troy, she says, he took me by the hand and urged me (among other things) to remarry if he had not returned by the time his son (the newly born Telemachus) had reached manhood (V). Penelope acknowledges that her son is a grown man. Consequently, she must now remarry. In other words, it is her absolute fidelity to, and trust in, Odysseus' parting words to her, twenty years ago, that have brought about the decision so hateful to her (but which is going to mean, though she does not know it, reunion with her husband).

Second, the trial of the bow. Penelope decides to find a new husband by setting up the axes and challenging the suitors to string the bow and shoot an arrow through them. What this actually means is disputed: it is probable that Homer only dimly envisaged it (certainly no Greek artist that we know of depicted it). Now this bow has a long and compelling history. It belonged to Eurytus, and he was the great bowman who had been taught by the archer-god himself, Apollo (III). This was the bow that had come into Odysseus' hands when he was sent as a youth on an embassy to Messene: it was a guest-gift from Eurytus' son, Iphitus. But, as the poet gently says, Odysseus used it only for hunting and never took it to Troy (21.38–41). For twenty years it, and its arrows, have lain unused in Penelope's store-room. When she goes to fetch them, in a poignant gesture she lays them on her knees and weeps (21.55–6). It is as if she is saying her final farewell. The youthful Telemachus sets up the axes, and tries to string the bow himself. He would have done it, says Homer, if Odysseus had not stopped him: true son of his father (21.117–29). The suitors fail hopelessly. But when Odysseus finally gets his hands on his old bow, twenty years on, he checks it first for woodworm before stringing it like a singer stringing a lyre, and plucking it. It gives a swallow's note. Why a swallow? As every Greek knew, swallows migrate and return to the nest they previously inhabited. Odysseus aims and shoots through the axes (21.343–423). If Homer passes over the moment with supreme casualness, in his fashion, the reader cannot help but wonder whether, twenty years on, Odysseus will have lost his strength or his finesse. The lyre simile (21.405–9) is important. Apollo is god of the lyre. He is also god of the bow. And the day of the suitors' slaughter is Apollo's feast day (20.276–8).

Third, the recognition scene between Odysseus and Penelope. So persuasive is Odysseus in his disguise as a beggar – Penelope swallows completely his story that he was Aethon, brother of Idomeneus (19.165–88) – that she cannot bring herself to believe that this dirty beggar is her husband. She seeks therefore for a sign; and the sign she seeks relates to the bed which Odysseus himself constructed more than twenty years before when they were first married (IV). He had built the bedroom around the bole of an olive-tree, which formed one leg of their marriage-bed. Only Odysseus, she and a maid (Actoris) long since dead knew about it. So she innocently thanks the beggar for killing the suitors and says she will have the bed moved for him to sleep on. This bed has not been slept on for twenty years (Penelope sleeps upstairs in Odysseus' absence). When Odysseus explodes with indignation at how this could be, Penelope falls into his arms. The past has once again given the key to the present (23.171–209), as it does so often in the *Odyssey*. In an epic of return and recognition, how could it not? When Argus recognizes Odysseus, we go back to Odysseus' hunting days (17.291–317); when Eurycleia does, we go back to his naming ceremony (19.392–466); when Laertes does, we go back to the young Odysseus in his father's garden (24.336–44).

## Telemachus

One moment that Homer does not precisely record for us is the moment when the suitors invade the house. We know they arrived in the seventeenth year of Odysseus' absence (VIII), but that is about all. Why? One reason must be that Homer is interested primarily in the *consequences* of their intrusion, because this is what makes the return of Odysseus so urgent. But I suspect he did not know exactly how the suitors came to dominate the palace as they do in the twentieth year, and in particular, he would have been hard pressed to have depicted their arrival in detail without explaining why everyone acquiesced in it. What, in particular, was Laertes doing? Why did not Mentor summon help (V)? Homer suppresses these questions because it is not in his interest to have them asked. In particular, he has seen what a rich and complex situation can be created in Ithaca by thrusting the growing Telemachus into the limelight, and this requires that Odysseus' father Laertes, whom one would expect in normal circumstances to take over when his son left for Troy, be shunted quietly off the stage (VIII). With Laertes gone, the scene is now set for exploring the relationship between Penelope, the object of the suitors' desires and reason why the household's goods are being destroyed, and a Telemachus who never knew his father (V), but is growing to manhood and finds his inheritance being destroyed by a ruthless band of young men whom he is powerless to prevent courting his mother and wasting his substance.

It is worth remarking the skill with which Homer has set this situation up. Odysseus *could* return to a situation in which Telemachus is too young or too disaffected to help him. Homer does not go down that road. In so choosing, he presents himself with a problem: how can he make Telemachus interesting enough without either taking the limelight off Odysseus or reducing Telemachus to a mere cipher when his father returns? The answer is masterly: he makes the growing up of Telemachus an *issue* of the epic. Is this young man fit to be the son of such a hero? If so, how will he prove it? Homer is less successful in solving a similar problem with the companions of Odysseus in

9–12 – a generally rather colourless crew. On the other hand, it must be remembered that it is Odysseus who is 'telling' the story at this point: no one will steal *his* limelight.

Having taken the decision, Homer has another problem to solve. For how long must Odysseus be away so that his son can reach maturity? If his son is (say) aged seven when Odysseus leaves, Odysseus will have to be away thirteen years. Ten at Troy, three on the high seas . . . excellent. Again, Homer ignores that easy option. Had he chosen it, Telemachus would be a young man with memories of his great father, with a faint outline image of the example he had to imitate. Again, when the recognition came (16), it would be far less dramatic. So Homer elects to make Telemachus a newly born babe when Odysseus leaves for Troy (V). It is a brilliant decision. The young man will never have *known* his father, merely *heard* of him from others' lips. The reunion scene when it does come will be that much more poignant. But to engineer this, Homer has to find some way of keeping Odysseus away for twenty years. Hence, it appears, Calypso, with whom Odysseus was conveniently trapped for seven years.

One aspect of the story of Telemachus which causes problems for contemporary readers is the interminable speeches about the returns of heroes and the deeds of Odysseus to which Telemachus patiently listens on his embassy to Nestor in 3 and Menelaus in 4. Ostensibly, his purpose is to find out about Odysseus – is he alive or not? These heroes from the Trojan War may be able to help him. But Athene has another purpose in sending him – to gain him a good reputation. The word used – *kleos* – means, in fact, 'that true account of yourself which will live on after death' and is what every hero strives for. So, first, what Telemachus hears from Nestor and Menelaus (and Athene in disguise in 1 and 2) is that he has all the attributes of his father: his looks, stature and way with words. Second, the context for these remarks is the return of the great heroes of the Trojan War and the exploits of Odysseus. These fill out and complement the *Iliad* story (which ends before Troy even falls), but also establish for Telemachus a sense of the world which heroes inhabit. The young hero learns from what other heroes have to tell him, as much as from acting himself. Moreover, both Nestor and Menelaus (like Athene) challenge Telemachus with the example of Orestes. When Orestes' father Agamemnon, on return from the Trojan War, had been killed by Aegisthus, lover of his wife Clytaemnestra, Orestes had, in time, taken revenge on both of them. Could Telemachus match that example and take his revenge on the suitors who threatened himself, his mother and his livelihood? The climax of Telemachus' story comes at 21.128 when Homer says he would have strung his father's bow had Odysseus not stopped him, and at 24.513, when Laertes rejoices to see his son and grandson competing in valour against each other.

## Penelope

Penelope is a woman in conflict: with herself – should she stay or remarry?; with Telemachus – who is the master of this house?; with her servants, and with the suitors. The constant pressure under which she lives has the effect of turning her into a woman who hangs grimly on to the past, and finds solace and comfort only in the world of sleep and dreams, though even these can be painful for her. She clutches at every straw of hope (though she denies it) and fluctuates between hope that Odysseus may return and absolute certainty that he will not. But her intelligence and beauty are never in doubt, as the suitors acknowledge (2.116–22), and her loyalty to Odysseus remains constant, even up to the moment when she agrees to remarry (see p. xix above). The trick involving Laertes' shroud which keeps the suitors at bay for a while – and did she hope that the bow trial might do likewise? – shows that she is by no means helpless, and her trick to discover whether the beggar really is Odysseus is worthy of Odysseus himself (who is on the receiving end of it).

## The Suitors

The suitors themselves, apart from the two leading contenders Antinous and Eurymachus, and the 'good' suitor Amphinomus, are not clearly characterized. There are 108 of them, coming from Ithaca and the surrounding islands and mainland. For all their wickedness – and the moral lesson which Homer inserts into 1.1–43 leaves us in no doubt about it (see p. xxxvi below) – they are the leading young men of Ithaca, as Agamemnon comments at 24.107. They have taken over Odysseus' household in a gross perversion of the convention of *xenia* (the obligation to entertain outsiders) and their aim is to get their hands on its wealth and power. It is never precisely clear how marriage to Penelope will bring that about, but marriage to her is their immediate goal.

Something must be said briefly about *xenia*, this obligatory bond of solidarity between insiders and outsiders. It is noticeable how many such scenes there are in the *Odyssey*. Telemachus entertains Athene in 1, Nestor entertains Telemachus in 3, Menelaus entertains him in 4, Calypso welcomes Hermes in 5, Nausicaa and then the Phaeacians welcome Odysseus in 6 and 7, Cyclops treats Odysseus and his men to his special brand of *xenia* in 9, as do Aeolus and Circe in 10. Eumaeus is the soul of hospitality to the beggar Odysseus in 14 and 15. Care of strangers, as of suppliants, is Zeus' business (6.207–8): there is an obligation to help the unfortunate, as Menelaus implies (4.31–6). The suitors' wanton and conscious destruction of Odysseus' household and reckless disregard for the bond of *xenia* are enough to justify their deaths (see p. xlv below).

Of the two leading suitors, Antinous is vicious and uncompromising, Eurymachus oily and hypocritical (the contrasted pairing is typical of Homer: see p. xxxviii, 2, below). The most significant characteristic of the two, as of all the suitors, is that they constantly think one thing and say another (e.g. 17.66). Such duplicity is untypical of Homeric characters. In the *Iliad*, heroic thought and action are all of a piece: once a hero thinks of something, he does it. This is what gives the heroes so much of their uncomplicated and forthright liveliness. It is a mark of the suitors' villainy that they are not such simple creatures. This is why Odysseus and Telemachus need to scheme and deceive as they do in order to match, and then beat, them; hence the disguise of Odysseus, the patience of Telemachus, the shroud trick of Penelope (see especially 16.266–307).

It is a characteristic that has not always met with favour. Odysseus himself, as we shall see (pp. xliii–xlv below), has received a varying press, from the time when Homer first moulded him down to James Joyce and the twentieth century. But simplicity, straightforwardness and plain honest dealing *are* found in the *Odyssey*, not so much in the persons of the main characters as in the humbler supporting roles. Another of the great glories of the *Odyssey*, memorably matched in the *Iliad* in its similes, is the celebration of the humble life which surfaces in the stories of the faithful servants of Odysseus – especially Eumaeus and Eurycleia.

## Eurycleia and Eumaeus

Eurycleia was bought as a young girl by Laertes at a price of twenty oxen: a high valuation. Laertes honoured her equally with his wife, but never slept with her (for fear of his lady's displeasure, as Homer says: 1.429–33). Eumaeus was the son of Ctesius, king of two cities in a place called Syrie by Homer. Phoenicians on a trading mission there corrupted a slave-girl of the household to run away with them, and she took the little Eumaeus with her (he would, she said, fetch a good price). When the Phoenicians arrived in Ithaca, Laertes purchased the young boy (15.403–84). Eumaeus was raised by Odysseus' mother, Anticleia, together with her young daughter (Odysseus' sister), Ctimene. When the sister was married off, Eumaeus was sent to a country property. But after the death of Anticleia and the arrival of the suitors in the palace, Eumaeus has had no occasion to go there. His farm had flourished (15.353–79), and he could even afford a slave, Mesaulius (14.449–52).

Eurycleia and Eumaeus are clearly not slaves of the sort we associate with American plantation slavery of the nineteenth century. Indeed, slavery of that sort is unknown in the Greek world. The system Homer describes is patriarchal: a slave is a valued piece of property, attached to the family to serve it in any way the master prescribes. Homer's comment that Laertes did not sleep with Eurycleia suggests it was common to use slaves sexually. It was certainly the norm for female slaves to wet-nurse children, as Eurycleia did both Odysseus and Telemachus, and it is Eurycleia who demands that Odysseus' grandfather Autolycus name the baby. She even makes a suggestion herself, irreproducible in English, as to what the child's name should be: 'he was *Polyēratos*' ('Much-Prayed-For'), she says (19.401–4). Eurycleia was loved and trusted by Telemachus (it is only to her, not Penelope, that he confides his plans to travel abroad at 2.348–81). She is able to comfort Penelope when she hears the news (4.742–58). The foot-washing episode at 19.335–502 splendidly illustrates her shrewdness and tact, and her stumbling run up the stairs to tell Penelope that her husband has returned is one of the most memorable scenes in Homer (23.1–84).

Eumaeus is drawn with equal liveliness. Distant from the family he may be, but his grief at the loss of Odysseus is no less real for that (14 *passim*), and when Telemachus returns from his travels, Homer describes how Eumaeus greets him as a father greets a son. The simile is doubly poignant, since the meeting takes place in the presence of the beggar-Odysseus, who has not set eyes on his son since he left him as a new-born baby in Ithaca twenty years before (16.1–21). Whereas some of Odysseus' servants chose to defect to the suitors (Melanthius and Melantho are picked out for special mention by Homer), Eumaeus has remained loyal, guarding his master's wealth as best he can in the face of the suitors' depredations. Most of all, Eumaeus has a keen sense of right and wrong, and his simple piety and open, uncomplicated generosity to the beggar-Odysseus (although he is hardly the wealthiest of men) make us warm to him (14.1–108). This, our first glimpse of Eumaeus, is a brilliant cameo. Eumaeus and Eurycleia are, as Norman Austin says, 'stalwart paradigms of order' in a palace dominated by disorderly suitors. They represent what the palace used to be like – and will be again, when its master is restored.

Slavery is an abomination to us, and it is easy to hold in contempt slaves like Eurycleia and Eumaeus who acquiesce in their state. Such a view would have been incomprehensible to Homer and his audience, for whom slavery was a condition of existence and the inevitable consequence of pirate raiding and defeat in war (which explains why there are more female than male slaves: the males (except the very old and young) would all have been killed off – unless, of course, Homer intentionally removed the male slaves to increase the isolation of Odysseus in the battle in the hall against the suitors). If loyalty is rewarded, disloyalty is ferociously punished (22.461–77). No slave would have expected otherwise. It is wholly appropriate that Eumaeus and Philoetius should join Telemachus in the execution of the faithless maidservants and in the gruesome mutilation of Melanthius.

## ORAL POETRY

It is generally agreed that the *Iliad* and *Odyssey* were composed in the *style* of oral poetry. Whether they were *actually* orally composed is a matter of some debate. Since writing, developed from the Phoenician script, became increasingly accessible in Greece from about 700 BC,[1] and we date the *Odyssey* to about the same time, it is possible that Homer was literate, and used writing to help him construct, perhaps even compose, his epics. However that may be, the *style* of the poetry is oral.

Oral poetry was chanted to a lyre (*kitharis*, 8.67–9), which helped sustain rhythm and metre. It is distinguished from written poetry largely by the extent of its verbal repetitiveness. To compose orally in the complex metre of epic (hexameters), the poet needs a stock of prepackaged but highly flexible words and phrases ('formulae'), sentences, even complete scenes ('type'-scenes), to fit the metre, which can be adapted to whatever context the poet desires. This technique of oral composition is *learned* (one imagines long apprenticeships, attached to a master bard) and is very largely *traditional*, i.e. it has been handed down – with epic subject-matter too – over many generations.

These two characteristics of oral poetry account for two features of Homeric epic. First, every new reader of Homer is struck by the frequency with which Odysseus is 'resourceful',

1. As a result of recent analysis, some scholars date our earliest example of writing to *c.* 800 BC.

Penelope 'wise', Telemachus 'sensible', Dawn 'rosy-fingered', and how often the same actions are described in virtually the same words (see, for example, the scenes of feasting at 1.136–42, 4.52 ff., 7.172 ff., 10.368 ff., 15.135 ff., 17.91 ff.). This is the inevitable consequence of an oral style of composition. The new reader may find such repetitions odd to start with – is Telemachus *really* as 'wise/sensible/thoughtful' as he is made out to be in all his words and actions? – but should remember that these epithets describe *innate* qualities, rather as we should not hesitate to talk of a 'fast car' even when it was parked. In fact one soon gets used to the repetitions and begins to enjoy them: their effect is to remind us of the permanent, eternal qualities of the people and objects so described, and to reinforce our own sense of pleasure at the repeated, relaxing routines of existence.

The second feature will not be as apparent as the first. Since oral composition is traditional, much of the subject-matter of the poems has been handed down over hundreds of years. The result of this is that the poems as we have them do not faithfully reflect the cultural and social conditions of any particular time, but rather an amalgam of such conditions, spread over hundreds of years, some going back as far as the twelfth century BC. For example, the eighth century BC in which Homer lived was an iron age, but weapons and armour are constantly referred to as bronze. This reflects the bronze-age twelfth-century world. But when Homeric heroes die, they are not buried, as twelfth-century custom demanded, but cremated – the contemporary practice of the eighth-century world. It is as well to say here that the more we come to know about oral poetry, the clearer it becomes that the oral poet reflects his own society to a much greater degree than we had previously imagined. It is very difficult to believe that the *Iliad* and *Odyssey* should reflect anything of value to historians about the world which they seem to wish to describe: that of the great heroes of the bronze age and of the Trojan War, some five hundred years earlier.

However the poet learned the business of becoming a professional bard, he must in the process have fully assimilated the technique of oral reproduction of epic poetry, becoming master of the formulae, whole lines and type-scenes which allowed him to recite in the first place. He must have been *able* to improvise too, if required. But improvisation should surely not preclude intensive prior thought and rehearsal, even elements of recollection and memorization too, and, as we have seen, writing may have played a part somewhere.

But what was he to sing *about*? The tradition provided him with his material. In our *Odyssey* Phemius sings about the returns of heroes from Troy (1.326–7); and Nestor and Menelaus tell stories of heroes' returns (3.103 ff., 254 ff.; 4.81 ff., 351 ff.). (Nestor's is particularly confused, as if the stories were well known and could be drastically shortened.) Helen and Menelaus tell stories of Odysseus' exploits at Troy (4.235 ff., 266 ff.), and Demodocus the blind bard in Phaeacia sings of the quarrel between Odysseus and Achilles (8.73 ff., a unique story, occurring nowhere else in Greek literature) and of the wooden horse (8.499 ff.), as well as of the seduction of Aphrodite by Ares and their eventual entrapment by Aphrodite's husband Hephaestus (8.266 ff.). As well as stories about Troy and its aftermath, we know of other epic 'cycles' about, for example, the Titans, Jason and the Argonauts, and Oedipus.

But there was no law that forced the poet to stick to material within the traditional story. It is, for example, clear that the poet has introduced all sorts of non-Odyssean material into the *Odyssey*. The Ares–Aphrodite story just mentioned is obviously one. Calypso is probably an invention to allow time for Telemachus to grow up (see p. xxii above). Sometimes the joins in such material show. For example, the tales which Odysseus tells in 9–12 were almost certainly adapted from the Jason/Argonaut saga (Circe, the Wandering Rocks, the Sirens and Scylla and Charybdis were all probably Argonautic adventures before they became Odyssean ones too; cf. 12.70). The result is that in an epic where Poseidon is the main antagonist, Odysseus' men are finally destroyed by the sun-god. Again, consider the effect of the bow-contest upon the narrative. Athene is Odysseus' great patron, but the bow is Apollo's instrument: consequently, it is not until Odysseus has used up the arrows (22.116–25) that Athene enters the fray (22.205–6).

What we have to imagine then is a bard who is the absolute master of the technique of oral reproduction of traditional epic tales, and has at his disposal a large range of traditional material. Over a long period of time, and with much experimentation, he gradually welds this material into an epic the size of the *Odyssey*.

But to be sung to whom? And in what context? The *Iliad* (*c.* 15,000 lines) and the *Odyssey* (*c.* 12,000 lines) are uniquely massive. They would each have taken between twenty and thirty hours to sing. Who could possibly listen to them? We do not know, but the evidence of the activity of the bards in the *Odyssey* inclines me to believe that the context must be a royal palace, the audience the dining nobles. Encouraged by the stability of his employment and the applause of his audience, Homer set out to create a uniquely massive epic, and night after night, after dinner, regaled his masters with the developing story, in suitable 'bites'. The finished product – if the poet understood such a concept – must have been years in the making. I for one cannot see any other likely context in eighth-century Greece where an endeavour of this size and intricacy could be possible.

This raises another large and awesome problem. If Homer was in fact an oral poet, how did the poems come to be written down, and – given the freedom with which the oral poet adapts his material – what relation does our version bear to any version that Homer sang? Even if one believes that Homer could write, the problem will not go away. In the 550s BC the Athenian tyrant Peisistratus is said to have produced a definitive text of the Homeric epic for recitation at the great All-Athenian (Panathenaic) festival which he instituted. That suggests that there were many versions of 'Homer' in circulation at the time, and it is just as likely that there were alternative *Homeric* as well as *non-Homeric* versions. Consequently the issue of whether Homer could write is not central to the problem of authenticity. Besides, it is doubtful whether a bard who freely adapted others' material and saw his own equally freely adapted would have understood the concept of a single, definitive version. On the other hand, of course, a Homer who had been working up his uniquely complex and massive version over many years, possibly with the help of writing, may well have had a greater sense of a definitive version than the more typical travelling bard, orally improvising and adapting his far shorter songs to the needs of whatever audience he could gather.

## HOMER AND HISTORY

The Mycenaean age of Greece, so called after Mycenae, one of its leading power-centres, was a bronze age. This world flourished from the sixteenth to the twelfth century BC, when it collapsed, for reasons which are not entirely clear. It was a civilization centred on great palaces like those of Mycenae and Pylos, ruled by powerful and wealthy kings. It was aggressively expansionist, conquering Crete and taking over its centre Cnossus in the fourteenth century BC and (as the archaeological record shows) trading vigorously as far west as Spain, as far east as Syria and the Black Sea, and with contacts probably as far north as the Baltic, as far south as Africa.

Moreover, it was a civilization which knew writing. The script, now called Linear B, was preserved for us on clay tablets baked hard in the fires that destroyed the palaces, and subsequently excavated in their thousands. In 1952 it was discovered that Linear B was in fact a form of Greek, and since then the work of translating and making sense of it has gone on apace. The clay tablets have turned out to contain not literature, but the record of the economic transactions of the palace societies where they have been dug up (largely in Mycenaean Cnossus and Pylos). It is this world that Homer purports to be recording. Consequently, it may be significant that, in Homer, writing is mentioned but once, and there is no indication at all that his heroes had an economic *apparat* of such forbidding complexity and range as the Mycenaeans'. Perhaps such details are not the sort of thing that epic poetry would preserve anyway (heroes have better things to do than record that year's wool-tally). Perhaps they have been forgotten. At all events, the Linear B script died with the collapse of Mycenaean civilization in the twelfth century, and for four hundred years Greece was illiterate.

In 1870 the German adventurer Heinrich Schliemann dug

into a mound in modern Hisarlik in the north-west corner of Turkey. It lies in an area known since ancient times as the Troad, where Greeks and Romans alike located Homer's Troy (Hisarlik was known as 'Ilium' from at least the fourth century BC); there were two rivers near by, called, like Homer's, Scamander and Simoeis; the site lay on a plain, near the ancient (not the modern) coastline. No wonder that, when Schliemann discovered an ancient strongly fortified citadel there, he thought that he had discovered Troy. And it is perfectly possible that he had. This may well be the Troy that Greeks besieged in the thirteenth century and took after ten years, to become the subject of song for future generations.

It is equally possible that it is not. It must be stated firmly that place-names themselves mean nothing, since later generations were bound to try to identify the site of Homer's epics (we do the same, with about as much success, with for example the King Arthur legends). If Homer's descriptions of the walls and gates of Troy square with those discovered at Hisarlik – and in places they can be made to match – it has to be asked how specific the description has to be for a match to be certain (the argument takes the form of the fallacy: 'Homer says Troy has a sloping wall: this town has a sloping wall: therefore this is Troy'). Dates too are troublesome. Of the two main candidates for Homer's Troy, Troy level 7a seems to have been sieged and fired *c.* 1140 BC, by which time Mycenaean power had collapsed. Troy 6 was destroyed *c.* 1250, but probably by earthquake. Finally, there is no evidence that *Greeks* besieged Hisarlik, let alone Mycenaean Greeks.

But even if Schliemann's Troy was the site of a thirteenth-century Trojan war, everything we know about the transmission of oral poetry argues that Homer's retelling of tales originating in the thirteenth century can bear virtually no resemblance to what happened to Troy. Oral poets exploit traditional material to please their contemporary audience. Five hundred years of crowd-pulling, not to mention five hundred years of pressure exerted by traditional story-patterns, folk-tales and new material (especially from the east) would have ensured that no Odysseus-sprung-to-life would have recognized anything resembling the truth in Homer's retelling of the heroic adventures of the past.

Homer's epics are in fact far more likely to reflect his own world than that of the thirteenth century. That raises a large and interesting question: what is it about the eighth-century world that makes epics about Troy so important to it? Since the dialect of and locational knowledge shown by the poems suggest strongly that they were composed on or off the western coast of Greek-inhabited Ionia, not on the Greek mainland, it may well be that the Greeks who had come over to settle there since 1000 felt some special sympathy for epics about Greek triumphs in Ionia and successful returns back home to Greece. And it is conceivable that Homer himself knew Hisarlik and constructed his epic around its ruins. But that in itself is no evidence that there was a 'historical' Trojan war or that it took place there.

The eighth-century Greek world experienced dramatic growth and expansion. The collapse of Mycenaean civilization in the twelfth century had heralded a 'dark age': the destruction of the great palaces, the loss of writing, a dramatic fall in population, and general cultural and economic impoverishment. True, this is not the *universal* picture. On Lefkandi, for example, in Euboea, a massive heroic shrine, or possibly residential building, dating to 1000, has been uncovered, together with burial complexes filled with goods of eastern origin; and a large adjoining settlement still awaits excavation. Here at least, even during these 'dark ages', some people had the resources to celebrate the death of a lord with a wealthy funeral, and the labour-force to construct a building uniquely massive for its time (though it may be that archaeologists of earlier generations, lacking contemporary technology, have missed identifying such buildings because the materials out of which they were made – mud-brick, wood and thatch – can melt unidentifiably into the ground).

But whatever lessons Lefkandi may yet have to teach us about the 'dark ages', archaeology, especially of cemetery sites, testifies to a huge population explosion in the eighth-century Greek world, heavy colonization east to the islands and mainland of Ionia and the Black Sea, renewed contacts with the east, the introduction of writing, and most of all the establishment of large numbers of settlements. These clusters of villages, probably joining together for mutual self-protection, in some cases even fortifying themselves, present a vision of a society quite different from that of the Mycenaean world, where the great local palace and its overlord dominated and controlled the outlying settlements. When we observe that temple construction and the establishment of cults to a city deity consistently begin in such sites in the eighth century, we have good evidence for the beginnings of that sense of community solidarity and self-identification which act as the precursors of the tightly knit communities known as the *poleis* (singular *polis*), 'city-states', of fifth-century classical Greece, where democracy was invented.

How does Homer's *Odyssey* fit into this picture? I make some large assumptions here, but observe:

1. When Odysseus describes the Cyclopes, he emphasizes that they have no assemblies for making laws, no established legal codes, but everyone makes laws for himself and cares nothing for his neighbours (9.112–15). This description is clearly meant to stand *in contrast* with Odysseus' way of doing things. Law-making, assemblies and community solidarity are all hinted at here, priorities surely for any community at embryo stage.

2. Later on, Odysseus says the Cyclopes have no ships or shipwrights, so that they cannot visit foreign places as other nations do (9.125–30). This is surely a reference to a world of burgeoning trade, and fits well with other references to Greek contacts with Egypt (which started up again at roughly this time; cf. 4.351 ff.) and that great trading nation, the Phoenicians (modern Lebanon), which had established colonies and trading-posts as far west as Spain (15.403 ff.).

3. Homer's concept of monarchy is a shadowy one. He is aware that in the epic world kings are the norm, but how kingship worked is not clear to him. The common term for 'king' in Greek is *basileus*, but all the suitors on Ithaca are called *basileus*, and Alcinous in Phaeacia has a number of *basileis* (plural) as advisers. It is not at all clear how a top *basileus* emerged or, in

Odysseus' case, that any suitor who married Penelope would automatically become top *basileus* of Ithaca. The hereditary principle, too, does not seem to feature in Homer's thinking (1.386–98). This fluid situation, where aristocratic nobles such as the Ithacan suitors seem able to exert arbitrary power with little reference to anyone else (despite the presence of an assembly on Ithaca, 2.6 ff.; cf. 16.375), may well reflect a stage of transition between rule by kings to rule by aristocrats, a transition probably well in place by the eighth century.

In these three respects, Homer's *Odyssey* may well reflect contemporary or near-contemporary developments in the Greek world. But a warning is in order. We cannot date Homer with absolute accuracy, and while many people favour a late eighth-century date for him, there are others who would wish to place him in the seventh century. Linguistic considerations alone suggest strongly, but not conclusively, that the *Iliad* came before the *Odyssey*, and that both came before the farmer-poet Hesiod, who is certainly a seventh-century figure.

## REALITY AND FANTASY, IDENTITY AND DISGUISE

If there is much that is vividly realistic about Homer's portrayal of life in the palace of Ithaca – servants clearing up rooms (20.147–59), princes going to bed (1.425–44), dogs on dung-heaps (17.291 ff.), baths and dressing (10.348 ff.) – there is much fantasy too. Menelaus' tale at 4.351 ff. of his meeting with the mysterious Old Man of the Sea, Proteus, prepares us for the adventures that Odysseus will relate in 9–12 – adventures with one-eyed giants (Cyclops), witches (Circe), wind-gods (Aeolus), singers who know everything there is to know on the earth (the Sirens), and the whirlpool (Charybdis) on one side of a strait, opposite the man-eating Scylla on the other.

What is extraordinary is the way in which these worlds are (on the whole) so effortlessly blended. We see nothing strange about Odysseus sitting on the very seat which the god Hermes has just abandoned (5.195–6), or going to bed with a witch who has the power to turn men into pigs (10.347), or addressing the ghosts of the dead in Hades (11.90 ff.). Two of the reasons for the successful blending of these separate worlds are that Homer keeps the outrageous, the bizarre and the grotesque firmly at bay. It requires no great leap of the human imagination to envisage one-eyed giants who are cannibals, or witches who can tame animals, but excesses are firmly repressed. Second, these supernatural figures work within the norms of Greek civilization. Calypso knows how visitors should be entertained, just as Telemachus does (5.85 ff.). Circe has servants who prepare hot baths and lay tables as is done in Ithaca (10.348 ff.). Cyclops is a master-shepherd and cheese connoisseur, with a particularly commendable line in kitchen organization (9.219 ff.). The blending is especially noticeable in Phaeacia, the divinity of whose surroundings and human character of whose inhabitants – the bumbling, genial Alcinous, the delightful Nausicaa – produce an especially memorable mix.

The gods too know their place. In the *Iliad*, divine intervention is commonplace. Gods appear either as themselves or in disguise (usually the former) and are ever-present, helping their favourites and hindering their enemies. In the *Odyssey*, their presence is far less noticeable, and with the possible exception of 15.1–9, they appear only in disguise. Zeus himself remains on the whole apart from the action, and when he does intervene, he is a quite unIliadic god of human justice. Observe how Homer sets out the ethical programme of the *Odyssey* in the opening book: Odysseus' men brought their own death upon themselves by eating the cattle of the sun-god (1.7–9), and Aegisthus did likewise by ignoring divine warnings, killing Agamemnon and marrying Clytaemnestra (1.32–43). In other words, the gods are concerned about the justice of human behaviour in a way in which they are not in the *Iliad*. What, therefore, will be the consequences for the suitors of *their* behaviour in Odysseus' household? The moral lesson is firmly drawn at their slaughter (22.35–41, 23.63–7).

But there is one god with a high profile in the *Odyssey* –

Odysseus' patron, Athene. She stands by her favourite and guides his steps almost continually, and the teasing encounter they enjoy at 13.221 ff. is unique in Homer for the closeness of the relationship it depicts between god and mortal. It is tempting to say that Athene's continuing presence diminishes the stature of Odysseus. But it is important to emphasize that in Homer the gods help only those who are worthy of it. Athene's patronage does not diminish but enhances Odysseus' status as a hero. Her willingness to help his son Telemachus is a similar index of *his* value.

The fine dividing-line which separates human from divine in the *Odyssey* is matched by an even finer one separating the real from the unreal, especially real from unreal *identity*. The issue of Telemachus' identity has already been discussed (p. xxi), but if he has problems, what of Odysseus? Kept from human sight for seven years by Calypso (the name is based on a Greek root meaning 'conceal'), refusing to reveal himself to the Phaeacians until he tells his story at 9.16 ff., a 'No one' in the Cyclops' cave, a filthy beggar when he returns to Ithaca, a man who wishes he had died at Troy rather than be drowned at sea (5.306 ff.) – what sort of hero is this? The answer is, of course, a man of masterful cunning, as he is proclaimed to be at the very opening of the poem (which also fails to name him until line 21). This hero needs more than martial skills if he is to survive, return home (see p. xliii below) and restore his house to what it used to be. His cunning is evinced in many different episodes: consider, for example, his disguise at Troy (4.244 ff.), his speech to Nausicaa (6.148 ff.), the 'No one' trick in the Cyclops' cave (the Greek for 'No one', *mē tis*, when run together, makes *mētis*, Greek for 'resourcefulness, cunning', one of Odysseus' most common epithets), his acting-out of the part of the beggar, and his restraint in front of Penelope (19.203–12).

Restraint and endurance, deception and disguise: these Odyssean characteristics are shared, of course, by Athene, and willingly embraced by Telemachus when he is reunited with his father in 16. In the prevailing atmosphere of ignorance of the true nature of things in which characters wallow from the very beginning of the *Odyssey* (e.g. Telemachus at 1.158 ff.,

Eumaeus at 14.39 ff.), such characteristics help to generate a text dominated by irony, pathos, despair and joyously happy surprise (especially in the recognition scenes).

## READING HOMER

The ancients, of course, listened to Homer, and it is well worth following their example. But whether listening or reading, newcomers to Homer will find their pleasure heightened if they are aware of some typical features of his style and compositional technique.

1. Expect some degree of repetition at the level of word, phrase and sentence, most apparent in epithets attached to characters and objects, and in formulas of speaking and answering.

2. Expect repetition at the level of scene (e.g. feasting; see p. xxvii above), and in certain action sequences (e.g. departing from land; see 9.62–3, 105, 565–6; 10.77, 133–4). Expect also accumulation. Observe, for example, how Odysseus is attacked not once in his palace but four times – and once outside – (17–20), each attack building on the last. Odysseus' repeated lying stories come into the same category. Notice again how Homer doubles up his characters and plays them off in pairs: the two leading suitors, Antinous and Eurymachus, the two faithful servants Eumaeus and Philoetius, the two faithful maids Eurycleia and Eurynome, the two faithless servants Melanthius and Melantho – and is the Mentes of Athene's disguise in 1 the doublet of the old household friend Mentor?

3. Observe how, with certain larger-scale sequences, Homer combines fixity with flexibility. Take, for example, the scene of welcoming and entertaining a guest at 1.102 ff. The sequence can be analysed down to the following outline:

1. Athene *leaves* (102), 2. *arrives* (103), 3. *finds* a situation (106), 4. Telemachus *sees* her (113), 5. Telemachus *goes to meet* her (119), 6. he is *angry* that she has been ignored (119), 7. he *takes her hand* (121),

8. he *offers* food and greetings (123), 9. Athene is *led in* and her *spear taken* (125), 10. she is *seated* (130), 11. *food* is prepared and consumed (136), 12. *questions* begin (170). This sequence will occur again, with variations, at 3.1 ff., 4.1 ff., 5.50 ff. and in many other places.

In other words, the poet has a basic outline, but he plays the variations in it – not of sequence (that remains fixed) but of elaboration and digression within the sequence.

4. Digression is a common feature of epic. Homer digresses to describe exotic places (e.g. Calypso's cave at 5.55 ff., Alcinous' palace at 7.80 ff.), to tell stories (e.g. Menelaus' long tale at 4.351 ff.), to fill in the past (the scar story at 19.392 ff.), and so on. He keeps control of his narrative by returning at the end of the digression to the point at which he began it, with almost the same words. Take, for example, the scar episode. At 19.392, Eurycleia 'recognized the scar, the one Odysseus had received years before'. The story of the scar is told, and it ends (467): 'It was this scar that the old woman felt and recognized'. This feature is called 'ring-composition'. It is an extremely common controlling device in Homer.

5. At 1.81–95, Athene says (a) the gods should send Hermes to order Calypso to release Odysseus, and (b) she will go to Ithaca to instil spirit into the heart of Telemachus. Then she will send him (a) to Sparta and (b) to Pylos to find out about his father. As it so happens, Homer reverses this order of events. Athene goes to Ithaca first (1.96 ff.), and only then does Hermes go to Calypso (5.44 ff.). And Telemachus goes to Pylos first (3.1 ff.), and only then to Sparta (4.1 ff.). This device is typical of Homer: it is called 'hysteron-proteron' – 'the later earlier', or 'last first'.

6. The example quoted above characterizes another feature of Homeric narrative, that is, that events which one should expect to take place simultaneously are narrated as if they are taking place one after another, e.g. Athene goes to Ithaca and Telemachus tours the Peloponnese; then, and then only, does Hermes set off with his orders to Calypso. This feature is generally in line with what is known as the 'paratactic' nature of Homeric style; that is, that there is little grammatical and temporal

interweaving. One thing 'stands alongside' another without the relationship between them being strictly clarified. To put this in concrete terms, whereas we might subordinate a sentence and say '*Because* it was raining, we stayed in', Homer tends to say 'It was raining *and* we stayed in'.

7. Repetitions and lack of grammatical complexity both help to make Homer a swift, lively, vivid and easy read. Psychologically, too, there is a straightforwardness about Homeric characters quite different from those in the post-Freudian modern novel. Partly, this is because Homer lacks a wide conceptual and psychological vocabulary (there are, for example, no words for 'duty' or 'loyalty' in Homer). Homer's world is one of speaking and doing, where the will is almost the equivalent of the deed, and where motive remains largely unstated. But the fact that Homer does not have the vocabulary does not mean that his understanding of human behaviour is unsophisticated. If there is no overlay of authorial comment in Homer, the reason is that there is no need for it. It is all there in the words and the actions. Rich rewards await those who submit to careful literary analysis the ways in which characters speak and behave towards each other (e.g. Nausicaa and Odysseus in 6, Penelope and Odysseus in 19).

8. That said, however, while it is true that the *Odyssey* lays out an ethical programme in 1 which is fulfilled with the death of the suitors in 22 (see p. xxxvi above), one of the consequences of points 6 and 7 above is that it is often difficult to be certain about the interpretation of a speech or an action. Are we to read anything into the fact that Helen puts drugs into the drinks of her guests at 4.220–26? If Homer tells us that Odysseus' speech to Nausicaa at 6.148 is full of craft, what of the tone of Nausicaa's reply? Odysseus' heroism has caused debate to this day; can we certainly identify non-heroic traits where Homer remains silent? Is the relationship between Helen and Menelaus in 4 one of unalloyed bliss, or strained incompatibility? Both views have been quite recently urged.

## PROBLEMS IN THE *ODYSSEY*

The fifth-century BC historian Herodotus was the first person to say that Homer composed the *Iliad* and the *Odyssey* and did *not* compose a number of other epics associated with him (*Histories* 2.116–17). The ancients generally agreed with that judgement on their greatest poet. But when, at the behest of Ptolemy (the Greek King of Egypt and a great patron of the arts and sciences), scholars set to work in third-century BC Alexandria to produce a definitive text of Homer, they found that neither the honour in which Homer was held nor the Peisistratean recension (see p. xxx above) had prevented considerable divergences between the manuscripts. Still, they produced their text, and it is from this (edited by the great Alexandrian scholar Aristarchus) that our text ultimately derives. Aristarchus, of course, could have got it wrong. But it is a relief that he took the decision not to cut out what he regarded as dubious, but simply to mark it with a dash in the margin (*athetesis* is the technical term), especially since he tended to athetize repetitions, the very essence of oral poetry!

Debate about what is and what is not Homeric in our text did not begin with Aristarchus (we hear of scholars debating the issue in the sixth century BC), and it did not end with him either. 'Scholia', notes written by later scribes in the margins of our texts, and later commentaries which have survived (e.g. that of Eustathius, the twelfth-century AD Bishop of Thessalonica), often quote earlier commentaries on the *Odyssey* and as a result we can occasionally get a glimpse into Aristarchus' workshop. For example, we learn that both Aristarchus and another distinguished editor Aristophanes (*not* the comic poet) made 23.296 the 'end' of the *Odyssey*. Does that mean that everything after that is not Homeric? Or that it was an alternative Homeric version? Or should we translate 'end' as 'climax'? Before it was established that the Homeric poems were oral in style, it was common to take *inconsistencies* in story-line, language and cultural background as an index of 'multiple authorship' and from them to try to tease out a pure, Homeric 'core' which had been ruined by later editorial incompetents. This method of approach, known as 'analysis' (and commonly applied to the Bible and Shakespeare in the nineteenth century), was fiercely opposed by the 'unitarians', who regarded every word as the purest original.

Under these terms, for example, debate was joined on the following issues:

1. The travels of Telemachus in 3–4: what possible function can these serve since Athene knows all along that Odysseus is about to return?

2. Odysseus' descent into the Underworld in 11: Circe tells Odysseus to find out from Teiresias how to get home, but in fact her own instructions given on his return to her in 12 are far more informative.

3. Odysseus' disguise in 13: if you are disguised by a god, you expect to have to be undisguised to be recognized. This happens in 16. It is then entirely forgotten, and Odysseus acts as if he had been altered by time, not divine intervention.

4. Penelope and Odysseus in 18 and 19: are there signs here that they have recognized each other already?

5. Book 24, especially the final scenes: many readers have remarked on the pointless cruelty with which Odysseus treats Laertes, the feeble and perfunctory final battle with the suitors' relatives, and the bizarre behaviour of Zeus and Athene (she, having proposed a settlement, urges Odysseus into battle, at which Zeus hurls a thunderbolt at her).

These problems will not go away, but our understanding of them has been transformed by evidence that Homer's art is essentially that of an oral poet. Three points must be made.

1. No one ever notices these problems except when they are pointed out, or under the most intensive scrutiny of the text. In the recitation of the story, they surely passed unnoticed.

2. Inconsistencies do not of themselves mean that different people were responsible for the text. An oral poet experiments ceaselessly with his material, drawing it from many different sources. Some of it may be incompatible. Such inconsistencies may merely indicate where the poet made his own joins between incompatible source-material. Folk-motifs particularly can cause confusion. A hero can be disguised because of the passage of time or because of divine intervention. The poet must have known and handled both conventions. If he confuses them, doubtless he was not the first, and the overall effect of each recognition, however technically inconsistent, is highly dramatic.

3. Traditional stories often possess a logic of their own. Subject to rational analysis, they may not make perfect sense (was Little Red Riding Hood *really* that unobservant?). But we do not conclude from such an observation that 'multiple authorship' explains the problem.

However we care to argue these issues, we must be fully confident that we understand the logical, cultural and linguistic boundaries within which an oral poet operates before we can start condemning passages as 'non-Homeric'. The more we learn about oral poetry, the more difficult it becomes to define those boundaries accurately. That said, the sheer feebleness of the ending of the *Odyssey* makes it difficult for me at any rate to believe it is by Homer.

## ODYSSEUS: HERO OF A THOUSAND DISGUISES

There have been three common responses to the hero of the *Odyssey*. First, he is the loyal hero-husband, whose eyes are fixed on one goal only: return home. Whatever his trials, tribulations and temptations, everything is subsumed to this ultimate imperative. Second, he is the eternal wanderer, fired with a passion for knowledge and experience. Even when he returns home, he must set out again and continue wandering till death. Third, he is an anti-hero, a mean, selfish time-server who employs disguise and deceit often to gain the most disreputable ends (classical Greeks and Romans frequently saw him in this light).

Of these responses, it is fair to say that the second (initiated by Dante in his *Inferno* and developed by, for example, Tennyson in his *Ulysses*) is not Homeric. For Homer, Odysseus is driven, helpless and against his will, during his travels in 9–12. True, he does not need to explore the Cyclops' island, but it is hardly in a spirit of objective research that he visits it (he wants guest-gifts and food). He listens to the song of the Sirens because he is going that way anyway and Circe has told him how to do it. Nor does he dismiss Aeolus' offer of a wind to take him straight home with protestations about his anthropological interests.

The two other interpretations do arise naturally from the Homeric text. Odysseus leaves Calypso, who even offers him immortality, has no truck with the Lotus-eaters, parts from Circe when his men prompt him, and bids farewell to the luxury-loving Phaeacians. Despite the disasters he knows he will meet on the way and at his return (foretold by Teiresias at 11.113–18, though he is assured of final victory), return he will.

The seeds of Odysseus' anti-heroism are also sown in our text of the *Odyssey*. He undergoes disguise and degradation, even namelessness (the Cyclops believes him to be 'No one'), to achieve his ends. He heartlessly exploits Eumaeus. He harps on his hungry stomach to the point of embarrassment. It is easy to accuse of betrayal or bad leadership the man who cuts and runs from the Laestrygonians (10).

Many of these problems vanish if we regard Odysseus as a hero facing very different challenges from those on the battle-field. His disguises and deceptions are all means to a justifiable and suitably heroic end. But here perhaps is the greatest problem for readers of the *Odyssey*. However badly the suitors have behaved, is their mass slaughter an *appropriate* punishment, especially given that Odysseus not only kills them but also plans to seek compensation for their depredations by raiding their property (23.355–8)?

Four points need to be made on top of what has already been said about *xenia* on p. xxiv above. First, in the ancient world, the survival of any household depends on its ability to feed itself. Anyone who threatens the economic self-sufficiency of a family is, in the long term, threatening its very survival. Second, the suitors are unambiguously warned that their behaviour will lead to their destruction, but they ignore such warnings (2.170 ff., 20.345 ff.): Homer is careful to establish the ethical pattern of the *Odyssey* at its very start, with Zeus' speech that humans bring disaster upon themselves by ignoring divine warnings (cf. 1.32–43; cf. 1.7–9). Third, the suitors intend not merely to destroy Odysseus' household if they have to, but to kill Odysseus if he returns (2.244–51) and Telemachus while he is away (4.843). Fourth, without any sort of state intervention in matters of crime and punishment, responsibility for righting wrongs lies with the family. Whatever one may think of the severity of Odysseus' revenge, no Greek would have argued that he did not have a right to take it.

Odysseus, down the ages, has been a man of many parts. But the text of our *Odyssey* invites us to admire its multifariousness: it is the secret of its enduring hold on our imagination. Howard Clarke summarizes those qualities which make our *Odyssey* what it is:

> The *Odyssey* is broad and inclusive: it is an *epic* poem, not in the *Iliad*'s way, with men and nations massed in the first conflict of East and West, but epic in its comprehension of all conditions of men – good and bad, young and old, dead and alive – and all qualities of life – subhuman, human and superhuman, perilous and prosperous, familiar and fabulous. The Greek critic Longinus described it as an 'ethical' poem, a word that Cicero later explained (*Orator* 37, 128) by a definition that could well be applied to the *Odyssey* – 'adapted to men's natures, their habits and every fashion of their life'.

PVJ

# Introduction to the 1946 Edition

This version of the *Odyssey* is, in its intention at any rate, a genuine translation, not a paraphrase nor a retold tale. At the same time, and within the rules I have set myself, I have done my best to make Homer easy reading for those who are unfamiliar with the Greek world. Nevertheless, they are bound to find here much that is strange and I beg them to bear with me patiently through a few preliminary pages, so that I may provide them beforehand with the answers to some at least of the questions that will occur to them as they read.

Homer's *Iliad* and *Odyssey* have from time to time afforded a first-class battleground for scholars. In the nineteenth century in particular, German critics were at endless pains to show, not only that the two works are not the product of a single brain, but that each is a piece of intricate and rather ill-sewn patchwork. In this process Homer disappeared.

By now he has been firmly re-established on his throne and his readers may feel as sure that they are in one man's hands as they do when they turn to *As You Like It* after reading *King John*.[1] But this restoration depends on a judicious re-examination of the internal evidence and has brought little new to light about the man and his life. It is beyond question that he is the earliest surviving Greek writer; probable that he lived in the tenth century before Christ in one or other of those cities

1. This is not to say that in so ancient a text one or two lines here and there may not be later interpolations. Yet the only longer passage in the *Odyssey* which I find valid reasons for suspecting is that beginning at l.67 of Book 20, where Penelope, in a prayer addressed to the goddess Artemis, tells her a story in which she, Artemis, is referred to in the third person.

which the Greeks had established on the Aegaean coast of Asia Minor; and quite likely that he actually committed his poems to writing, though that art was still perhaps hardly known save to the minstrel fraternity to which he belonged. The rest, including his blindness, is legend or guesswork; and the reader who tries to glean from his poems something of the man, as apart from his art, will find himself baffled by the most impersonal and objective of authors.

The *Iliad* and *Odyssey* are twin aspects of a single theme – the story of the Trojan War and its aftermath. Together they constitute the first expression of the Western mind in literary form – the earliest, at all events, which we possess, for it will be obvious even to those who read them in translation that two such masterpieces could not have sprung into being without artistic antecedents. In form they are epic poems; but it will perhaps make their content clearer to the modern reader if I describe the *Iliad* as a tragedy and the *Odyssey* as a novel. It is in the *Iliad* that we hear for the first time the authentic voice of the Tragic Muse, while the *Odyssey*, with its well-knit plot, its psychological interest, and its interplay of character, is the true ancestor of the long line of novels that have followed it. And though it is the first, I am not sure that it is not still the best. Let the new reader decide for himself.

Each of the two poems is complete and independent as a work of art, with an atmosphere of its own, yet, as we have seen, they share a common background in the Trojan War; and of this war something must now be said.

The city of Troy or Ilium, which in Homer's account was besieged for ten years and finally sacked by the Greek king Agamemnon and his feudal supporters, has been identified by archaeologists with Hissarlik, an ancient settlement near the coast of the Aegaean in the north-west corner of Asia Minor, whose remains show traces of repeated demolition and rebuilding. It is quite likely that a marauding force from European Greece played a destructive part in its chequered life. But this is not to say that Homer's account is to be taken as history. Homer was neither a historian nor an archaeologist – the very ideas of history and archaeology were non-existent in his day –

and we shall be far nearer to the truth if we regard him as having worked up a mass of legendary and mythical material, of very ancient date and well known to his hearers, into a seemingly historical tale. His heroes and heroines were the supposed ancestors of the nobles before whom he recited his poems. It flattered his audience to hear of their doughty deeds and, in the absence of genuine pedigrees and records, to imagine these divinely-descended and godlike beings as separated from themselves by only a few generations. But in my view,[1] at any rate, they are mythical, and Homer's historical value to us lies, not in his attempt to describe an actual past, but in the picture which, in the course of this attempt, he cannot help giving us of the life and manners of his own day.

Before introducing the reader to the scene he will meet with in the *Odyssey*, we must briefly describe the action of the *Iliad*, which is no more than an episode in the ten years' siege of Troy. The ships of the Greek expeditionary force are lined up on the beach; the troops are encamped in huts beside them; the fighting takes place on the rolling plain between these huts and the city walls. Agamemnon, son of Atreus, the Greek overlord, with his brother Menelaus of Sparta, has induced the princes who owe him allegiance to join forces with him against Troy and Priam, its king, because Paris, one of Priam's many sons, has abducted Menelaus' wife, the beautiful Helen. The narrative covers only the short period of Achilles' withdrawal from the fighting after a quarrel with Agamemnon, his resumption of arms, and the death at his hands of the Trojan prince, Hector, whose body is recovered from Achilles for burial by the personal efforts of his father, King Priam. With Hector's funeral the *Iliad* ends. Homer left it to the lesser epic poets who followed him to fill the story out at either end.

His own work he resumed[2] in the *Odyssey*, which, though with many a backward look at the actual fighting, starts at a point in the tenth year after its end and deals with the adventures of the Greek chieftains on their homeward way. All the principal

1. A view that I express with some diffidence, for I feel that I have many scholars against me.

2. There are some slight suggestions that he wrote the *Iliad* first.

heroes are carefully accounted for, but the fate of one of them, Odysseus, King of Ithaca, an island off the western coast of Greece, is for artistic purposes selected as the central theme. Menelaus, Agamemnon, and Nestor receive special treatment. The adventures of Menelaus, indeed, are given at such length in Book 4 and bear so suggestive a resemblance to those of Odysseus that we are tempted to think that in the material at his disposal Homer found the legend of the Wandering Prince attached to the names of both Menelaus and Odysseus, and gave us two versions of the tale. At any rate there is a puzzle here for those who would have us believe that the pair are historical figures. Incidentally, it is noteworthy that apart from the death of Priam's daughter, Cassandra, Homer, who shows such meticulous care in winding up the Greek side of the business, concerns himself not at all with the destinies of the Trojans and their allies after the Sack.

But to return to the *Odyssey* – I am not going to spoil my readers' pleasure by an analysis of the plot. Homer is the world's best story-teller, and I can safely leave them in his hands. A few words, however, on the opening scenes may not come amiss. The tale begins with a council of the Olympian gods – of whom more anon – in the tenth year after the Fall of Troy. Zeus takes the chair, and comments first on the fate of Agamemnon, murdered on his return from Troy by Clytaemnestra, his wife, and her lover, Aegisthus; a tragic tale which Homer introduces here, and many times again, by way of pointing the contrast between Clytaemnestra's infamy and the sterling virtue of Penelope, Odysseus' queen. Next, Odysseus himself is discussed, and it is felt that this unhappy wanderer, who, mainly through the enmity of the sea-god Poseidon, has for ten years failed to reach his home in Ithaca, should be brought back to his kingdom. At the moment he is detained against his will in the remote island of Ogygia by the nymph Calypso, a lesser goddess who has for seven years exercised her charms in vain upon him; and it is there (in Book 5) that we first meet him, and not till Book 9 that we hear what he did in the first three years of his ten years' wanderings after the Sack of Troy.

Meanwhile, to return to Book 1, after suggesting that Hermes, the Envoy of the gods, should be dispatched to release Odysseus, the goddess Athene, Odysseus' champion and protector, visits his palace in Ithaca to stir his young son Telemachus to take active steps towards the discovery of his long-lost father, or, failing this, to bring to an end the intolerable situation that has arisen during his long absence. For we find that his faithful wife Penelope is besieged in her own house by a host of amorous and ambitious princelings from Ithaca itself and the neighbouring isles, each eager to wed the still attractive queen and even more eager to step into King Odysseus' shoes. It is the doom of these Suitors that is slowly but surely worked up to in the magnificent climax of Book 22.

But I undertook to introduce the reader only to the opening scene. Nor, having done this, do I propose to add one more to the many appreciations of the *Odyssey* that have been penned. I will content myself by drawing his attention to one or two aspects of Homer's genius which have struck me with even greater force during the long period of intimate study which translation involves than they did when I tackled him as a task at school.

I put first the extraordinary insight, delicacy, and truth with which he handles his hero's relations with members of the other sex – I cannot simply say women, for at least three goddesses are involved, though they are by no means the less feminine for being divine. The princess Nausicaa is a peculiarly attractive figure to modern readers. Some of us, steeped in the traditions of later fiction, may regret Homer's failure to pursue Nausicaa's romance to a more exciting conclusion, or may console ourselves by reading a broken heart into her last words with Odysseus. But Homer was neither a sex-ridden romantic nor a disillusioned realist, with the happy result that his picture of Nausicaa is as fresh and lovely now as when it was painted three thousand years ago.

Next, in an age which in spite of two savage wars is still too ready to look askance at the barbarity of its predecessors and to censure the occasional brutalities that Homer seems to condone, I cannot help dwelling on the tenderness which he expresses (or rather, in some subtle manner, causes *us* to feel) for all those whom fate or their own follies have afflicted or cast down. I am thinking of the luckless young Elpenor, 'not much of a fighting man, nor very strong in the head'; of the woman-slave grinding corn in the handmill, who was 'not so vigorous as the rest'; of the stricken Calypso's lament; of Odysseus' mother, pining in heartache 'for his wise and gentle ways'; of the great Otus and Ephialtes, destroyed 'before the down came curling on their cheeks'; of Cassandra's dying cry, which lingered so long in Agamemnon's ears; of the lonely Circe, 'decking herself out' in vain to meet Odysseus; of the faithful Eumaeus, braving the inclement night to sleep with his pigs; of his Phoenician nurse cut off in the midst of her successful crime by Artemis with her gentle darts; of the suitor Amphinomus, 'a thoroughly decent fellow', who had his warning but did not heed it; of the dog Argus, too old and weak to greet his master with more than a wag of the tail; of the netted birds, 'who meet death where they had only looked for sleep'; of the souls of the vanquished Suitors 'following the Deliverer down the dark paths of decay'; of Odysseus' old father, Laertes, expressing his misery in rustic clothes; and of the blinded Cyclops with his words of endearment to his darling ram – perhaps the most interesting case of all, for here Homer actually succeeds in enlisting our sympathy for a cruel and disgusting monster, and does so to the detriment of his own hero, much as in Shakespeare's *Tempest* the more our hearts are wrung for the unfortunate Caliban the more thoroughly do we dislike the ruthless master who 'works upon him'.

By now I have at least mentioned the chief human actors in the tale. It remains for me to repair an omission and say something of that galaxy of Olympian gods whom the reader is faced with at the very beginning of the poem and will meet as individuals on almost every page. This is no place for a disquisition on Greek religion, but it is worth while, before describing these gods and their functions, to pause for a moment and inquire what Homer's attitude towards them was.

The wrong conclusion to jump to, though I have often been

tempted to make the mistake, is that Homer's attitude is detached and sophisticated. He does believe in his gods, and that very vividly, but whereas the Christian conception of godhead is based on our creation by God in his image and likeness, with imperfections introduced by Satan, Homer regards his gods, though immortal, as made in the image and likeness of man. Mixed with his deep respect for their almost unlimited powers and his aesthetic appreciation of their beauty, he betrays a very tolerant understanding of their motives and frailties. This leads quite often, as in the famous Lay of Demodocus in Book 8, to a treatment that we can only regard as humorous. But it was neither flippant nor irreverent. These powerful beings, who were so intimately connected with men's passions and desires, were there to administer, not necessarily to obey, man's moral code. Christian apologists of a later age made a mistake when they suggested that the pagans had invented the gods and their iniquities as an excuse for themselves. Homer never censures a god nor lets a mortal use a god's misdeeds as a pretext for his own.

So much, however inadequate, about Homeric religion. It remains to touch briefly on the artistic use which Homer made of the superhuman realm. The most casual reader must at every page be struck by the contrast between the carefree happiness of the Olympian company and the toiling, anxious world of men. This contrast is woven into the very texture of the *Iliad* and *Odyssey*, and is nowhere turned to better account than when Odysseus refuses immortality as a gift from Calypso. To us the device may seem artificial. Yet how effective an artifice! Modern novelists might well envy Homer its use.

And now a few words on the individual gods who play a part in Odysseus' story. *Zeus*, son of Cronos, is supreme – the Father of gods and men. It is left a little doubtful to what extent he is independent of Fate,[1] but at all events it is he who administers the fate of men. Justice and the punishment of the transgressor are in his hands. So is mercy, and, perhaps because supreme power engenders confidence, he is more compassionate in his

1. See the curious passage about Sarpedon, *Iliad*, 16.440 ff.

dealings than most of his fellow-Olympians. He was conceived by Greek artists as a handsome bearded man in early middle age. His consort, *Here*, is little more than mentioned in the *Odyssey*.

His brother *Poseidon*, the god of the earthquake, who rules the sea, as Zeus rules the heavens, is a far less attractive and imposing figure, at any rate in the *Odyssey*, where he is represented as persecuting the hero with implacable though not unjustified resentment.

*Hades* is another brother of Zeus. Remote from Olympus, he and his consort *Persephone* are the austere and dreaded powers that rule in the realm of the dead.

The youthful and attractive *Hermes* we have already met in his capacity as Ambassador of Zeus. He also serves as Guide to the dead. And Homer makes many references to his great exploit in slaying Argus, the monster with the hundred eyes.

*Ares*, the War-god; laughter-loving *Aphrodite*, the goddess of Love; and lame *Hephaestus*, the Master-craftsman, though frequently heard of in the *Iliad*, play only incidental parts in the *Odyssey* and may be summarily dealt with here. So may *Phoebus Apollo*, the Archer-king, and *Artemis*, the Virgin Huntress, though both are often mentioned in the poem as responsible for sudden deaths.

There are other and lesser deities whom we need not here describe, since Homer himself introduces them with sufficient clarity, but there remains one major figure, *Pallas Athene*, who commands our attention, since she plays a leading, if not the heroine's, part in the plot. Athene is a daughter of Zeus, and inherits many of his powers and qualities. She is not all-powerful nor all-wise. Her impetuosity is sometimes curbed by Zeus, and she dreads her uncle Poseidon; but subject to these Olympian limitations she stands in Homer for the intellectual and moral qualities which were most admired in man and with which he so liberally endows Odysseus – cunning, resolution, industry, and unfaltering courage. It is she too who has given Penelope her outstanding gifts, 'her skill in fine handicraft, her excellent brain, and that genius she has for getting her way'. When Homer does not describe the disguise she has for the moment adopted, we may think of her as a tall and beautiful woman, with brilliant eyes, clad in a white robe, with the *aegis*, a goatskin cloak, across her breast, a crested helmet on her head, and a long spear in her hand. Most vivid and alive of Homer's gods, she dominates the *Odyssey*. And this is true even though there are moments when we are at a loss to say whether the poet means us to imagine her actual presence or to understand only that his characters are exercising the mother-wit which she personifies. Finally, though the rest of Homer's gods are by no means distinguished for nicety in their ideas of fun, he has endowed his favourite goddess with a sense of humour as delicate as his own.

I do not propose to embarrass the reader with elaborate rules for the pronunciation of the names of these gods and the other proper names in Homer; but two hints may be useful. The final *-e* should be sounded (Athene has three syllables, Penelope four, Here two). And secondly, *-eus* is a diphthong (Zeus rhymes with *puce*, and Odysseus has three syllables only). Here too, while on the subject of names, I must point out that although I have talked, throughout this introduction, of *Greece* and the *Greeks*, the reader will not come across these names in the text. They were not used by Homer, nor were the terms *Hellas* and *Hellenes* applied by him to the whole of what we call Greece, except in one highly doubtful case. The people he describes were known to him as *Achaeans*, and their country as *Achaea*, though he calls them also *Argives* and *Danaans* with an apparent impartiality that we need not inquire into here.

The rest of what I have to say is addressed more especially to those who know Greek and are interested in the problems involved in the translation of Homer. It has been my aim to present the modern reader with a rendering of the *Odyssey* which he may understand with ease and read with appreciation. I realize that in Homer, as in all greater writers, matter and manner are inseparably blended, and I have sought, in so far as English prose usage allowed it, not only to give what he says but to give it in his own way. But style is one thing and idiom another. In the very attempt to preserve some semblance of the original effect, I have often found it necessary – in fact my duty as translator – to abandon, or rather to transform, the idiom and the syntax of the Greek. Too faithful a rendering defeats its own purpose; and if we put Homer straight into English words, neither meaning nor manner survives.

Consider the following version of 21.402–3, by a pair of scholarly translators whom I quote with awe, for my generation was brought up on their work: 'Oh, that the fellow may get wherewith to profit withal, just in such measure as he shall ever prevail to bend the bow!' That is a tolerably close translation, but quite apart from the fact that the modern reader can scarcely get at the meaning without retranslating the sentence, it cannot fail to suggest to him that Homer must have sounded uncommonly turgid to his original audience. And this, we have good reason to suppose, is not the fact.

Take, again, the famous phrase 'winged words'. I submit that nobody knows what this means in English, though it may be beautiful. Are we then to leave it at that, or should we seek to discover and to reproduce the effect aimed at by the original *cliché*? For such I believe it to have been; and an examination of all the passages where it is used leads me to think that it indicates an utterance delivered with particular care and emphasis, or under the influence of some strong emotion – and I have tried to translate accordingly.

Much the same applies to the expression 'What a word has escaped you by the fence of your teeth!' This is intelligible, but unidiomatic, English for 'What nonsense!' Must we flout English usage to preserve it, if we feel convinced, as I do, that Homer took it over, as an idiom discounted by familiar use, from a long line of bardic ancestors, much as he inherited the epithet 'fast' for ships, and has, as a result, to talk of a 'swift fast ship' when he means a real clipper?

This brings me to the vexed question of the recurrent epithets. They are a marked feature of Homer's style, and as such I have endeavoured to deal with them faithfully (though not without an element of variety), since there are few cases[1] where English is altogether recalcitrant to their use. I think that, whether used

1. One occurs in 22.439, where the servants are *told* to use 'porous sponges'.

for ornamental or for deictic purposes, they too were a legacy from the past. But genius has a way of its own with traditional material; and Homer not only added to his legacy but extended its use in several interesting and subtle ways. For instance, Odysseus and other princes are 'godlike' in right of their divine descent, and as a rule the word has no more significance than 'royal'. But in 21.254 the context surely gives it the full value of its original meaning: Odysseus is a superman. Then there are a number of curious cases in which, unless we credit him with self-conscious art, Homer must be regarded either as having used a stereotyped expression in a meaningless way, or as having 'nodded' – which would amount to the same thing for such a stylist. I take it as an axiom that Homer never nods, and I suggest that where (in 24.57) he gives the Achaeans their usual epithet 'great-hearted', though they are behaving like cowards, he does so in order to produce an exactly opposite effect – and succeeds. Again, Phemius' lyre is called 'tuneful' on an occasion when it is not only silent (which would not matter) but likely to remain silent for ever as far as Phemius is concerned (22.332). Or, if this is pushing the idea too far, consider the one occasion in the whole work when 'early' Dawn is late yet Homer persists in calling her 'early'. The artifice, if such it is, is untranslatable. But there is a kind of half-way usage where we can almost follow the Greek. Dogs are styled 'noisy', and rightly so in 14.29, where they bark at a stranger, but somewhat surprisingly also in 16.4 where they are greeting a friend and are expressly stated not to have barked. Here the meaning, and the translation, 'usually so obstreperous', are easily arrived at.

I have cited these instances to make my point that Homer does a great deal with his adjectives and does not always use them in a conventional manner. In his handling of the personal epithets, in particular, we can see how Homer the novelist triumphed over Homer the traditional bard. Just as 'noisy' dogs do not always bark, and all 'fast' ships are not clippers, so 'prudent' Penelope, the 'wise' Telemachus, and the 'stalwart' or 'resourceful' Odysseus are often found, as their characters evolve in the hands of their maker, to behave in a manner far removed from exemplary wisdom, patience, and sagacity.

Indeed they are much too human and too well-drawn for such dull and uniform perfection.[1] And I feel that Homer often leaves them their epithets in cases where they do not apply, because their use will actually sharpen his hearers' perception of the characters he is building up. Nor, curiously enough, does his apparently inconsequent use of the epithets on inappropriate occasions detract from their effect when more pertinently used. I feel, at any rate, that there are cases where adverbial translation is justified, and I have acted accordingly, though I should be hard put to it if I were asked to lay down formal rules for such procedure.

Two points of detail, and I have done. Over the 'wine-dark' sea I have abandoned my own principles and thrown up my pen in despair. I know that it is wrong and ought to be 'wine-faced' or something to that effect. But the English language has failed me, just as it fails me, though for other reasons, when I am tempted to write of the 'fishy' sea. What a pity it is that so natural an epithet should have been reserved by us for such unsavoury uses.

But if there are some occasions when a translator of Homer may justly inveigh against the shortcomings of modern English, there are many more, I fear, when it is his own that are to blame. And I had better come to an end, rather than invite too close a scrutiny of these, or, worse still, fall into the most heinous crime that a translator can commit, which is to interpose the veil of his own personality between his original and the reader.

EVR

*May 1945*

1. Apollonius Rhodius, always careful not to copy Homer, is more sparing in his use of laudatory epithets, but presents us with even greater contrasts between the traditional reputation of his characters and their actual behaviour. As often as not, Jason is left speechless and paralysed by situations that call for heroic action.

## Note on the 14th Printing, 1959

Michael Ventris' decipherment of Linear B in 1952 marks the beginning of a new era in Homeric studies. One of the leading pioneers in the field is Professor T. B. L. Webster, who in his brilliant work *From Mycenae to Homer*, London (Methuen) 1958 and New York (Praeger), has even proved able, through a minute examination of the Homeric poems, to give us some idea of the nature of Mycenaean poetry, none of which has as yet come to light. But though all who wrote about Homer before 1952 must already be feeling that their words will eventually stand in need of considerable revision, much work remains to be done; and at the moment I content myself by stating in the Introduction that I seem to have antedated Homer by at least a century.

EVR

*June 1959*

# Further Reading

## Commentaries on *The Odyssey* in English

Peter V. Jones, *Homer's 'Odyssey': A Companion to the Translation of Richmond Lattimore* (Bristol: Bristol Classical Press, UK, and Carbondale: Southern Illinois University Press, USA, 1988). The *Companion* comments on the text by line-number, with a gloss, and has full introductions to each book. It is usable with this, and any other accurate, translation.

R. D. Dawe, *The Odyssey: Translation and Analysis* (Lewes: Book Guild, 1993). This massive 879-page tome (translation with commentary underneath) takes the *Odyssey* apart in minute, scholarly detail.

## Commentaries on *The Odyssey* in Greek

W. B. Stanford, *Homer's 'Odyssey' 1–12* and *13–24* (two vols., London: Macmillan, 1959).

A. Heubeck, S. West and J. B. Hainsworth, *A Commentary on Homer's 'Odyssey'*, vol. i, *Books 1–8* (Oxford: Clarendon Press, 1988).

A. Heubeck and A. Hoekstra, *A Commentary on Homer's 'Odyssey'*, vol. ii, *Books 9–16* (Oxford: Clarendon Press, 1989).

J. Russo, M. Fernandez-Galiano and A. Heubeck, *A Commentary on Homer's 'Odyssey'*, vol. iii, *Books 17–24* (Oxford: Clarendon Press, 1992).

## Books about Homer and *The Odyssey*

Howard W. Clarke, *The Art of the 'Odyssey'* (Englewood Cliffs, NJ: Prentice Hall, 1967; reprinted by Bristol Classical Press with corrections and additions, 1990).

M. I. Finley, *The World of Odysseus* (Harmondsworth: Pelican Books, second edition, 1979).

Jasper Griffin, *Homer: The 'Odyssey'* (Cambridge: Cambridge University Press, 1987).

J. Latacz, *Homer: His Art and his World*, transl. J. P. Holoka (Ann Arbor: University of Michigan Press, 1996).

I. Morris and B. B. Powell (eds.), *A New Companion to Homer* (Leiden, Netherlands: Brill, 1997).

Beaty Rubens and Oliver Taplin, *An Odyssey round Odysseus* (London: BBC Books, 1989).

S. V. Tracy, *The Story of the 'Odyssey'* (Princeton: Princeton University Press, 1992).

## Books about the Influence of The Odyssey

Howard Clarke, *Homer's Readers* (Cranbury, NJ: Associated University Presses, 1981).

Beaty Rubens and Oliver Taplin, *An Odyssey round Odysseus* (London: BBC Books, 1989).

W. B. Stanford, *The Ulysses Theme* (Oxford: Blackwell, second edition, 1963).

## Learning Ancient Greek

Peter Jones, *Learn Ancient Greek* (London: Duckworth, 1998), a simple introduction, based on a series in the *Daily Telegraph*.

## Classics Today

There are two associations for members of the general public who live in the UK:

*Friends of Classics*. This is for adults with a love of the ancient world, however creaky their knowledge of it. It organizes seminars, social events and outings, and produces a biennial colour magazine (ed. Peter Jones). Write to Jeannie Cohen, 51 Achilles Road, London NW6 1DZ.

*The Classical Association*. The CA organizes lectures at local universities, school reading competitions and an AGM, and publishes regular newsletters. Write to The CA, Institute of Classical Studies, Senate House, Malet Street, London WC1E 7HU.

For details of classical summer schools for students and adults in ancient Greek, Latin, and Greek and Roman history and culture, write to: The Joint Association of Classical Teachers, Institute of Classical Studies, Senate House, Malet Street, London WC1E 7HU.

PVJ

Greece and the Ionian Islands in the eighth century BC

# The Odyssey

# I
# ATHENE VISITS TELEMACHUS

*Tell me, Muse, the story of that resourceful man who was driven to wander far and wide after he had sacked the holy citadel of Troy. He saw the cities of many people and he learnt their ways. He suffered great anguish on the high seas in his struggles to preserve his life and bring his comrades home. But he failed to save those comrades, in spite of all his efforts. It was their own transgression that brought them to their doom, for in their folly they devoured the oxen of Hyperion the Sun-god and he saw to it that they would never return. Tell us this story, goddess daughter of Zeus, beginning at whatever point you will.*

All the survivors of the war had reached their homes by now and so put the perils of battle and the sea behind them. Odysseus alone was prevented from returning to the home and wife he yearned for by that powerful goddess, the Nymph Calypso, who longed for him to marry her, and kept him in her vaulted cave. Not even when the rolling seasons brought in the year which the gods had chosen for his homecoming to Ithaca was he clear of his troubles and safe among his friends. Yet all the gods pitied him, except Poseidon, who pursued the heroic Odysseus with relentless malice till the day when he reached his own country.

Poseidon, however, was now gone on a visit to the distant Ethiopians, in the most remote part of the world, half of whom live where the Sun goes down, and half where he rises. He had gone to accept a sacrifice of bulls and rams, and there he sat and enjoyed the pleasures of the feast. Meanwhile the rest of the gods had assembled in the palace of Olympian Zeus, and the Father of men and gods opened a discussion among them. He had been thinking of the handsome Aegisthus, whom Agamemnon's far-famed son Orestes killed; and it was with Aegisthus in his mind that Zeus now addressed the immortals:

'What a lamentable thing it is that men should blame the gods and regard *us* as the source of their troubles, when it is their own transgressions which bring them suffering that was not their destiny. Consider Aegisthus: it was not his destiny to steal Agamemnon's wife and murder her husband when he came home. He knew the result would be utter disaster, since we ourselves had sent Hermes, the keen-eyed Giant-slayer, to warn him neither to kill the man nor to court his wife. For Orestes, as Hermes told him, was bound to avenge Agamemnon as soon as he grew up and thought with longing of his home. Yet with all his friendly counsel Hermes failed to dissuade him. And now Aegisthus has paid the final price for all his sins.'

The goddess of the flashing eyes, Athene, answered him at once: 'Father of ours, Son of Cronos, King of Kings, Aegisthus' end is just what he deserved. May all who act as he did share his fate! It is for Odysseus that my heart is wrung, the wise and unlucky Odysseus, who has been parted so long from all his friends and is pining on a lonely island far away in the middle of the seas. The island is well-wooded and a goddess lives there, the child of the malevolent Atlas, who knows the depths of all the seas and supports the great columns that hold earth and sky apart. It is his daughter who is keeping the unhappy man from home, grieving. Day after day she does her best to banish Ithaca from his memory with soft, persuasive words; and Odysseus, who would give anything for the mere sight of the smoke rising up from his own land, can only yearn for death. Yet your Olympian heart is quite unmoved. Tell me, did the sacrifices he made you by the Argives' ships on the plains of Troy find no favour in your sight? Why are you at *odds* with *Odysseus*,[1] Zeus?'

'Nonsense, my child!' replied the Gatherer of the Clouds. 'How could I ever forget the admirable Odysseus? He is not only the wisest man alive but has been the most generous in his

1. Athene ventures a pun with her august Father.

offerings to the immortals who live in the wide heaven. It is Poseidon, Sustainer of the Earth, who is so implacable towards him on account of the Cyclops, godlike Polyphemus, the most powerful of the Cyclopes, whom Odysseus blinded. His mother was the Nymph Thoosa, daughter of Phorcys, Lord of the Salt Sea Waves; and it was Poseidon who gave her this child when he slept with her in her cavern hollowed by the sea. That is why, ever since Polyphemus was blinded, Poseidon the Earth-shaker has kept Odysseus in exile, though he stops short of killing him. But come now, let all of us here together contrive a plan to bring him home. Poseidon will relent. For he will not be able to struggle on alone against the united will of the immortal gods.'

Bright-eyed Athene answered him: 'Father of ours, Son of Cronos, King of Kings, if it is now the pleasure of the blessed gods that the wise Odysseus shall return to Ithaca, let us send our Messenger, Hermes the Giant-killer, to the isle of Ogygia, so that he can immediately tell Calypso, the Nymph with the plaited tresses, of our unalterable decision that the patient Odysseus must now set out for home. Meanwhile I myself will go to Ithaca to instil more spirit into Odysseus' son and encourage him to call the long-haired Achaeans to an assembly and speak his mind to that crowd of Suitors who spend their time in the wholesale slaughter of his jostling sheep and his shambling cattle with their twisted horns. After that I shall send him to Sparta and to sandy Pylos[1] to seek news of his father's return. It is possible that he may hear of him, and so win the praise of men.'

This said, Athene bound on her feet her lovely sandals of untarnishable gold, which carried her with the speed of the wind over the water or the unending land, and seized her heavy spear with its point of sharpened bronze, the huge long spear with which she breaks the ranks of noble warriors when she, the Daughter of the mighty Father, is angry with them. She flashed down from the heights of Olympus, and on reaching Ithaca she took her stand on the threshold of the court in front of Odysseus' house; and to look like a visitor she assumed the appearance of

1. Sparta and Pylos were the cities where lived Menelaus and Nestor, fellow commanders with Odysseus of the Achaean army at Troy.

a family friend, the Taphian chieftain Mentes, bronze spear in hand.

She found the insolent Suitors sitting in front of the door on hides of oxen they themselves had slaughtered, playing with counters; their squires and pages were busy round them, some blending wine and water in the mixing-bowls,[1] and others carving meat in lavish portions and wiping down the tables with sponges before they set them ready.

The first to see her was Telemachus the godlike youth, who was sitting disconsolate among the Suitors, imagining how his noble father might come back out of the blue, drive the Suitors headlong from the house, and so regain his royal honours, and reign over his own once more. Full of these visions he caught sight of Athene and set off at once for the porch, ashamed that a stranger should be kept standing at the gates. He went straight up to his visitor, grasped his right hand, took his bronze spear and gave him cordial greetings. 'Welcome, friend!' he said. 'You can tell us what has brought you here when you have had some food.'

With this he led the way and Pallas Athene followed. Once inside the lofty hall, he took her spear and put it by one of the great pillars in a wooden rack among the many spears of the patient Odysseus. He then conducted her to a beautiful carved chair, over which he spread a linen cloth, and seated her there with a stool for her feet. For himself he drew up an ornate easy-chair, well away from the crowd of Suitors, for fear that his guest might take offence at the uproar, and finding himself in such ill-mannered company turn with distaste from his meal. Moreover, he wished to question him about his absent father.

Presently a maid came with water in a fine golden jug and poured it out over a silver basin for them to rinse their hands. She then drew a polished table to their side, and the faithful housekeeper brought some bread and set it by them with a choice of delicacies, helping them liberally to all she could offer. Meanwhile a steward served them plates of various meats he had selected from his board, and put gold cups beside them,

1. Wine was diluted with water in various ratios, 1:3 being the average.

which a steward filled with wine as he passed on his frequent rounds.

The Suitors came swaggering in and sat down in rows on the seats and chairs. Their squires poured water on their hands and the maids put piles of bread in bowls beside them, while the pages filled the mixing-bowls to the brim with wine. They helped themselves to the good things spread before them; and when all had satisfied their hunger and thirst, the Suitors turned their thoughts to other activities, music and dancing, which add to the pleasures of a banquet. A herald brought a beautiful lyre and handed it to Phemius, the minstrel whom they had forced into their service. He had just struck the first notes for some delightful song, when Telemachus spoke to bright-eyed Athene, with his head close to hers so that the others could not hear:

'Friend, will you be angry if I say something? How easy it is for that gang over there to think of nothing but music and songs! They are living free off another man – a man whose white bones are rotting in the rain upon some distant land or rolling in the salt sea waves. One glimpse of him in Ithaca, and they'd pray for a faster pair of legs rather than gold or rich clothes! But as it is, he has come to some dreadful end. No one on earth can bring us a spark of comfort by telling us that he'll come back. The day for that is gone for ever.

'But tell me honestly who you are and where you come from. What is your native town? Who are your parents? And since you certainly cannot have come on foot, what kind of vessel brought you here? How did the crew come to land you in Ithaca, and who did they claim to be? And tell me the truth – I'd like to know – is this your first visit to Ithaca, or has my father received you before – he used to entertain in our house just as often as he visited abroad.'

'I will tell you everything honestly,' answered the bright-eyed goddess Athene. 'My father was the wise prince Anchialus. My own name is Mentes, and I am chieftain of the sea-faring Taphians. As for my arrival in Ithaca, I came with my own ship and crew across the wine-dark sea. We are bound for the foreign port of Temesa with a cargo of gleaming iron, which we mean to trade for bronze. My ship is not berthed near the city, but over there by the open country, in Rheithron Cove, under the woods of Neion. As for our families, the ties between them go a long way back, as the old lord Laertes would tell you if you went and asked him. For I gather that he no longer comes to the town, but lives a miserable existence on his distant farm with an old woman-servant, who puts his food and drink before him when he has tired himself out by dragging himself up and down his vineyard on the hill.

'The reason for my presence here is this. I actually heard that *he* was home – I mean your father. But the gods must be hindering his return, because the good Odysseus is not dead, but alive somewhere on this earth. He must be on some distant island out in the sea, in the hands of enemies, savages no doubt, who keep him there by force. Now I am no seer or soothsayer, but I will venture on a prophecy to you which the immortal gods put into my mind. I am certain it will come true. Your father will not be exiled much longer from the land he loves so well, not even if he's kept in iron chains. He will think of a way to return – he is endlessly resourceful.

'But are you really Odysseus' son? How you have grown! You certainly have his head and fine eyes. The likeness is startling to one who met him as often as I did, though that was before he and the other great men of Argos all set out for Troy in their hollow ships. From that day to this, Odysseus and I have never set eyes on each other.'

'My friend,' answered the courteous Telemachus, 'I will be honest too. My mother certainly says I am Odysseus' son; but for myself I cannot tell. No man can be certain of his parentage. Ah, if only I were the son of some lucky man overtaken by old age among his own belongings! As it is, and since you ask me, the man whose son they say I am is the most unfortunate man that ever lived.'

'And yet,' said the goddess of the flashing eyes, 'with Penelope for your mother, I cannot think that your house is doomed to an inglorious future. But here is another matter I should like you to explain. What is the banquet for? Who are all these people? How are *you* concerned? Is it a private dinner or a wedding feast? Obviously these men have not brought their own food. At any rate these banqueters in your house strike me as domineering and insolent. Any decent man would be disgusted at the sight of such disgraceful behaviour.'

'My friend,' the courteous Telemachus replied, 'you may well ask. There was a time when this house was by way of being prosperous and respectable, when Odysseus was still among us. But since then, the gods have had other and more sinister designs; and they have served him as they never served a man before: they have made him vanish. His death itself, if he had fallen among his men at Troy or died in friendly arms at home with all his fighting done, would have caused me less distress. For in that case the whole Achaean[1] nation would have joined in building him a mound, and he would have left a great name for his son to inherit. But there was to be no famous end for him; the Storm-Fiends have snatched him away. He has gone where he cannot be seen or found and to me has left nothing but sorrow and tears. Nor is it only on his account that I am sighing and grieving, for the gods have gone on piling other troubles on my head. Of all the island-chieftains in Dulichium, in Same, and in wooded Zacynthus, all the nobles in rocky Ithaca, there is not one that isn't courting my mother and wasting my property. As for her, though she hates the idea of remarrying, she cannot bring herself to take the final step of rejecting all the Suitors or accepting one of them. Meanwhile they are eating me out of house and home. And they will very soon destroy me too.'

Pallas Athene was moved. 'How disgraceful!'[2] she cried. 'O how you miss your father, how much you need him to lay hands on this dissolute mob! If only he could show himself at this moment at the palace gates, with his helmet, his shield, and his two spears, just as he was when I first saw him, drinking and in happy mood in our house, that time he came up from Ephyre after a long visit to Mermerus' son Ilus. He had sailed there in

1. I have kept the terms Homer uses – Achaeans, Argives and Danaans – rather than call them all Greeks.

2. The Greek is 'O popoi', an interjection used to express astonishment, displeasure, wrath or grief, which I have translated variously as 'Dammit!' 'Well I'll be –ed!' and 'Well! Well!' to suit the speaker and the occasion.

search of a deadly poison to smear on the bronze tips of his arrows, and Ilus, a god-fearing man, refused to supply him; but my father, who loved him dearly, gave it to him. Yes, if only Odysseus, as he then was, could confront these Suitors, there'd be a quick death and a sorry wedding for them all. But such matters, of course, lie in the lap of the gods. They must decide whether or not he's to come back and settle accounts in his palace.

'Meanwhile I do urge you to find some way of ridding the house of these Suitors. Listen carefully to what I suggest. Tomorrow morning call the Achaean lords to Assembly and announce your decision to them all, asking the gods to witness what you say. Tell the Suitors to leave and go home. As for your mother, if she is set on marrying, let her go back to her father's house. He is a man of consequence, and the family will arrange a marriage and see that she has a generous dowry, as is only right for a beloved daughter.

'For yourself, here is my advice. It is sound, and I hope you will take it. Choose your best ship, man her with twenty oarsmen, and set out to inquire after your long absent father. Someone may be able to tell you about him, or you may pick up one of those rumours from Zeus that so often turn out to be true. Go to Pylos first and question the excellent Nestor; then on to Sparta to see auburn-haired Menelaus, since he was the last of the bronze-armoured Achaeans to reach home. If you hear that your father is alive and on his way back, you should reconcile yourself to a year more of this wastage. But if you hear that he is dead and gone, return to your own country, build a mound with all the proper funeral rites, and give your mother in marriage to a new husband. This settled and done, you must think of some way of destroying this mob in your house, either by cunning or in open fight. You are no longer a child: you must put childish thoughts away. Have you not heard what a name Orestes made for himself in the world when he killed the cunning Aegisthus for murdering his noble father? You, my friend – and what a tall and splendid young man you have grown! – must be as brave as Orestes. Then future generations will sing your praises.

'But my crew must be tired of waiting for me, and I must now go to my good ship. I leave the matter in your hands. Think over what I have said.'

'Sir,' said the thoughtful Telemachus, 'you have spoken to me out of the kindness of your heart like a father talking to his son; and I shall never forget your words. Though you are anxious to be on your way, stay a little longer so that you can bathe and refresh yourself. Then you can go to your ship in a happy frame of mind, taking with you as a keepsake from myself something precious and beautiful, the sort of present that one gives to a guest who has become a friend.'

'No,' said the bright-eyed goddess. 'I am eager to be on my way; do not detain me now. As for the gift you kindly suggest, let me take it home with me on my way back. Make it the best you can find, and you won't lose by the exchange.'

The goddess spoke and the next moment she was gone, vanishing like a bird through a hole in the roof. In Telemachus' heart she had implanted spirit and daring, and had brought the image of his father to his mind even more strongly than before. He felt the change and was overcome with awe, for he realized a god had been with him. Then, godlike himself, he rejoined the Suitors.

He found them listening in silence to a song which their famous bard was singing to them about the Achaeans' return from Troy and the disasters that Pallas Athene made them suffer. In her room upstairs, Penelope, the gracious daughter of Icarius, took in the words of his stirring ballad and came down from her quarters by the steep staircase, not alone, but with two waiting-women in attendance. When she came near her Suitors the great lady drew a fold of her shining veil across her cheeks and took her stand by a pillar of the massive roof, with one of her faithful maids on either side. Then, bursting into tears, she broke in on the inspired minstrel.

'Phemius,' she said, 'with your knowledge of the ballads that poets have made about the deeds of men or gods you could enchant us with many other tales, rather than this. Choose one of those now for your audience here, and let them drink their wine in peace. But give us no more of your present song. It is too sad; it never fails to wring my heart. For in that catastrophe no one was dealt a heavier blow than I, who pass my days in mourning for the best of husbands, the man whose name rings through the land from Hellas to the heart of Argos.'

But the prudent Telemachus intervened. 'Mother,' he said, 'why grudge our loyal bard the right to entertain us as the spirit moves him? Surely it is not the poets who are responsible for what happens, but Zeus himself, who deals with each of us toilers on earth as he sees fit? We cannot blame Phemius if he chooses to sing of the Danaan's tragic fate, for it is always the latest song that an audience applauds the most. You must be brave and nerve yourself to listen, for Odysseus is not the only one who has never returned from Troy. Troy was the end of many another man. So go to your quarters now and attend to your own work, the loom and the spindle, and tell the servants to get on with theirs. Making decisions must be men's concern, and mine in particular; for I am master in this house.'

Penelope was taken aback, but she retired to her own apartments, for she took her son's sensible words to heart. Attended by her maids, she went upstairs to her bedroom, and there she wept for Odysseus, her beloved husband, till bright-eyed Athene closed her eyes in sweet sleep.

Meanwhile in the shadowy hall the Suitors burst into uproar, and each man voiced a prayer that he might sleep with her.

But the thoughtful Telemachus called them to order. 'Gentlemen,' he cried, 'from you who court my mother this is sheer insolence. For the moment, let us dine and enjoy ourselves, but quietly, for it is a lovely thing to listen to a minstrel such as we have here, with a voice like a god's. But in the morning I propose that we all take our places in assembly, so that I can announce my demand that you quit my palace. Yes, you can feast yourselves somewhere else and eat your provisions in each other's homes. But if you think it a sounder scheme to destroy one man's estate and not make restitution, then eat your fill, while I pray that Zeus will bring a day of reckoning, when in this house *I* will destroy *you* – and not make restitution.'

It amazed them all that Telemachus should have the audacity to adopt this tone, and they could only bite their lips. But at last

Antinous, Eupeithes' son, spoke up in answer: 'It is obvious that the gods are teaching you this bold and haughty way of speaking. Being your father's son, you are heir to this island realm. Heaven grant that you may never be its king!'

'Antinous,' the prudent Telemachus answered, 'it may disappoint you to learn that I would gladly accept that office from the hands of Zeus. Perhaps you argue that nothing worse could happen to a man? I on the contrary, maintain that it is no bad thing to be a king – to see one's house enriched and one's authority enhanced. However, the Achaeans are not short of princes; young and old they swarm in sea-girt Ithaca. And since the great Odysseus is dead, let one of *them* succeed him. But *I* intend at least to be master of my own house and the servants whom my royal father won for me in war.'

This time it was Eurymachus son of Polybus who answered him: 'Telemachus, the gods must of course decide who is to be our king in sea-girt Ithaca. But by all means keep your own belongings and rule your own house. I pray that no one comes and lays violent hands on your property, as long as there are people in Ithaca. But, my dear Telemachus, do tell us something about that guest of yours. Where did the man come from? What account does he give of his country? Who might his people be? And what is his native land? Does he bring news of your father's coming, or is he here on business of his own? He looked distinguished, but he jumped up and was gone so suddenly that he gave one no time to get to know him.'

'Eurymachus,' the sensible Telemachus replied, 'it is certain that my father will never come back. So I no longer believe any rumours whatever their source, nor have I any use for the skill of such diviners as my mother may call in for consultation. As for my guest, he is an old friend of my father from Taphos. He introduced himself as Mentes, the son of wise Anchialus, and chieftain of the sea-faring Taphians.' This is what Telemachus said, but in his heart he knew her for an immortal goddess.

From then till dusk they gave themselves up to the pleasures of dancing and the delights of song. Night fell and found them still revelling but at last they went off to bed, each to his own house. Telemachus, busy with his thoughts, retired to his own bedroom, a lofty chamber in the fine courtyard with a clear view on every side. He was escorted by the faithful Eurycleia, who carried a blazing torch. This Eurycleia was the daughter of Ops and granddaughter of Peisenor. Laertes had procured her at his own cost long ago, when she was still a girl, for the price of twenty oxen. He had treated her in his home with all the respect due to a loyal wife, though for fear of his wife's displeasure he had not slept with her. It was she who now served as torch-bearer to his grandson; and she who of all the household women loved him most, for she had nursed him as a child.

Telemachus threw open the door of his solidly built room, sat down on the bed and took off his soft tunic, which he put in the wise old woman's hands. After folding it and smoothing it out, she hung it on a peg by the wooden bedstead and withdrew from the bedroom, pulling the door to by the silver handle and shooting the bolt home by means of its leather thong. And there, all the night long, under his woollen blanket, Telemachus lay planning in his mind the journey that Athene had suggested.

## 2

# THE DEBATE IN ITHACA

As soon as Dawn appeared, fresh and rosy-fingered, Odysseus' son got up from his bed and put his clothes on. He slung a sharp sword from his shoulder, bound a stout pair of sandals on his glistening feet and strode from his bedroom looking like a god. He at once gave orders to the clear-voiced criers to call the long-haired Achaeans to Assembly. The heralds cried their summons and the people quickly gathered. When all had arrived and the Assembly was complete, Telemachus himself set out for the meeting-place, bronze spear in hand, escorted only by two hunting-dogs. Athene endowed him with such supernatural grace that all eyes were turned on him in admiration when he came up. The elders made way for him as he took his father's seat.

Aegyptius, an old lord bent with years and rich in wisdom, was the first to speak. His own soldier son Antiphus had sailed with godlike Odysseus in the big ships to Ilium the city of horses, only to be killed by the savage Cyclops in his cavern home when he made the last of his meals off Odysseus' men. And although he had three other sons, Eurynomus, who had joined with the Suitors, and two who worked steadily on their father's estate, Antiphus was always in his mind. His grief was inconsolable; and it was with tears for this lost son that he now rose to address the gathering:

'My fellow-countrymen, listen to what I have to say. Not once since the good Odysseus sailed have we been called to Assembly or Council meeting here. Who has summoned us now? Was it one of the young men or one of the older generation? And what is his pressing need? Perhaps he has heard of an army's approach, and wishes to tell us the early news he has received? Or is there some other matter of public concern that he intends to raise for discussion? "Good man!" I say in any case. Our blessing on him! May Zeus reward him with his heart's desire!'

His auspicious words delighted Odysseus' son. Eager to speak, he left his seat without further ado and took his stand in the middle of the Assembly. The herald Peisenor, a shrewd, experienced counsellor, thrust the speaker's staff into his hand; and Telemachus, turning first to old Aegyptius, began:

'Venerable sir, you shall have the truth at once. The man who summoned this gathering is not far to seek. It was I – I am in great distress. Of an army's approach I have heard nothing to tell you. Nor is it some other question of public concern that I propose to bring forward, but my own private business, the affliction, the double affliction, that has fallen on my house. In the first place I have lost my good father, who was once king among you here and gentle as a father to you all. But now there is a far greater calamity, one which will bring my house to utter ruin and rob me of any livelihood I have. A crowd of Suitors are pestering my mother with their unwanted attentions, and these Suitors are actually the sons of those who are your leaders here. Too cowardly to present themselves at her father's house, for Icarius to make terms for his daughter's hand with the claimant he prefers, they spend all day in and out of our house. They slaughter our oxen, our sheep, our fatted goats; they feast themselves and drink our sparkling wine – with never a thought for all the wealth that is being wasted. The truth is that there is no one like Odysseus in charge to purge the house of this blight. We are not able to defend it ourselves: we would prove miserably weak, quite untrained to fight. Yet I would willingly fight if I had the strength. For I tell you, the things they do are past all bearing.

'The destruction of my house is an injustice which you, gentlemen, should resent not only on your own behalf but as a scandal to our neighbours who live round about. You should shrink from the wrath of the gods. Have you no fear that they may be outraged at your wickedness and turn on you? In the name of Olympian Zeus, in the name of Themis, who summons and dissolves the councils of men, I beg you, my friends, to leave me alone with my bitter grief – unless by any chance you think that my good father harmed the well-greaved[1] Achaeans out of malice, and you are trying to repay me with equal malice by the encouragement you give these men? If only it were you men of Ithaca who were devouring our treasure and our flocks, I think we should be better off. For in that case we should not have far to look for compensation. We should simply hound you up and down the town for the restitution of our goods till every item was repaid. As it is, you fill my heart with a pain for which I find no cure.'

As he spoke his passion rose; and at the end he burst into tears and flung the staff on the ground. A wave of pity swept through the gathering. Nobody made a move, nobody had the heart to give Telemachus a sharp reply, and the silence was unbroken till Antinous retorted:

'What a speech, Telemachus, and what a temper! So you'd put us to shame, would you, and fix the blame on *us*? You are wrong. We Suitors plead "Not guilty". It is your own mother, that incomparable schemer, who is the culprit. Listen. For three whole years – in fact close on four – she has been leading us on, giving us all some grounds for hope, and in her private messages to each making promises that she has not the slightest intention of keeping. And here's another example of her duplicity. On her loom in her house she set up a great web and began weaving a large and delicate piece of work. She said to us: "My lords, my Suitors, now that noble Odysseus is dead, restrain your ardour, do not urge on this marriage till I have done this work, so that the threads I have spun may not be altogether wasted. It is a shroud for Lord Laertes. When he succumbs to the dread hand of remorseless Death that stretches all men out at last, I must not risk the scandal there would be among my countrywomen here if one who had amassed such wealth were laid to rest without a shroud." That's what she said; and we magnanimously consented. So by day she used to weave at the great web, but every night had torches set beside it and undid the work.

1. Greaves were shin-guards.

For three years she took us in by this trick. A fourth began, and the seasons were slipping by, when one of her women who knew all about it gave her mistress away. We caught her unravelling her beautiful work, and she was forced reluctantly to complete it.

'Here is the Suitors' answer, Telemachus, and I want you and all the people to be quite clear about it. Send your mother away and make her marry the man whom her father chooses and whom she prefers. She must beware of trying our young men's patience much further and counting too much on the matchless gifts that she owes to Athene, her skill in fine handicraft, her excellent brain, and that genius she has for getting her way. In that respect I grant she has no equal, not even in story. For of all the Achaean beauties of former times, not Tyro, nor Alcmene, nor Mycene of the lovely diadem, had at her command such wits as she. Yet in the present case Penelope has misused those wits. For I assure you that so long as she maintains this attitude that the gods have guided her to adopt, the Suitors will continue to eat you out of house and home. She may be winning a great name for herself, but at what expense to you! So we will not return to our own estates, nor go anywhere else, until she makes her choice and marries one of us.'

'Antinous,' the thoughtful Telemachus replied, 'it is quite impossible for me to cast out, against her will, the mother who bore me and who brought me up, with my father somewhere at the world's end, perhaps alive, perhaps dead. Think what I would have to pay Icarius if I were to send my mother back to him. I would suffer at his hands and the gods would send me further disasters, because my mother as she left would call down on me the Avenging Furies. And I would incur the wrath of my countrymen. You may be sure that I will never give the word. If you feel angry about this then quit my palace and feast somewhere else, eating your own food in each other's houses. But if you think it a sounder scheme to destroy one man's estate and not make restitution, then eat your fill, while I pray that Zeus will bring a day of reckoning, when in this house *I* will destroy *you* – and not make restitution.'

In answer to his words, Zeus the Thunderer urged two eagles

into flight from the mountain-top. For a while they sailed down the wind with outstretched pinions, wing to wing. But as soon as they were directly over the meeting-place, where the sound of voices filled the air, they began to flap their wings and wheel about, glancing down at the faces of the crowd with looks foreboding death. Then with their talons they clawed at each other's cheeks and neck, and so swooped eastward over the house-tops of the busy town. The people stared at the birds in amazement, and asked themselves what was to come of it. At last the old hero Halitherses, Mastor's son, spoke out. He knew more of bird-lore and soothsaying than any man of his generation, and had his countrymen's welfare at heart when he rose now to address them:

'People of Ithaca, hear what I have to say. And my pronouncement is meant particularly for the Suitors. A great calamity is about to engulf them. Odysseus is not going to be parted from his friends much longer. At this very moment he is close at hand, sowing the seeds of a bloody doom for the Suitors one and all, which means disaster to many others of us who live under the clear skies of Ithaca. Let us plan to stop these men, before it happens. Or rather, won't they stop of their own accord – which would be the better course? I am not unskilled in prophecy: I speak from ripe experience. Consider Odysseus. Has not everything happened as I warned that self-reliant man when he embarked for Ilium with the Argive army? I said he would return home in the twentieth year, after much suffering, having lost all his comrades, and that no one would know him when he came. And now all this is coming true!'

It was Eurymachus, Polybus' son, who rose to reply. 'That's enough, old man!' he said. 'Run home and read omens to your children, or some disaster may happen to them. And leave me to interpret these signs. I am better at that than you. After all, plenty of birds go about their business in the sunny air, but it isn't every one that is a bird of omen. As for Odysseus, he has met his fate abroad. If only you had shared his fate! We should then have been spared this tedious prophesying from your mouth, and you wouldn't be fuelling Telemachus' anger. No doubt you expect him at some time to make a gift to your household. But now *I* will make a prophecy, and this *will* come true. If you, his senior, with the lore of the ages at your disposal, misuse your eloquence to incite this young man to violence, in the first place it will be all the worse for him; and secondly for you, old man, there will be the extremely unpleasant consequence that we shall impose on you a fine it will break your heart to pay.

'For Telemachus, here is my own advice: I give it openly, before you all. Let him tell his mother to return to her father's house, where they will make arrangements for her wedding and see that she has a generous dowry, as is only right for a much-loved daughter. Not till that is done can I see the sons of the Achaeans giving up their unwelcome suit. For we are afraid of no one at all – certainly not of Telemachus, for all his rhetoric. Nor, old man, do we pay the slightest attention to those prophecies that fall from your lips. They come to nothing and only make you even more hated. No; Telemachus must see his wealth ruthlessly consumed without hope of restitution, so long as Penelope keeps us kicking our heels in this matter of her marriage. Meanwhile we stay, and, instead of each seeking a suitable bride, we feed our hopes from day to day on the thought of the incomparable prize for which we are competing.'

'Eurymachus,' the thoughtful Telemachus replied, 'and all you distinguished Suitors, I make no further appeal; I have said my say. The gods and the whole people here have heard my case. So now give me a fast ship and a crew of twenty to see me to my journey's end and back. For I am going to Sparta and to sandy Pylos to inquire after my long-lost father in the hope that someone may be able to tell me about him or that I may pick up one of those rumours from Zeus that so often turn out to be true. If I hear that he is alive and on his way back, then, harassed though I am, I will hold out for one more year. But if I learn that he is dead and gone, I shall come home, build him a mound with all the proper funeral rites, and give my mother in marriage to a new husband.'

Telemachus resumed his seat and Mentor rose to speak. Mentor was an old friend of Odysseus, to whom the king had entrusted his whole household when he sailed, with orders to defer to the aged Laertes and keep everything safe and sound. He spoke now from the goodness of his heart.

'My fellow-citizens,' he said, 'kindness, generosity, and justice should no longer be the aims of any man who wields the royal sceptre – in fact he might just as well devote his days to tyranny and lawless deeds, since none of those whom the godlike Odysseus ruled with a father's loving care give a thought to him today. Of course it is not for me to pass judgement on the villainy of these black-hearted Suitors – it is their own skins they are risking when they squander Odysseus' estate in the belief that he is gone for ever. No, it is the rest of you sitting there in silence that stir my indignation. They are few and you are many. Yet not a word have they had from you in condemnation or restraint!'

Up sprang Leocritus, Euenor's son. 'Mentor, you crazy fool,' he shouted at him, 'what are you saying, inciting the people to stop us? It's expecting much of men to take up arms over a *meal*, even with the odds in their favour. Even if Odysseus of Ithaca himself came back and took it into his head to drive us nobles from the palace because he found us dining in his hall, his wife would have no joy of his return, much as she may have missed him. Then and there he'd come to an ignominious end, fighting alone against so many. So what you suggest is out of the question. But enough of this. Break up the meeting, and each man go back to his own estate, while Mentor and Halitherses, as old friends of his father, speed Telemachus on his way, though I have an idea that he will never bring this journey off, but will find himself sitting in Ithaca for many a long day, gathering news as best he can.'

The assembled people were quick to accept this dismissal and now scattered to their homes, while the Suitors made their way to King Odysseus' palace.

In the meantime Telemachus sought the solitude of the seashore, where he washed his hands in the grey surf and lifted them in prayer to Athene. 'Hear, I beg you, you that in your godhead came yesterday to my house. It was your command that I should sail across the misty seas to find out whether my long-lost father is ever coming back. But my countrymen, and above all those Suitors that besiege my mother, are thwarting me at every point.'

This was his prayer. Athene drew near to him, and assuming the form and voice of Mentor, addressed him with winged words. 'Telemachus, you will be neither a coward nor a fool in the future, if your father's manly vigour has descended on you – and what a man *he* was in word and deed! This journey of yours will not prove futile or fruitless. It is only if you were not the true son of Odysseus and Penelope that I would think your plans might come to nothing. Few sons, indeed, are like their fathers. Generally they are worse; but just a few are better. And since you are by no means lacking in Odysseus' resourcefulness, and since you will be no fool or coward in the future, you can hope to succeed in this undertaking. So forget the Suitors now and dismiss their plots and machinations from your mind. They are fools, and there is no sense in them. Nor have they any inkling of the dark fate that is stalking so near and will strike them all down in a single day.

'You, meanwhile, will soon be starting this journey you have set your heart on. For am I not your father's friend, and ready to find you a fast ship and sail with you myself? Go home now and show yourself to the Suitors. Then get provisions ready and stow them all in containers, the wine in jars, and the barley-meal, that gives men strength, in strong skins. Meanwhile, I will soon collect a crew of volunteers in the town. And there are plenty of ships, old and new, in sea-girt Ithaca. I myself will pick out the best for you, and we'll have her rigged in no time and launch her on the open sea.'

Athene, Daughter of Zeus, had spoken, and there was no loitering there for Telemachus when he heard the voice of the goddess. He set off at once for home, though with an anxious heart. At the palace he found the high and mighty Suitors skinning goats and singeing fatted hogs in the courtyard. Antinous, with a laugh, ran up to him, seized his hand and, loudly calling his name, said: 'Telemachus, my fiery young orator, enough now of hard words and thoughts of violence. Let me see you eat and drink with us as usual. Our people will make all arrangements on your behalf for a ship and a picked crew to speed you on your way to sacred Pylos on your noble father's trail.'

But sagacious Telemachus replied: 'Antinous, it is out of the question for a man to sit down to a quiet supper and take his ease with a rowdy mob like you. Isn't it enough that all this time, under pretext of your suit, you have been robbing me of my best, while I was still too young to understand? I tell you, now that I'm old enough to learn from others what happened and to feel my own strength at last, I will do my best to send you all to perdition, whether I go to Pylos or stay here in Ithaca. And I shall not be thwarted over this journey of mine. I am going, if only as a passenger, since it seems to have suited you better that I should not be allowed a ship or crew of my own.' With this, Telemachus calmly withdrew his hand from Antinous'.

The Suitors, who had been preparing a meal, greeted this speech with a storm of insults and derision. 'I do believe,' said one arrogant young man, 'that Telemachus wants to cut our throats! And he's off to sandy Pylos to get help. Perhaps he'll go as far as Sparta and back, since he's so thirsty for our blood. Or it may occur to him that the fertile soil of Ephyre is worth a visit. He'll come home with a deadly poison, drop it in the wine-bowl, and kill us all off.'

And another insolent youth chimed in: 'Ah, but who knows? If he too takes to sea-faring, he may stray from home and be lost like Odysseus, far from his friends. And what a nuisance that would be for us! All the extra trouble of dividing his property between us and presenting his house to his mother and her bridegroom!'

Telemachus let them talk, and went down to his father's store-room, a big and lofty chamber stacked with gold and bronze, and with chests full of clothing, and stores of fragrant oil. There too, packed close along the wall, stood jars of mellow vintage wine, full of the true unblended juice, waiting for the day when Odysseus, after all his suffering, should find his way home again. There were locks to the closely fitting, double doors; and day and night the room and its treasures were in charge of the housekeeper, Eurycleia, daughter of Ops, Peisenor's son, who had all her wits about her.

Calling her now to the store-room, Telemachus said: 'Listen, nurse dear, will you draw some flagons of wine for me? And let it be the choicest you have, next to the vintage you keep with such care for your unlucky king, always hoping that he may escape his fate and return home. Fill twelve flagons and put their stoppers on. And pour out some barley-meal in strong leather bags – twenty measures, please, of mill-crushed grain. Not a word to anyone else! Get all the provisions together, and in the evening I will fetch them myself when my mother has gone upstairs for the night. I am off to Sparta and sandy Pylos on the chance of finding out something about my dear father's return.'

At this his nurse, Eurycleia, gave a shriek and burst into tears and poured out winged words.

'Dear child, what on earth has put this idea into your head? Why must you go wandering all over the world, you an only son, the apple of your mother's eye; and Odysseus, favourite of Zeus, dead and gone, far from his home in foreign parts? The moment your back is turned those men will be plotting mischief against you; and when they've done you to death, they'll share all this between them. Stay here at home where you belong. There's no call for you to go looking for trouble all over the barren seas.'

'Have no fears, nurse dear,' the prudent Telemachus replied. 'There's a god's hand in this. But you must swear to me that you won't tell my good mother for at least a dozen days, or till she misses me herself and finds I'm gone. We don't want tears to spoil her lovely cheeks.'

The old woman swore by all the gods that she would keep his secret, and when she had solemnly taken her oath she drew off the wine for him in flagons and ran the barley-meal into strong bags. Telemachus rejoined the company in the hall.

The bright-eyed goddess Athene now had another idea. Disguising herself as Telemachus, she went all through the town, picked out her twenty men and passed them each the word to forgather by the good ship at nightfall. The vessel itself she begged of Noemon son of Phronius, a prominent Ithacan, who willingly promised to give it to her.

The sun went down and all the ways grew dark. The goddess now ran the good ship into the water and stowed in her all the gear that big ships carry. This done, she moored her in the far corner of the harbour. When the good ship's company had gathered round, the goddess had an encouraging word for each of them.

The bright-eyed goddess Athene now had yet another idea. She made her way to godlike Odysseus' palace and lulled the Suitors there into a state of pleasant drowsiness, clouding their wits as they drank, and striking the wine-cups from their hands. Their eyelids heavy with sleep, they lingered no more at table, but went off to the town to their beds. Then bright-eyed Athene, assuming Mentor's form and voice once more, called Telemachus out of the palace to her side. 'Telemachus,' she said, 'your well-greaved companions are sitting at their oars, waiting for your word to start. Come; we do not want to delay the journey.'

With this, Pallas Athene led the way swiftly, and Telemachus followed in the footsteps of the goddess. When they came down to the sea and reached the boat they found their long-haired crew waiting on the beach, and the noble Telemachus addressed them.

'My friends, follow me; we must get the stores on board. They are all stacked and ready at the palace. My mother knows nothing of this, nor do the servants, except one woman whom I took into my confidence.'

He led off and the crew followed. They brought down all the stores and stowed them in their well-built ship, taking their orders from Odysseus' son. Telemachus then followed Athene on board. She took her seat on the afterdeck and he sat down beside her. The men cast the hawsers off, climbed in, and took their places at their oars. And now, out of the West, Athene of the flashing eyes called up for them a steady following wind and sent it singing over the wine-dark sea. Telemachus shouted to the crew to rig the ship and they leapt to his orders. They hauled up the pine mast, placed it in its hollow box, made it fast with stays, and hoisted the white sail with plaited oxhide ropes. The sail billowed out in the wind, and a dark wave hissed loudly round her keel, as the vessel gathered way and sped on her course through the seas.

When all was made fast in the swift black ship, they took out the mixing-bowls, filled them to the brim with wine and poured libations to the immortal gods who live for ever, and above all to the Daughter of Zeus, the Lady of the gleaming eyes. And all night long and into the dawn the ship ploughed her way through the sea.

# 3
# TELEMACHUS WITH NESTOR

Leaving the waters of the splendid East, the Sun leapt up into the brazen firmament to bring light to the immortals and to mortal men on the fruitful earth. The travellers now came to Pylos, the stately citadel of Neleus, where they found the people on the sea-shore sacrificing jet-black bulls to Poseidon, Lord of the Earthquake, god of the sable locks. There were nine companies seated there, with five hundred men in each; and every company had nine bulls to sacrifice. They had just tasted the victims' entrails and were burning the thigh-bones in the god's honour, as the travellers brought their trim ship to land. The crew brailed up and furled the sail, moored their vessel, and disembarked with Athene leading the way; Telemachus was the last to leave.

The goddess with the flashing eyes turned to him now and said: 'Telemachus, you must forget your diffidence: there is no occasion for it here at all. Why have you crossed the seas, if not to find out where your father's bones lie buried and how he met his end? Go straight up, then, to Nestor, the tamer of horses; we are here to learn the wisdom hidden in his heart. But you yourself must appeal to him to tell you the honest truth, though a man as wise as he is will not lie.'

'But, Mentor,' the thoughtful Telemachus asked, 'how am I to go up to him? How shall I greet him? I have had no practice in making speeches; it is embarrassing for a young man to question one so much his senior.'

'Telemachus,' replied bright-eyed Athene, 'where your own intelligence fails, a god will inspire you. For I think the gods have blessed both your birth and your progress to manhood.'

With this, Pallas Athene led off quickly, and Telemachus followed in the steps of the goddess till they reached the place where the people of Pylos were assembled. There sat Nestor with his sons; their followers around them were piercing meat with skewers or roasting it in preparation for the banquet. But as soon as they caught sight of the strangers they all made a move in their direction, took them by the hand and invited them to join them. Nestor's son, Peisistratus, who was the first to reach them, took them both by the hand and gave them places at the banquet on downy fleeces spread over the sandy beach, near his brother Thrasymedes and his father. Then he helped them to the victims' inner parts, filled a gold cup with wine and welcomed Pallas Athene, Daughter of Zeus who bears the aegis,[1] with these words:

'Pray to the god, my friend. This feast that you find us holding is in the Lord Poseidon's honour. When you have made your drink-offering[2] and your prayer, as our rites dictate, pass on the cup of mellow wine to your companion here, so that he may do the same. For he too must be a worshipper of the immortal gods of whom all men stand in need. But since he is the younger, in fact a man of my own age, I hand this golden beaker to you first.' And he placed the cup of sweet wine in Athene's hands.

The goddess was delighted at the good manners which the young man had shown in giving her the golden beaker first, and at once began an earnest prayer to the Lord Poseidon: 'Hear me, Poseidon, Sustainer of Earth, and do not grudge us, your suppliants, the fulfilment of our wishes. First of all, grant glory to Nestor and his sons. Consider next these others, and recompense all in Pylos for their sumptuous offerings. Grant, lastly, that Telemachus and I may successfully accomplish the task that brings us here in our swift black ship and afterwards reach home safely.'

1. The aegis (meaning originally 'goatskin') seems to have been some sort of armour worn for defence, or of weapon brandished in attack, used by Zeus and Athene.

2. In the ceremony of libation the first few drops of wine were poured on to the ground or on to the fire as an offering to the gods.

So the goddess prayed, and as each petition left her lips she herself made its fulfilment sure. Then she passed the fine two-handled beaker to Telemachus, and Odysseus' son repeated her prayers. The outer flesh from the victims was now roasted and drawn off the spits, portions were carved for all, and they began their sumptuous feast.[1] When they had satisfied their appetite and thirst, Nestor, the Gerenian charioteer, said:

'Now that our visitors have eaten well, it is the right moment to put some questions to them and enquire who they are. Who are you, friends? From what port have you sailed over the highways of the sea? Is yours a trading venture; or are you sailing the seas recklessly, like roving pirates, who risk their lives to ruin other people?'

Telemachus, inspired by Athene, who was anxious for him to question the king about his father's disappearance and so win a good name among men, now plucked up the courage to make him a spirited reply:

'Nestor son of Neleus, great glory of the Greeks, you ask where we come from. I will tell you. We are from Ithaca, which lies at the foot of Mount Neion. We have come on private, not on public, business. I am searching through the length and breadth of the land for news of my noble father, the long-suffering Odysseus, who, it is said, fought by your side years ago at the sack of Troy. We can account for all the others who took part in the war. We know where each man met his pitiful death. But Zeus has wrapped even the death of Odysseus in utter mystery; and no one can tell us for certain when he died, whether he was the victim of some hostile tribe on land, or whether he was lost at sea in Amphitrite's waves. So I have come here to plead with you in the hope that you will tell me the truth about my father's unhappy end, if by any chance you witnessed it yourself or heard the story from some wanderer like him. For if ever a man was born to suffer, it was he. Do not soften your account out of pity or concern for my feelings, but faithfully

1. At a sacrifice to the gods, the thigh-bones of the slaughtered victim were wrapped in fat and burned with some of the flesh in honour of the gods. The sacrificers then tasted some of the offal, and then had their real feast of the good flesh roasted on spits or skewers.

describe the scene that met your eyes. I beseech you, if ever my good father Odysseus in the hard years of war at Troy gave you his word and kept it, remember what he did and tell me all you know.'

'Ah, my friend,' exclaimed Nestor, the Gerenian charioteer, 'what memories the name of Troy brings back! The miseries we fierce Achaeans endured there – raid after raid across the misty seas in search of plunder wherever Achilles led, fight after fight around the very walls of royal Priam's town! There our best men fell. There warlike Ajax lies. There lies Achilles, there Patroclus, wise in counsel as the gods. There too Antilochus, my own dear son, as strong as he was handsome, a fast runner, and what a fighter too! Nor is *that* the full sum of what the noble Achaeans endured at Troy. There is no man on earth who could unfold to you the whole disastrous tale, not though you sat and questioned him for half a dozen years, by which time you would have grown weary and gone home.

'For nine years we struggled to bring them down by every stratagem we could devise – but Zeus made it very difficult for us to achieve victory. And all the time there was not a man that dared to match his wits against the admirable Odysseus, who in every kind of strategy proved himself supreme – your father, if you really are his son. Indeed, I cannot help looking at you in awe: you talk exactly as he did, and I should have sworn no young man could so resemble him in speech. In all those years, whether at the general assembly or in the council of the kings, not once did Odysseus and I find ourselves speaking on opposite sides. We seemed to share a single mind, so well did we agree when, with our good sense and judgement, we advised the Argives on the best policies.

'After we had destroyed Priam's towering city we left in our ships. But then the gods scattered the fleet. Zeus planned disaster for our homeward journey because we had not all behaved sensibly and honestly, and many came to grief through the fatal anger of the bright-eyed Daughter of that mighty Sire. It happened like this. She began by making the two sons of Atreus quarrel. Acting on the spur of the moment and with no regard for procedure, they summoned the whole Achaean army to assemble at sunset, so that the troops arrived drunk, and told them the reason for the assembly. Menelaus put it to them all that their first concern should be to get to their distant homes across the seas. But this was not at all to Agamemnon's liking. He was for keeping them there and making ceremonial offerings to Athene, in the hope of appeasing her terrible wrath, not realizing in his folly how implacable she would prove; for it is not so easy to divert the immortal gods from their purpose. Well, the pair of them stood there exchanging hard words, till the soldiers, themselves divided in opinion, broke up the assembly in indescribable uproar. That night we rested, nursing vindictive feelings against our comrades-in-arms; for Zeus was making ready to strike us the fatal blow. In the morning half of us ran our ships down into the tranquil sea, and stowed in them our spoils and the captive women in their low-girdled dresses. Then, though the rest still held back and stayed where they were with Agamemnon the commander-in-chief, our party embarked and set out.

'Our ships sailed fast, for a god had levelled the deep swell of the sea. We soon reached Tenedos, and there, eager to be home, we sacrificed to the gods. But Zeus had no intention of letting us reach home so soon, and he mercilessly stirred dissension among us once more. As a result, one squadron swung the curved prows of their vessels round and turned back towards Troy. These were the followers of Odysseus, that wise and subtle king, falling in once more with the wishes of Agamemnon son of Atreus. But I, well aware of the god's sinister designs, fled with the massed ships that formed my company. Warlike Diomedes did the same, bringing his party with him, and later on auburn-haired Menelaus followed too. He caught us up at Lesbos, where we were pondering over the long sea journey, whether to sail north of the rugged coast of Chios and by way of Psyria, keeping that island on our left, or to sail south of Chios past the windy heights of Mimas. We prayed for a sign, and the god made it clear that we should cut straight across the open sea to Euboea to get out of harm's way as quickly as possible. A whistling wind blew up, and our ships made splendid running down the teeming sea-ways, reaching Geraestus during the night. And many a bull's thigh we laid on Poseidon's altar after spanning that weary stretch of water.

'It was on the fourth day that the company of Diomedes, son of Tydeus, the tamer of horses, brought their fine craft to anchor in Argos. But I held on for Pylos, and the breeze never dropped from the moment when the god made it blow. Consequently, dear child, I got back without any news of the men we had left behind, and have no idea who escaped or who was lost. But all the news that has come to me as I sit here at home you shall have, as is only right, and I'll keep nothing back. In the first place, they tell me that the Myrmidon spearmen reached home in safety under the great Achilles' noble son; and that Poias' son, the brilliant Philoctetes, fared equally well. Again, Idomeneus brought all his men to Crete, all, that is, who had survived the war. The sea got none from him.

'As for Agamemnon, though you live far away, you must have heard how he had no sooner got back than he fell a wretched victim to Aegisthus' plot. And a grim reckoning there was for Aegisthus! Which shows what a good thing it is, when a man dies, for a son to survive him, as Orestes survived to take revenge on the treacherous Aegisthus who had killed his noble father. So you, my friend – and what a tall and splendid young man you have become! – be as brave as Orestes. Then future generations will sing your praises.'

The thoughtful Telemachus replied: 'King Nestor son of Neleus, great glory of the Achaeans, that was revenge indeed! Orestes' fame will travel throughout Achaean lands and live in song for generations. Ah, if the gods would only give me strength like his to exact revenge for the Suitors' vicious crimes, their wilful disregard of what is right, and the ways they have humiliated me. But they have no such happiness in store for me, nor for my father. I must just endure.'

'My friend,' said Nestor the Gerenian charioteer, 'now that your own remarks have put me in mind of it, they *do* say a whole crowd of your mother's Suitors are wreaking havoc in your house as uninvited guests. Tell me, do you tamely submit to this, or have the people of Ithaca been listening to some rumour inspired by a god that has turned their hearts against you? Who knows whether some day Odysseus may not come back, alone perhaps, or with all his followers, and pay these Suitors out for their violence? I only wish that bright-eyed Athene could show towards you some of the loving care she devoted to your illustrious father in the course of our hard campaigns at Troy. For never in my life have I seen the gods display such open affection as Pallas Athene showed in her championship of Odysseus. Ah, if only she would love and care for you like that, some of those gentlemen would soon have all thoughts of courtship knocked out of their heads for ever.'

'Venerable Lord,' said the thoughtful Telemachus, 'I see no hope whatever of your words proving true. You speak of the impossible. You amaze me. For all my hopes, that will never happen, even if the gods were to will it.'

'Telemachus,' the goddess of the flashing eyes exclaimed, 'what are you saying? A god who wills it can bring anyone safely home however far away he may be. And for myself I would rather live through untold hardships to reach home in the end and see that happy day, than come straight back and die at my own hearth, as Agamemnon died by the wiles of his wife and Aegisthus. But it is our common lot to die, and the gods themselves cannot rescue even one they love, when Death that stretches all men out lays its dread hand upon him.'

'Mentor,' the thoughtful Telemachus replied, 'let us not discuss these painful matters any more. We can no longer count on my father's return. The gods who never die have already set his feet on the dark path that leads to death. But there is something else I would like to ask Nestor, whose knowledge of men's ways and thoughts is unrivalled. They tell me he has been king through three generations, and when I look at him I seem to gaze on immortality itself. Nestor, son of Neleus, tell me what really happened. How did imperial Agamemnon, son of Atreus, meet his end? Where was Menelaus, and by what cunning snare did that treacherous Aegisthus contrive to kill a man far braver than himself? Was Menelaus away from Achaean Argos and wandering abroad? Is that why Aegisthus plucked up the courage to strike?'

'My child,' Nestor, the Gerenian charioteer, answered, 'I will tell you the whole story. You can imagine for yourself what would have happened had Agamemnon's brother, auburn-haired Menelaus, come back from Troy and caught Aegisthus in the house alive. No mound would have honoured *his* remains! Flung on the plain outside the city walls, he'd have made meat for the dogs and birds of prey, and there's no woman in Achaea who would have shed a tear for him. His was indeed no petty crime. While we who were besieging Troy toiled at heroic tasks, he spent his leisured days, right in the heart of Argos where the horses graze, busy charming Agamemnon's wife with his seductive talk.

'At first Queen Clytaemnestra turned a deaf ear to his dishonourable schemes. She was a sensible woman, and besides, she had a minstrel with her, to whom Agamemnon when he left for Troy had given orders to watch over his queen. But when the fatal day came, appointed by the gods for her to yield, Aegisthus took this minstrel to a desert isle, left him there as carrion for the birds of prey, and carried Clytaemnestra off to his own house, fond lover, willing lady. After this great achievement he heaped the holy altars of the gods with thigh bones, and hung the temple walls with fine fabrics and gold, thank-offerings for a success beyond his wildest dreams.

'Meanwhile we were sailing together over the sea from Troy, Menelaus and I, the best of friends. But when we were abreast of the sacred cape of Sunium, where Attica juts out into the sea, Phoebus Apollo shot one of his painless arrows at Menelaus' helmsman and killed him, with the tiller of the running ship still in his hands. This man, Phrontis son of Onetor, had been the world's best steersman in a gale, and Menelaus, though anxious to journey on, was kept at Sunium till he could bury his comrade with the proper rites. But when he too had got away over the wine-dark sea in those great ships of his and had run as far as the steep headland of Malea, far-seeing Zeus brought disaster on their journey, and sent them a howling gale with giant waves. Then and there he split the fleet in two.

'He drove one group towards Crete and the Cydonian settlements on the River Iardanus. Now where the lands of Gortyn end, out in the misty sea, there is a precipitous cliff that falls abruptly to the water, and the south-westerly gales drive the great rollers against a headland to the west, in towards Phaestus, with nothing but this puny reef to keep their violence in check. When one party reached this spot, the crews by a hair's breadth escaped destruction, though their ships were splintered on the rocks by the fury of the seas. Meanwhile Menelaus with the remaining five vessels of his blue-prowed fleet was driven on by wind and wave to Egypt. And so it was that he was cruising in those foreign lands, amassing a fortune in goods and gold, while Aegisthus schemed this wickedness at home. After he had killed Agamemnon, the usurper reigned in golden Mycenae and kept the people in subjection for seven years. But the eighth brought him disaster, in the shape of Orestes; for that brave youth, returning from Athens, killed Aegisthus, his noble father's murderer, and so the slayer was slain. When Orestes had done the deed, he invited his friends to a funeral banquet for his hateful mother and the cowardly Aegisthus; and on the selfsame day he was joined by Menelaus of the loud war-cry, bringing in all the treasures that had filled his holds.

'Be warned yourself, my friend! Don't stray too long or too far from home, nor leave your wealth unguarded with such a set of arrogant brutes in the place, unless you want them to share it out, to eat up all you have, so making your journey futile. I do urge you, however, to pay Menelaus a visit. For he has only just returned home from a region so remote that one might well give up all hope of return once the winds had blown one astray into that wide expanse of sea, which is so vast and perilous that even the birds cannot cross it in a year. So set off now with your ship and crew; or, if you prefer to go by land, I have a chariot and horses at your disposal and my sons are at your service too, to escort you to lovely Lacedaemon where auburn-haired Menelaus lives. Appeal to him in person if you want the truth from his lips, though as wise a man as he is will not lie.'

As Nestor came to an end, the sun went down and darkness fell. It was the bright-eyed goddess Athene who spoke next: 'Venerable Lord, your tale was well told. But come, cut up the victims' tongues and mix the wine, so that we can pour out offerings to Poseidon and the other immortals before we think of sleeping. It is time for bed, now that the light has faded into dusk. It is not right to remain any longer at this feast of the gods. We should return home.'

It was the Daughter of Zeus who had spoken; her words did not fall on deaf ears. The squires sprinkled their hands with water, while the young attendants filled the mixing-bowls to the brim and then, after pouring a few drops first in each man's cup, they served them all with wine. The tongues were thrown into the flames; the company rose and sprinkled libations on them. And when they had made their offerings and drunk their fill, Athene and Prince Telemachus both made a move to return to their hollow ship. But Nestor stopped them, protesting loudly:

'May Zeus and the other immortal gods forbid that you should go to your ship and turn aside from my house as though it belonged to some destitute pauper who hasn't enough blankets and rugs for himself and his guests to sleep between in comfort! Indeed, I have good bedding for all; and I swear that the son of my friend Odysseus shall not lie down to sleep on his ship's deck so long as I am alive or sons survive me here to entertain all visitors that come to my door.'

'Well said, my Lord,' replied the goddess of the flashing eyes; 'and it is right for Telemachus to accept your invitation. He will go with you now and sleep in your palace, while I return to the black ship to reassure the men and tell them everything. For I am the only senior in the party; all the rest are young men of much the same age as the great-hearted Telemachus and follow him out of companionship. I intend to sleep there by the black ship's hull tonight, and in the morning to set out on a visit to the great-hearted Cauconians, who owe me a long-standing debt – not a small one either. But since Telemachus has become your guest, send him on in a chariot with one of your sons and give him the fastest and strongest horses in your stable.'

As she finished, bright-eyed Athene took the form of a vulture and flew off. They were all amazed. The old King marvelled at the sight.

'Telemachus, dear boy!' he exclaimed, seizing him by the

hand. 'There is no chance that you will ever be a coward or weakling when, young as you are, you already have your guardian gods at your side. For of all that live on Olympus, this was no other than the Daughter of Zeus, the august Lady of Triton, who honoured your noble father too among the Argives. Goddess, be gracious and grant fame to me and to my sons and to my honoured wife. In return you shall have a yearling heifer, broad in the brow, whom no one yet has broken in and led beneath the yoke. She shall be sacrificed to you with gilded horns.'

That was his prayer, and Pallas Athene heard him; and now the Gerenian charioteer Nestor led the way towards his stately home, followed by his sons and his sons-in-law. When they came to the royal palace, they took their places on the seats and chairs, and the old man prepared a bowl of mellow wine for his guests, from a jar that had stood for ten years until the moment when the maid undid the cap and opened it. When the old King had mixed a bowl of this vintage, he poured a little out, with earnest prayers to Athene, Daughter of Zeus who holds the aegis.

They made their libations and quenched their thirst, after which the rest went to their homes for the night. But Nestor the Gerenian charioteer arranged for the noble Odysseus' son Telemachus to sleep at the palace itself, on a wooden bedstead in the echoing portico, with the spearman Peisistratus, that leader of men, next to him; he was the only unmarried son left at home. The King himself retired to rest in his room at the back of the high building, where the Queen his wife prepared his bed.

When Dawn came, fresh and rosy-fingered, Nestor the Gerenian charioteer got up from his bed, went out, and seated himself on a smooth white bench which stood, gleaming and polished, in front of his lofty doors. Here his father Neleus used to sit and give counsel as wise as the gods'; but he had long since died and gone to Hades' Halls. So now Nestor of Gerenia sat there in his turn, sceptre in hand, a Warden of the Achaean race. His sons all came from their rooms and gathered round him, Echephron and Stratius, Perseus and Aretus, and the noble

Thrasymedes. The heroic Peisistratus came last and made the sixth. The godlike Telemachus was ushered to a seat at their side; and Nestor the Gerenian charioteer now made his wishes known:

'Quick, my dear sons, do what I want so that I can pay my devotions to Athene, who of all the gods has first claim upon them, since it was she who came in person to me at the god's sumptuous banquet. One of you go to the meadow for a heifer to be brought here as quickly as the cowherd can drive her. And one go down to great-hearted Telemachus' black ship and bring all his crew here except two; another summon the goldsmith Laerces to gild the heifer's horns. The rest of you stay with me here, and tell the servants indoors to prepare a feast in the palace and to fetch seats and firewood and fresh water.'

They all busily set about their tasks. The heifer came from the meadows; bold Telemachus' crew came from his good ship; the smith came, equipped with the bronze tools of his trade, anvil, hammer, and the strong tongs he used for working gold; Athene also came, to accept the sacrifice. Then Nestor the old charioteer gave out the gold, with which the smith gilded the heifer's horns by way of embellishment to please the goddess's eye. Next Stratius and Echephron led the heifer forward by the horns. Aretus came from the store-room carrying in his right hand a flowered bowl of lustral water, and in the other a basket with the barley-meal. The stalwart Thrasymedes, gripping a sharp axe, stood by to strike the victim down, and Perseus held the dish to catch its blood.

The old charioteer Nestor now started the ritual with the lustral water and the scattered grain, and offered up his earnest prayers to Athene as he began the sacrifice by throwing a tuft of hair from its head on the fire.

When they had prayed and sprinkled the barley-meal, Nestor's son, the high-spirited Thrasymedes, stepped up and struck. The axe cut through the tendons of the heifer's neck and it collapsed. At this, the women raised their celebratory cry – Nestor's daughters and his daughter-in-law, and his honoured wife Eurydice, Clymenus' eldest daughter. The men lifted the heifer's head from the trodden earth and held it up while that leader of men, Peisistratus, cut its throat. When the dark blood had gushed out and life had left the heifer's body, they swiftly dismembered the carcass, cut out the thigh bones in the usual way, wrapped them in folds of fat and laid raw meat above them. The venerable King burnt these on the firewood, sprinkling red wine over the flames, while the young men gathered round with five-pronged forks in their hands. When the thighs were burnt up and they had tasted the inner parts, they carved the rest into small pieces, pierced them with skewers and held the sharp ends to the fire till all was roasted.

The beautiful Polycaste, King Nestor's youngest daughter, now bathed Telemachus. When she had bathed him and rubbed him with olive-oil, she gave him a tunic and arranged a fine cloak round his shoulders, so that he stepped from the bath looking like an immortal god. He then went and sat down by Nestor, the shepherd of the people.

When they had roasted the outer flesh and taken it off the skewers, they sat down to dine, with squires to wait on them and fill their golden cups with wine. After they had satisfied their appetite and thirst, Nestor the Gerenian charioteer said: 'Now my sons, fetch Telemachus a pair of long-maned horses and harness them to a chariot so that he can be on his way.'

They obeyed him promptly and soon had a pair of fast horses harnessed to a chariot, in which the housekeeper had packed bread and wine together with delicacies of the kind that the favourites of the gods eat. Telemachus took his place in the handsome chariot, and Nestor's son, that leader of men Peisistratus, got in beside him, took the reins in his hands, and flicked the horses with the whip to urge them forward. The willing pair flew off towards the plains, putting the high city of Pylos behind them, and all day long the yoke rose and fell on their necks.

The sun went down and all the ways grew dark. They reached Pherae, where they drove up to the house of Diocles, son of Ortilochus, whose father was Alpheius. There they spent the night and received the gifts that hospitality dictates. As soon as Dawn appeared, fresh and rosy-fingered, they harnessed their horses once again and mounted the burnished chariot. Out past the echoing portico and through the gates they drove. A flick of the whip to speed them on, and the pair flew on with a will. They came to the wheat plains and hastened on to their journey's end with all the speed of their thoroughbred horses. The sun went down and all the ways grew dark.

# 4
# MENELAUS AND HELEN

And so they came to the rolling lands of Lacedaemon, deep in the hills, and drove up to the palace of the illustrious Menelaus. They found him entertaining a large company of relatives in his house to celebrate the impending weddings of his son and of his lovely daughter. He was sending the princess as a bride to the son of Achilles, that breaker of the battle-line, as he had promised long ago in Troy. So now by the gods' will the marriage was soon to take place, and Menelaus was sending her with chariot and horses to the capital of the Myrmidons, of whom her bridegroom was the King. As bride for his beloved son, the gallant Megapenthes, he was bringing Alector's daughter from Sparta. A slave had borne this son to Menelaus, for the gods had given no other child to Helen after Hermione, that lovely girl with golden Aphrodite's beauty.

They were banqueting then under the high roof of the great hall, these relatives and friends of the illustrious Menelaus, in festive mood, while a minstrel in the company sang divinely to the lyre, and two acrobats danced in time to his tune, and whirled in and out among the guests.

The two travellers, brave Telemachus and Nestor's noble son, brought their chariot to a halt at the courtyard gate. The lord Eteoneus, energetic squire of the great Menelaus, came out and saw them there, and set off at once through the palace to inform the King. He stood near him and said urgently, 'Menelaus, favourite of Zeus, we have some strangers here at the gates – men whom I take by their looks to be of divine descent. Tell me whether we should unharness their horses for them or send them on to find someone else to entertain them.'

Auburn-haired Menelaus answered him indignantly. 'Eteoneus, son of Boethus, you have not always been a fool; but at the moment you are talking nonsense like a child. You and I enjoyed much hospitality from strangers before we reached our homes and could expect that Zeus might grant us a life without suffering in time to come. Unyoke their horses at once, and bring our visitors to join us at the feast.'

Eteoneus ran off through the hall, shouting to his assistants to hurry up and follow him. They led the sweating horses from under the yoke and tied them up at the mangers in the stable, throwing down beside them a feed of grain mixed with white barley. Then they tilted the chariot against the burnished wall by the gate and ushered the newcomers into the royal buildings. Telemachus and his friend opened their eyes in wonder at all they saw as they passed through the King's palace. It seemed to them that this lofty hall of illustrious Menelaus was lit by something of the sun's or the moon's splendour.

When they had feasted their eyes on the sight, they went and bathed in polished baths, and after the maids had washed them, rubbed them with oil and dressed them in thick cloaks and tunics, they took their places on chairs at the side of noble Menelaus, son of Atreus. A maid came with water in a beautiful golden ewer and poured it out over a silver basin for them to rinse their hands. She then drew a polished table to their side, and the faithful housekeeper brought some bread and set it by them with a choice of delicacies, helping them liberally to all she could offer. Meanwhile a carver served them with plates of various meats he had selected from his board, and put gold cups beside them.

Auburn-haired Menelaus now greeted them, saying, 'Welcome. Do begin your meal. After you've dined we shall inquire who you may be. Your lineage has left a stamp upon your looks; you are the sons of kings, those sceptred favourites of Zeus, for inferior parents could not breed such men as you.'

As he spoke, with his own hands he passed them the rich piece of roast that had been given him as the portion of honour, and they helped themselves to the good things spread before them. When they had satisfied their appetite and thirst,

Telemachus spoke to Nestor's son, leaning close so that the rest might not hear him: 'Look round this echoing hall, son of Nestor, friend of my heart. The whole place gleams with bronze and gold, amber and silver and ivory. What an amazing quantity of treasures! The court of Zeus on Olympus must be like this inside. The sight fills me with awe.'

Auburn-haired Menelaus caught what he was saying and spoke words that flew. 'No mortal can compete with Zeus, dear boys. His house and all his possessions are everlasting. But when it comes to men, I feel that few or none can rival me in wealth, for it took me seven years and great hardship to amass this fortune and bring it home in my ships. My travels took me to Cyprus, to Phoenicia, and to Egypt. Ethiopians, Sidonians, Erembians, I visited them all; and I saw Libya too, where the lambs grow horns almost immediately and their ewes lamb three times in the course of the year; where nobody from king to shepherd need go without cheese or meat, or fresh milk either, since the ewes provide milk all the year round.

'But while I was wandering in those parts, making my fortune, an enemy of our house struck down my unsuspecting brother, caught off his guard through the treachery of his accursed wife. So it gives me little pleasure to call myself the lord of all this wealth, since, as you must have heard from your fathers, whoever they may be, I have had much sorrow in my life and have already lost one lovely dwelling full of precious things. How happy I could be, here in my house, with even a third of my former estate, if those friends of mine were still alive who died long ago on the broad plains of Troy, so far from Argos where the horses graze!

'And yet, though I miss them all and often grieve for them as I sit here in our halls till sorrow finds relief in tears and the tears cease to fall (for mourning is bleak and one soon tires of it), I do not mourn for that whole company, disconsolate as I am, so much as for one man among them, whose loss when I brood over it makes sleep and eating hateful to me. For of all the Achaeans who strove at Troy it was Odysseus who strove the hardest and achieved the most. Yet all that labour was to end in misery for him, and in a haunting sense of loss for me, so long has he been gone, leaving us in ignorance of whether he is dead or not; though I suppose his people are already mourning for him as dead – the old man Laertes, loyal Penelope, and Telemachus, whom he left a new-born baby in his home.'

Menelaus' words stirred in Telemachus an overwhelming desire to weep, and when he heard about his father he let the tears roll down his cheeks to the ground and with both hands held up his purple cloak in front of his eyes. Menelaus recognized him and deliberated for a while within himself whether to wait for the young man to mention his father, or to put searching questions to him straight away. In the midst of his perplexity, Helen came down from her lofty perfumed room, looking like Artemis with her golden distaff. Adreste drew up for her an elegant chair; Alcippe brought a rug of the softest wool; and Phylo carried her silver work-basket, a gift from Alcandre, wife of Polybus, who lived in Egyptian Thebes, where the houses are furnished in more sumptuous style than anywhere else in the world. This man had given Menelaus two silver baths, a pair of three-legged cauldrons, and ten talents in gold; in addition his wife gave Helen beautiful gifts for herself, including a golden spindle and a basket that ran on wheels that were made of silver finished with a rim of gold. This was the basket that her lady, Phylo, brought in and put beside her. It was full of fine-spun yarn, and the spindle with its dark wool was laid across it. Helen sat down on the chair, with a footstool for her feet, and at once asked her husband about everything.

'Menelaus, favourite of Heaven, have we been told the names of these men who have come to our house? Shall I withhold the truth, or speak the truth? I feel that I must speak. For never in man or woman have I seen such a likeness before – I am lost in admiration. Surely this must be great-hearted Odysseus' son Telemachus, whom his father left as a new-born baby in his home, when you Achaeans came to Troy with war in your hearts for my sake, shameless creature that I was!'

'Lady,' replied the auburn-haired Menelaus, 'you point out a resemblance I can see too. Odysseus' feet were just the same, and so were his hands, the movement of his eyes, the shape of his head and the way his hair grew. Only a moment ago when I was talking of Odysseus as I remembered him, and saying how much he had done and suffered for my sake, the tears came streaming down his cheeks and he covered his face with his purple cloak.'

Nestor's son Peisistratus now said, 'Menelaus, son of Atreus, favourite of Heaven, leader of your people, you are right in supposing that my friend here is Odysseus' son. But he is modest, and on a first visit like this he is too bashful to speak uninvited in front of you, whose conversation gives us as much pleasure as we would get from listening to a god. So Nestor of Gerenia sent me with him for escort, as Telemachus was anxious to see you, in case you might help with advice or suggest some line of action. For a son, when his father is gone, has many difficulties to cope with at home, especially if there is nobody to help him, as is the case with Telemachus, whose father is abroad and who has no other friends at home to protect him from injustice.'

'Who would have thought it!' exclaimed the auburn-haired Menelaus. 'He was indeed a well-loved friend, the friend who undertook all those heroic tasks for my sake: and now his son has come to my house! I had meant to favour him above all others of our race when he came back, if an all-seeing Zeus had allowed the two of us to bring our good ships safely home across the sea. I'd have built him a house and transplanted him from Ithaca with all his possessions and his son and his people too. Yes, I'd have emptied one of the towns round here in my own dominions and given him a town in Argos to live in. We would have lived in the same country and met continually. Nor could anything have intervened to spoil our pleasure in each other's company, till the darkness of death had swallowed us up. But a jealous god must have thought otherwise, and so ensured that that unhappy man was the only one who never reached his home.'

Menelaus' words stirred in them all a longing for tears. Helen of Argos, child of Zeus, broke down and wept. Telemachus and Menelaus, son of Atreus, did the same. Nor could Nestor's son keep his eyes dry when he thought of his brother, the handsome Antilochus, whom the splendid son of the bright Dawn had killed. Remembering him he turned to Menelaus now.

'Menelaus, son of Atreus,' he said, 'whenever we talked of you at home and asked one another about you, Nestor my old father used always to speak of you as the wisest of men. Please be persuaded now by me, and contain your grief, if you possibly can, since I for one take no delight in weeping as I dine – and besides, it's almost dawn. Not that I think it wrong to shed a tear for any man who meets his fate and dies. Indeed, what other tribute can one pay to poor mortality than a lock of hair from the head and a tear on the cheek? I have my own dead too, a brother, not by any means the worst soldier in the Argive camp. You must have met Antilochus, though I never knew him myself, nor even saw him. They say he excelled above all others, a superb runner and a great fighter.'

'My friend,' replied the auburn-haired Menelaus, 'in saying all you said just now, you spoke and acted with the discretion of a much older man. You talk such good sense, you're the true son of your father. Good breeding cannot be hidden when a man's father has himself been blessed by Zeus at his birth and at his marriage, like Nestor. He was lucky from first to last through all his life, and is now serenely ageing in his home, with sons about him who combine good spearmanship and intelligence. Well, let us forget the tearful mood that we had fallen into, and turn our thoughts once more to supper, when they have poured some water on our hands. In the morning Telemachus and I shall have many important matters to discuss with each other.'

Asphalion, one of noble Menelaus' busy squires, poured water on their hands, and they helped themselves to the good food that was spread before them. Helen, meanwhile, the child of Zeus, had had an idea. Into the bowl in which their wine was mixed, she slipped a drug that had the power of robbing grief and anger of their sting and banishing all painful memories. No one that swallowed this, dissolved in wine, could shed a single tear that day, even for the death of his mother and father, or if they put his brother or his own son to the sword and he were there to see it done. It was one of many drugs which had been given to the daughter of Zeus by an Egyptian woman, Polydamna, the wife of Thon. The fertile soil of Egypt is very rich in herbs, many of which are beneficial in solution, though many are poisonous. And in medical knowledge Egyptians are supreme among men. They are true sons of Paeeon the Healer.

When Helen had dropped the drug into the wine and seen that their cups were filled, she turned to the company once more and said: 'Menelaus, son of Atreus, favourite of the gods, and my young and noble guests, each of us has his good times, and each his bad times – Zeus in his omnipotence sees to that. Then let us sit at dinner in this hall and enjoy ourselves listening to each other's stories. I have just the one for the occasion. It is, of course, beyond me to describe or even number all the daring feats of dauntless Odysseus. But here is one marvellous exploit which he had the nerve to conceive and carry through in Troy when you Achaeans were hard pressed.

'He disfigured himself with appalling lacerations and then, with dirty rags on his back, looking like a slave, he slunk into the broad streets of the enemy city. Disguised as a beggar he looked utterly different from the Odysseus of the camp by the ship. He made his way like this into the Trojan city, and was not detected by anyone. I was the only one who penetrated his disguise, but whenever I questioned him he was clever enough to evade me. However, when I bathed and anointed him, gave him some clothes to wear and solemnly swore that I would not disclose his name to the Trojans before he returned to the huts by the ships, he gave me full details of the Achaeans' plans. And after killing a number of Trojans with his long sword, he got back to the Argive camp with a great deal of information. The other women of Troy were loud in their lamentations, but I rejoiced, for I was already longing to go home again. I had suffered a change of heart, repenting the blindness which Aphrodite sent me when she brought me to Troy from my own dear country and made me forsake my daughter, my bridal chamber, and a husband who lacked nothing in intelligence and looks.'

'My dear,' said the auburn-haired Menelaus, 'your tale was well and truly told. I have wandered far in this world, I have looked into many hearts and heard the counsels of the great, but never have I set eyes on a man of such endurance as the indomitable Odysseus. What he did inside the Wooden Horse is another example of the man's steadfastness and iron resolution. We sat inside it with the pick of the Argive army, waiting to bring havoc and slaughter on the Trojans, when you came up, prompted, I can only suppose, by some god who wished to give victory to Troy, for Prince Deiphobus came with you. Three times you circled round our hollow lair, feeling the outside with your hands, and you called out the name of all the Argive captains in turn, altering your voice to mimic each man's wife. Diomedes and I, who were sitting right in the middle with the good Odysseus, heard you calling and were both tempted to jump up and come out or give an instant answer from within. But Odysseus held us back and checked our impetuosity. The rest of the warriors stayed absolutely still, though Anticlus still wanted to give you some reply. But Odysseus clapped his great hands relentlessly on the man's mouth and so saved the whole army, holding him tight till Pallas Athene had induced you to go away.'

Here the thoughtful Telemachus addressed the King: 'Menelaus, son of Atreus, favourite of the gods, leader of the people, it only makes things worse to think that such qualities as these could not shield Odysseus from disaster. Even a heart of iron could not have saved him. But come, let us retire for the night to find pleasure in sweet sleep.'

At this Helen of Argos instructed her maids to put two bedsteads in the portico and to lay fine purple fleeces on them, and spread rugs over these, and some thick coverlets on top. Torch in hand, the maids went out of the hall and made the beds, to which a squire then conducted the guests. And so the heroic Telemachus and Nestor's royal son spent the night in the forecourt of the palace, while Menelaus slept in his room at the back of the high buildings and the lady Helen of the long robes lay by his side.

As soon as Dawn appeared, fresh and rosy-fingered, Menelaus of the loud war-cry rose from his bed and put on his clothes. He slung a sharp sword from his shoulder, bound a fine pair of sandals on his glistening feet and strode from his bedroom looking like a god. He went to Telemachus and, with a word of greeting, took a seat beside him. 'Telemachus,' he asked, 'what brought you here over the wide seas to our pleasant land of Lacedaemon? Was it public business or private affairs? Tell me the truth.'

'Menelaus, son of Atreus, favourite of the gods, leader of your people,' the thoughtful Telemachus replied, 'I came to find out whether you could give me any news of my father. I am eaten out of house and home, my rich estate has gone to ruin, and my palace is packed with a set of implacable enemies, who spend their days in the wholesale slaughter of my jostling sheep and shambling cattle with their twisted horns; and in competing for my mother's hand in all their brutal pride. I am here to plead with you in the hope that you will tell me the truth about my father's unhappy end, if by any chance you witnessed it yourself or heard the story from some other wanderer like him. For if ever a man was born to suffer it was he. Do not soften your account out of pity or concern for my feelings, but faithfully describe the scene that met your eyes. I beseech you, if ever my good father Odysseus, in the hard years of war at Troy, gave you his word and kept it, remember what he did, and tell me all you know.'

Auburn-haired Menelaus was hot with indignation. 'How disgraceful!' he cried. 'So the cowards want to creep into the brave man's bed? It's just as if a deer had put her two little unweaned fawns to sleep in a mighty lion's den and gone to range the high ridges and the grassy dales for pasture. Back comes the lion to his lair, and the fawns meet a grisly fate – as will the Suitors at Odysseus' hand. Once, in the pleasant isle of Lesbos I saw him stand up to Philomeleides in a wrestling-match and bring him down with a mighty throw which delighted all the Achaeans. By Father Zeus, Athene, and Apollo, that's the Odysseus I should like to see these Suitors meet. A swift death and a sorry wedding there would be for all!

'But to answer your appeal and the questions you asked me – I have no wish to deceive you or to put you off with evasive answers. On the contrary, I shall pass on to you without concealment or reserve every word that I heard myself from the infallible lips of the Old Man of the Sea.

'It happened in Egypt. I had been anxious for some time to

get home, but the gods delayed me there, for I had omitted to make them the correct offerings, and they never allow one to forget their commandments. There is an island called Pharos in the rolling seas off the mouth of the Nile, a day's sailing for a ship with a roaring wind astern. In this island is a sheltered cove where sailors put in to draw their water from a well and afterwards launch their trim ships into the deep sea. It was here that the gods kept me for twenty days; and all that time there was never a sign of the off-shore breezes that speed ships out and into the open sea. All our supplies would have disappeared and the men's strength been exhausted, if one of the gods had not taken pity on me. It was Eidothee, the daughter of the mighty Proteus, the Old Man of the Sea, who came to my rescue. The sight of me touched her heart deeply when she met me walking by myself, away from my men, whom the pangs of hunger scattered every day round the coast to angle with barbed hooks for fish.

'She approached me and said, "Sir, are you an utter fool? Are you completely stupid? Or have you simply given up, and enjoy suffering so much that you allow yourself to be imprisoned all this time in the island and can find no means of escape though your men are growing weaker day by day?" To which I replied, "I do not know what goddess you may be, but I assure you that I have no wish to linger here. I must have offended the immortals who live in the wide heavens. You gods know everything; so tell me which of you it is that has confined me here and cut my voyage short; and tell me also how I can return home across the teeming seas."

'The fair goddess answered me at once: "Sir, I will tell you all you need to know. This island is the haunt of that immortal seer, Proteus of Egypt, the Old Man of the Sea, who owes allegiance to Poseidon and knows the depth of all the seas. He is my father too, so people say. If you could contrive somehow to lie in wait and catch him, he would tell you about your journey and the distances to be covered, and direct you home across the teeming seas. Not only that, favourite of Zeus, he will tell you, if you want to know, all that has happened in your palace, good or bad, while you have been away on your long weary travels." "Will you," I replied, "suggest a way by which we can waylay this ancient god? I am afraid that he might see me first, or hear of my plans in advance and keep away. A god is not easily defeated by a mortal."

'"I will tell you the plan in detail," she replied. "When the sun has climbed to its highest point the sage old sea-god emerges from his native salt, hidden by the dark ripples stirred by the West Wind. Once out, he makes for his sleeping-place in the shelter of a cave, and the seals, the children of the sea-nymphs, heave themselves up from the grey surf and go to sleep in herds around him, exhaling the pungent smell of the salt sea depths. Pick three men from your crew with care, the best you have on board, and at daybreak I will lead you to the spot and find you each a place to lie in. But I must tell you how the old sorcerer proceeds. First he will go his round and count the seals; then, when he has counted them and seen that all are there, he will lie down among them like a shepherd with his flocks of sheep. Directly you see him settled, summon all your strength and courage and hold him down, however hard he strains and struggles to escape. He will try all kinds of transformations, and change himself into every sort of beast on earth, and into water and blazing fire. But hold him fast and grip him all the tighter. And when he speaks at last and asks you questions in his natural shape, just as he was when you saw him lie down to rest, relax your pressure, let the old man go, and ask him which god is making difficulties for you and how to reach your home along the teeming sea-ways."

'After giving me this advice she disappeared into the billowing waves, and I went to where my ships were resting on the sand. My heart was dark and troubled. When I had reached the sea and found my ship, we prepared our supper. The solemn night descended on us and we lay down to sleep at the water's edge.

'As soon as Dawn appeared, fresh and rosy-fingered, I set out, with many prayers to heaven, along the shore of the far-flung sea, accompanied by the three men from my crews whom I could most rely on in any emergency.

'Eidothee had vanished under the wide waters of the sea, but she now returned carrying the skins of four seals, all freshly flayed, as part of the plan to deceive her father. She scooped out lairs for us in the sandy beach and sat down to await our arrival. When we came up to her, she ensconced us in our places and covered each man with a skin. Our vigil might have been insupportable, because the vile smell of the fish-fed seals was peculiarly trying. Who would choose a monster of the deep for bed-fellow? However, the goddess herself thought of a miraculous remedy and came to our rescue with some ambrosia, which she applied to each man's nostrils. It was sweet-smelling stuff and killed the stench of the seals.

'So there we waited patiently right through the morning. Then multitudes of seals came up from the sea and lay down in rows along the beach to sleep. At midday the old man himself emerged; found his sleek seals already there, and went the rounds to make his count. Entirely unsuspicious of the fraud, he included us as the first four in his flock. Then he too lay down to sleep. With a shout, we charged and grabbed hold of him. But the old man's skill and cunning had not deserted him. He began by turning into a bearded lion and then into a snake, and after that a panther and a giant bear. He changed into running water too and a great tree in leaf. But we set our teeth and clung on grimly.

'When at last the old man who knew so many tricks grew weary, he broke into speech and began asking me questions. "Tell me now, Menelaus," he said, "which of the gods conspired with you to waylay and capture me? And why did you need to do it?" "Old man," I answered, "why are you prevaricating? You know as well as I do how long I have been a prisoner on this island, unable to escape and growing weaker every day. So tell me now, in your divine omniscience, which god it is that has confined me here and interrupted my journey; and tell me also how I can reach my home across the teeming deep." "Before embarking," said the old man in reply, "you should have offered rich sacrifice to Zeus and all the other gods, if you wished to get home fast across the wine-dark sea. It is not your fate to reach your own country and see your friends and fine house again until you have sailed the heaven-fed waters of the Nile once more and made ceremonial offerings to the everlasting gods who live in the broad sky. When that is done, the gods will let you start this voyage that you have set your heart on."

'Now when I heard him tell me to make the long and weary trip over the misty seas to Egypt once again, my heart sank. Nevertheless I found my voice and made him this reply: "Old man, I shall do exactly what you advise. But there is something else I wish you to tell me. Did all of my countrymen whom Nestor and I left behind when we sailed from Troy reach home in safety with their ships, or were there any who came to grief in some accident at sea, or died in their friends' arms though the fighting was over?" "Son of Atreus," he replied, "why do you question me on these matters? You have no need to know or to probe my understanding. I warn you that your tears will flow soon enough when you have listened to my tale. For many were killed, though many too were spared. Yet only two of the commanders of your armies lost their lives when homeward bound – I need not speak of the fighting, since you took part in that yourself – but there is a third who, though still alive, is a prisoner somewhere in the vastness of the seas.

'"Ajax, to take him first, was wrecked in his long-oared ships by Poseidon, who drove him on to the great cliff of Gyrae and then rescued him from the surf. In fact, he would have evaded his doom, in spite of Athene's enmity, if in his blind folly he had not talked so arrogantly, boasting that he had escaped from the hungry jaws of the sea in defiance of the gods. His loud-voiced blasphemy came to the ears of Poseidon, who seized his trident in his powerful hands, struck the Gyraean rock and split it into two. One half stood firm, but the fragment he had severed, where Ajax had been resting when the blind impulse took him, crashed into the sea and carried him with it into the vast and rolling depths, where he drank the salt water and drowned.

'"But your brother Agamemnon contrived somehow to circumvent his fate, and slipped away in his great ships with the goddess Hera's help. Yet when he had nearly reached the heights of Cape Malea, a hurricane caught him, and with heavy groans he found himself driven over the teeming seas towards the borders of the land where Thyestes in the old days and now his son Aegisthus had their home. But in due course there came the chance of a safe return even from there. The gods turned the winds round and home they came.

'"Agamemnon set foot on the land of his fathers with a happy heart, and as he touched it kissed his native earth. The warm tears rolled down his cheeks, he was so glad to see his country again. But his arrival was observed by a spy in a watch-tower, whom the cunning Aegisthus had posted there with the promise of two talents of gold for his services. This man had been on the lookout for a year in case the King should land unannounced, slip by, and himself launch an attack. He went straight to the palace and informed the usurper. Then Aegisthus devised a clever trap. He selected twenty of the best soldiers from the town, left them in ambush in one part of the palace and, after ordering a banquet to be prepared in another part, set out in a chariot to bring home the King, with his heart full of ugly thoughts. Agamemnon, never guessing that he was going to his doom, came up with him from the coast, and Aegisthus feasted him, then killed him as a man might fell an ox at its manger. Not a single one of the King's following was left, nor of Aegisthus' company either. They were killed in the palace, to a man."

'This was his story, and it broke my heart. I sat down on the sands and wept. I had no further use for life, no wish to see the sunshine any more. But when I had had enough of tears and writhing on the sands, the old Sea Prophet spoke to me again. "Menelaus," he said, "you have wept too long. Enough of this incontinent grief, which gains us nothing. Better make every effort to get back to your own land as quickly as you can. For either you will find Aegisthus still alive or Orestes will have forestalled you by killing him, and you may be in time for the funeral feast." At these words, in spite of my distress, my heart and spirits were cheered.

'"You have accounted for two," I said. "But who is the third, the one who is still alive but a prisoner somewhere in the vastness of the seas? Or is he dead by now? I wish to hear, whatever sorrow it may cause me." "The third," said Proteus, "is Odysseus, Laertes' son, whose home is in Ithaca. I caught a glimpse of him on an island, in the Nymph Calypso's home, with tears streaming down his cheeks. She keeps him captive there, for without a ship and crew to carry him so far across the sea it is impossible for him to reach his home.

'"And now, Menelaus, favourite of Zeus, hear your own destiny. It is not your fate to die in Argos where the horses graze. Instead, the immortals will send you to the Elysian Fields at the world's end, to join auburn-haired Rhadamanthus in the land where living is made easy for mankind, where no snow falls, no strong winds blow and there is never any rain, but day after day the West Wind's tuneful breeze comes in from the Ocean to refresh its people. This is because you are the husband of Helen and, in the eyes of the gods, son-in-law to Zeus."

'The old man finished, and sank into the heaving waters of the sea, while I went off towards the ships with my heroic comrades, my heart in a turmoil. When I had reached the sea and found my ship we prepared our supper. The solemn night descended on us and we lay down to sleep on the surf-beaten shore.

'As soon as Dawn appeared, fresh and rosy-fingered, we first of all ran our fleet down into the good salt water and put the masts and sails on board our trim ships. The crews then climbed in, found their places at the oars, and struck the grey surf rhythmically with their blades. And so I returned to the heaven-fed waters of the Nile, where I moored, made the proper ritual offerings, and after appeasing the deathless gods built a mound of earth so that the glory of Agamemnon would last for ever. When all this was done I set out for home, and the immortals sent me a favourable wind and brought me quickly back to my own beloved land.

'And now, my friend, do stay on in my palace. Stay for twelve days or so, and then I'll send you off in style. You shall have glorious gifts from me – three horses and a splendid chariot. I'll give you a lovely cup as well to remind you of me all your life when you make drink-offerings to the immortal gods.'

'Son of Atreus,' the thoughtful Telemachus replied, 'do not keep me here on a lengthy visit. It is true that your tales and talk so delight me that I could easily stop with you for a year and never feel homesick for Ithaca or my parents. But my friends must already be tired of waiting for me in sacred Pylos; and now you prolong my stay. As for the gift you offer me, please make it a keepsake I can carry. Horses I will not take to Ithaca. I'd rather leave them here to grace your own stables. For your kingdom is a broad plain, where clover and galingale grow in plenty, with wheat and rye and broad-eared white barley; whereas in Ithaca there is no room for horses to run, nor any meadows at all. It is a pasture-land for goats and more attractive to my eyes than the sort of land where horses thrive. None of the islands that slope down to the sea is rich in meadows or suitable for chariots, Ithaca least of all.'

These remarks made Menelaus of the loud war-cry smile. He patted Telemachus with his hand and replied: 'I like the way you talk, dear boy: one can see that you have the right blood in your veins. Very well, I will change my gift – it is easily done. You shall have the loveliest and most precious of the treasures that my palace holds. I'll give you a mixing-bowl of wrought metal. It is solid silver with a rim of gold round the top, and was made by Hephaestus himself. I had it from Phaedimus, the heroic King of Sidon, when I stayed at his palace on my journey home. That is the present I should like you to take.'

During their talk, the guests began to arrive at the great King's palace. They drove up their own sheep and brought heart-warming wine; their bread was sent in for them by their elegantly dressed wives. This was how they prepared for their banquet in Menelaus' hall.

In front of Odysseus' palace, the Suitors in their usual high and mighty way were once again amusing themselves with throwing the discus and the javelin on the levelled ground. Antinous and the handsome Eurymachus, the boldest spirits in the gang and its acknowledged leaders, were sitting by, when Phronius' son Noemon came up to them with a question for Antinous.

'Have we any idea,' he asked him, 'when Telemachus comes back from sandy Pylos, or don't we know? He has gone off with my ship; and I happen to need it, to cross over to Elis, where the fields are big and I keep twelve brood mares, with their sturdy mules, not yet weaned or broken in. I want to drive one off and train him.'

His news filled them with consternation, for they had no idea that Telemachus had gone to Pylos, but thought he was somewhere in the neighbourhood on the farm, among the flocks perhaps, or with the swineherd. Antinous, Eupeithes' son, turned to him and said, 'I want the truth. When did he leave and what young men went with him? Did he take men from the town or did he make up a crew from his own serfs and servants, as he easily might? And tell me this too, so that I can be quite clear. Did he use force and go off with your ship against your wishes? Or did you give it willingly when he asked?'

'I gave it to him,' said Noemon, 'of my own accord. What would anyone do when asked a favour by a man of his standing with so much trouble on his mind? It would be very hard to refuse him. As for the young men who went with him, they're the best in the land next to ourselves. For captain, they had Mentor. I saw him embark – him or some god. Anyhow it was exactly like him. And that's what puzzles me. I saw the good Mentor here, only yesterday at dawn. Yet he certainly boarded my ship for Pylos that night.'

With this, Noemon went back to his father's house, leaving the two proud lords appalled and furious. They made the rest leave their games and sit down together, while Antinous, Eupeithes' son, held forth and gave vent to his fury. His heart was seething with black passion, and his eyes were like points of flame.

'Damnation take it!' he cried out. 'What a coup Telemachus has had the audacity to bring off – this expedition that we swore would come to nothing. With all of us against him, the young puppy calmly sets out, after picking the best men in the place and getting them to launch a ship for him! He is going to give us still more trouble. I hope Zeus clips his wings before he reaches manhood! However, give me a fast ship and a crew of twenty, and I'll lie up for him in the straits between Ithaca and the bluffs of Samos, and catch him on his way. And a grim ending there'll be to this sea-trip of his in search of his father!' The others welcomed the scheme and told him to carry it out. They then got up and moved off to the palace.

Before long Penelope heard about the plot that her Suitors

were hatching. It was Medon, the herald, who let her know. For while they were working out the plot in the courtyard, he had been eavesdropping outside and heard all they said. He set off straight away through the palace to tell Penelope. Immediately he crossed the threshold of her room she said: 'Herald, what errand have the young lords given you? Is it to tell King Odysseus' maids to drop their work and prepare them a feast? Oh how I hate their pursuit of me and the way they swarm around! They'd never feast here again, if I could stop them. Yes, the whole gang of you that come here day by day, fleecing us of our livelihood, my prudent son's inheritance. I suppose you never listened years ago when you were children and your fathers told you how Odysseus treated them – never a harsh word, never an injustice to a single person in the land. How different from the usual run of kings, favouring one man, persecuting the next. Whereas Odysseus never wronged a soul. Which only serves to show you and your shameful behaviour up, and proves how easily past kindness is forgotten.'

'My Queen,' replied the fair-minded Medon, 'I only wish that this were the worst of your troubles. Your Suitors are planning a far greater and more shocking crime. Zeus grant that they may not succeed! They are all set now on assassinating Telemachus with their sharp swords as he comes home – he has gone to holy Pylos and Lacedaemon to seek news of his father.'

When Penelope heard this her knees trembled and her heart grew faint. For a long time she found it impossible to speak; her eyes filled with tears; the words stuck in her throat. At length she managed to say: 'Tell me, herald, why has my son gone? There was no call whatever for him to venture on these fast ships that sailors use like chariots, to drive across the wide seas. Does he wish his very name to be forgotten in the world?'

The astute Medon replied: 'I do not know whether some god urged him on or his own feelings suggested this journey to Pylos, but his purpose was to find out about his father's return, or to learn what end he met.'

Medon went off through the palace. Penelope was overwhelmed by the anguish that racked her. She could not even bear to sit on one of the many chairs in her apartments, but sank down on the threshold[1] of her lovely room, weeping bitterly, while all the maids of her household, young and old, stood round her sobbing.

'Listen, my friends,' she said between her sobs. 'Is there a woman of my time whom Zeus has treated worse than me? I had a husband years ago, the best and bravest of the Danaans, a lion-hearted man, famous from Hellas to the heart of Argos. That husband I have lost. And now the whirlwinds have snatched my darling son from the house without a word. I was not even told that he had gone; not even by you, who must have known it well enough. How cruel of you all not to have thought of rousing me from my bed when he went to his hollow black ship! For had I known that he had this journey in mind, I swear he would have stayed, however determined to go, or left me dead at home.

'But hurry, one of you, and call my old servant Dolius, whom my father gave me when I came here and who looks after my orchard now. He shall go straight to Laertes, sit down beside him, and tell him the whole story. Perhaps Laertes may hit upon some scheme and come out of his retreat to appeal to the people, who seem intent on wiping out his and Odysseus' royal line.'

'Dear lady,' said Eurycleia, the fond old nurse, 'whether you kill me with the cruel knife or let me live on in the palace, I cannot hold my tongue. I knew the whole thing; it was I who gave him bread and wine and all he asked for. But he made me solemnly promise not to tell you for a dozen days or till you missed him yourself and found that he had started. He didn't want the tears to spoil your lovely cheeks.

'Come, go and wash and put on some fresh clothes. Then go to your room upstairs with your waiting-women and pray to Athene, Daughter of Zeus. She may still save him, even from the jaws of death. And don't trouble an old man who has troubles enough already. I cannot believe that the happy gods detest Arceisius' line. Someone surely will survive to own these lofty halls and the fertile fields beyond.'

1. Between rooms in Homeric houses there was a wooden or stone 'threshold', a raised structure into which the door jambs were fixed.

In this way Eurycleia hushed Penelope's sobs and cleared her eyes of tears. So the Queen Penelope, when she had washed and changed her clothes, went to her room upstairs with the waiting-women, filled a basket with sacrificial grains, and prayed to Athene:

'Hear me, Atrytone, Unwearied One, Daughter of Zeus who bears the aegis! If ever Odysseus in his wisdom burnt the fat thighs of a heifer or sheep to honour you in his palace, remember his offerings now, save my dear son for me, and guard him from harm at the hands of these brutal Suitors.'

At the end of her prayer she uttered a great cry. The goddess heard her petition, but in the shadowy hall the Suitors broke into uproar. One of the callous youths called out, 'It sounds as if our much-courted Queen is going to give us a wedding. Little does she know that her son's death has been arranged.'

This was their boastful way, though it was they who little guessed what had really been arranged. Antinous, however, rose up and silenced them. 'Are you mad?' he cried. 'None of this boasting, or somebody may go inside and tell. Keep your mouths shut now and disperse. You know the plan we all agreed on. Let's carry it out.'

Without further ado he picked the twenty best men, and they left for their ship and the sea-shore, where they began by running the black vessel down into deep water, then put the mast and sail on board, fixed the oars in their leather slings, all shipshape, and spread the white sail out. Meanwhile their eager squires had brought down their armour. They moored the boat well out in the water and came on shore, where they had their supper and waited for evening to fall.

Wise Penelope lay there in her upper room, without touching food or drink, wondering whether her innocent son would escape death or fall a victim to her brutal Suitors. Doubts and fears chased through her mind as they do through a lion's when he finds himself surrounded by the beaters and stands in terror as they stealthily close in. But at last a comforting sense of drowsiness overcame her; she sank back, she fell asleep, and all her limbs relaxed.

Athene of the flashing eyes now had another idea. King Icarius had another daughter besides Penelope, called Iphthime, who had married Eumelus and lived in Pherae. The goddess made a phantom now, exactly like this woman, and sent it to Odysseus' palace to save the unhappy and weeping Queen from more distress and further floods of tears. It entered her bedroom by the strap that worked the bolt, stood by her head and spoke to her:

'Are you asleep, Penelope, worn out with grief? I do assure you that the gods, who live such easy lives themselves, do not mean you to be so distressed, for it is settled that your son shall come home safe. The boy has done no wrong in their eyes.'

'Sister, what brings you here?' Penelope replied out of her sweet sleep at the Gate of Dreams. 'We are not used to seeing you with us, living as you do so far away. You tell me to forget my sorrows and all these anxieties that give my mind and heart no rest from pain. As though I had not married and then lost the best and bravest of our race, my noble lion-hearted husband, famous from Hellas to the heart of Argos! And now my beloved son, for whom I grieve even more than for his father, has sailed away in a great ship – a child like him, untrained for action or debate. I tremble for him when I think what they may do to him where he has gone or what may happen to him on the sea. He has so many enemies plotting against him and thirsting for his blood before he reaches home.'

'Be brave and conquer these wild fears,' said the shadowy wraith in reply. 'He has gone with such escort as any man might pray to have beside him – Pallas Athene in all her power. And it is she who in pity for your grief has sent me here to bring this message to you.'

'If you are really divine,' the wise Penelope said in reply, 'and have heard the voice of a god, tell me about his unfortunate father too. Is he alive somewhere and can he see the sunshine still; or is he dead by now and down in Hades' Halls?'

'Of Odysseus, whether alive or dead,' said the shadowy wraith, 'I will not give you any news at all. It does no good to utter empty words.'

With that, it slipped past the bolt by the door-post and into the breath of the wind. But Icarius' daughter, waking with a start, drew a warm sense of comfort from the vividness of this dream that had flown to her in the dark of the night.

Meanwhile her Suitors had embarked and were sailing the high seas with murder for Telemachus in their hearts. Out in the open strait, midway between Ithaca and the rugged coast of Samos, lies the rocky isle of Asteris, which, small as it is, can offer ships a harbour with two entrances. It was here that the Achaean lords set their ambush for Telemachus.

# 5
# CALYPSO

When Dawn had risen from the bed where she sleeps beside illustrious Tithonus, to bring daylight to immortals and to mortals, the gods sat down in assembly, and among them Zeus the Thunderer, the greatest of them all. The imprisonment of Odysseus in Calypso's home was heavy on Athene's heart, and she now recalled the tale of his misfortunes to their minds.

'Father Zeus, and you other blessed gods who live for ever, kindness, generosity and justice should no longer be the aims of any man who wields a royal sceptre – in fact he might just as well devote his days to tyranny and lawless deeds. Look at Odysseus, that admirable King! Today, not one of the people he once ruled like a loving father gives him a single thought. He is left to languish in misery in the island home of the Nymph Calypso, who keeps him captive there. Not that he could reach Ithaca in any case, for he has neither ships fitted with oars nor crew to carry him so far across the sea. Meanwhile his beloved son has gone to sacred Pylos and blessed Lacedaemon for news of his father, and they mean to murder him on the way back.'

'My child,' replied the Gatherer of the Clouds, 'what are you saying? Did you not plan all this yourself? Was it not your idea that Odysseus should return and take revenge on these men? As for Telemachus, use your own skill – you have the power – to bring him back to Ithaca safe and sound, and let the Suitors sail home again in their ship with nothing accomplished.'

Zeus now turned to Hermes, his beloved son. 'Hermes,' he said, 'as you are our usual Messenger, convey our final decision to that Nymph of the plaited tresses. The long-enduring Odysseus must now set out for home. On the journey he shall have neither gods nor men to help him. He shall set out on a raft put together by his own hands, and on the twentieth day, after great hardship, reach Scherie, the rich country of the Phaeacians, who are close to the gods. They will take him to their hearts and treat him like a god. They will convey him by ship to his own land, giving him bronze, gold and woven materials in such quantities as he could never have won for himself from Troy, even if he had come away with his fair share of the spoil. This is how it is ordained that he shall see his friends and come to his high-roofed house and his native land once more.'

Zeus had spoken. His Messenger, the Giant-killer, obeyed. Immediately he bound on his feet the lovely sandals of untarnishable gold that carried him with the speed of the wind over the water or the boundless earth; and he picked up the wand which he can use at will to cast a spell upon men's eyes or waken them from sleep. With this wand in his hand, the mighty Giant-killer made his flight. From the upper air he dropped to the Pierian range, and from there swooped down on the sea, and skimmed the waves like a sea-gull drenching the feathers of its wings with spray as it pursues the fish down fearsome troughs of the unharvested deep. So Hermes rode wave after wave, till at length he reached the remote island, where, leaving the blue waters of the sea, he came to the great cavern where the Nymph of the lovely locks was living.

He found her at home. A large fire was blazing on the hearth and the scent from burning logs of juniper and cedar was wafted far across the island. Inside, Calypso was singing with her beautiful voice as she went to and fro at her loom, weaving with a golden shuttle. The cave was sheltered by a copse of alders and fragrant cypresses, which was the roosting-place of wide-winged birds, horned owls and falcons and cormorants with long tongues, birds of the coast, whose business takes them down to the sea. Trailing round the mouth of the cavern was a thriving garden vine, with great bunches of grapes; from four separate but neighbouring springs four crystal rivulets were channelled to run this way and that; and in soft meadows on either side iris and wild celery flourished. It was indeed a spot where even an immortal visitor must pause to gaze in wonder and delight.

The Messenger, the Giant-killer, stood and gazed at the scene. When he had gazed at it all to his heart's content he passed into the great cavern. The goddess Calypso knew him the moment she raised her eyes to his face, for none of the immortal gods is a stranger to his fellows, even though his home may be remote from theirs. As for the lion-hearted Odysseus, Hermes did not find him in the cave, for he was sitting disconsolate on the shore in his accustomed place, tormenting himself with tears and sighs and heartache, and looking out across the barren sea with streaming eyes.

The divine Calypso seated Hermes on a brightly polished chair, and asked him: 'Hermes of the golden wand, what brings you here? You are an honoured and welcome guest, though in the past your visits have been few. Tell me what is in your mind, and I will gladly do what you ask of me, if I can and if it must be so. But first follow me inside and let me offer you hospitality.'

The goddess now put some ambrosia on a table, drew it to his side, and mixed him a cup of red nectar. The Messenger, the Giant-killer, began to eat and drink, and when he had dined and refreshed himself, he answered Calypso's questions:

'As one immortal to another, you ask me what has brought me here; since you command me, I shall tell you frankly. It was Zeus who sent me; it was no wish of mine to come. For who would choose to race across that vast expanse of salt water? It seemed unending. And not a city on the way, not a mortal soul to offer a choice sacrifice to a god. But when Zeus, who bears the aegis, makes up his mind, it is impossible for any other god to thwart him or evade his will.

'He says that you have with you here a man who has been dogged by misfortune, more so indeed than any of those with whom he shared the nine years of fighting round the walls of Troy and left for home when they had sacked it in the tenth. In setting out they gave offence to Athene, who raised a violent gale and heavy seas against them. His noble companions were lost to a man, but he himself was swept here by the wind and waves. And now Zeus bids you send him off without delay. He is not doomed to end his days on the island, away from all his friends. He is destined to see his friends and come to his high-roofed house and his native land once more.'

At his words the divine Calypso shuddered. Her words winged their way to him. 'You are hard-hearted, you gods, and unmatched for jealousy. You are outraged if a goddess sleeps openly with a man even if she has chosen him as her husband. You were the same when rosy-fingered Dawn fell in love with Orion. Free and easy yourselves, you were outraged at her conduct, and in the end chaste Artemis of the golden throne rose, attacked him in Ortygie with her gentle arrows and left him dead. And so again, when the lovely Demeter gave way to her desire and made love with her beloved Iasion in the field of the three ploughed furrows, Zeus heard of it quickly enough and struck him dead with his blinding thunderbolt.

'And now it is my turn to incur the envy of you gods for living with a mortal man – a man whom I rescued from death as he was drifting alone astride the keel of his ship, when Zeus had shattered it with his lightning bolt out on the wine-dark sea, and all his fine comrades were lost. But he was driven to this island by the wind and waves and I welcomed him with open arms; I tended him; I offered to make him immortal and ageless. But now, since no god can evade or thwart the will of aegis-bearing Zeus, let him go. If Zeus insists that he should leave, let him be gone across the barren water and good riddance to him! But I will not help him on his way, not I. I have no ship fitted with oars, no crew to carry him so far across the seas. Yet I do promise with a good grace and unreservedly to give him such directions as will bring him safe and sound to his native land.'

'Then send him off at once,' the Messenger, the Giant-killer, said, 'and so avoid provoking Zeus, or he may be angry and punish you one day.' With this the mighty Giant-killer took his leave.

The Nymph at once went to the valiant Odysseus, for the message from Zeus had not fallen on deaf ears. She found him sitting on the shore. His eyes were wet with weeping, as they always were. Life with its sweetness was ebbing away in the tears he shed for his lost home. For the Nymph had long since ceased to please. At nights, it is true, he had to sleep with her in the vaulted cavern, cold lover, ardent lady. But the days found him sitting on the rocks or sands, torturing himself with tears, groans and heartache, and looking out with streaming eyes across the watery wilderness.

The goddess came and stood beside him now. 'My unhappy friend,' she said, 'don't go on grieving, don't waste any more of your life on this island. For I am ready with all my heart to help you leave it. Come now, fell some tall trees with an axe, make a wide raft and fit half-decks on top so that it can carry you across the misty seas. I will stock it myself with bread and water and red wine to your liking, so that you need be in no fear of starvation; and I'll give you clothing too, and send you a following wind, so that you may reach your own country safe and sound, if it please the gods of the broad sky, who have more power to plan and to ordain than I have.'

The stalwart good Odysseus shuddered at this and addressed her with words that flew. 'Goddess, it is surely not my safety you are thinking about but something else, when you tell me to cross this formidable sea in such a craft. Even the fastest sailing-ships do not cross it, though they like nothing better than the winds of heaven. So I shall not entrust myself to a raft unless I can count on your goodwill, and you give me your solemn oath that you will not plot some other mischief against me.'

Calypso, the divine goddess, smiled and stroked him with her hand. 'Odysseus,' she protested, 'what a rogue you are to say such a thing! It shows the crafty way your mind works. Now let Earth be my witness, with the broad Sky above, and the waters of Styx that flow below – the greatest and most solemn oath the blessed gods can take – that I plot no other mischief against you but am considering only what I should do on my own behalf if I found myself in such a plight. For I have some sense of what is fair; and *my* heart is not made of iron. I know what pity is.' With these words the gracious goddess moved swiftly away, and he followed her.

The goddess and the man reached the great cavern together and Odysseus seated himself on the chair that Hermes had just left. The Nymph placed at his side the various kinds of food and drink that mortal men consume, and sat down facing the noble Odysseus. Her maids set ambrosia and nectar beside her, and the two helped themselves to the meal spread before them. When they had enjoyed the food and drink, the goddess Calypso began to speak.

'So you are determined, son of Laertes, favourite of Zeus, ingenious Odysseus, to leave at once for home and your beloved Ithaca? Even so I wish you happiness. Yet had you any inkling of the full measure of misery you are bound to endure before you reach your native land, you would stay and share this home with me, and take on immortality, however much you long to see that wife of yours, who is never out of your thoughts. And yet I claim to be by no means her inferior in looks or figure, for surely it would be most unseemly for a woman to compete with a goddess in form and face.'

To this the nimble-witted Odysseus replied: 'My lady goddess, do not be angry at what I am about to say. I too know well enough that my wise Penelope's looks and stature are insignificant compared with yours. For she is mortal, while you have immortality and unfading youth. Nevertheless I long to reach my home and see the day of my return. It is my never-failing wish. And what if one of the gods does wreck me out on the wine-dark sea? I have a heart that is inured to suffering and I shall steel it to endure that too. For in my day I have had many bitter and painful experiences in war and on the stormy seas. So let this new disaster come. It only makes one more.'

By now the sun had set and it grew dark. So the two retired to a recess in the cavern and there in each other's arms they found pleasure in making love.

As soon as Dawn appeared, fresh and rosy-fingered, Odysseus put on his tunic and cloak, and the Nymph dressed herself in a long silvery mantle of a fine and elegant material, with a splendid golden belt round her waist, and a scarf over her head. Then she planned her noble guest's departure. First she gave him a great axe of bronze. Its double blade was sharp, and the shapely handle of olive-wood fixed firmly to its head was comfortable to hold. Next she handed him an adze of polished metal, and led the way to the farthest part of the island, where the trees grew tall, alders and poplars and towering firs, all dry timber that had long since lost its sap and would make buoyant material for his raft. When she had shown him the place where the trees were tallest the gracious goddess went home, and Odysseus began to cut down the trees. He worked fast and felled twenty in all and lopped their branches with his axe, then trimmed them in a workmanlike manner and with a line made their edges straight.

Presently Calypso brought him boring-tools. With these he drilled through all his planks, cut them to fit each other, and fixed this flooring together by means of dowels driven through the interlocking joints, giving the same width to his raft as a skilled shipwright would choose in rounding out the hull for a broad-bottomed trading vessel. He next put up the decking, which he fitted to ribs at short intervals, finishing with long gunwales down the sides. He made a mast to go in the raft, and constructed a half-deck and a rudder to keep it on its course. And from stem to stern he fenced its sides with plaited osier twigs and a plentiful backing of brushwood, as some protection against the heavy seas. Meanwhile the goddess Calypso had brought him cloth with which to make the sail. This too he skilfully made; then lashed the braces, halyards and sheets in their places on board. Finally he dragged it down on rollers into the bright sea.

By the end of the fourth day all his work was done, and on the fifth the goddess Calypso saw him off from the island. She bathed him first and dressed him in sweet-smelling clothes. She had also stowed two skins in his boat, one full of dark wine, the other larger one of water, as well as a leather sack of grain and quantities of appetizing meats. And now a warm and gentle breeze sprang up at her command.

It was with a happy heart that the noble Odysseus spread his sail to catch the wind and skilfully kept the raft on course with the rudder. There he sat and never closed his eyes in sleep, but kept them on the Pleiads, or watched the late-setting Bootes slowly fade, or the Great Bear, sometimes called the Wain, which always wheels round in the same place and looks across at Orion the Hunter with a wary eye. It was this constellation, the only one which never sinks below the horizon to bathe in Ocean's Stream, that the wise goddess Calypso had told him to keep on his left hand as he sailed across the sea. So for seventeen days he sailed on his course, and on the eighteenth there came into view the shadowy mountains of the Phaeacians' country, which jutted out to meet him. The land looked like a shield laid on the misty sea.

But now Poseidon, Lord of the Earthquake, who was on his way back from his visit to the Ethiopians, observed him from the distant mountains of the Solymi. The sight of Odysseus sailing over the seas enraged him. He shook his head and said to himself: 'Damnation! I had only to go to Ethiopia for the gods to change their minds about Odysseus! And there he is, close to the Phaeacians' land, where he is destined to bring his long ordeal to an end. Nevertheless I mean to let him have a bellyful of trouble yet.'

With that he marshalled the clouds and, seizing his trident in his hands, stirred up the sea. He roused the stormy blasts of every wind that blows, and covered land and water alike with a canopy of cloud. Darkness swooped down from the sky. The East Wind and the South Wind and the tempestuous West Wind clashed together, and the North Wind came from the upper sky, rolling a great wave in front of it. Odysseus' knees shook and his spirit failed. In anguish he communed with his great heart:

'Poor wretch that I am, what will become of me after all? I fear the goddess prophesied all too well when she told me I should have my full measure of misery on the sea before I reached my native land. Every word she said is coming true. At Zeus' command the whole sky is heavy with clouds, the sea is seething, squalls from every quarter hurtle together. There is nothing for me now but sudden death. Three and four times blessed are those countrymen of mine who fell long ago on the broad plains of Troy in loyal service to the sons of Atreus. If only I too could have met my fate and died the day the Trojan hordes let fly at me with their bronze spears over Achilles' corpse! I should at least have had my burial rites and the Achaeans would have spread my fame abroad. But now it seems I was predestined to an ignoble death.'

As he spoke, a mountainous wave, advancing with awesome speed, crashed down upon him from above and whirled his raft around. The rudder was torn from his hands, and he himself was tossed off the raft; at the same moment the warring winds joined forces in one tremendous gust, which snapped the mast in two and flung the sail and half-deck far out into the sea. For a long time the water kept him under. Weighed down by the clothes which the goddess Calypso had given him, he could not quickly fight his way up against the downrush of that mighty wave. But at last he reached the air and spat out the bitter brine that poured down his face. Exhausted though he was, he did not forget his raft, but struck out after it through the surf, scrambled up, and sitting in the middle of it avoided the finality of death. The heavy seas thrust him with the current this way and that. Like the North Wind at harvest-time tossing about the fields a ball of thistles that have stuck together, the gusts drove his craft hither and thither over the sea. Now the South Wind would toss it to the North to play with, and now the East would leave it for the West to chase.

But there was a witness of Odysseus' plight. This was the daughter of Cadmus, Ino of the slim ankles, who was once a mortal woman speaking like ourselves, but now lives in the salt depths of the sea, and, as Leucothoe the White Goddess, has been acknowledged by the gods. She took pity on the forlorn and afflicted Odysseus, rose from the water like a sea-gull on the wing, and settled on his raft.

'Poor man,' she said to him, 'why is Poseidon, Lord of the Earthquake, so violently at odds with you that he puts all these disasters in your path? At any rate he shall not kill you, however hard he tries. Now do exactly what I say, like the sensible man you seem to be. Take off those clothes, leave your raft for the winds to play with, and swim for your life to the Phaeacian coast, where deliverance awaits you. Here; take this veil and wind it round your waist. With its divine protection you need not be afraid of injury or death. But directly you touch the dry land with your hands, undo the veil and throw it far out from the shore into the wine-dark sea; and as you do so turn your eyes away.'

As she spoke the goddess gave him the veil, and then like a gull she dived back into the turbulent sea and the dark waters swallowed her up. Stalwart Odysseus was left in perplexity and distress, and once more took counsel with his indomitable soul, saying with a groan, 'I'm afraid this is one of the immortals setting a snare to catch me, with her advice to abandon my raft. No, I will not leave the raft for the moment. I saw with my own eyes how far the land is where she promised me salvation. I shall do what I myself think best. As long as the joints of the planks hold fast, I shall stay where I am and endure the suffering. But when the seas break up my raft, I'll swim for it. I cannot think of anything better.'

As Odysseus was turning this over in his heart and mind, Poseidon the Earthshaker sent him another monster wave. Grim and menacing it curled above his head, then hurtled down and scattered the long timbers of his raft, as a boisterous wind will toss a dry heap of chaff and scatter it in all directions. Odysseus scrambled on to one of the beams, and sitting astride like a rider on horseback cast off the clothes that the divine Calypso had given him. Then he wound the veil round his waist, and with arms outstretched plunged headlong into the sea and boldly struck out.

The Lord Poseidon saw him, shook his head and said to himself: 'So much for you! Now make your miserable way across the sea, until you come into the hands of a people favoured by the gods. Even so I don't think you'll find any fault with your buffeting!' With this, Poseidon lashed his long-maned horses and drove to Aegae, where he had his famous palace.

At this point Athene, Daughter of Zeus, decided to intervene. She checked all the other winds in their courses, bidding them calm down and go to sleep. She summoned the strong North Wind with which she flattened the waves in the swimmer's path, so that Odysseus, favourite of Zeus, might be rescued from the jaws of death and come into the hands of the sea-faring Phaeacians.

For two nights and two days he was driven by the heavy seas. Time and again he thought he was doomed. But in the morning of the third day, which Dawn with her beautiful tresses opened in all her beauty, the wind dropped, a breathless calm set in, and Odysseus, keeping a sharp look-out, caught a glimpse of land close by as he was lifted by a mighty wave. He felt all the relief that a man's children feel when their father, who has been in bed wasting away with a long, painful illness, in the grip of some malignant power, passes the crisis by the gods' will and they know that he will live. Odysseus' happiness was like that when he caught that welcome glimpse of earth and trees. He swam quickly on in his eagerness to set foot on solid ground. But when he had come within shouting distance of the shore, he heard the thunder of surf on a rocky coast. With an angry roar the great seas were battering at the rocky land and all was veiled in spray. There were no coves, no harbours that would hold a ship; nothing but headlands jutting out, sheer rock and jagged reefs. When he realized this, Odysseus' knees grew weak and his heart failed. In his misery he communed with his courageous spirit:

'O misery!' he groaned. 'Against all hope Zeus let me see land after I won my way across that vast expanse of water, only to find there is no escape from the foaming sea, and all my efforts will have been in vain. Off shore, the pointed reefs; all around, a raging sea; behind, a smooth sheer cliff; deep water near the shore; no place where a man can touch bottom and scramble to safety. If I try to land, I may be lifted by a roller, dashed against the solid rock – and I'd have had my trouble for nothing. If I swim further down the coast, on the chance of finding a natural harbour where the waves strike the beach sideways, I'm afraid another squall will snatch me, and drag me out groaning into the teeming deep. Or some demon may let loose against me one of the many monsters that the great Amphitrite breeds in her seas, and I am well aware that the famed Earthshaker is at odds with me.'

This inward debate was cut short by a tremendous wave which swept him forward to the rugged shore, where his skin would have been torn off him and all his bones broken, had not the bright-eyed goddess Athene put it into his head to grab hold of a rock with both hands as he was swept in. He clung there groaning while the great wave swept by. But no sooner had he escaped its fury than its backward rush caught him with full force and flung him far out to sea. Pieces of skin stripped from his sturdy hands were left sticking to the crag, like the pebbles that stick to the suckers of a squid when it is torn from its lair. The great surge hid him and there the unhappy man would have come to an unpredestined end, if Athene had not given him a good idea.

He struggled to the surface, swam clear of the coastal breakers, and then swam along outside them, keeping an eye on the land, in the hope of lighting on some natural harbour with shelving beaches. Presently his progress brought him to the mouth of a fast-running stream, which seemed to be the best place, because it was clear of rocks and sheltered from the winds. The current told him that he was at a river's mouth, and in his heart he prayed to the god of the stream:

'Hear me Lord, whoever you are. I come to you, as many others have come, with a prayer. I am a fugitive from the sea and from Poseidon's malice. Any poor wanderer who comes in supplication is given respect, especially by the immortal gods. I am such a man, and I now turn to you after much suffering and seek the sanctuary of your stream. Take pity on me, Master. I am your suppliant.'

In answer to his prayer the River checked its current, and holding back its waves made the water smooth in the swimmer's path, and so brought him safely to land at its mouth. Odysseus' knees gave way and his sturdy arms sagged; he was exhausted by his struggle with the sea. All his flesh was swollen and streams of brine gushed from his mouth and nostrils. Winded and speechless he lay there too weak to stir, overwhelmed by a terrible fatigue. Yet directly he got his wind and breath came into his lungs, he unwound the goddess's veil from his waist and let it drop into the river as it rushed out to sea. The strong current swept it downstream and in a moment it was in Ino's hands. Odysseus turned away from the river, threw himself down in the reeds and kissed the bountiful earth.

And now in perplexity he communed with his mighty spirit. 'Oh, what will happen to me now?' he groaned. 'What will become of me after all? If I stay by the river and keep awake all through the wretched night, bitter frost and drenching dew together may do for me. I'm already at my last gasp. And a cold wind can blow up from a river just before dawn. But if I climb up the slope into the thick woods and lie down in the dense undergrowth and shake off my chill and my exhaustion, and fall into a sound sleep, I'm afraid that I may make a meal for beasts of prey.'

However, in the end he decided that this was the better course and set off towards the wooded ground. Not far from the river he found a copse in a clearing. Here he crept under a pair of bushes, one an olive, the other a wild olive, which grew from the same stem with their branches so closely intertwined that when the damp winds blew not a breath could enter, nor the rays of the sun penetrate their shade, nor the rain soak through. Odysseus crawled into his shelter, and at once heaped up the dry leaves into a wide bed – the ground was littered with piles of them, enough to provide covering for two or three men in the hardest winter weather. The noble long-suffering Odysseus was delighted with his bed, and lay down in the middle of it, covering himself with a blanket of leaves. This he did as carefully as a farmer on a lonely farm far away from any neighbours buries a glowing log under the black ashes to keep his fire alive and save himself from having to seek a light elsewhere. And now Athene filled his eyes with sleep and sealed their lids – sleep to soothe his pain and utter weariness.

# 6
# NAUSICAA

So there he slept, the much-enduring patient Odysseus, conquered by sleep and weariness, but Athene came to the country and city of the Phaeacians. These Phaeacians had once lived in the broad lands of Hypereie, and been neighbours to the Cyclopes, a domineering people, who used to take advantage of their greater strength to ravage their land, till the day when the godlike Nausithous took them and settled them in Scherie, far from ordinary hard-working people. There he laid out the walls of a new city, built houses, put up temples to the gods, and divided up the land for cultivation. But he had long since met his fate and gone to Hades' Halls; and it was now the divinely inspired Alcinous who ruled them. To his palace the bright-eyed goddess Athene made her way, intent on her plans for the great-hearted Odysseus' return.

The mighty Alcinous had a young daughter called Nausicaa, tall and beautiful as a goddess. She was asleep now in her richly decorated room, with two of her maids, both blessed with beauty by the Graces, lying asleep by the door-posts, one on either side. The polished doors were closed; but Athene swept through like a breath of air to the girl's bed, leant over her head and spoke to her, taking the form of the daughter of a ship's captain named Dymas, a girl of Nausicaa's own age and one of her closest friends.

In the form of this girl, bright-eyed Athene said: 'Nausicaa, how did your mother come to have such a lazy daughter as you? All your shining clothes have been left lying about neglected, but you may soon be married and need beautiful clothes, not only to wear yourself but to provide for your bridegroom's party. That is how a bride gains a good reputation with people, which brings great pleasure to her father and her mother. Let us go and do some washing together the first thing in the morning. I will go with you and help, so that you can get it done as soon as possible, because you certainly won't remain unmarried long. Every nobleman in Phaeacia, where you yourself were born and bred, wants you for his wife. Ask your royal father in the morning to have a waggon made ready for you with a couple of mules. It can take the sashes and robes and bright rugs, and it would be much better for you yourself to ride than to go on foot; it's a long way from the city to the washing-pools.'

When she had finished, bright-eyed Athene withdrew to Olympus, where people say the gods have made their everlasting home. Shaken by no wind, drenched by no showers, and invaded by no snows, it is set in cloudless limpid air with a white radiance playing over all. There the blessed gods spend their days in pleasure, and there the Lady of the Bright Eyes went when she had spoken to the girl.

Soon after, Dawn enthroned herself in the sky, and woke up Nausicaa in her lovely gown. She was amazed at her dream and set out at once through the palace to tell her father and her mother. She found them both in the house. Her mother was sitting at the hearth with her ladies, spinning yarn dyed with sea-purple; and she met her father just as he was going out to join the distinguished princes at a conference to which the Phaeacian nobles had called him. She went close to her dear father and said:

'Father dear, I wonder if you could tell them to get me a high-sided waggon with strong wheels, so that I can take all the fine clothes that I have lying about dirty to the river to wash? And indeed it is only proper for you yourself when you are discussing affairs of state with important people to have clean linen on your back. Then there are five sons of yours in the palace, two married, and three active bachelors who are always asking for clothes straight from the wash to wear at dances. It is I who have to think of all these things.'

She spoke in this way because she was too shy to mention to

her father the subject of marriage and all it promises. But he understood completely and replied: 'I don't grudge you the mules, my child, or anything else. You may go; and the servants shall get you a fine high-sided waggon with a hood to it.'

He called to his men and they obeyed. While they prepared a smooth-running mule cart outside, led the mules under the yoke and harnessed them to it, Nausicaa fetched the gaily coloured clothing from the room and packed it in the polished waggon. Meanwhile her mother filled a box with various kinds of appetizing provisions and delicacies to go with them, and poured some wine into a goatskin bottle. The girl climbed into the waggon and her mother handed her a golden flask of soft olive-oil, so that she and her ladies could rub themselves with it after bathing. And now Nausicaa took the whip and the gleaming reins, and flicked the mules to make them start. There was a clatter of hooves, and they stepped out eagerly, taking the clothes and their mistress along. But as her ladies followed and kept her company, she was not alone.

They reached the lovely river with its never-failing pools, in which there was enough clear water always bubbling up and swirling by to clean the dirtiest clothes. Here they unharnessed the mules and drove them along the eddying stream to graze on the sweet grass. Then they lifted the clothes by the armful from the waggon, carried them to the dark water and trod them down briskly in the washing-pools, vying with each other in the work. When they had rinsed them till no dirt was left, they spread them out in a row along the sea-shore, just where the waves washed the shingle clean as they came tumbling up the beach. Next, after bathing and rubbing themselves with olive-oil, they took their meal at the riverside, waiting for the sunshine to dry the clothes.

Presently, when mistress and maids had all enjoyed their food, they threw off their headgear and began playing with a ball, while Nausicaa of the white arms sang and kept time for their game. She looked like Artemis the Archeress, coming down from the mountain along the high ridge of Taygetus or Erymanthus for the joy of chasing the wild boar or the nimble deer, and the Nymphs of the countryside (daughters of aegis-bearing

Zeus) join with her in the sport. And her mother Leto's heart is gladdened, because she is a head taller than any of them and even though all are beautiful there is no question which is she. So did this young girl stand out among her maids.

When she was about to yoke the mules and fold the beautiful clothes and set out for home, the bright-eyed goddess Athene had other ideas and arranged for Odysseus to wake up and see this lovely girl who was to serve as his escort to the Phaeacian city. Accordingly, when the princess threw the ball to one of her maids, it missed her and fell into the deep, eddying current. At this they all gave a loud shriek. The noble Odysseus awoke, and, sitting up, wondered to himself.

'What country have I come to this time?' he said with a groan. 'What people are there here? Hostile and uncivilized savages, or kindly and god-fearing people? There's a shrill echo in my ears, as though some girls were shrieking – Nymphs, who haunt the steep hill-tops, the springs of rivers, and the grassy meadows. Or am I by any chance among human beings who can talk as I do? Well, I must go and use my own eyes to find out.'

So the noble Odysseus crept out from under the bushes, after breaking off with his great hand a leafy bough from the thicket to conceal his naked manhood. Then he advanced on them like a mountain lion who sallies out, defying wind and rain in the pride of his power, with fire in his eyes, to hunt down the oxen or sheep or pursue the wild deer. Forced by hunger, he will even attack flocks in a well-protected fold. So Odysseus, naked as he was, made a move towards these girls with their braided hair; necessity compelled him. Grimy with salt he was a gruesome sight, and the girls went scuttling off in every direction along the jutting spits of sand.

Alcinous' daughter Nausicaa was the only one to stand firm. Athene put courage into her heart and took the fear from her limbs, and she stood her ground and faced him. Odysseus considered whether he should throw his arms round the beautiful girl's knees and beg for help, or just keep his distance and beg her with all courtesy to give him clothing and direct him to the city. He decided that as the lady might take offence if he embraced her knees it would be better to keep his distance and courteously plead his case. In the end, his address was both courteous and full of subtlety:

'Princess, I am at your knees. Are you some goddess or a mortal woman? If you are one of the gods who live in the wide heaven, it is of Artemis, the Daughter of almighty Zeus, that your beauty, grace and stature most remind me. But if you are one of us mortals who live on earth, then thrice-blessed indeed are your father and your lady mother; thrice-blessed your brothers too. How their hearts must glow with pleasure every time they see their darling join the dance! But he is the most blessed of them all who with his wedding gifts can win you and take you home as a bride. Never have I set eyes on any man or woman like you. I am overcome with awe as I look at you. Only in Delos have I seen the like, a fresh young palm-tree shooting up by the altar of Apollo, when my travels took me there – with a fine army at my back, that time, though the expedition was doomed to end so fatally for me. For a long time I stood spellbound at the sight, for no such sapling ever sprang from the ground.

'And it is with just the same wonder and veneration that I look at you, my lady, and I dare not clasp your knees, though my sufferings are serious enough. Only yesterday, after nineteen days, I made my escape from the wine-dark sea. It took all that time for the waves and the tempestuous winds to carry me here from the island of Ogygia. And now some god has flung me on this shore, no doubt to suffer more disasters here. For I have no hope that my troubles will come to an end: the gods have plenty in store for me before that can be. Pity me, princess. You are the first person I have met after all I have been through, and I do not know a soul in this city or this land. Do direct me to the town and give me some rags to put round myself, if only the cloth wrappings you may have brought when you came here. And may the gods grant you your heart's desire; may they give you a husband and a home, and the blessing of harmony so much to be desired, since there is nothing better or finer than when two people of one heart and mind keep house as man and wife, a grief to their enemies and a joy to their friends, and their reputation spreads far and wide.'

'Sir,' said the white-armed Nausicaa, 'since your manners show you are not a bad man or a fool – it is Olympian Zeus himself who assigns good fortune to men, good and bad alike, as he wills, and must have sent you your personal misfortune – and you must just endure it – but now since you have come to our country and our city here, you certainly shall not want for clothing or anything else that an unfortunate suppliant has the right to expect from those he meets. I will show you the way to the town and tell you who we are. This country and the city belong to the Phaeacians. I myself am the daughter of great-hearted Alcinous, who is the source of the might and majesty of the Phaeacian people.'

Here she turned and called out to her maids: 'Stop, girls. Where are you flying to at the sight of a man? Don't tell me you take him for an enemy. There is no man on earth, nor ever will be, who would dare to set hostile feet on Phaeacian soil. The gods are too fond of us for that. Remote, we are at the edge of the world and come in contact with no other people. This man is an unfortunate wanderer who has strayed here, and we must look after him, since all strangers and beggars come under the protection of Zeus, and to such people a small gift can mean much. So give him food and drink, girls, and bathe him in the river where there's shelter from the wind.'

The girls stood still, each urging the others on. Then they led Odysseus to a sheltered place where he could sit down as Nausicaa, the daughter of the great-hearted Alcinous, had ordered. On the ground beside him they laid a tunic and cloak for him to wear, and, giving him some soft olive-oil in a golden flask, they told him to wash himself in the running stream.

Then the good Odysseus said to them, 'Ladies, stand back over there and leave me to wash the brine from my shoulders and rub my body with olive-oil. It's a long time since olive-oil has touched my skin. I am not going to take my bath with you looking on. I should be ashamed to stand naked in the presence of elegant ladies.'

At this they withdrew and told their young mistress about it. Meanwhile with river-water Odysseus was washing off the salt that encrusted his back and his broad shoulders, and scrubbing his head free of the scurf left there by the barren sea. When he had thoroughly washed and rubbed himself with oil and had put on the clothes which the girl had given him, Athene, daughter of Zeus, made him seem taller and sturdier and caused the bushy locks to hang from his head thick as the petals of a hyacinth in bloom. Just as a craftsman trained by Hephaestus and Pallas Athene in the secrets of his art puts a graceful finish to his work by overlaying silverware with gold, she endowed his head and shoulders with beauty. When Odysseus retired to sit down by himself on the sea-shore, he was radiant with grace and beauty. Nausicaa gazed at him in admiration and said to her beautiful-haired attendants:

'Listen, my white-armed girls, to what I am saying. This man's arrival among the godlike Phaeacians was not opposed by *all* the gods of Olympus. When we first met I thought him repulsive, but now he looks like the gods who live in heaven. I wish I could have a man like him for my husband, if only he were content to stay and live here. But come, girls, give the stranger something to eat and drink.'

Her maids at once carried out her orders and set food and drink before the stalwart Odysseus, who ate and drank with avidity, for it was a long time since he had tasted any food.

Nausicaa of the white arms now turned her mind to other matters. After folding up the clothing, she stowed it in her fine waggon, harnessed the strong-hooved mules, and herself climbed in. Then she called to Odysseus.

'Come, sir, and make a move towards the city, so that I can direct you to my good father's house, where I can assure you that you will meet all the Phaeacian nobility. But this is what you must do – and I take you for a man of understanding. So long as we are passing through the country and the farmers' lands, walk quickly with my maids behind the waggon and the mules, following me.

'But once we come to our city – it is surrounded by high battlements; it has an excellent harbour on each side and is approached by a narrow causeway, where the curved ships are drawn up to the road and each owner has his separate landing-place. Here is the people's meeting-place, built up next to the fine temple of Poseidon with blocks of quarried stone bedded deeply in the ground. It is here too that the sailors attend to the rigging of the black ships, their cables and sails, and smoothe their oars. For the Phaeacians have no use for the bow and quiver, but only for masts and oars on the graceful craft they take pride in sailing across the grey seas.

'Now it is their unpleasant gossip that I wish to avoid. I am afraid they might give me a bad name, for they are supercilious people, and I can well imagine one of the cruder ones saying after he had seen us: "Who is this tall and handsome stranger with Nausicaa? Where did she find him? Her future husband no doubt! She must have rescued some shipwrecked foreigner who had strayed this way, since we have no neighbours. Or perhaps some god has answered her insistent prayers and stooped from heaven to make her his for ever. And it is better that way – better that she should look around and find a husband from abroad. For she obviously despises her fellow Phaeacians though so many of the best would like to marry her." That is how they will talk, and my good name would suffer. Indeed I should blame any girl who behaved like that – who behind her family's back, while her parents were still alive, associated with men before being properly married.

'So listen carefully to my directions if you want my father's help for your homeward journey as soon as possible. You will see near the path a fine poplar wood sacred to Athene, with a spring welling up in the middle and a meadow all round. That is where my father has his estate and fertile garden within calling distance of the city. Sit down there and wait a little till we get into the town and reach my father's house. When you think we have had time to do so, go into the city yourself and ask for the palace of my father, the great-hearted Alcinous. It is quite easy to recognize: any little child could show it to you. For the houses of the rest are not built in anything like the style of the palace of King Alcinous, my father.

'Directly you have passed through the courtyard and into the buildings, walk quickly through the great hall till you reach my mother, who sits in the firelight by the hearth, spinning yarn dyed with sea-purple – a marvellous sight – with her chair against a pillar and her ladies sitting behind. My father's throne is close to hers, and there he sits drinking his wine like a god. Slip past him and clasp my mother's knees if you wish to see the day of your homecoming and rejoice, however far away it is. For if she is sympathetic to you, you may confidently expect to see your friends again, to reach your own fine house and your native land.'

When she had finished, Nausicaa used her shiny whip on the mules, and they soon left the flowing river behind them, their legs weaving a pattern as they trotted steadily along. She drove so as to allow the maids and Odysseus to keep up with her on foot, and used her judgement in laying on the whip. As the sun was setting they reached the famous grove, the sacred place of Athene. Here the good Odysseus sat down and prayed to the Daughter of almighty Zeus.

'Hear me, Atrytone, Unwearied One, Child of Zeus who bears the aegis, and hear my prayer this time; you turned a deaf ear to me before, when I was shipwrecked and the great Earthshaker shattered my raft. Grant that the Phaeacians may receive me with kindness and compassion.'

Pallas Athene heard his prayer but still refrained from appearing before him, out of deference to her Father's brother Poseidon, who persisted in his rancour against the noble Odysseus until he reached his own land.

# 7
# THE PALACE OF ALCINOUS

So the much-enduring Odysseus prayed in Athene's grove, and the two sturdy mules brought the princess to the city. When she reached her father's famous palace, she drew up at the entrance, and her brothers, looking like the immortals, gathered round her, unharnessed the mules from the cart, and carried the clothes indoors. She herself retired to her own apartments, where a fire was lit for her by her waiting-woman Eurymedusa, an old Aperaean woman. She had been brought by ship from Aperaea years ago and selected as a prize for Alcinous, the King of all the Phaeacians and idolized by the people as a god. It was this woman who had nursed the white-armed Nausicaa at home, and who now lit a fire and prepared supper in the inner room.

Then Odysseus started for the town. Athene, in her concern for his welfare, enveloped him in a thick mist, in case some high-handed Phaeacian who crossed his path insulted him and asked him who he was. He was just about to go into the pleasant town when the bright-eyed goddess herself came to meet him, disguised as a young girl carrying a pitcher, and halted in front of him.

'My child,' said the good Odysseus, 'I wonder if you could show me the way to the house of Alcinous, the King of this country? I've had a hard time; I'm a stranger here from a distant land and don't know a single soul in the city or the country around.'

'Sir,' replied the bright-eyed Athene, 'certainly, I'll show you the house you want, since it lies close to my good father's place. But you must follow my lead without a word, look at nobody and ask no questions. For the people here have little affection for strangers and do not welcome visitors with open arms. They put their trust in fast ships that carry them across the far-flung seas, for that is a privilege granted by Poseidon, and these ships of theirs are as swift as a bird or as thought itself.'

With this Pallas Athene led the way quickly, and Odysseus followed in the steps of the goddess. The Phaeacians, those famous seamen, failed to observe him as he passed them by on his way through the town. For the formidable goddess Athene of the lovely hair prevented it, shedding a magic mist round her favourite in her concern for his safety. As he walked, Odysseus marvelled at the harbours with their trim ships, at the meeting-place of the sea-lords and at their long and lofty walls, surmounted by palisades, presenting a wonderful sight.

When they reached the King's famous palace, the bright-eyed goddess Athene said: 'Here, sir, is the house that you asked me to show you. You will find princes, favourites of Zeus, feasting there, but go straight in and have no qualms. For it is the bold man who always succeeds in his enterprises even if he comes from far away. The first person you will find in the palace will be the Queen. Her name is Arete and she comes from the same family as Alcinous the King. Nausithous, the first of the line, was the son of Poseidon the Earthshaker and of Periboea, the loveliest woman of her time. She was the youngest daughter of the great Eurymedon, who was once King of that overweeningly proud race, the Giants, but led that wicked race to its destruction, and his own too. Poseidon slept with Periboea and by her had the great-hearted Nausithous, who became King of the Phaeacians. And Nausithous had two sons, Rhexenor and Alcinous. Rhexenor had not long been married and had as yet no son when he was killed in his palace by Apollo with his silver bow.

'But he left one daughter, Arete. Alcinous made her his wife and gave her such honour as no other woman receives who keeps house under her husband's eye in the world today. Such is the extraordinary and heartfelt devotion which she has enjoyed in the past and still enjoys, both from her children and Alcinous himself, and from the people, who look on her as a goddess, and greet her when she walks through the town. For she is also a wise woman, and when her sympathies are enlisted she settles even men's disputes. So if only you can secure her friendly interest, you may well hope to see your friends once more, to return to the high roof of your own house and to your native land.'

Athene finished, and now left the pleasant land of Scherie, crossed the unharvested seas, and came to Marathon and the broad streets of Athens, where she entered the great palace of Erechtheus.

Now Odysseus approached Alcinous' splendid dwelling. His heart was filled with varied emotions and he kept on stopping before he reached the bronze threshold. A kind of radiance, like that of the sun or moon, played upon the high-roofed halls of the great King. Bronze walls, topped by a frieze of dark-blue enamel, ran round to left and right from the portals to the back of the court. The interior of the well-built mansion was guarded by golden doors hung on posts of silver which were set in the bronze threshold. The lintel they supported was of silver too, and the door-handle of gold. On either side stood gold and silver dogs, which Hephaestus had made with consummate skill, to keep watch over the palace of the great-hearted Alcinous and serve him as immortal sentries never doomed to age. Inside the hall, tall chairs were ranged along the walls on either side, right round from the threshold to the chamber at the back, and each was draped with a delicately woven cover that the women had worked. Here the Phaeacian chieftains used to sit and enjoy the food and wine of which there was always a lavish supply. Golden statues of youths, fixed on solid pedestals, held flaming torches in their hands to light the banqueters in the hall by night.

The house keeps fifty maids employed. Some grind apple-golden corn in the handmill, some weave at the loom, or sit and twist yarn, their hands fluttering like the leaves of a tall poplar, while soft olive-oil drips from the close-woven fabrics they have finished. For the Phaeacians' extraordinary skill in handling ships at sea is matched by the dexterity of their womenfolk at the loom, for Athene has given them outstanding skill in beautiful crafts and such fine intelligence.

Just outside the entrance to the courtyard, surrounded by a wall, lies a large orchard of four acres – pears and pomegranates, apple trees with glossy fruit, sweet figs and luxuriant olives. Their fruit never fails nor runs short, winter and summer alike. It comes at all seasons of the year, and there is never a time when the West Wind's breath is not assisting, here the bud, and there the ripening fruit; so that pear after pear, apple after apple, cluster on cluster of grapes, and fig upon fig are always coming to perfection.

In the same enclosure there is a fruitful vineyard, in one part of which is a warm patch of level ground, where some of the grapes are drying in the sun, while others are being gathered, or trodden in the wine-press, and on the foremost rows hang unripe bunches that have just dropped their blossom or show the first faint tinge of purple. Beyond the furthest row, vegetable beds of various kinds are neatly laid out, luxuriantly productive all the year round. In the garden are two springs; one flows in channels to all parts of it; the other, starting next to it, first provides a watering-place for the townspeople and then runs under the courtyard gate towards the great house itself. Such were the glorious gifts the gods had bestowed on Alcinous' home.

Patient, good Odysseus stood before the house and drank it all in. When he had admired it to his heart's content he stepped briskly over the threshold and entered the palace. There he found the captains and counsellors of the Phaeacians pouring libations from their cups to the keen-eyed Giant-slayer Hermes. It was their custom to pour the last cup to him before retiring to bed. But the much-enduring good Odysseus walked straight up the hall, wrapped in the mist that Athene shed about him, till he reached Arete and King Alcinous and threw his arms around Arete's knees. At the same moment the magic mist that had hidden him rolled away, and at the sight of this man in their midst a silence fell on all the banqueters up and down the hall. They stared at Odysseus in amazement while he made his petition:

'Arete, daughter of godlike Rhexenor, as one who has suffered much I come a suppliant to your husband, to you and to your guests. May the gods grant them happiness for life and may each bequeath to his sons the treasures of his house and the honours bestowed on him by the people. But for me please arrange an escort to my own country, as soon as may be, for I have had to live through many hardships far from my friends.'

His petition made, he sat down in the ashes by the hearth, close to the fire. From that whole company there came not a sound. At last the silence was broken by the venerable lord Echeneus, a Phaeacian elder, an eloquent speaker, rich in the wisdom of his forefathers. He now made his friendly counsel heard:

'Alcinous, it is unseemly and unlike your royal ways to let a stranger sit in the ashes at the hearth, while the guests around you must patiently await your lead. Sir, tell him to get up and sit on one of the silver chairs, and tell your squires to mix some more wine so that we can make a fresh libation, to Zeus the Thunderer, patron of suppliants, who deserve respect. And let the housekeeper give him a meal from all she has available.'

The mighty King Alcinous listened to what Echeneus said, took the wise and subtle Odysseus by the hand, raised him from the hearth and seated him on a tall polished chair, from which he moved the friendly Laodamas, his favourite son, who was sitting next to him. A maid came with water in a beautiful golden jug and poured it out over a silver basin to rinse his hands. Then she drew a wooden table to his side, and the faithful housekeeper brought some bread and put it by him with a choice of delicacies, helping him liberally to all she could offer. While the much-enduring, good Odysseus ate and drank, mighty Alcinous gave an order to his squire:

'Pontonous, mix a bowl of wine and fill the cups of all the company in the hall, so that we may now make a drink-offering to Zeus the Thunderer, patron of suppliants, who deserve respect.'

So Pontonous prepared a bowl of mellow wine, from which he poured out a few drops in each man's cup. Then, when they had made their libations and drunk their fill, Alcinous addressed them:

'Captains and Counsellors of the Phaeacians, listen while I tell you what is in my mind. Now you have dined, disperse to your homes for the night; and in the morning we will summon a fuller gathering of the elders to entertain our visitor here and to sacrifice to the gods. We will then take up the matter of his passage so as to ensure him without trouble or anxiety the happiness of a speedy return to his country under our escort, however far away it is. We will safeguard him on the way from any further hardship or accident till he sets foot on his own land. After which he must suffer whatever Destiny and the relentless Fate spun for him with the first thread of life when he came from his mother's womb.

'But if he is one of the immortals come down from heaven, then the gods must be playing some new trick on us. For in the past they have always shown themselves to us without disguise when we have offered them their sumptuous sacrifices; and at our banquets they sit at our side. Even when a traveller meets them on his lonely way, they make no concealment; for we are special to them, like the Cyclopes and the wild tribes of the Giants.'

'Alcinous,' the shrewd Odysseus replied, 'put that idea out of your mind. I have neither the looks nor the stature of the immortal gods who live in heaven, but those of a human being. Think of the wretches who in your experience have borne the heaviest load of sorrow, and I will match my griefs with theirs. Indeed I think that I could tell an even longer tale of woe, if I gave you an account of what by the gods' will I have suffered. But, in spite of all my troubles, give me leave to eat my supper. For nothing in the world is so shamelessly demanding as a man's confounded stomach. However afflicted he may be and sick at heart, it calls for attention so loudly that he is bound to obey it. Such is my case: my heart is sick with grief, yet my stomach insists that I eat and drink. It makes me forget all I have suffered and forces me to eat my fill. But at daybreak do make arrangements for landing this unfortunate guest of yours in his own country. I have had hard times indeed. Once let me see my own estate, my servants, and the high roof of my great house, and I shall be content to breathe my last.'

They all applauded his speech and agreed that the stranger should be escorted home, for he had talked good sense. Then after making a libation and satisfying their thirst, they retired for the night to their several homes, leaving good Odysseus sitting in the hall beside Arete and the godlike Alcinous, while the maids cleared the dinner things away.

White-armed Arete was the first to break the silence, for in the fine cloak and tunic she saw him wearing she recognized some clothes that she herself had made with her women's help. 'Sir,' she said, with words on wings, 'I myself will question you and ask you this first. Who are you? Where do you come from? And who gave you those clothes? Didn't you say you came here from wandering over the seas?'

'My Queen,' the shrewd Odysseus replied, 'it would be wearisome to tell you all my troubles from first to last, for the gods have sent me so many. But I will tell you this much in answer to your questions. Far out at sea there is an island called Ogygia, where Atlas' daughter, the artful Calypso, lives, the awesome goddess with braided hair. No god or mortal man comes near her. And yet I had the misfortune to be brought by some power to her hearth. I was alone, for with one of his blinding bolts Zeus had smashed my good ship to pieces out in the wine-dark sea. My loyal company all lost their lives. But with both arms I clasped the curved ship's keel and for nine days kept afloat. In the blackness of the tenth night the gods washed me ashore on Ogygia, the home of Calypso, that formidable goddess with the beautiful locks. She took me in and looked after me with loving care. She offered me immortality and eternal youth. But never for a moment did she win my heart. Seven whole years I stayed, soaking with my tears the imperishable clothes Calypso gave me.

'But at last, when the eighth came round in its course, she urged me to be gone, either in obedience to a message from Zeus or because her own feelings had changed. She sent me off in a solidly made raft, after providing me generously with bread and sweet wine, and giving me imperishable clothes to wear. She also caused a warm and kindly wind to blow. So for seventeen days I sailed across the sea and on the eighteenth the shadowy mountains of your land loomed up, and I rejoiced. Too soon, poor man, for I was destined to meet further troubles, which Poseidon the Earthshaker was yet to send me. Rousing the winds against me, he stopped me from making headway; and as I sat groaning there he stirred the sea to such unspeakable fury that the waves made it impossible for me to stay on my raft – a squall smashed it to pieces. However, I managed by swimming to make my way across that stretch of water, till the winds and the waves brought me to your coast.

'There I tried to scramble ashore, but a wave took and dashed me on the great rocks of that inhospitable coast. So I gave up the plan and swam away from the shore. In the end I reached a river, which seemed to offer the best possible landing-place, clear of rocks and sheltered from the wind. I struggled out and lay there till I could rally my strength. Meanwhile the solemn night came on. After climbing up from the bed of that heaven-fed river I lay down in a thicket, heaped leaves over my body and with a god's help fell into a sound sleep. I was exhausted and slept there in the leaves all night and right through the morning into the middle of the day. The sun was on his downward path when I awoke from my refreshing sleep to find your daughter's ladies playing on the beach. The princess herself was with them, looking like a goddess. I asked her help. And she proved what good sense she has, acquitting herself in a way you would not expect in one so young – young people are thoughtless as a rule. But she gave me plenty of bread and sparkling wine, bathed me in the river and provided me with the clothes you see. That is the truth of the matter, painful as it is to tell it.'

'Sir,' said Alcinous, 'in one respect my daughter's judgement is faulty. She should have brought you home with her maids. After all, she was the first person you had begged for help.'

'My lord,' replied the resourceful Odysseus, 'do not rebuke your peerless daughter. She did tell me to follow along with the servants. But in my modesty I shrank from doing so, fearing that you might be indignant at the sight. We men are naturally suspicious.'

'My friend,' replied Alcinous, 'I am not one to take offence for no good reason; it is always better to be reasonable. I wish – by Zeus and Athene and Poseidon – I wish that a man like you, like-minded with myself, could have my daughter and remain here as my son-in-law – I would give you a house and riches. That is, if you were willing to stay. But not one of us

Phaeacians shall detain you. God forbid such a thing! And to set your mind at rest, I now appoint a day for your departure home: tomorrow. You shall lie deep in sleep while they row you over tranquil seas, till you come to your own country and your house or anywhere else where you would like to go. Nor does it matter if the place is even more remote than Euboea, which is said to be at the world's end by those of our sailors who saw it, that time they took auburn-haired Rhadamanthus to visit Tityus, the son of Earth. They got there and returned in one day without fatigue. But you shall learn from your own experience the surpassing excellence of my ships and how good my young men are at whipping up the water with their oars.'

Odysseus' patient heart filled with happiness as he listened, and he raised his voice in prayer: 'O Father Zeus, grant that Alcinous may accomplish all that he has promised; then his fame would never die anywhere on the fruitful Earth, and I should come again to the land of my fathers.'

While they were conversing, white-armed Arete gave her maids instructions to put a bed in the portico and to furnish it with the finest purple rugs, spread coverlets over these, and add warm blankets on top. The servants, torch in hand, went out of the hall and busied themselves at this task. When they had spread the bed-clothes on the bed, they came up to Odysseus and invited him to retire. 'Come along, sir,' they said, 'your bed is made.' The prospect of sleep seemed very sweet to him.

So the long-suffering good Odysseus slept there in the echoing portico on a wooden bed. Alcinous lay down for the night in his room at the back of the lofty palace with his wife, who shared his bed.

# 8
# THE PHAEACIAN GAMES

As soon as Dawn appeared, fresh and rosy-fingered, the mighty Alcinous left his bed and conducted Odysseus, favourite of Zeus, sacker of cities, who had risen at the same time, to the place by the ships where the Phaeacians held their assemblies; and there they sat down side by side on seats of polished marble. In the meantime Pallas Athene, pursuing her plans for the great-hearted Odysseus' return, went through the town disguised as a herald from wise Alcinous. She went up to each of the citizens and gave them this message:

'Captains and Counsellors of the Phaeacians, follow me to the assembly, where you will hear about the stranger who has just arrived at our wise King's palace after being driven to wander over the seas; he looks like an immortal god.'

These words acted as inspiration and encouragement to them all. In a short time not only the seats but all parts of the meeting-place were filled by the throng that crowded in; and many eyes were fixed in admiration on Laertes' keen-witted son. Athene invested his head and shoulders with a divine beauty, and made him seem taller and broader, so that he would inspire the whole Phaeacian people not only with affection but with fear and respect, and might emerge successfully from the many tests they later subjected him to. When they had all assembled, Alcinous rose to address them:

'Captains and Counsellors of the Phaeacians, listen while I tell you what is in my mind. The stranger at my side – I do not know his name, nor whether he has come from Eastern or from Western lands – has in the course of his travels come to my palace. He asks for his passage home and begs us to assure him this favour. In accordance with our custom, let us make immediate arrangements to escort him. For there has never been a time when anyone who has come to my house has had to complain of being kept here for lack of escort. So let us run a black ship down into the friendly sea for her maiden voyage, and from the town pick fifty-two young oarsmen who have proved their excellence. This crew, when they have all fixed their oars in place, may leave the ship and come on to my house, where they can quickly share a meal: I will make ample provision for all. These are my orders for the ship's company.

'As for the rest, I invite you who are sceptred princes to my palace to entertain our visitor indoors. Let no one refuse. And summon our divine bard, Demodocus; a god has given him the special gift of delighting our ears with his song, at whatever point he chooses to begin.'

When Alcinous had finished speaking he led the way, and the princes followed him. His squire set out in search of the divine minstrel, and meanwhile fifty-two young men were chosen and made their way, as he had directed, to the shore of the barren sea. When they reached the ship at the edge of the sea, they dragged the black vessel into deep water, put the mast and sails on board, fixed the oars in their leather loops, all shipshape, and hauled up the white sail. Then they moored her well out in the water, and proceeded to the great palace of their wise King, where the galleries and the courts, as well as the apartments themselves, were filled with a throng of people, both young and old. Alcinous sacrificed for them a dozen sheep, eight white-tusked boars, and two shambling oxen. These they flayed and made ready for the table, and so prepared a heart-warming feast.

The squire now came, leading their favourite bard, whom the Muse loved above all others, though she had mingled good and evil in her gifts, robbing him of his eyes but granting him the gift of sweet song. Pontonous placed a silver-studded chair for him in the centre of the company, with its back to one of the great pillars, and the squire hung his tuneful lyre on a peg just above his head and showed him how to lay his hand upon it. At his side he put a handsome table, with a bowl of bread and a cup of wine to drink when the spirit moved him. Then they all helped themselves to the delicious food that was spread before them.

When they had satisfied their appetite and thirst, the Muse set the bard to sing the famous deeds of heroes, that part of a lay well known by then throughout the world, the Quarrel of Odysseus and Achilles son of Peleus. It told how these two had clashed in a violent altercation at a festival of the gods, though Agamemnon King of men was secretly delighted to see the Achaean leaders at loggerheads, because their quarrel fulfilled the prophecy[1] that Phoebus Apollo had made to him in sacred Pytho when he crossed the marble threshold to consult the oracle. Those events were the beginning of the great wave of disasters that was rolling towards Trojan and Danaans alike, by the will of mighty Zeus.

This was the theme of the famous minstrel's lay, but Odysseus with his sturdy hands drew his purple cloak over his head and hid his handsome face, as he was ashamed to be seen weeping by the Phaeacians. Whenever the glorious minstrel paused in his song, he wiped the tears away and, removing the cloak from his head, reached for his two-handled cup and made libations to the gods. But whenever Demodocus started singing again, encouraged by the Phaeacian lords, who were enjoying the tale, Odysseus once more hid his face and sobbed. He managed to conceal his tears from everyone except Alcinous. But the King, sitting next to Odysseus, felt and noticed his distress and heard his heavy sighs. He spoke up before long and said to the sea-loving Phaeacians:

'Captains and Counsellors of the Phaeacians, listen to me. We have eaten together and listened to the lyre, that goes with good food, to our heart's content. Let us go outside now and try skills at various sports, so that when our guest has reached his home he can tell his friends that at boxing, wrestling, jumping and running there is no one who can beat us.'

1. The prophecy stated that Agamemnon would capture Troy after the noblest Greeks had quarrelled. In the event it was not after this quarrel, but after Agamemnon's quarrel with Achilles, that the prophecy was fulfilled.

With these words he led the way and was followed by the others. The squire hung Demodocus' tuneful lyre on its peg, took the bard's hand and guided him out of the palace, in the wake of the Phaeacian nobility as they set out to see the games. They all made for the place of assembly and were followed there by a vast crowd.

There was no lack of fine young men to compete – Acroneos, Ocyalus, Elatreus, Nauteus, Prymneus, Anchialus, Eretmeus, Ponteus, Proreus, Thoon, and Anabesineos, Amphialus son of Polyneus and grandson of Tecton, and Euryalus too, the son of Naubolus,[1] who looked a match for Ares the man-killing War-god and was the most handsome and strongest of all the Phaeacians next to the peerless Laodamas. Alcinous' three sons, Laodamas, Halius and godlike Clytoneus, also took part.

The first event was a race. They ran at full speed from the start, raising a cloud of dust on the track as they flew along. By far the quickest was the excellent Clytoneus, who shot ahead, and when he reached the crowd at the post he had left the rest behind by as much as the width of a fallow field that mules can plough in a day. Next came the painful sport of wrestling; and here it was Euryalus' turn to beat all the champions. Amphialus won the jump; at throwing the discus, Elatreus was by far the best; and at boxing, Laodamas, Alcinous' handsome son. When they had all enjoyed the games, it was Laodamas who made a suggestion to the rest:

'Come, friends, and let us ask our visitor here if he's an expert in any form of sport. He is well enough built: look at his thighs and legs, look at his hands, and that great neck – all that great strength, and he's not so old, either, just broken down by hardships. I tell you, there's nothing like the sea to break a man, however strong.'

'Laodamas,' said Euryalus, 'I like your idea. Go and have a word with the man yourself and challenge him.'

1. The names of these Phaeacian sailors, so grandiloquent to our ears, are all punning names – 'Topship and Quicksea and Paddle, Seaman and Poopman, Beacher and Oarsman etc.' – W. H. D. Rousse. It is the same with many of the main characters: Antinous means 'Contrarymind', Eurymachus means 'Wide-fighter'.

When he heard this Alcinous' handsome son made his way to the centre and addressed Odysseus: 'Come, sir, won't you take part in our games, if you're good at any sport? It is only right that you should be an athlete, for nothing makes a man so famous during his lifetime as what he can achieve with his hands and feet. Come along and have a try, casting your cares aside; for it won't be long before you are off on your journey. Your ship is launched already and the crew are standing by.'

'Laodamas,' the nimble-witted Odysseus answered him, 'why are you trying to provoke me with your challenges, you and your friends? I am too sick at heart to think of games. I have been through many bitter and exhausting experiences, and all I seek now is my passage home, which is why I am sitting here in your assembly to plead help from your King and your whole nation.'

Euryalus now interposed and insulted him to his face: 'You are quite right, sir. I should never have taken you for an athlete, good at any of the games men play. You are more like a skipper of a merchant crew, who spends his life on a hulking tramp, worrying about his outward freight, or keeping a sharp eye on the cargo when he comes home with his extortionate profits. No: one can see you are no athlete.'

With a black look the nimble-witted Odysseus retorted: 'That, sir, was an unbecoming speech; you strike me as a presumptuous fool. And it shows that the gods do not grace men equally with the attributes of good looks, brains and eloquence. A man may be quite insignificant to look at but the gods can grace his words with charm: people watch him with delight as he speaks unfalteringly with winning modesty. He stands out in the gathering and is stared at like a god when he passes through the town. Another may be as handsome as an immortal, yet quite deficient in the graceful art of speech. Now you, sir, are distinguished in appearance – the gods themselves could not improve it – but you are short of brains.

'You have stirred me to anger with your inept remarks. I am no novice at sport, as you suggest, but consider myself to have been in the first rank so long as I was able to rely on the strength of my youth. But as things are, all the misfortunes and hardships

I have endured in warfare and in fighting my way through hostile seas weigh heavily upon me. All the same, and in spite of what I have gone through, I'll try my hand at the sports. For your words have stung me and put me on my mettle.'

With this he leapt to his feet and, not even troubling to remove his cloak, picked up the biggest discus of all, a huge weight, more massive by far than the Phaeacians normally used. With one swing he launched it from his mighty hand, and the stone hummed on its course. The Phaeacians, lords of the sea and champions of the long oar, cowered down as it hurtled through the air; and flying smoothly from his hand it overshot the marks of all the other throws. Athene, pretending to be one of the crowd, marked the distance, and spoke out.

'Look, sir,' she called, 'even a blind man could pick out your peg, by feeling with his hands. The others are all in a bunch, but yours stands right out in the front. In this event at any rate you have nothing to fear. None of the Phaeacians will make as good a throw, let alone a better.'

Her words delighted the much-enduring Odysseus, who was happy to find a real friend in the arena and now addressed the Phaeacians with a lighter heart: 'Now beat that, you young men! But presently I expect to send along another just as far or even further. And since you have thoroughly provoked me, come out, if any of you like the idea and have the spirit, come out and take me on – at boxing, wrestling, or even running, I don't care which. Laodamas, whose guest I am, is the only one among you all whom I except, for who would fight his host? Only a fool or a nonentity would challenge the friend who is entertaining him in a strange country. That would be to spite himself. But of the rest of you, there is no one I'll back away from and no one I'll consider beneath me. I'm ready to meet and match myself against all comers.

'I am not bad at any kind of manly sport. I can handle the polished bow well and I would be the first to pick off my man with an arrow in the enemy ranks, however many of my side might be standing by and shooting at the enemy. When we Achaeans had to use our bows in the fighting at Troy, Philoctetes was the only archer better than me. Of all the others now alive and eating their bread on the face of the earth, I claim to be by far the best, though I should not care to compete with the men of the past, with Heracles, for instance, or Eurytus of Oechalia, who as bowmen even challenged the gods. In fact that was why the great Eurytus came to a sudden end and never lived to see old age in his home, but was killed by Apollo, whom he had offended by challenging him to a match. As for the javelin, I can throw it further than anyone else can shoot an arrow. It is only in running that I am afraid some of you might outstrip me. I was too badly knocked about by the rough seas, for in my raft my stores gave out, and as a result my legs have lost their power.'

Odysseus finished speaking, and they stood still and silent, leaving it to Alcinous to reply.

'My friend,' said the King, 'we don't resent what you say – you want to prove your natural prowess – you were angry at the way this man came up and insulted you in the competition. No one who knew how to talk sense would have belittled your prowess in this way. But listen now to what I have to say. When you are banqueting in your own home with your wife and your children beside you, and the talk turns to the Phaeacian prowess, I want you to be able to tell your noble friends that Zeus has given us too certain skills, which we have possessed from our forefathers' time to the present day. Though our boxing and wrestling are not outstanding, we can run fast and we are first-rate seamen. But the things in which we take a perennial delight are the feast, the lyre, the dance, frequent changes of clothes, hot baths and our beds.

'So forward now, my champion dancers, and show us your steps, so that when he gets home our guest may be able to tell his friends how far we surpass all other people in seamanship, in speed of foot, in dancing and in song. And one of you run and fetch Demodocus his tuneful lyre. It is somewhere in my house.'

At the godlike Alcinous' word, a squire set off to fetch the resonant lyre from the palace, and the nine official stewards took matters in hand. These were public servants who supervised all the details during such displays. They now swept the dancing-floor and cleared a ring wide enough for the performance. The squire came up to Demodocus and handed him his tuneful lyre. The minstrel then moved forward to the centre; a group of expert boy dancers, all in the first bloom of youth, took up their positions round him, and began the divine dance; their flashing feet filled Odysseus with admiration as he watched.

Presently the bard struck up and lifted his fine voice in song. His theme was the love of Ares and Aphrodite of the beautiful diadem, how they first made love secretly in her husband Hephaestus' palace; how Ares gave her many gifts and how he dishonoured the Lord Hephaestus' marriage-bed. But the Sun had witnessed their loving embraces and came to inform Hephaestus, who, when he heard the bitter truth, went straight to his workshop with his heart full of evil plans, laid his great anvil on the block and forged a network of chains which could neither be broken nor undone, to bind them there. His fury with Ares inspired him as he worked, and when the snare was finished he went to the room where his marriage-bed stood and threw the netting right round the legs. A number of further lengths were attached to the rafter overhead and hung down like fine spiders' webs, quite invisible even to the blessed gods. It was a masterpiece of cunning work.

When he had surrounded the bed in this way and set his trap, he made a pretence of leaving for the pleasant town of Lemnos, his favourite place on earth. Meanwhile Ares of the Golden Reins had not kept watch for nothing. Directly he saw Hephaestus, the illustrious Master-craftsman, leave, he made his way to his house, filled with a passionate desire for Aphrodite of the lovely diadem. She had recently returned from seeing her mighty Father, Zeus, and had just sat down when Ares came in at the door, clasped her hand and greeted her fondly.

'Come, my beloved,' he said, 'let us go to bed and find pleasure in love, for Hephaestus is no longer around. He has gone to somewhere in Lemnos, to visit his barbarous Sintian friends.' Aphrodite desired nothing better than to sleep with him; so the two went to bed and lay down. Immediately the netting which Hephaestus' ingenuity had contrived fell around them in such a way that they could not move or lift a limb. They found too late that there was no escape. And now the great lame god himself approached. For the Sun, acting as his spy, had given him word; and he hurried home in anguish. Standing there in the entrance, in the grip of fierce anger, he let out a terrible yell and called aloud to all the gods.

'Father Zeus and you other blessed gods who live for ever, come here and see a comic and cruel thing. Zeus' Daughter Aphrodite has always despised me for my lameness, and now she has given her heart to this butcher Ares just because he is good-looking and sound of limb, while I was born a weakling. And whom have I to blame for that, if not my father and my mother? I wish they had never begotten me! But see where these two have crept into my bed and are sleeping in each other's loving arms. The sight is like a sword in my heart. Yet I have an idea that they won't be eager to prolong that embrace, no, not for a moment, not for all their love. Theirs is a sleep that both will soon be tired of. But my cunning meshes are going to keep them just where they are, till her Father hands me back every one of the gifts I made him to win this brazen bitch, who may be his daughter and a lovely creature but is the slave of her passions.'

At his words the gods came thronging to the house with the bronze floor. Up came Poseidon the Sustainer of the Earth; Hermes, the Swift Runner; and Apollo, Lord of the Bow; but the goddesses, out of modesty, all stayed at home. So there they stood in front of the doors, the immortals who are the source of all our blessings; and when they caught sight of Hephaestus' clever device a fit of unquenchable laughter seized the blessed gods.

'Bad deeds don't prosper,' said one of them with a glance at his neighbour; 'the tortoise catches up the hare. See how our slow-moving Hephaestus has caught Ares, though no god on Olympus can run as fast. Hephaestus may be lame, but he has won the day by his cunning. And now Ares will have to pay him an adulterer's fine.'

This was the kind of comment made. The Lord Apollo, Son of Zeus, turned to Hermes and said: 'Hermes, Son of Zeus, Guide and Giver of good things, would you care, though tied down by those unyielding chains, to lie in bed by golden Aphrodite's side?'

To which the Guide, the Giant-slayer replied: 'Lord Apollo, royal Archer, I only wish I could. Though the chains that kept me prisoner were three times as many, and though all you gods and all the goddesses were looking on, yet would I gladly sleep by golden Aphrodite's side.'

At his words laughter arose among the immortal gods. But Poseidon did not laugh; he kept begging the great craftsman Hephaestus to free Ares from the net. 'Let him go,' he said, and his words flew, 'and I promise you that he shall make full and proper atonement, as required by you, in the presence of the immortal gods.'

'Poseidon, Girdler of the Earth,' replied the illustrious lame god, 'do not press me. Pledges for the worthless are worthless. How could I throw *you* in chains while the immortal gods looked on if Ares were to wriggle out of his debt as well as out of his chains?'

'Hephaestus,' said Poseidon the Earthshaker, 'if Ares does repudiate his debt and abscond, I myself will pay you the fine.'

'To such an offer from you,' replied the great lame god, 'I cannot and I must not answer no.'

With that the mighty Hephaestus undid the chains, and the two of them, freed from the shackles that had proved so strong, leaped up and fled, Ares to Thrace, and laughter-loving Aphrodite to Paphos in Cyprus, where she has her sacred sanctuary and altar fragrant with incense. There the Graces bathed her and anointed her with the celestial oil that is like a bloom on the limbs of the immortal gods. And they dressed her in lovely clothes that were a marvel to behold.

This was the song that the famous minstrel sang, to the delight of Odysseus and the rest of his audience, the Phaeacians, those famous and intrepid mariners.

After this Alcinous ordered Halius and Laodamas to dance by themselves, since no one could compete with them. Polybus, a skilled craftsman, had made them a beautiful purple ball, which they took in their hands, and one of them, bending right back, would throw it up towards the shadowy clouds, and the other, leaping up from the ground, would catch it skilfully before his feet touched earth again. After showing their skill at this high play, they began tossing the ball quickly to and fro as they moved in their dance on the bountiful earth, while the other youths stood at the ringside beating time, till the air was filled with sound, and the noble Odysseus turned to his host and said: 'Lord Alcinous, most illustrious of all your people, you claimed just now that your dancers are supreme. Your claim is made good. I marvel at the sight of them.'

His praise delighted the great Alcinous, who turned at once to his sea-faring subjects and said: 'Listen, Captains and Counsellors of the Phaeacians, I find a nice discernment in this guest of ours. Let us make him parting gifts, as is appropriate. Our people have for their chiefs and rulers twelve eminent princes – thirteen with myself. Let each one of us present him with a fresh cloak, a tunic and a talent of sterling gold. Let us quickly gather all our gifts together, so that the stranger can receive them and come to supper in a happy frame of mind. As for Euryalus, he must make amends to him by a personal apology, and a present as well, for the incivility of his comments.'

They all approved his suggestions and gave their instruction. Each of the princes dispatched his squire to fetch the gifts, and Euryalus spoke up in answer: 'Lord Alcinous, most illustrious of your people, I shall make atonement to the stranger, as you have ordered. I will give him this sword of bronze, which has a silver hilt and a sheath of newly carved ivory to hold it – it will be a very valuable possession.'

He then laid the sword with its silver mounting in Odysseus' hands, and addressed him with words that flew: 'Honoured guest, I salute you. If some offensive words escaped my lips, let the storm-winds take and blow them away, and may the gods grant that you may reach home again and see your wife, since you have lived a hard life for so long away from your friends.'

'Friend,' said the nimble-witted Odysseus, 'I return your kindly greeting. May the gods bless you! And I only hope you will not one day miss the sword you have given me here with words that make full amends.' And as he spoke he slung the silver-studded weapon from his shoulder.

By sunset he was in possession of all their splendid gifts, which were then carried to Alcinous' palace by their well-born squires. There the good King's sons took charge of them and placed the magnificent collection at their honoured mother's feet. Meanwhile great Alcinous brought the rest of the company to his house, where they seated themselves on high-backed seats, and mighty Alcinous called to Arete.

'My dear,' he said, 'bring a really splendid coffer here, the best we have, and put a fresh cloak and a tunic in it as your own gift. Then heat a copper over the fire and warm some water for our guest, so that when he has had his bath and seen that all the gifts which the Phaeacian nobles have brought him here are properly packed, he can dine at his ease and enjoy the minstrel's lay. I shall give him this beautiful golden chalice of mine, so that he may have me in mind for the rest of his days when he makes drink-offerings in his house to Zeus and to the other gods.'

Arete told her maidservants to put a large three-legged cauldron on the fire at once. They set the cauldron for the bath-water on the glowing embers, filled it with water, and brought firewood which they kindled beneath it. The flames began to lick round the belly of the cauldron and the water was heated. Meanwhile Arete brought out from the inner chamber a fine chest for their guest, in which she packed the splendid gifts of clothing and of gold which the Phaeacians had made him. To these, on her own account, she added a cloak and a tunic of fine quality, and then addressed Odysseus with words that flew.

'See to the lid yourself, now, and tie the knot, so that you may not be robbed on your journey when you're enjoying a sweet sleep later on as the black ship carries you along.'

Noble, much-enduring Odysseus took her advice and fixed the lid on at once, fastening it neatly with a complicated knot that the Lady Circe had once taught him. Immediately after that the housekeeper invited him to have a bath. It was a pleasure for him to see a hot bath again, for he had not been used to such comforts since leaving the home of Calypso of the lovely hair, where he had received constant attention like a god. When the maids had bathed and rubbed him with oil, and clothed him in a fine tunic and cloak, he left the bath to join the men at their wine.

Now Nausicaa, in all her heaven-sent beauty, was standing by one of the pillars that supported the massive roof. She was filled with admiration when she saw him there before her eyes, and when she spoke it was with winged words:

'Good luck be with you, my friend,' she said, 'so that when you are in your own country you will remember me sometimes, since it is chiefly to me that you owe your life.'

'Nausicaa, daughter of great-hearted Alcinous,' answered the resourceful Odysseus, 'I do indeed pray to Zeus the Thunderer, husband of Hera, to let me reach my home and see the day of my return. If he does, then I will pray to you as a divinity all the rest of my days. For it was you, lady, who gave me back my life.'

With this he took a chair by the side of King Alcinous, for they were already serving portions of food and mixing the wine. A squire now came in leading their beloved bard Demodocus, the people's favourite. He seated him in the centre of the company with his back against one of the high columns, and at once the resourceful Odysseus, carving a portion from the chine of a white-tusked boar – there was plenty left – with rich fat on either side, called to a squire and said:

'Here, give this helping to Demodocus to eat, with kindly greetings from my unhappy self. All men honour and respect bards, for the Muse has taught them songs and she loves the minstrel fraternity.'

The squire took the meat and handed it to the illustrious Demodocus, who accepted it with pleasure. The company now helped themselves to the delicious food that was spread before them, and when they had satisfied their thirst and hunger, the resourceful Odysseus said to the minstrel:

'Demodocus, I admire you above all men. Either Zeus' Child, the Muse, or Apollo must have been your teacher. For it is remarkable how accurately you sing the tale of the Achaeans' fate and of all their achievements, sufferings and struggles. It is almost as though you had been with them yourself or heard the story from one who was. But now change your theme and sing to us of the stratagem of the Wooden Horse, which Epeius built with Athene's help, and which the good Odysseus contrived to get taken one day into the citadel of Troy as an ambush, manned by the warriors who then sacked the town. If you can tell this story as it really happened I shall proclaim to the world how generously the god has endowed you with the heavenly gift of song.'

Odysseus finished speaking, and the bard, beginning with an invocation to the gods, unfolded the tale. He took it up at the point where the Argives after setting fire to their huts had embarked on their ships and were sailing away, while the renowned Odysseus and his party were already sitting in the assembly-place in Troy, concealed within the Horse, which the Trojans had themselves dragged into the citadel. There stood the Horse, with the Trojans sitting round it endlessly arguing. Three policies commended themselves. Some were for piercing the wooden frame with a pitiless bronze spear; others would have dragged it to the edge of the heights and hurled it down the rocks; others again wished to let it stand as a magnificent offering to appease the gods – and that was what happened in the end. For it was destiny that they should perish when Troy received within her walls that mighty Wooden Horse, laden with the flower of the Argive might bringing doom and slaughter to the Trojans.

He went on to sing how the Achaean warriors, leaving their hollow ambush, poured out from the Horse to ravage Troy; how they scattered through the steep streets of the city leaving ruin in their wake; and how Odysseus, looking like Ares himself, went straight to Deiphobus' house with the gallant Menelaus. And there, sang the bard, he engaged in the most terrible of all his fights, which in the end he won with the help of the indomitable Athene.

While the famous minstrel was singing, Odysseus' heart was melting with grief and his cheeks were wet with the tears that ran down from his eyes. He wept as a woman weeps when she throws her arms round the body of her beloved husband, fallen in battle in the defence of his city and his comrades, fighting to save his city and his children from the evil day. She has found him gasping in the throes of death; she clings to him wailing and lamenting. But the enemy come up and beat her back and shoulders with spears, as they lead her off into slavery and a life of miserable toil, with her cheeks wasted by her pitiful grief. Equally pitiful were the tears that now welled up in Odysseus' eyes, and though he succeeded in hiding them from everyone else, Alcinous could not help observing his condition; he was sitting next to him and heard his heavy groans. He spoke up at once and said to the Phaeacian sea-captains:

'Hear me, Captains and Counsellors of the Phaeacians. Let Demodocus stop playing his tuneful lyre; the theme of his song is not to everybody's liking. Since we began our meal and our divine minstrel struck up, our guest here has been weeping bitterly without a pause. Some poignant sorrow must have overwhelmed his feelings. Let the bard stop playing, so that we can all be merry, hosts and guest alike. How much pleasanter that is! For it was on account of our worthy guest that all this has been arranged, this farewell and these friendly gifts that we give as welcoming hosts. To any man with the slightest claim to common sense, a guest and suppliant is as close as a brother.

'And now, sir, do not, for some crafty reason, withhold the answers to the questions I may ask. Frankness is better. Tell me the name by which you were known at home to your mother and father and your friends in the town and country round. No one, after all, whether of low or high degree, goes nameless once he has come into the world; everybody is named by his parents when he is born. You must also tell me where you come from, to what people and to what city you belong, so that my sentient ships may plan the right course to convey you there. For the Phaeacian ships have no helmsmen or rudders such as other craft possess. Our ships know by instinct what their crews are thinking and propose to do. They know every city, every fertile land; and hidden in mist and cloud they make their swift passage over the sea's immensities with no fear of damage and no thought of wreck.

'At the same time, I must tell you of a warning I had from my father Nausithous, who used to say that Poseidon grudged us our privilege of giving safe-conduct to all comers without ourselves coming to any harm. He prophesied that some day the god would wreck one of our fine vessels on the misty sea as she came home from such a journey, and would surround our city with a wall of mountains. That is what the old King used to say; and the god may do it, or may let things be. It is for him to decide as he pleases.

'And now, speak and tell us truly: where have you been driven in your wanderings? What parts of the inhabited world have you visited? What lovely cities did you see, what people in them? Did you meet hostile tribes with no sense of right and wrong, or did you fall in with hospitable and god-fearing people? Explain to us also what sorrow makes you weep as you listen to the tragic story of the Argives and the fall of Troy. The gods were responsible for that, weaving catastrophe into men's lives to make a song for future generations. Perhaps one of your kinsmen by marriage fell before Ilium, a brave man, your son-in-law possibly or your father-in-law, who are nearest after one's own flesh and blood? Or perhaps some true friend, a kindred spirit? For a friend with an understanding heart can be quite as dear as a brother.'

# 9
# THE CYCLOPS

In answer to the King, this is how Odysseus, the man of many resources, began his tale:

'King Alcinous, most illustrious of all your people, it is indeed a lovely thing to hear a bard such as this, with a voice like the voice of the gods. I myself feel that there is nothing more delightful than when the festive mood reigns in the hearts of all the people and the banqueters listen to a minstrel from their seats in the hall, while the tables before them are laden with bread and meat, and a steward carries round the wine he has drawn from the bowl and fills their cups. This, to my way of thinking, is perfection.

'However, your heart has prompted you to ask me about my troubles, and that intensified my grief. Well, where shall I begin, where end, my tale? For the list of woes which the gods in heaven have sent me is a long one. I shall start by giving you my name: I wish you all to know it so that in times to come, if I escape the evil day, I may always be your friend, though my home is far from here.

'I am Odysseus, Laertes' son. The whole world talks of my stratagems, and my fame has reached the heavens. My home is under the clear skies of Ithaca. Our landmark is Mount Neriton with its quivering leaves. Other islands are clustered round it, Dulichium and Same and wooded Zacynthus. But Ithaca, the farthest out to sea, lies slanting to the west, whereas the others face the dawn and rising sun. It is a rough land, but nurtures fine men. And I, for one, know of no sweeter sight for a man's eyes than his own country. The divine Calypso was certainly for keeping me in her cavern home because she yearned for me to be her husband and with the same object Circe, the Aeaean witch, detained me in her palace; but never for a moment did they win my heart. So true it is that a man's fatherland and his parents are what he holds sweetest, even though he has settled far away from his people in some rich home in foreign lands. However, let me tell you of the disastrous voyage Zeus inflicted on me when I started back from Troy.

'The same wind that wafted me from Ilium brought me to Ismarus, the city of the Cicones. I sacked this place and destroyed its menfolk. The women and the vast plunder that we took from the town we divided so that no one, as far as I could help it, should go short of his proper share. And then I said we must escape with all possible speed. But my fools of men refused. There was plenty of wine, plenty of livestock; and they kept on drinking and butchering sheep and shambling crooked-horned cattle by the shore. Meanwhile the Cicones went and raised a cry for help among other Cicones, their inland neighbours, who are both more numerous and better men, trained in fighting from the chariot and on foot as well, when the occasion requires.

'At dawn they were on us, thick as the leaves and flowers in spring, and disaster, sent by Zeus to make us suffer, overtook my doomed companions and me. They fought a pitched battle by the swift ships and exchanged volleys of bronze spears. Right through the early morning and while the blessed light of day grew stronger we held our ground and kept their greater force at bay; but when the sun began to drop, towards the time when the ploughman unyokes his ox, the Cicones gained the upper hand and broke the Achaean ranks. Six of my strong-greaved comrades from each ship were killed. The rest of us eluded our fate and got away alive.

'We sailed on from Ismarus with heavy hearts, grieving for the loss of our dear companions though rejoicing at our own escape; and I would not let the curved ships sail before each of our poor comrades who had fallen in action against the Cicones had been three times saluted with a ritual call. Zeus, who marshals the clouds, now sent my fleet a terrible gale from the north. He covered land and sea alike with a canopy of cloud; darkness swept down on us from the sky. Our ships pitched and plunged in the wind, and the force of the gusts tore their sails to shreds and tatters. With the fear of death upon us, we lowered them on to the decks, and rowed the bare ships to the land with all our might.

'We rested on land for two days and two nights on end, with exhaustion and anxiety gnawing at our hearts. But on the third morning, which bright-haired Dawn had ushered in, we stepped the masts, hauled up the white sails, and took our places in the ship. The wind and the helmsmen kept our vessels straight. In fact I should have reached my own land safe and sound, had not the swell, the current and the North Wind combined, as I was rounding Malea, to drive me off my course and send me drifting past Cythera.[1]

'For nine days I was chased by those accursed winds across the teeming seas. But on the tenth we reached the country of the Lotus-eaters, a race that eat the flowery lotus fruit.[2] We disembarked to draw water, and my crews quickly had a meal by the ships. When we had eaten and drunk, I sent some of my followers inland to find out what sort of human beings might be there, detailing two men for the duty with a third as herald. Off they went, and it was not long before they came upon the Lotus-eaters. Now these natives had no intention of killing my comrades; what they did was to give them some lotus to taste. Those who ate the honeyed fruit of the plant lost any wish to come back and bring us news. All they now wanted was to stay where they were with the Lotus-eaters, to browse on the lotus, and to forget all thoughts of return. I had to use force to bring them back to the hollow ships, and they wept on the way, but once on board I tied them up and dragged them under the benches. I then commanded the rest of my loyal band to embark with all speed on their fast ships, for fear that others of them might eat the lotus and think no more of home. They came on board at once, took their places at their oars and all together struck the white surf with their blades.

1. Malea and Cythera are the last places on Odysseus' journey that can be found on a map. Scholars have naturally enjoyed speculating about the rest of his journey.
2. A mythical fruit.

'So we left that country and sailed with heavy hearts. And we came to the land of the Cyclopes, a fierce, lawless people who never lift a hand to plant or plough but just leave everything to the immortal gods. All the crops they require spring up unsown and untilled, wheat and barley and vines with generous clusters that swell with the rain from heaven to yield wine. The Cyclopes have no assemblies for the making of laws, nor any established legal codes, but live in hollow caverns in the mountain heights, where each man is lawgiver to his own children and women, and nobody has the slightest interest in what his neighbours decide.

'Not very far from the harbour of the Cyclopes' country, and not so near either, there lies a luxuriant island, covered with woods, which is the home of innumerable goats. The goats are wild, for the footsteps of man never disturb them, nor do hunters visit the island, forcing their way through forests and ranging the mountain tops. Used neither for grazing nor for ploughing, it lies for ever unsown and untilled; and this land where no man goes supports only bleating goats. The Cyclopes have nothing like our ships with their crimson prows; they have no shipwrights to build merchantmen that could give them the means of sailing across the sea to visit foreign towns and people, as other nations do. Such craftsmen would have turned the island into a fine colony for the Cyclopes.

'It is by no means a poor country, but capable of yielding any crop in due season. Along the shore of the grey sea there are lush water-meadows where the grapes would never fail; and there is land level enough for the plough, where they could count on cutting a tall-standing crop at every harvest because the subsoil is exceedingly rich. Also it has a safe harbour, in which there is no need of moorings – no need to cast anchor or make fast with hawsers: all your crew need do is beach their ship and wait till the spirit moves them and the right wind blows. Finally, at the head of the harbour there is a stream of fresh water, running out of a cave in a grove of poplar-trees.

'This is where we came to land. Some god must have guided us through the murky night, for it was impossible to see ahead. The ships were in a thick fog, and overhead not a gleam of light came through from the moon, which was obscured by clouds. Not a man among us caught sight of the island, nor did we even see the long breakers rolling up to the coast, before our good ships ran aground. It was not till they were beached that we lowered sail. We then jumped out on to the shore, fell asleep where we were and so waited for the blessed light of day.

'As soon as Dawn appeared, fresh and rosy-fingered, we were delighted with what we saw of the island, and set out to explore it. Presently the Nymphs, those children of Zeus, set the mountain goats on the move to ensure my companions a meal. Directly we saw them we fetched our curved bows and our long spears from the ships, separated into three parties, and began shooting at the goats; and in a short time the god had sent us plenty of game. When it was shared out, nine goats were allotted to each of the twelve ships under my command, but to me alone they made an allotment of ten.

'So the whole day long till the sun set we sat down to rich supplies of meat and mellow wine, since the ships had not yet run dry of our red vintage. There was still some in the holds, for when we took the sacred citadel of the Cicones, every member of the company had drawn off a generous supply in jars. There we sat, and as we looked across at the neighbouring land of the Cyclopes, we could see the smoke from their fires and hear their voices and the bleating of their sheep and goats. The sun went down, night fell, and we lay down to sleep on the sea-shore.

'As soon as Dawn appeared, fresh and rosy-fingered, I assembled my company and spoke to them. "My good friends," I said, "for the time being stay here, while I go in my ship with my crew to find out what kind of men are over there, and whether they are aggressive savages with no sense of right or wrong or hospitable and god-fearing people."

'Then I climbed into my ship and told my men to follow me and loose the hawsers. They came on board at once, took their places at the oars and all together struck the white surf with the blades. It was no great distance to the mainland. As we approached its nearest point, we made out a cave close to the sea, with a high entrance overhung by laurels. Here large flocks of sheep and goats were penned at night, and round the mouth a yard had been built with a great wall of quarried stones and tall pines and high-branched oaks. It was the den of a giant, who pastured his flocks alone, a long way away from anyone else, and had no truck with others of his kind but lived aloof in his own lawless way. And what a formidable monster he was! He was quite unlike any man who eats bread, more like some wooded peak in the high hills, standing out alone apart from the others.

'At this point, I told the rest of my loyal companions to stay there on guard by the ship, but I myself picked out the twelve best men in the company and advanced. I took with me in a goatskin some dark and mellow wine which had been given to me by Maron son of Euanthes, the priest of Apollo, the tutelary god of Ismarus, because we had protected him and his child and wife out of respect for his office. He lived in a wooded grove sacred to Phoebus Apollo. This man had given me some fine presents: seven talents of wrought gold, with a mixing-bowl of solid silver, and he drew off for me a dozen jars of mellow unmixed wine as well. It was a wonderful drink. It had been kept secret from all his serving-men and maids, in fact from everyone in the house but himself, his good wife and a housekeeper. To drink this red and honeyed vintage, he would pour one cupful of wine into twenty of water, and the bouquet that rose from the bowl was pure heaven – those were occasions when abstinence could have no charms.

'Well, I filled a big goatskin with this wine and also took some food in a bag with me; for I had an instant foreboding that we were going to find ourselves face to face with some barbarous being of colossal strength and ferocity, uncivilized and unprincipled. It took us very little time to reach the cave, but we did not find its owner at home: he was tending his fat sheep in the pastures. So we went inside and looked in amazement at everything. There were baskets laden with cheeses, and the folds were thronged with lambs and kids, each group – the spring ones, the summer ones, and the new-born ones – being separately penned. All his well-made vessels, the pails and bowls he used for milking, were swimming with whey.

'To start with my men begged me to let them take away some of the cheeses, then come back, drive the kids and lambs quickly out of the pens down to the good ship, and so set sail across the salt water. But though it would have been far better so, I was not to be persuaded. I wished to see the owner of the cave and had hopes of some friendly gifts from my host. But when he did appear, my men were not going to find him a very likeable character.

'We lit a fire, made an offering to the gods, helped ourselves to some of the cheeses, and when we had eaten, sat down in the cave to await his arrival. At last he came up, shepherding his flocks and carrying a huge bundle of dry wood to burn at supper-time. With a great crash he threw this down inside the cavern, giving us such a fright that we hastily retreated to an inner recess. Meanwhile he drove some of his fat flock into the wider part of the cave – all the ones he was milking – the rams and he-goats he left out of doors in the walled yard. He then picked up a huge stone, with which he closed the entrance. It was a mighty slab; twenty-two four-wheeled waggons could not shift such a massive stone from the entrance, such was the monstrous size of the rock with which he closed the cave. Next he sat down to milk his ewes and his bleating goats, which he did methodically, putting her young to each mother as he finished. He then curdled half the white milk, collected the whey, and stored it in wicker cheese-baskets; the remainder he left standing in pails, so that it would be handy at supper-time when he wanted a drink. When he had efficiently finished all his tasks, he re-lit the fire and spied us.

'"Strangers!" he cried. "And who are you? Where do you come from over the watery ways? Is yours a trading venture; or are you cruising the main on chance, like roving pirates, who risk their lives to ruin other people?"

'Our hearts sank. The booming voice and the very sight of the monster filled us with panic. Still, I managed to find words to answer him. "We are Achaeans," I said, "on our way back from Troy – driven astray by contrary winds across a vast expanse of sea – we're making our way home but took the wrong way – the wrong route – as Zeus, I suppose, intended that we should. We are proud to say that we belong to the forces of Agamemnon, Atreus' son, who by sacking the great city of Ilium and destroying all its armies has made himself the most famous man in the world today. We find ourselves here as suppliants at your knees, in the hope that you may give us hospitality, or even give us the kind of gifts that hosts customarily give their guests. Good sir, remember your duty to the gods; we are your suppliants, and Zeus is the champion of suppliants and guests. He is the god of guests: guests are sacred to him, and he goes alongside them."

'That is what I said, and he answered me promptly out of his pitiless heart: "Stranger, you must be a fool, or must have come from very far afield, to order me to fear or reverence the gods. We Cyclopes care nothing for Zeus with his aegis, nor for the rest of the blessed gods, since we are much stronger than they are. I would never spare you or your men for fear of incurring Zeus' enmity, unless I felt like it. But tell me where you moored your good ship when you came. Was it somewhere along the coast, or nearby? I'd like to know."

'His words were designed to get the better of me, but he could not outwit someone with my knowledge of the world. I answered with plausible words: "As for my ship, it was wrecked by the Earthshaker Poseidon on the borders of your land. The wind had carried us on to a lee shore. He drove the ship up to a headland and hurled it on the rocks. But I and my friends here managed to escape with our lives."

'To this the cruel brute made no reply. Instead, he jumped up, and reaching out towards my men, seized a couple and dashed their heads against the floor as though they had been puppies. Their brains ran out on the ground and soaked the earth. Limb by limb he tore them to pieces to make his meal, which he devoured like a mountain lion, leaving nothing, neither entrails nor flesh, marrow nor bones, while we, weeping, lifted up our hands to Zeus in horror at the ghastly sight. We felt completely helpless. When the Cyclops had filled his great belly with this meal of human flesh, which he washed down with unwatered milk, he stretched himself out for sleep among his flocks inside the cave.

'On first thoughts I planned to summon my courage, draw my sharp sword from the scabbard at my side, creep up to him, feel for the right place with my hand and stab him in the breast where the liver is supported by the midriff. But on second thoughts I refrained, realizing that we would seal our own fate as well as his, because we would have found it impossible with our unaided hands to push aside the huge rock with which he had closed the great mouth of the cave. So with sighs and groans we waited for the blessed light of day.

'As soon as Dawn appeared, fresh and rosy-fingered, the Cyclops re-lit the fire and milked his splendid ewes and goats, all in their proper order, putting her young to each. Having efficiently completed all these tasks, he once more snatched up a couple of my men and prepared his meal. When he had eaten, he turned his plump flocks out of the cave, removing the great doorstone without an effort. But he replaced it once more, as though he were putting the lid on a quiver. Then, with frequent whistles, he drove his plump flocks off towards the mountain, and I was left, with murder in my heart, scheming how to pay him out if only Athene would grant me my prayer. The best plan I could think of was this.

'Lying by the pen the Cyclops had a huge staff of green olive-wood, which he had cut to carry in his hand when it was seasoned. To us it looked more like the mast of some black ship of twenty oars, a broad-bottomed merchantman such as makes long sea-voyages. That was the impression which its length and thickness made on us. Standing beside this piece of timber I cut off a fathom's length, which I handed over to my men and told them to smooth it down. When they had done this I stood and sharpened it to a point. Then I hardened it in the fire, and finally I carefully hid it under the dung, of which there were great heaps scattered throughout the cave. I then told my company to cast lots for the dangerous task of helping me to lift the pole and twist it in the Cyclops' eye when he was sound asleep. The lot fell on the very men that I myself would have chosen, four of them, so that counting myself we made a party of five.

'Evening came, and with it the Cyclops, shepherding his plump flocks, every one of which he herded into the broad cave, leaving none out in the walled yard, either because he suspected something or because a god had ordered him to. He lifted the great doorstone, set it in its place, and then sat down to milk his ewes and bleating goats, which he did methodically, giving each mother its young one in due course. When he had efficiently completed all these tasks, he once more snatched two of us and prepared his supper. Then with an olive-wood bowl of my dark wine in my hands, I went up to him and said: "Here, Cyclops, have some wine to wash down that meal of human flesh, and find out for yourself what kind of vintage was stored away in our ship's hold. I brought it for you as an offering in the hope that you would take pity on me and help me on my homeward way. But your savagery is more than we can bear. Hard-hearted man, how can you expect ever to have a visitor again from the world of men? You have not behaved rightly."

'The Cyclops took the wine and drank it up. And the delicious drink gave him such exquisite pleasure that he asked me for another bowlful. "Give me more, please, and tell me your name, here and now – I would like to make you a gift that will please you. We Cyclopes have wine of our own made from the grapes that our rich soil and rains from Zeus produce. But this vintage of yours is a drop of the real nectar and ambrosia."

'So said the Cyclops, and I handed him another bowlful of the sparkling wine. Three times I filled it for him; and three times the fool drained the bowl to the dregs. At last, when the wine had fuddled his wits, I addressed him with soothing words.

' "Cyclops," I said, "you ask me my name. I'll tell it to you; and in return give me the gift you promised me. My name is Nobody. That is what I am called by my mother and father and by all my friends."

'The Cyclops answered me from his cruel heart. "Of all his company I will eat Nobody last, and the rest before him. That shall be your gift."

'He had hardly spoken before he toppled over and fell face upwards on the floor, where he lay with his great neck twisted to one side, and all-compelling sleep overpowered him. In his drunken stupor he vomited, and a stream of wine mixed with morsels of men's flesh poured from his throat. I went at once and thrust our pole deep under the ashes of the fire to make it hot, and meanwhile gave a word of encouragement to all my men, to make sure that no one would hang back through fear. When the fierce glow from the olive stake warned me that it was about to catch alight in the flames, green as it was, I withdrew it from the fire and my men gathered round. A god now inspired them with tremendous courage. Seizing the olive pole, they drove its sharpened end into the Cyclops' eye, while I used my weight from above to twist it home, like a man boring a ship's timber with a drill which his mates below him twirl with a strap they hold at either end, so that it spins continuously. In much the same way we handled our pole with its red-hot point and twisted it in his eye till the blood boiled up round the burning wood. The scorching heat singed his lids and brow all round, while his eyeball blazed and the very roots crackled in the flame. The Cyclops' eye hissed round the olive stake in the same way that an axe or adze hisses when a smith plunges it into cold water to quench and strengthen the iron. He gave a dreadful shriek, which echoed round the rocky walls, and we backed away from him in terror, while he pulled the stake from his eye, streaming with blood. Then he hurled it away from him with frenzied hands and raised a great shout to the other Cyclopes who lived in neighbouring caves along the windy heights. Hearing his screams they came up from every quarter, and gathering outside the cave asked him what the matter was.

' "What on earth is wrong with you, Polyphemus? Why must you disturb the peaceful night and spoil our sleep with all this shouting? Is a robber driving off your sheep, or is somebody trying by treachery or violence to kill you?"

'Out of the cave came mighty Polyphemus' voice in reply: "O my friends, it's Nobody's treachery, not violence, that is doing me to death."

' "Well then," came the immediate reply, "if you are alone and nobody is assaulting you, you must be sick and sickness comes from almighty Zeus and cannot be helped. All you can do is to pray to your father, the Lord Poseidon."

'And off they went, while I laughed to myself at the way in

which my cunning *notion*[1] of a false name had taken them in. The Cyclops, still moaning in agonies of pain, groped about with his hands and pushed the rock away from the mouth of the cave. Then he sat himself down in the doorway and stretched out both arms in the hope of catching us in the act of slipping out among the sheep. What a fool he must have thought me! Meanwhile I was cudgelling my brains for the best possible course, trying to hit on some way of saving my friends as well as myself. I thought up plan after plan, scheme after scheme. It was a matter of life or death: we were in mortal peril.

'This was the scheme that eventually seemed best. The rams of the flock were of good stock, thick-fleeced, fine, big animals in their coats of black wool. These I quietly lashed together with the plaited willow twigs which the inhuman monster used for his bed. I took them in threes. The middle one was to carry one of my followers, with its fellows on either side to protect him. Each of my men thus had three rams to bear him. But for myself I chose a full-grown ram who was the pick of the whole flock. Seizing him by the back, I curled myself up under his shaggy belly and lay there upside down, with a firm grip on his wonderful fleece and with patience in my heart. In this way, with sighs and groans, we waited for the blessed Dawn.

'As soon as she arrived, fresh and rosy-fingered, the he-goats and the rams began to scramble out and make for the pastures, but the females, unmilked as they were and with udders full to bursting, stood bleating by the pens. Their master, though tortured and in terrible agony, passed his hands along the backs of all the animals as they stopped in front of him; but the idiot never noticed that my men were tied under the chests of his own woolly rams. The last of the flock to come up to the doorway was the big ram, burdened by his own fleece and by me with my thoughts racing. As he felt him with his hands the great Polyphemus broke into speech:

'"Sweet ram," he said, "why are you the last of the flock to

1. The Greek for 'no one' is *me tis*, but run together as *metis* it means 'wily scheme, resourcefulness'. Odysseus laughs to himself because *metis* (no one/resourcefulness) has foiled the Cyclops. '*No*tion' is an attempt to get the pun.

pass out of the cave like this? You have never before lagged behind the others, but always step so proudly out and are the first of them to crop the lush shoots of the grass, first to make your way to the flowing stream, and first to want to return to the fold when evening falls. Yet today you are the last of all. You must be grieved for your master's eye, blinded by a wicked man and his accursed friends, when he had robbed me of my wits with wine. Nobody was his name; and I swear that he has not yet saved his skin! Ah, if only you could feel as I do and find a voice to tell me where he's hiding from my fury! I'd hammer him and splash his brains all over the floor of the cave, and my heart would find some relief from the suffering which that nothing, that Nobody, has caused me!"

'So he let the ram pass through the entrance and when we had put a little distance between ourselves and the courtyard of the cave, I first let go my ram and then untied my men. Then, quickly, though with many a backward look, we drove our long-striding sheep and goats – a rich, fat flock – right down to the ship. My dear companions were overjoyed when they caught sight of us survivors, but broke into loud lamentations for the others. With nods and frowns I indicated silently that they should stop their weeping and hurry to bundle the fleecy sheep and goats on board and put to sea. So they went on board at once, took their places at the oars, and all together struck the white water with the blades.

'But before we were out of earshot, I shouted out derisive words at Polyphemus. "Cyclops! So he was not such a weakling after all, the man whose friends you meant to overpower and eat in your hollow cave! And your crimes were bound to catch up with you, you brute, who did not shrink from devouring your guests. Now Zeus and all the other gods have paid you out."

'My words so enraged the Cyclops that he tore the top off a great pinnacle of rock and hurled it at us. The rock fell just ahead of our blue-painted bows. As it plunged in, the water surged up and the backwash, like a swell from the open sea, swept us landward and nearly drove us on to the beach. Seizing a long pole, I pushed the ship off, at the same time commanding my crew with urgent nods to bend to their oars and save us from disaster. They leant forward and rowed with a will; but when they had taken us across the water to twice our previous distance I was about to shout something else to the Cyclops, but from all parts of the ship my men called out, trying to restrain and pacify me.

'"Why do you want to provoke the savage in this obstinate way? The rock he threw into the sea just now drove the ship back to the land, and we thought it was all up with us. Had he heard a cry, or so much as a word, from a single man, he'd have smashed in our heads and the ship's timbers with another jagged boulder from his hand. We're within easy range for him!"

'But my temper was up; their words did not dissuade me, and in my rage I shouted back at him once more: "Cyclops, if anyone ever asks you how you came by your blindness, tell him your eye was put out by Odysseus, sacker of cities, the son of Laertes, who lives in Ithaca."

'The Cyclops gave a groan. "Alas!" he cried. "Those ancient prophecies have come back to me now! We had a prophet living with us once, a great and mighty man, Eurymus' son Telemus, the best of soothsayers, who grew old as a seer among us Cyclopes. All that has now happened he foretold, when he warned me that a man called Odysseus would rob me of my sight. But I always expected some big handsome man of tremendous strength to come along. And now, a puny, feeble good-for-nothing fuddles me with wine and then puts out my eye! But come here, Odysseus, so that I can give you some friendly gifts and prevail on the great Earthshaker, Poseidon, to see you safely home. For I am his son, and he is proud to call himself my father. He is the one who will heal me if he's willing – a thing no other blessed god nor any man on earth could do."

'To which I shouted in reply: "I only wish I could make as sure of robbing you of life and breath and sending you to Hell, as I am certain that not even the Earthshaker will ever heal your eye."

'At this the Cyclops lifted up his hands to the starry heavens and prayed to the Lord Poseidon: "Hear me, Poseidon, Sustainer of the Earth, god of the sable locks. If I am yours indeed and you claim me as your son, grant that Odysseus, sacker of cities and son of Laertes, may never reach his home in Ithaca. But if he is destined to see his friends again, to come once more to his own house and reach his native land, let him come late, in wretched plight, having lost all his comrades, in a foreign ship, and let him find trouble in his home."

'So Polyphemus prayed; and the god of the sable locks heard his prayer. Once again the Cyclops picked up a boulder – bigger, by far, this time – and hurled it with a swing, putting such tremendous force into his throw that the rock fell only just astern of our blue-painted ship, narrowly missing the tip of the rudder. The water heaved up as it plunged into the sea; but the wave that it raised carried us on towards the further shore.

'And so we reached our island, where the rest of our good ships were all waiting for us, their crews sitting round disconsolate and keeping a constant watch for our return. Once there, we beached our ship, jumped out on the shore, and unloaded the Cyclops' flocks from the hold. We then divided our spoil so that no one, as far as I could help it, should go short of his proper share. But my comrades-in-arms did me the special honour, when the sheep and goats were distributed, of presenting me with the big ram in addition. Him I sacrificed on the beach, burning slices from his thighs as an offering to Zeus of the Black Clouds, the Son of Cronos, who is lord of us all. But Zeus took no notice of my sacrifice; his mind must already have been full of plans for the destruction of all my fine ships and of my loyal band.

'So the whole day long till sundown we sat and feasted on our rich supply of meat and mellow wine. When the sun set and darkness fell, we lay down to sleep on the sea-shore. As soon as Dawn appeared, fresh and rosy-fingered, I roused my men and ordered them to go on board and cast off. They climbed on board at once, took their places at the oars and all together struck the white surf with the blades. Thus we left the island and sailed on with heavy hearts, grieving for the dear friends we had lost but glad at our own escape from death.'

# 10
# CIRCE

'We next came to the floating island of Aeolia, the home of Aeolus son of Hippotas, who is a favourite of the immortal gods. All round this isle there runs an unbroken wall of bronze, and below it the cliffs rise sheer from the sea. Aeolus shares his house with his family of twelve, six daughters and six grown-up sons; and he has given his daughters to his sons in marriage. With their father and their estimable mother they are always feasting. Countless delicacies are laid before them, and all day long the house is filled with the savoury smell of roasting meat, and the courtyard echoes to the sounds of banqueting within. At night they sleep, each with his loving wife, on ornate beds, with plenty of rugs.

'To this domain of theirs and this magnificent palace we now came. For a whole month Aeolus entertained me and questioned me on everything – Troy, the Achaean navy and our return – and I told him everything, exactly as it was. When it came to my turn and I asked him whether I might now continue my journey and count on his help, he gave it willingly. He made arrangements for my journey and presented me with a leather bag, made from the flayed skin of a full-grown ox, in which he had imprisoned the boisterous energies of all the winds. Zeus had put him in charge of the winds, with power to lay or rouse them each at will. This bag he stowed in the hold of my ship, securing it tightly with a burnished silver wire to prevent the slightest leakage. Then he called up a breeze from the West to blow my ships and their crews across the sea. But his measures were doomed to failure, for we came to grief, through our own senseless stupidity.

'For nine days and nights we sailed on; and on the tenth we were already in sight of our homeland, and had even come near enough to see people tending their fires, when I fell fast asleep. I was utterly exhausted, for in my anxiety to speed our journey home I handled the sheet of my ship myself without a break, giving it to no one else.

'The crew began to discuss matters among themselves, and word went round that I was bringing home a fortune in gold and silver which the great-hearted Aeolus son of Hippotas had given me. And this is what they said as they exchanged glances: "It's not fair! What a captain we have, valued wherever he goes and welcomed in every port! Back he comes from Troy with a splendid haul of plunder, though we who have gone every bit as far come home with empty hands – and now Aeolus has given him all this into the bargain, as a favour for friendship's sake! Come on; let's find out and see how much gold and silver is hidden in that bag."

'After talk like this evil counsels prevailed. They undid the bag, the winds all rushed out, and in an instant the tempest was upon them, carrying them headlong out to sea, in tears, away from their native land. When I awoke my spirit failed me. I debated within myself whether to jump overboard and drown or stay among the living and quietly endure. I stayed and endured. Covering my head with my cloak, I lay where I was in the ship. So all my ships, with their distraught crews, were driven back to the island of Aeolus.

'We disembarked and collected water, and the men straightaway had a quick meal by the ships. But as soon as we had had something to eat and drink I took a messenger and one of my comrades to accompany me and set out for the palace of Aeolus, whom we found at dinner with his wife and family. We went in and sat down on the threshold by the door-posts.

'They were astounded at the sight of us. "Odysseus?" they exclaimed. "How do *you* come to be here? What evil power has dealt you this blow? We did our best to help you on your way home to Ithaca or any port you might choose."

'I replied sorrowfully, "An untrustworthy crew and a fatal sleep were my downfall. Put things right for me, my friends.

You easily could." It was with these placatory words that I appealed to them.

'They remained silent. Then the father answered. "Get off this island instantly! The world holds no one more damnable than you, and it is not right for me to entertain and equip a man detested by the blessed gods. Your returning like this *shows* they detest you. Get out!"

'Thus he dismissed me from his palace, causing me deep distress. We left the island and resumed our journey in a state of gloom; and the heart was taken out of my men by the wearisome rowing. But it was our own stupidity that had deprived us of the wind.

'For six days and six nights we sailed on, and on the seventh we came to Telepylus, Lamus' stronghold in the Laestrygonian land, where herdsmen bringing in their flocks at night exchange greetings with other herdsmen driving out at dawn. For in this land nightfall and morning tread so closely on each other's heels that a man who could do without sleep might earn two wages, one for herding cattle and the other for shepherding flocks of white sheep. Here we found an excellent harbour, closed in on all sides by an unbroken ring of precipitous cliffs, with two jutting headlands facing each other at the mouth so as to leave only a narrow channel in between.

'The captains of my squadron all steered their curved craft straight into the harbour and tied up in the sheltered waters within. They remained close together, for it was obvious that there was never any swell there, slight or strong, but always a flat calm. But I did not follow them. Instead I brought my black ship to rest outside the harbour and made her fast with a cable to a rock at the end of the point. I then climbed the headland to get a view from the top. But no cultivated fields or herds of cattle were visible; all we saw was a wisp of smoke rising up from the countryside. So I sent a party inland to find out what sort of people the inhabitants were, two of my men, together with a messenger.

'When they had left the ships they found a well-worn track used by waggons bringing timber down from the high mountains to the town. Presently they came across a strong girl drawing water outside the town, the daughter of Antiphates, the Laestrygonian chief. She had come down to a bubbling spring called Artacie, from which the townspeople drew their water. When they went up and asked her who the ruler of the country was and what his people were called, she pointed at once to the high roof of her father's dwelling. When they entered his palace they were confronted by Antiphates' wife, a woman of mountainous proportions; the sight of her appalled them. She called her husband, the famous Antiphates, from the assembly-place, who promptly made his murderous intentions clear, pouncing on one of my men to eat him for supper. The other two sprang back and fled, and managed to make their way back to the ships.

'Meanwhile Antiphates raised a hue and cry through the town, which brought countless numbers of powerful Laestrygonians running up from every side, more like Giants than men. Standing at the top of the cliffs they began pelting my flotilla with lumps of rock such as an ordinary man could barely lift; and the din that now rose from the ships, where the groans of dying men could be heard above the splintering of timbers, was appalling. They carried them off like fishes on a spear to make their loathsome meal. But while this massacre was still going on in the deep harbour, I drew my sword from my hip, slashed through the hawser of my blue-prowed vessel, and shouted to the crew to bend to their oars if they wished to save their lives. With the fear of death upon them they struck the water like one man, and to our relief and joy we shot out to sea and left those frowning cliffs behind. My ship was safe. But that was the end of all the rest.

'We travelled on with heavy hearts, grieving for the loss of our dear friends though rejoicing at our own escape. In due course we came to the island of Aeaea, the home of the beautiful Circe, a formidable goddess, with a mortal woman's voice. She is the sister of the baleful Aeetes, both being children of the Sun who lights the world, by the same mother, Perse the Daughter of Ocean. We brought our ship into the shelter of the harbour without making a sound. Some god guided us in. And when we had disembarked, we lay on the beach for two days and nights, utterly exhausted and eating our hearts out with grief.

'When Dawn with her beautiful tresses ushered in the third day, I took my spear and sword, left the ship, and struck inland, making for a vantage-point from which I might see signs of cultivation or hear men's voices. I climbed a rocky height, and on reaching the top I was able to see the smoke rising from the distant place where Circe's house lay in a clearing among the dense oak-scrub and forest trees. That glimpse I had of reddish smoke left me in two minds whether or not to press forward and reconnoitre. After some thought I decided the better course would be to return first to my ship on the beach, give my men a meal, and send out an exploring party.

'And then some god was moved to pity by my forlorn condition. For when I had almost reached the ship, he sent a great antlered stag right across my path. The fierce heat of the sun had driven him down from the forest pastures to drink at a stream, and as he came up from the water I struck him on the spine half-way down his back. My bronze spear went right through him, and with a bellow he fell in the dust and was dead. With one foot on his carcass I dragged the bronze spear out of the wound, laid it on the ground, and left it there while I broke off creepers and shoots from undergrowth and willows, which I twisted into a fathom's length of rope carefully plaited from end to end. With this I tied the monster's feet together, and, slinging him round my neck, I made for the ship, using my spear as a staff. I could not possibly have balanced him on one shoulder with my free hand – he was a massive brute. When I reached the ship, I threw the stag down in front of it, and going up to each man in turn heartened them with a cheerful word.

' "My friends," I said, "we may be miserable, but we are not going down to the house of Hades yet, not till our time has come. Get up, and while there's food and drink on board, let us have something to eat instead of dying here of starvation."

'This was advice they took readily enough. They at once flung off their rugs, and there on the desolate sea-shore they gazed open-mouthed at the stag; he really was a monster. When they had feasted their eyes on the sight they washed their hands and prepared a glorious meal. So the whole day long till sundown we sat down to a feast of unlimited meat and mellow wine. When the sun set and darkness fell, we lay down to sleep on the sea-shore. As soon as Dawn appeared, fresh and rosy-fingered, I gathered my men round me and addressed them.

'"Comrades in suffering, friends, listen to me. We are utterly lost. We do not know where East or West is; where the light-giving Sun rises or where he sets. So the sooner we decide on a sensible plan the better – if one can still be found, which I doubt. For when I climbed the crag I found that this is an island, and low-lying; all round it in a ring the sea stretches away to the horizon. But what I did see, right in the middle, through dense oak-scrub and forest, was a wisp of smoke."

'When they heard my report they broke down completely. They could not help remembering what Antiphates the Laestrygonian had done, and the unbridled savagery of the man-eating Cyclops. They burst into loud sobs and the tears streamed down their cheeks. But they might have spared themselves their lamentations for all the good they did.

'In the end I divided my well-armed crew into two parties with a leader for each. Of one party I myself took charge; the other I gave to the noble Eurylochus. Then we shook lots in a bronze helmet and out jumped the lot of the great-hearted Eurylochus, so he went off with his twenty-two men, a tearful company, leaving us, who stayed behind, weeping too. In a clearing in a glade they came upon Circe's house, built of polished stone. Prowling about the place were mountain wolves and lions that Circe had bewitched with her magic drugs. They did not attack my men, but rose on their hind legs to fawn on them, with much wagging of their long tails, like dogs fawning on their master as he comes from table for the tasty bits he always brings. In the same way these wolves and lions with great claws fawned round my men. Terrified at the sight of the formidable beasts, they stood in the palace porch of the goddess with the lovely tresses. They could hear Circe within, singing in her beautiful voice as she went to and fro at her great and everlasting loom, on which she was weaving one of those delicate, graceful and dazzling fabrics that goddesses make.

'Polites, an authoritative man and the one in my party whom I liked and trusted most, now took the lead. "Friends," he said, "there is someone in the castle working at a loom. The whole place echoes to that lovely voice. It's either a goddess or a woman. Let us call to her immediately."

'So they called and Circe came out at once, opened the polished doors, and invited them to enter. In their innocence, the whole party followed her in. But Eurylochus suspected a trap and stayed outside. Circe ushered the rest into her hall, gave them seats and chairs to sit on, and then prepared them a mixture of cheese, barley-meal, and yellow honey flavoured with Pramnian wine. But into this dish she introduced a noxious drug, to make them lose all memory of their native land. And when they had emptied the bowls which she had handed them, she drove them with blows of a stick into the pigsties. Now they had pigs' heads and bristles, and they grunted like pigs; but their minds were as human as they had been before. So, weeping, they were penned in their sties. Then Circe flung them some forest nuts, acorns and cornel-berries – the usual food of pigs that wallow in the mud.

'Meanwhile Eurylochus came back to the swift black ship to report the catastrophe his party had met with. He was in such anguish that he could not utter a single word; his eyes were filled with tears, and he felt on the verge of breaking down. Exasperated, we all bombarded him with questions, till at length he came out with the story of his comrades' fate.

'"We went – as you ordered – through the woods – noble Odysseus. In a clearing, in a glade, we came to a well-built house of polished stone. Someone inside was singing in a clear voice as she went to and fro at her great web – either a goddess or a woman. My men called and she came out, immediately opened the polished doors, and invited us to enter. In their innocence, the whole party followed her in. But I suspected a trap and stayed outside. And now the whole party has been wiped out. Not a single man reappeared, though I sat there a long time, watching."

'When I heard this story I slung my big bronze silver-studded sword in its silver scabbard over my shoulder, then my bow, and I told Eurylochus to take me back with him by the way he had come. But he threw his arms round my knees in supplication and broke into a pitiful appeal.

'"Favourite of Zeus," he said, "leave me behind; don't force me to go with you there. You will never come back yourself and you won't rescue a single man of your crew. I am certain of it. Let us get away quickly with those that are left here. We might still escape the evil day."

'"Very well, Eurylochus," I replied; "stay where you are, and eat and drink by the black ship's hull. But I shall go. I have absolutely no choice."

'With this, I turned my back on the ship and the sea, and struck inland. But, threading my way through the enchanted glades, I was nearing the sorceress's palace when I met Hermes, god of the golden wand, looking like a young man at that most charming age when the beard first starts to grow. He took my hand in his and greeted me amiably.

'"Where are you off to now, my poor fellow," he said, "wandering alone through the wilds in unknown country, with your friends in Circe's house penned like pigs in their crowded sties? Have you come here to free them? I think you are more likely to stay with them yourself and never see your home. However, I will save you and deliver you from your trouble. Look: here is a drug of real virtue that you must take with you into Circe's palace; it will make you immune from evil. I will tell you how she works her black magic. She will begin by preparing you a mixture, into which she will put her drug. But even with its help she will be unable to enchant you, for this antidote that I am going to give you will rob it of its power. I will tell you exactly what to do. When Circe strikes you with her long stick, you must draw your sword from your side and rush at her as though you mean to kill her. She will shrink from you in terror and invite you to her bed. You must not refuse the goddess's favours, if you want her to free your men and look after you. But make her swear a solemn oath by the blessed gods not to try any more of her tricks on you, or when she has you stripped naked she may rob you of your courage and your manhood."

'Then the Giant-killer handed me a herb he had plucked from the ground, and showed me what it was like. It had a black root and a milk-white flower. The gods call it moly, and it is a dangerous plant for mortal men to dig up. But the gods, after all, can do anything.

'Hermes went off through the island forest, making for high Olympus, while I with a heart oppressed by many dark forebodings pursued my way to Circe's home. I stood at the doors of the lovely goddess's palace and called out. Circe heard me, came out immediately, and, opening the polished doors, invited me in. Filled with misgivings, I followed her indoors and she offered me a beautiful silver-studded chair with a stool for my feet. She prepared a brew in a golden bowl for me to drink and with evil in her heart dropped in the drug. She gave me the bowl and I drained it, but without suffering any magic effects. She struck me with her stick and shouted, "Off to the pigsty, and lie down with your friends." Whereupon I snatched my keen sword from my hip and rushed at Circe as though I meant to kill her. But with a shriek she slipped below my blade, clasped my knees and burst into tears.

' "Who are you and where do you come from?" she asked, and her words had wings. "Where is your native town? Who are your parents? I am amazed to see you take my drug and suffer no magic change. For never before have I known a man who could resist that drug once he had taken it and swallowed it down. You must have a heart in your breast that is proof against all enchantment. I am sure you are Odysseus, that resourceful man; the man whom the Giant-killer with the golden wand always told me to expect here on his way back from Troy in his swift black ship. But now put up your sword and come with me to my bed, so that in making love we may learn to trust one another."

' "Circe," I answered her, "how can you order me to be gentle with you, you who have turned my friends into pigs here in your house, and now that you have me too in your clutches are inveigling me to your bedroom and inviting me into your bed, to strip me naked and rob me of my courage and manhood? Nothing, goddess, would induce me to come into your bed unless you can bring yourself to swear a solemn oath that you have no other mischief in store for me."

'Circe at once swore as I ordered her. So when she had duly sworn the oath, I went with the goddess to her beautiful bed.

'Meanwhile the four maids who do the housework for Circe were busying themselves in the palace. They are the daughters of Springs and Groves and sacred Rivers that flow out into the sea. One of them threw linen covers over the chairs and spread fine purple rugs on top. Another drew silver tables up to the chairs and placed golden dishes upon them; the third mixed the sweet and mellow wine in a silver bowl and set out the golden cups; and the fourth fetched water and lit a fire under the big cauldron, and the water grew warm.

'When the shining bronze vessel was boiling, she sat me in a bath and washed me with water from the great cauldron mixed with cold to a comfortable heat, sluicing my head and shoulders till all the painful weariness was gone from my limbs. My bath done, she rubbed me with olive-oil, clothed me in a tunic and a splendid cloak, and seated me on a beautiful silver-studded chair with a foot-stool beneath. Next came another maid with water in a splendid golden ewer. She poured it out over a silver basin so that I could rinse my hands, and then drew up a polished table to my side. A trusty housekeeper brought some bread, which she put by me with a variety of delicacies; and after helping me liberally to all she could offer she invited me to eat. But I had no heart for eating. As I sat there my thoughts were elsewhere and my mind was full of forebodings.

'When Circe saw me sitting so quiet and not helping myself to the food, she knew that I was in deep anguish. So she came and stood by me and said with words that flew:

' "Odysseus, why are you sitting like this as though you were dumb, and feeding on your own thoughts instead of helping yourself to meat and wine? Do you suspect another trap? You need have no fears: I have given you a solemn oath to do you no harm."

' "Circe," I answered her, "could any honourable man bear to taste food and drink before he had freed his men and seen them face to face? If you are sincere in asking me to eat and drink, give them their liberty and let me set eyes on my loyal followers."

'Stick in hand, Circe went straight out of the hall, threw open the pigsty gate, and drove them out, looking exactly like full-grown swine. When they were all in front of her she went in among them and smeared them each in turn with some new ointment. Then the bristles which her first deadly potion had caused to sprout dropped off their limbs, and they became men again and looked younger and much more handsome and taller than before. They recognized me now, and one after the other seized my hand. We were so moved that we all wept tears of happiness, till the walls echoed with the mournful sound. Even the goddess felt pity, and came to me and said: "Favourite of Zeus, son of Laertes, Odysseus of the many devices, go down now to your ship by the sea-shore, drag her straight away on to dry land, stow your possessions and all the ship's tackle in a cave, and then come back yourself with the rest of your loyal company."

'At this my proud heart was convinced. I went to the ship and the sea-shore. I found my good companions by the ship, lamenting pitifully, with the tears streaming down their cheeks. But as soon as they caught sight of me they were all round me in a weeping throng. It was like the scene at a farm when cows in a drove come home full-fed from the pastures to the yard and are welcomed by all their frisking calves, who burst out from the pens to gambol round their mothers, lowing excitedly. My men were as deeply moved as if they had reached their homeland and were standing in their own town in rugged Ithaca, where they were born and bred.

'"Favourite of Zeus," they said between their sobs, "we are as happy to see you back as we would be to set foot on our own island of Ithaca. But tell us how our comrades met their end."

'I gave them a soothing reply. "Our first business," I said, "is to drag up the ship on to dry land and stow our possessions and the tackle in a cave. Then you must get ready and all come with me and see your friends eating and drinking in Circe's enchanted palace, where they have enough to last them for ever."

'They were quick to be convinced by my suggestion. Only

Eurylochus was against me and did his best to keep the whole company back. "Where are we poor wretches off to now?" he cried with winged words. "Why are you looking for trouble – going to Circe's palace, where she will turn you all into pigs or wolves or lions, and force you to keep watch over that great house of hers? We have had all this before, with the Cyclops, when our friends found their way into his fold with this foolhardy Odysseus. It was this man's reckless folly that cost *them* their lives."

'Now when Eurylochus said that, I considered drawing the long sword from my sturdy side and lopping his head off to roll in the dust, even though he was a close kinsman of mine. But my men held me back and calmed me down.

' "Favourite of Zeus," they said, "let's leave this man here to guard the ship, if that is your order. But you lead us to Circe's enchanted castle."

'So they left the ship and the sea and struck inland. Eurylochus came with us after all. He was not going to be left by the ship; he was afraid of the stinging rebuke I might give him.

'Circe meanwhile had graciously bathed the members of my party in her palace and rubbed them with olive-oil. She gave them all tunics and warm cloaks to wear, so that on our arrival we found them having dinner together in the hall. When the two companies came face to face and they all recognized each other, they burst into tears and the whole house echoed to their sobs. But then the goddess approached me.

' "Heaven-born son of Laertes," she said, "resourceful Odysseus, check this immoderate grief. I know as well as you all you have gone through on the teeming seas and suffered at the hands of savages on land. But now eat your food and drink your wine, till you are once more the men you were when first you sailed from your homes in rugged Ithaca. You are worn out and dispirited, always brooding on the hardships of your travels. Your sufferings have been so continuous that you have lost all pleasure in living."

'My gallant company were not difficult to persuade. We stayed on day after day for a whole year, feasting on lavish quantities of meat and mellow wine. But as the months went by and the seasons passed and the long days returned, my loyal companions called me aside one day and said: "What possesses you to stay on here? It's time you thought of Ithaca, if the gods mean you to escape and get back to your ancestral home in your own country." This was enough: my proud heart was convinced.

'For the rest of that day till sunset we sat and feasted on lavish quantities of meat and mellow wine. When the sun sank and night fell, my men settled down for sleep in the darkened hall. But I went to Circe's beautiful bed and there clasped the goddess's knees in supplication, and she listened to my winged words:

'"Circe," I said, "keep that promise which you once made me, to send me home. I am eager now to be gone, and so are all my men. Whenever you are not present they stand around and exhaust me with their complaints."

'"Heaven-born son of Laertes, resourceful Odysseus," the goddess answered me, "do not stay on unwillingly. But first you have to make another journey and find your way to the Halls of Hades and dread Persephone, to consult the soul of Teiresias, the blind Theban prophet. His faculties are unimpaired, for dead though he is, Persephone has granted him, and him alone, continuing wisdom. The others there are mere shadows flitting to and fro."

'This news broke my heart. Sitting there on the bed I wept. I had no further use for life, no wish to see the sunshine any more. But when at last I had satisfied my need for tears and for tossing and turning on the bed, I began to question her: "Circe, who is to guide me on the way? No one has ever sailed a black ship into Hell."

'"Heaven-born son of Laertes, resourceful Odysseus," the goddess answered me, "do not think of lingering on shore for lack of a pilot. Set up your mast, spread the white sail and sit down in the ship. The North Wind will blow her on her way; and when she has brought you across the River of Ocean, you will come to a wild coast and Persephone's Grove, where the tall poplars grow, and the willows that so quickly shed their seeds. Beach your boat there by Ocean's swirling stream and go on into Hades' Kingdom of Decay. There, at a rocky pinnacle, the River of Flaming Fire and the River of Lamentation, which is a branch of the Waters of Styx, meet and pour their thundering streams into Acheron. When you reach this place, do as I tell you, my lord; dig a trench as long and as wide as a man's forearm. Go round this trench and pour offerings to all the dead, first with a mixture of honey and milk, then with sweet wine, and last of all with water. Over all this sprinkle white barley and then begin your prayers to the helpless ghosts of the dead. Promise them that once you are in Ithaca you will sacrifice a barren heifer in your palace, the best that you have, and will heap the pyre with treasures, and make Teiresias a separate offering of the finest jet-black sheep in your flock.

'"When you have finished your invocations to the glorious company of the dead, sacrifice a ram and a black ewe, holding their heads down towards Erebus while you turn your own aside, to face the River of Ocean. The spirits of the dead and departed will come up in their multitudes. Then you must immediately order your men to flay the sheep that are lying there slaughtered by your pitiless blade, and burn them sacrificially, praying to the gods, to mighty Hades and august Persephone. Sit still yourself meanwhile, with your drawn sword in your hand, and do not let any of the helpless ghosts come near to the blood till you have questioned Teiresias. Presently the prophet himself will come to you, my Lord King. And he will prophesy your route, the stages of your journey and how you will reach home across the teeming seas."

'Circe finished, and soon after, Dawn rose from her throne of gold. The Nymph dressed me in my tunic and cloak and herself put on a long robe of silvery sheen, of a light fabric charming to the eye. Round her waist she fastened a splendid golden belt, and she put a veil over her head. Then I walked through the palace and made the round of my men, rousing them each with a cheerful word. "Wake up," I said, "and bid your pleasant sleep farewell. It's time to go. My lady Circe has made everything clear."

'My gallant band agreed gladly enough. But even this time I did not lead them all safely away. There was one called Elpenor, the youngest of the party, not much of a fighting man and not very clever. This young man had got drunk, and longing for fresh air had left his friends and gone to sleep on the roof of Circe's enchanted palace. Roused in the morning by the bustle and din of the departure, he leapt up suddenly, and forgetting to go to the long ladder and take the proper way down, he toppled headlong from the roof. He broke his neck and his soul went to Hades.

'When the rest of the party joined me I said to them: "You no doubt imagine that you are bound for home and our beloved Ithaca. But Circe has marked us out for a very different route – to the Halls of Hades and dread Persephone, where we must seek advice of the spirit of Theban Teiresias."

'When I told them this they were heart-broken. They sat down where they were and wept and tore their hair. But their lamentations achieved nothing.

'We made our way to our ship and the beach with heavy hearts and with many tears. Meanwhile Circe had gone ahead and tethered a ram and a black ewe by the ship. She had slipped past us with ease; when a god wishes to remain unseen, what eye can observe his coming or going?'

# 11
# THE BOOK OF THE DEAD

'Our first task, when we came down to the sea and reached our ship, was to run her into the bright salt water and put the mast and sails on to the black ship. We then picked up the sheep and goats and put them on board, after which we ourselves embarked, heavy-hearted and weeping bitterly. However, Circe of the lovely tresses, the powerful goddess with a human voice, sent us the friendly escort of a favourable breeze, which sprang up from astern and filled the sail of our blue-prowed ship. So, after putting the tackle in order fore and aft, we sat down, while the wind and the helmsman kept her straight. With a taut sail she sped across the sea all day, till the Sun went down and all the ways grew dark.

'So she reached the furthest parts of the deep-flowing River of Ocean where the Cimmerians live, wrapped in mist and fog. The bright Sun cannot look down on them with his rays, either when he climbs the starry heavens or when he turns back from heaven to earth again. Dreadful Night spreads her mantle over that unhappy people.

'Here we beached our ship and, after putting our flocks ashore, made our way along the banks of the River of Ocean till we reached the place that Circe had described. There, while Perimedes and Eurylochus kept hold of the sacrificial victims, I drew my sharp sword from my side and dug a trench as long and as wide as a man's forearm. There I poured libations to all the dead, first with a mixture of honey and milk, then with sweet wine, and last of all with water. Over all this I sprinkled some white barley, and then began my prayers to the insubstantial presences of the dead, promising them that directly

I got back to Ithaca I would sacrifice a barren heifer in my palace, the best I had, and heap the pyre with treasures, and make Teiresias a separate offering of the finest jet-black sheep in my flocks.

'When I had finished my prayers and invocations to the communities of the dead, I took the sheep and cut their throats over the trench so that the dark blood poured in. And now the souls of the dead came swarming up from Erebus – brides, unmarried youths, old men who had suffered greatly, once-happy girls with grief still fresh in their hearts, and a great throng of warriors killed in battle, their spear-wounds gaping and all their armour stained with blood. From this multitude of souls, as they fluttered to and fro by the trench, there came an eerie clamour. Panic drained the blood from my cheeks. I turned to my comrades and told them quickly to flay the sheep I had slaughtered with my sword and burn them, and to pray to the gods, to mighty Hades and august Persephone. But I myself sat on guard, bare sword in hand, and prevented any of the insubstantial presences from approaching the blood before I questioned Teiresias.

'The first spirit that came up was that of my own comrade Elpenor, for he had not yet been buried in the wide bosom of Earth. So urgent had our other task been that we had left his corpse unburied and unwept in Circe's palace. Now, when I saw him, tears started to my eyes and I was stirred with pity for him.

'I called across to him with winged words: "Elpenor! How did you come here, to the land of shadows? You have been quicker on foot than I in my black ship."

'I heard him groan, and then his answer came: "Son of Laertes, favourite of Zeus, Odysseus of the nimble wits, the malicious decree of some god and too much wine were my undoing. I had lain down to sleep on the roof of Circe's palace, and forgot to go to the long ladder and take the right way down, and so fell headlong from the roof. My neck was broken and my soul came down to Hades. And now, I beseech you, by all the absent friends we left behind, by your wife, by the father who looked after you as a child, and by Telemachus, your only son, whom you left at home – since I know for certain that when you leave this kingdom of the dead you will put in with your good ship at the Isle of Aeaea, Circe's isle – I beg you, master, to remember me then and not to sail away and forsake me utterly nor leave me there unburied and unwept, in case I bring down the gods' curse on you. So burn my body there with all the arms I possess, and raise a mound for me on the shore of the grey sea, in memory of an unlucky man, so that men yet unborn may learn my story. Do this for me, and on my barrow plant the oar I used to pull when I was alive and with my comrades."

'To which I answered: "All this, my poor Elpenor, I will do. Nothing shall be forgotten."

'Thus we sat facing each other across the trench exchanging joyless words, I on the one side, with my sword stretched out above the blood, and on the other the ghost of my comrade pouring out his tale.

'Next came the soul of my dead mother, Anticleia, the daughter of the great Autolycus, who had still been alive when I left her and sailed for sacred Ilium. My eyes filled with tears when I saw her there, and I was stirred to compassion. Yet, deeply moved though I was, I would not allow her to approach the blood first, before I had questioned Teiresias. And the spirit of the Theban prophet now came up, with a gold sceptre in his hand, saw who I was, and addressed me.

'"Favourite of Zeus, son of Laertes, Odysseus of the nimble wits, what has brought you, the man of misfortune, to forsake the sunlight and to visit the dead in this joyless place? Step back now from the trench and hold your keen sword aside, so that I can drink the blood and prophesy the truth to you."

'I drew back, sheathing my silver-studded sword in its scabbard. And when the illustrious prophet had drunk the dark blood he uttered these words: "My Lord Odysseus, you seek a happy way home. But a god is going to make your journey hard. For I cannot think that you will escape the attention of the Earthshaker, who still nurses resentment against you in his heart, enraged that you blinded his beloved son. Even so, you and your friends may yet reach Ithaca, though not without suffering, if only you have the strength of will to control your men's appetites and your own from the moment when your good ship leaves the deep blue sea and approaches the isle of Thrinacie. There you will find at their pasture the cattle and the fat flocks of the Sun-god, whose eyes and ears miss nothing in the world. If you leave them untouched and fix your mind on returning home, there is some chance that all of you may yet reach Ithaca, though not without suffering. But if you hurt them, then I predict that your ship and company will be destroyed, and if you yourself contrive to escape, you will reach home late, in a wretched state, upon a foreign ship, having lost all your comrades. You will find trouble too in your house – insolent men eating up your livelihood, courting your royal wife and offering wedding gifts. It is true that you will take revenge on these men for their misdeeds when you reach home.

'"But when you have killed these Suitors in your palace, by stratagem or in a straight fight with the naked sword, you must set out once more. Take a well-cut oar and go on till you reach a people who know nothing of the sea and never use salt with their food; crimson-painted ships and the long oars that serve those ships as wings are quite beyond their experience. And this will be your sign – a very clear one, which you cannot miss. When you fall in with some other traveller who refers to the object you are carrying on your shoulder as a 'winnowing-fan', then plant your shapely oar in the earth and offer Lord Poseidon the rich sacrifice of a ram, a bull and a breeding-boar. Then go back home and make ceremonial offerings to the immortal gods who live in the broad heavens, to all of them this time, in due precedence.

'"As for your own end, Death will come to you far away from the sea, a gentle Death. When he takes you, you will die peacefully of old age, surrounded by a prosperous people. This is the truth that I have told you."

'"Teiresias," I answered him, "no doubt these are the threads of destiny which the gods themselves have spun. But tell me this, and tell me truthfully. I see the spirit of my dead mother. She sits in silence by the blood and cannot bring herself to look her own son in the face or say a single word to him. Tell me, my lord, how can I make her recognize who I am?"

'"There is a simple rule," said Teiresias, "which I will explain.

Any ghost to whom you give access to the blood will speak the truth; any to whom you deny it will withdraw.”

‘The spirit of Lord Teiresias had spoken his prophecies and now withdrew into the Halls of Hades. But I kept steady at my post and waited till my mother came up and drank the dark blood. She recognized me at once; she gave a cry of grief and her words winged their way to me.

‘“My child, how did you come here to this murky realm, you who are still alive? This is no easy place for living eyes to find. For between you and us flow wide rivers and fearful waters, first of all Oceanus, whose stream a man could never cross on foot, but only in a well-found ship. Have you come here now from Troy and been wandering over the seas in your ship with your comrades ever since you left? Have you not been to Ithaca yet, nor seen your wife in your palace?”

‘“Mother,” I answered her, “I had to come down to Hades and consult the soul of Theban Teiresias. For I have not yet been near to Achaea, nor set foot on our own land, but have been a wretched wanderer from the very day when I sailed with King Agamemnon for Ilium, the city of fine horses, to fight the Trojans. But tell me what happened to you. What death overtook you? Did you have some lingering illness? Or did Artemis the Archeress visit and kill you with her gentle darts? And tell me of my father and the son I left behind. Is my kingdom safe in their hands, or was it taken by some other man when it was assumed that I would never return? And what of my good wife? How does she feel and what does she intend to do? Is she still living with her son and keeping our estate safe? Or has the best of her countrymen already married her?”

‘“Of course she is still living in your home,” my royal mother replied.[1] “She has schooled her heart to patience, though her eyes are never free from tears as the slow nights and days pass sorrowfully by. Your fine kingdom has not yet passed into other hands. Telemachus is in peaceful possession of the royal lands and attends all public banquets such as justices are expected to

1. Anticleia answers Odysseus’ questions in reverse order. The ancients called this ordering Homeric last-first.

give, for every one of them invites him. But your father lives alone on his farm and never goes down to the city now. He has no proper bed with laundered sheets and blankets to sleep on. Instead, he lies down in the winter-time with the labourers at the farm in the ashes by the fire, and goes about in rags. But when the summer and the mellow autumn days come round, he makes himself a humble bed of fallen leaves anywhere on the high ground of his vineyard. There he lies in his misery, with old age pressing hard upon him, and nursing his grief and yearning for you to come back. That was my undoing too; it was that that brought me to the grave. It was not that the keen-eyed Archeress sought me out in our home and killed me with her gentle darts. Nor was I attacked by any of the malignant diseases that so often make the body waste away and die. No, it was my heartache for you, my glorious Odysseus, and for your wise and gentle ways, that brought my life with all its sweetness to an end."

'These were my mother's words. Without knowing whether I could, I yearned to embrace her spirit, dead though she was. Three times, in my eagerness to clasp her to me, I started forward. Three times, like a shadow or a dream, she slipped through my hands and left me pierced by an even sharper pain.

'"Mother!" I cried with words that winged their way to her. "Why do you not wait for me? I long to reach you, so that even in Hell we may throw our loving arms round each other and draw cold comfort from our tears. Or is this a mere phantom that august Persephone has sent me to increase my grief?"

'"Alas, my child," came my revered mother's reply, "ill-fated above all men! This is no trick played on you by Persephone, Daughter of Zeus. It is the law of our mortal nature, when we come to die. We no longer have sinews keeping the bones and flesh together; once life has departed from our white bones, all is consumed by the fierce heat of the blazing fire, and the soul slips away like a dream and goes fluttering on its ways. But now quickly make for the light! And bear in mind all you have learnt here, so that one day you can tell your wife."

'Such was the talk that we two had together. And now,

impelled by august Persephone, there came up all the women who had been the wives or the daughters of the great, and gathered round the black blood in a throng. I considered how to question each in turn, and in the end decided that the best plan was to draw my long sword from my strong thigh and prevent them from drinking the dark blood all at the same time. So they came forward and announced their lineage one by one, and I was able to question them all.

'The first I saw was highborn Tyro, who told me she was the daughter of the noble Salmoneus, and had married Cretheus, Aeolus' son. She fell in love with the god of the River Enipeus, the loveliest river that flows on earth, and often wandered on the banks of this beautiful stream. One day the Lord of the Earthquake, the Sustainer of the Earth, disguised himself as the river-god and made love to her at the mouth of the eddying river. A dark wave gathered mountain-high, curled over them, and hid the woman and the god. He then unclasped her virgin girdle and sealed her eyes in sleep.

'And when the god had made love to her, he took her hand in his, and said: "Lady, be happy in this love of ours. When the year completes its course – a god's embrace is never fruitless – you will give birth to beautiful children, whom you must nurse and rear with care. But now go home, and guard your tongue. Tell no one; but the truth is I am Poseidon, the Shaker of the Earth." The god then plunged under the heaving sea. Tyro conceived, and gave birth to Pelias and Neleus, who both became powerful servants of mighty Zeus. Pelias lived in the spacious lands of Iolcus, and his wealth lay in his flocks; Neleus' home was in sandy Pylos. This illustrious Queen had other sons by Cretheus – Aeson and Pheres and Amythaon, the dashing charioteer.

'The next I saw was Antiope, the daughter of Asopus, who claimed to have slept in the arms of Zeus. She had two sons, Amphion and Zethus. They founded Thebes, the city of Seven Gates, and walled it round, since for all their prowess they were unable to inhabit so vast a city unfortified. After Antiope I saw Alcmene, Amphitryon's wife, who lay in the loving arms of mighty Zeus and brought the all-daring, lion-hearted

Heracles into the world. Megare I also saw, proud Creon's daughter, who married the indomitable Heracles, Amphitryon's son.

'Then I saw Oedipus' mother, the lovely Epicaste.[1] She in her ignorance did a terrible thing; she married her son. For Oedipus killed his father and took his mother to wife. But the gods soon let the truth come out. They devised a cruel plan: Oedipus remained to suffer the tortures of remorse as King of the Cadmeians in the lovely city of Thebes; but Epicaste, tormented by anguish, hanged herself with a long rope she made fast to the roof-beam overhead, and so came down to the House whose gates the mighty Hades guards, leaving Oedipus to suffer all the horrors that the Avenging Furies of a mother can inflict.

'Next came the great beauty Chloris, the youngest daughter of Amphion son of Iasus, the powerful Minyan King of Orchomenus. Neleus married her for her beauty and paid a fortune for her hand. So she was Queen in Pylos, and bore Neleus glorious children, Nestor and Chromius and princely Periclymenus as well as the beautiful Pero, the wonder of her age, whom all the young men of the neighbourhood wished to marry. But Neleus announced that he would give her hand to no one but the man who succeeded in driving away the cattle of the mighty Iphiclus from Phylace. It was a dangerous task to round up these shambling broad-browed cattle. A certain gifted seer, Melampus,[2] was the only man who undertook the venture. But because of the cruel decree of a god he ended up in chains as a prisoner of the savage herdsmen. The days passed and mounted up to months. But it was not until a year had run its course and the seasons came round once more, that the mighty Iphiclus set him free in return for divulging all that the gods had decreed. In this way the will of Zeus was accomplished.

'Then I saw Leda, wife of Tyndareus, who bore him those stout-hearted twins, Castor trainer of horses, and Polydeuces the great boxer, both of whom are still alive, though the fruitful Earth has received them in her lap. For even in the world below

1. Usually known as Jocasta.

2. The sequel to this story is to be found in 15.223 ff.

they have been singled out by Zeus; each is a living and a dead man on alternate days, and they are honoured like the gods.

'My eyes fell next on Iphimedeia, the consort of Aloeus. She told me that she had slept with Poseidon, and was the mother of those short-lived twins, the godlike Otus and Ephialtes famed in story, the largest men Earth ever nourished, and finer by far than all but the glorious Orion. In their ninth year they were nine cubits across the shoulders and nine fathoms tall. It was this pair that threatened to go to war with the very gods on Olympus in the din and turmoil of battle. It was their ambition to pile Mount Ossa on Olympus, and wooded Pelion on Ossa, to make a stairway up to heaven. And this they would have accomplished had they reached their youthful prime. But Apollo, the son whom Leto of the lovely tresses bore to Zeus, destroyed them both before their beards had begun to grow and cover their cheeks with the soft down of youth.

'Phaedra I also saw, and Procris, and the lovely Ariadne, that daughter of baleful Minos whom Theseus once attempted to carry off from Crete to the hill of sacred Athens. But he had no joy of her, for before their journey's end Dionysus brought word to Artemis, who killed her in sea-girt Dia. Maera too, and Clymene I saw, and the hateful Eriphyle,[1] who bartered her own husband's life for gold. Indeed I could not tell you the tales, not give you the names, of all the great men's wives and daughters whom I saw, for before I could finish, the ambrosial night would have slipped away.

'But now the time has come for me to go and sleep, whether I join the crew on board or remain in your palace. My journey home is in the gods' hands and yours.'

Odysseus stopped speaking. Held by the spell of his words they all remained silent and still throughout the shadowy hall. At last white-armed Arete broke the silence.

'Phaeacians,' she said, 'what do you think of this man, his looks, his presence and the quality of his mind? He is my guest, but each of you shares that honour with me. So do not send him

1. She was bribed to persuade her husband to go on an expedition on which he knew he was doomed to die.

on his way with undue haste, nor stint your generosity to one who stands in such need. For the gods have filled your homes with riches.'

The venerable lord Echeneus, the oldest man among the Phaeacians, now spoke. 'My friends, our wise Queen's words are most apt and are just what we might have expected. Do as she says, though of course it is for Alcinous here to say the word and act on it.'

Alcinous replied: 'As I live and rule this nation of sailors, it shall be so. But our guest, though longing to return home, must make up his mind to stay till tomorrow, to give me time to add to my gifts. Meanwhile his passage home shall be the concern of all the people, and my own in particular, since I am sovereign in this land.'

'Alcinous, my most worshipful prince,' replied Odysseus, the master-schemer, 'I would be happy if you pressed me to stay among you even for a year, as long as you saw me safely back and loaded me with your splendid gifts. It would be a great advantage to me to arrive in my own dear country with more possessions. For thus enriched I would win a warmer welcome and greater respect from everyone who saw me on my return to Ithaca.'

'Odysseus,' said Alcinous, 'we are far from regarding you as one of those impostors and cheats whom this dark world brings forth in such profusion to spin their lying yarns which nobody can test. On the contrary, you have eloquence and sound judgement too, and you have told us the story of your own and all your companions' terrible misfortunes with all the artistry of a bard. But now continue and tell us truly; did you see any of those heroic comrades of yours who joined you on the expedition to Ilium and met their death there? We have endless time ahead of us tonight; it's too early for us to go to our beds. Tell me more of your marvellous adventures. I could stay here till the blessed dawn, if only you could bring yourself to remain in this hall and continue the tale of your misfortunes.'

In response to this the resourceful Odysseus went on with his story. 'Lord Alcinous, my most worshipful prince,' he began, 'there is a time for long tales, but there is also a time for sleep.

However, if you really wish to hear me further, I will not refuse to tell you an even more tragic tale than you have heard already. I will tell you the sad fate of my comrades-in-arms who perished after the sack of Troy and escaped from the perils and turmoil of the Trojan War only to be slaughtered on reaching home, through the will of a wicked woman.

'In the end, holy Persephone drove off the women's ghosts. They scattered in all directions, and I was approached by the soul of Agamemnon, son of Atreus. He came in sorrow, and round about him were gathered the souls of all those who had met their doom and died with him in Aegisthus' palace. As soon as he had drunk the dark blood, he recognized me, uttered a loud cry and burst into tears, stretching his arms out in my direction in his eagerness to reach me. But this he could not do, for all the strength and vigour had gone for ever from those once supple limbs. Moved to compassion at the sight, I too gave way to tears and spoke to him with winged words:

' "Illustrious son of Atreus, Agamemnon, King of men, what mortal stroke of fate laid you low? Did Poseidon rouse fearful squalls and tempestuous winds and overwhelm your ships? Or did you fall to some hostile tribe on land as you were driving off their cattle and their flocks or fighting with them for their town and women?"

' "Royal son of Laertes, Odysseus of the nimble wits," he answered me at once, "Poseidon did not wreck my ships with fearful squalls and tempestuous winds, nor did I fall to any hostile tribe on land. It was Aegisthus who plotted my destruction and with my accursed wife put me to death. He invited me to the palace, he feasted me, and he killed me as a man fells an ox at its manger. That was my most pitiful end. And all around me my companions were cut down in ruthless succession, like white-tusked swine slaughtered in the mansion of some rich and powerful lord, for a wedding, or a banquet, or a sumptuous private feast. You, Odysseus, have witnessed the deaths of many men in single combat or in the thick of battle, but none with such horror as you would have felt had you seen us lying there by the wine-bowl and the laden tables in the hall, while the whole floor swam with our blood.

'"Yet the most pitiable thing of all was the cry I heard from Cassandra,[1] daughter of Priam, whom that treacherous schemer Clytaemnestra murdered at my side. I raised my hands, but then beat them on the ground, dying, thrust through by a sword. The bitch turned her face aside, and could not even bring herself, though I was on my way to Hades, to shut my eyes with her hands or to close my mouth. There is nothing more degraded or shameful than a woman who can contemplate and carry out deeds like the hideous crime of murdering the husband of her youth. I had certainly expected a joyful welcome from my children and my servants when I reached my home. But now, in the depth of her villainy, she has branded with infamy not herself alone but the whole of her sex, even the virtuous ones, for all time to come."

'"Alas!" I exclaimed. "All-seeing Zeus has indeed proved himself a relentless foe to the House of Atreus from the beginning, working his will through women's crooked ways. It was for Helen's sake that so many of us met our deaths, and it was Clytaemnestra who hatched the plot against her absent lord."

'"Yes," replied Agamemnon. "Never be too trustful even of your wife, nor show her all that is in your mind. Reveal a little of your plans to her, but keep the rest to yourself. Not that *your* wife, Odysseus, will ever murder you. Icarius' daughter is far too loyal in her thoughts and feelings. The wise Penelope! She was a young woman when we said goodbye to her on our way to the war. She had a baby son at her breast. And now, I suppose, he has begun to take his seat among the men. Fortunate young man! His loving father will come home and see him, and he will kiss his father. That is how things should be. Whereas that wife of mine refused me even the satisfaction of setting eyes on my son – she killed me before I could. And now I will give you a piece of advice; take it to heart. Do not sail openly into port when you reach your home-country. Make a secret approach. Women, I tell you, are no longer to be trusted. But can you give me the truth about my son? Have you and your friends heard

1. Brought home by Agamemnon as a prize of war.

of him as still alive, in Orchomenus possibly, or sandy Pylos, or maybe with Menelaus in the plains of Sparta? For my good Orestes has not yet died and come below."

'"Son of Atreus," I answered him, "why ask me that? I have no idea whether he is alive or dead. It does no good to utter empty words."

'So we stood there grieving, exchanging joyless words as the tears rolled down our cheeks. And now there came the soul of Peleus' son Achilles, of Patroclus, of the handsome Antilochus, and of Ajax, who in stature and in manly grace was second to none of the Danaans except the handsome son of Peleus. The soul of Achilles, the great runner, recognized me. "Favourite of Zeus, son of Laertes, Odysseus, master of stratagems," he said in mournful tones, "what next, dauntless man? What greater exploit can you plan to surpass your voyage here? How did you dare to come below to Hades' realm, where the dead live on as mindless disembodied ghosts?"

'"Achilles," I answered him, "son of Peleus, far the strongest of the Achaeans, I came to consult with Teiresias in the hope of finding out from him how I could reach rocky Ithaca. For I have not managed to come near Achaea yet, nor set foot on my own island, but have been dogged by misfortune. But you, Achilles, are the most fortunate man that ever was or will be! For in the old days when you were on Earth, we Argives honoured you as though you were a god; and now, down here, you have great power among the dead. Do not grieve at your death, Achilles."

'"And do not you make light of death, illustrious Odysseus," he replied. "I would rather work the soil as a serf on hire to some landless impoverished peasant than be King of all these lifeless dead. Come, give me news of that fine son of mine. Did he follow me to the war to play a leading part or not? And tell me anything you have heard of the noble Peleus. Does the Myrmidon nation still do him homage, or do they dishonour him in Hellas and Phthie because old age has made a cripple of him? For I am not up there in the sunlight to protect him as I once protected the Argives and laid the champions of the enemy low on the broad plains of Troy. If I could return for a single moment to my father's house as I then was I would make those who forcibly rob him of his position of honour cringe before the might of my unconquerable hands."

'"Of the handsome Peleus," I answered Achilles, "I have heard nothing. But of your dear son Neoptolemus I will tell you the whole truth, as you ask, since it was I who brought him from Scyros in my own fine ship to join the Achaean army. And there in front of the city of Troy, when we used to discuss our plans, he was always the first to speak and always spoke to the point. Godlike Nestor and I were his only betters in debate. And when we Achaeans gave battle on the Trojan plain, he was never content to hang back in the ranks or with the crowd. That spirit of his gave place to none, and he would run far ahead of the others. Many were the men he brought down in mortal combat. I could not tell you of all those he killed in battle for the Argives, nor give you their names; but well I remember how the heroic Eurypylus son of Telephus fell to his sword, and how many of his Hittite men-at-arms were slaughtered at his side, all on account of a bribe that a woman had taken. He was the handsomest man I ever saw, next to the godlike Memnon.

'"Then again, when we Argive captains took our places in the Wooden Horse that Epeius had constructed and it rested with me to throw the door of our ambush open or to keep it shut, all the other Danaan chieftains and officers were wiping the tears from their eyes and every man's legs were trembling beneath him. But not once did I see your son's handsome face turn pale or catch him brushing a tear from his cheek. On the contrary he begged me time and time again to let him jump out from the Horse, and kept handling his sword-hilt and his heavy bronze spear in his eagerness to inflict disaster on the Trojans. And when we had brought Priam's city tumbling down in ruins, he took his share of the spoils and his special prize, and embarked safe and sound on his ship without a single wound either from a flying spear or from a sword at close quarters. Such wounds are common in battle: the War-god in his fury is no respecter of persons."

'When I had done, the soul of swift-footed Achilles passed

with great strides down the meadow of asphodel, rejoicing in the news I had given him of his son's renown.

'The mourning ghosts of all the other dead and departed pressed round me now, each with some question for me on matters that concerned him. The only soul that stood aloof was that of Ajax son of Telamon. He was still embittered by the defeat I had inflicted on him at the ships in the contest for the arms of Achilles, whose divine mother had offered them as a prize, with the Trojan captives and Pallas Athene for judges. I wish I had never won such a prize – the arms that brought Ajax to his grave, the heroic Ajax, who in looks and valour surpassed all the Danaans except the handsome son of Peleus. I called to him now, and sought to placate him:

' "Ajax, son of the noble Telamon; could not even death itself make you forget your anger with me on account of those fatal arms? It was the gods that made them a curse to us Argives. What a tower of strength we lost when you fell! We have never ceased to mourn your death as truly as we lament Achilles, Peleus' son. No one else is to blame but Zeus, that bitter foe of the Danaan army. He it was who brought you to your doom. Draw near, my lord, and hear what I have to say. Curb your anger and conquer your obstinate pride."

'So I spoke. He made no reply but went away into Erebus to join the souls of the other dead. There, for all his bitterness, he might yet have spoken to me, or I to him, had not the wish to see the souls of other dead men filled my heart.

'And indeed I saw King Minos there, glorious son of Zeus, sitting, gold sceptre in hand, and delivering judgement to the dead, who sat or stood all around, putting their cases to him for decision within the House of Hades, to which the gate is wide. My eyes fell next on the giant hunter Orion, who was rounding up the game on the meadow of asphodel, the very beasts his living hands had killed among the lonely hills, armed with a club of solid indestructible bronze.

'And I saw Tityus, son of the great goddess Earth, stretched on the ground and covering nine roods as he lay. A pair of vultures sat by him, one on either side, plucking at his liver, penetrating deep into his body; and his hands were powerless to drive them off. This was his punishment for assaulting Leto, the glorious consort of Zeus, as she made her way to Pytho across the pleasant plains of Panopeus.

'I also saw the awful agonies that Tantalus[1] has to bear. The old man was standing in a pool of water which nearly reached his chin, and his thirst drove him to unceasing efforts; but he could never reach the water to drink it. For whenever he stooped in his eagerness to drink, it disappeared. The pool was swallowed up, and all there was at his feet was the dark earth, which some mysterious power had drained dry. Trees spread their foliage high over the pool and dangled fruits above his head – pear-trees and pomegranates, apple-trees with their glossy burden, sweet figs and luxuriant olives. But whenever the old man made to grasp them in his hands, the wind would toss them up towards the shadowy clouds.

'Then I witnessed the torture of Sisyphus,[2] as he wrestled with a huge rock with both hands. Bracing himself and thrusting with hands and feet he pushed the boulder uphill to the top. But every time, as he was about to send it toppling over the crest, its sheer weight turned it back, and once again towards the plain the pitiless rock rolled down. So once more he had to wrestle with the thing and push it up, while the sweat poured from his limbs and the dust rose high above his head.

'Next after him I observed the mighty Heracles – his wraith, that is to say, since he himself banquets at ease with the immortal gods and has for wife Hebe of the slim ankles, the daughter of almighty Zeus and golden-sandalled Hera. From the dead around him there rose a clamour like the noise of wild fowl taking off in alarm. He looked like black night, and with his naked bow in hand and an arrow on the string he glanced ferociously this way and that as though about to shoot. Terrible too was the golden belt he wore as a baldric over his breast,

1. Tantalus was a son of Zeus, but ejected from the gods' company for stealing their food to give to mortals, and for serving the gods with the flesh of his son Pelops at a banquet.

2. Sisyphus was the crafty and avaricious King of Corinth, who twice tricked the god Death, once by blinding him and once by persuading him to let him return to earth.

depicting miraculous scenes – bears, wild boars and glaring lions, conflict and battle, bloodshed and the massacre of men. That baldric was a masterpiece that no one should have made. May the craftsman who conceived the work never make another!

'One look was enough to tell Heracles who I was, and he greeted me with winged words. "Heaven-born son of Laertes, Odysseus, master of stratagems, unhappy man! So you too are working out some such miserable doom as I endured when I lived in the light of the sun. Though I was a son of Zeus, unending troubles came my way. For I was bound in service to a master far beneath my rank, who used to set me the most arduous labours. Once, thinking that no other task could be more difficult for me, he sent me down here to bring back the Hound of Hell. And under the guiding hands of Hermes and bright-eyed Athene, I did succeed in capturing him and leading him out of Hades' realm."

'Heracles said no more, but withdrew into the House of Hades, while I lingered on there, in the hope that I might yet be visited by other men of note who had perished long ago. And now I might have seen men of still earlier times whom I so much wanted to see, Theseus and Peirithous, those legendary children of the gods. But before that could happen, the tribes of the dead came up and gathered round me in their tens of thousands, making their eerie clamour. Sheer panic turned me pale. I feared that dread Persephone might send up from Hades' Halls the gorgon head of some ghastly monster. I hurried off to my ship and told my men to embark and loose the hawsers. They climbed in at once and took their seats by the oars, and the current carried her down the River of Ocean, helped at first by our oars and later by a friendly breeze.'

# 12
# SCYLLA AND CHARYBDIS

'From the flowing waters of the River of Ocean my ship passed into the wide spaces of the open sea; and so reached the island of Aeaea, where, ever-fresh, Dawn has her home and her dancing-lawns, and where the Sun rises. Here we beached the ship on the sands and climbed out on to the shore, where we fell into a sound sleep, awaiting the coming of ethereal Dawn.

'As soon as she appeared, fresh and rosy-fingered, I sent off a party to Circe's house to fetch the dead body of Elpenor. We quickly chopped some logs, and then, with the tears streaming down our cheeks, performed the funeral rites on the summit of the boldest headland of the coast. When the corpse was burnt, and with it the dead man's armour, we built him a barrow, hauled up a stone for monument, and planted his shapely oar on the top of the mound.

'When we had completed each of these rites, Circe became aware of our return from Hades, adorned herself, and came hurrying up with handmaidens laden with bread, a plentiful supply of meat and sparkling red wine.

' "What audacity," said the glorious goddess, as we gathered round her, "to descend alive into the House of Hades! Other men die once; you will now die twice. But come, spend the rest of the day here, enjoying this food and wine, and at daybreak tomorrow you shall sail. I myself will give you your route and make everything clear, to save you from the disasters you may suffer as a result of evil scheming on land or sea."

'We were not difficult to persuade. So the whole day long till sunset we sat and feasted on our rich supply of meat and mellow wine. When the sun sank and darkness fell, my men settled down for the night by the ships; but Circe took me by the hand, led me away from my good comrades, and made me sit down and tell her everything as she lay beside me. When I had given her the whole tale from first to last the lady Circe said:

'"Very well; all that is done with now. But listen to my words – and some god will recall them to your mind. Your next encounter will be with the Sirens, who bewitch everybody who approaches them. There is no homecoming for the man who draws near them unawares and hears the Sirens' voices; no welcome from his wife, no little children brightening at their father's return. For with their high clear song the Sirens bewitch him, as they sit there in a meadow piled high with the mouldering skeletons of men, whose withered skin still hangs upon their bones. Drive your ship past the spot, and to prevent any of your crew from hearing, soften some beeswax and plug their ears with it. But if you wish to listen yourself, make them bind you hand and foot on board and place you upright by the housing of the mast, with the rope's ends lashed to the mast itself. This will allow you to listen with enjoyment to the Sirens' voices. But if you beg and command your men to release you, they must add to the bonds that already hold you fast.

'"When your crew have carried you past the Sirens, two routes will be open to you. Though I cannot give you precise advice – you must choose for yourself – I will tell you about both. One leads to those sheer cliffs which the blessed gods know as the Wandering Rocks. Here blue-eyed Amphitrite sends her great breakers thundering in, and the very birds cannot fly by in safety, even the shy doves that bring ambrosia to Father Zeus; even of them the smooth rock always takes one, and the Father has to send one more to make their number up. For any sailors who bring their ship to the spot, there is no escape whatever. They end as flotsam on the sea, timbers and corpses tossed in confusion by the waves or licked up by tempestuous and destroying flames. Of all ships that go down to the sea one only has made the passage, and that was the celebrated *Argo*, homeward bound from Aeetes' coast. And the waves would soon have dashed her upon those mighty crags, if Hera, for love of Jason, had not helped her past.

'"In the other direction lie two rocks, one of which rears its sharp peak up to the very sky and is capped by black clouds that never stream away nor leave clear weather round the top, even in summer or at harvest-time. No man on earth could climb to the top of it or even get a foothold on it, not even if he had twenty hands and feet to help him, because the rock is as smooth as if it had been polished. But half-way up the crag there is a murky cavern, facing the West and running down to Erebus, past which, illustrious Odysseus, you will probably steer your ship. Even a strong young bowman could not reach the gaping mouth of the cave with an arrow shot from a ship below.

'"It is the home of Scylla, the creature with the dreadful bark. It is true that her yelp is no louder than a new-born pup's, but she is a repulsive monster nevertheless. Nobody could look at her with delight, not even a god if he passed that way. She has twelve feet, all dangling in the air, and six long scrawny necks, each ending in a grisly head with triple rows of fangs, set thick and close, and darkly menacing death. Up to her waist she is sunk in the depths of the cave, but her heads protrude from the fearful abyss, and thus she fishes from her own abode, groping greedily around the rock for any dolphins or seals or any of the larger monsters which Amphitrite breeds in the roaring seas. No crew can boast that they ever sailed their ship past Scylla unscathed, for from every blue-prowed vessel she snatches and carries off a man with each of her heads.

'"The other of the two rocks, Odysseus, is lower, as you will see, and the distance between them is no more than a bowshot. A great fig-tree with luxuriant foliage grows upon the crag, and it is below this that dread Charybdis sucks the dark waters down. Three times a day she spews them up, and three times she swallows them down once more in her horrible way. Heaven keep you from the spot when she does this because not even the Earthshaker could save you from destruction then. No, you must hug Scylla's rock and with all speed drive your ship through, since it is far better to lose six of your company than your whole crew."

'"Yes, goddess," I replied, "but tell me this. I must be quite clear about it. Could I not somehow steer clear of the deadly Charybdis, yet ward off Scylla when she attacks my crew?"

'"Obstinate fool," the beautiful goddess replied. "Again you are spoiling for a fight and looking for trouble! Are you not prepared to give in to immortal gods? I tell you, Scylla was not born for death: she is an undying fiend. She is a thing of terror, intractable, ferocious and impossible to fight. No, against her there is no defence, and the best course of action is flight. For if you waste time by the rock in putting on your armour, I am afraid she may dart out once more, make a grab with all six heads and snatch another six of your crew. So drive your ship past with all your might, and call on Cratais, Scylla's mother, who whelped her into the world to be the bane of mankind. She will prevent her from pouncing out again.

'"Next you will reach the island of Thrinacie, where many of the Sun-god's cattle and plump sheep graze. There are seven herds of cattle and as many flocks of beautiful sheep, with fifty head in each. No births increase or deaths decrease their numbers. And to shepherd them they have goddesses with braided hair, the Nymphs, Phaethusa and Lampetie, children of Hyperion the Sun-god by the resplendent Neaera, whom their mother, when she had brought them up, took away to this new and distant home in Thrinacie to watch over their father's sheep and crooked-horned cattle. Now if you leave them untouched and fix your mind on getting home, there is some chance that all of you may yet reach Ithaca, though not without suffering. But if you hurt them, then I predict the destruction of your ship and your company. And if you yourself contrive to escape, you will reach home late, in a wretched state, having lost all your comrades."

'As Circe came to an end, Dawn mounted her golden throne. The glorious goddess left me and made her way inland, while I went to my ship and ordered my men to embark and untie the hawsers. They did so promptly, went to the oars, sat down in their places and all together struck the grey surf with their blades. Then Circe, that formidable goddess with the beautiful hair and a woman's voice, sent us the friendly escort of a favourable wind, which sprang up from astern and filled the sail of our blue-painted ship. We set the tackle in order fore and aft, then sat down, and the wind and the helmsman kept her on her course.

'Then, perturbed in spirit, I addressed my men. "My friends," I said, "it is not right that only one or two of us should know the prophecies that divine Circe has made to me, and I am going to pass them on to you, so that we may all be forewarned, whether we die, or escape the worst and save our lives. Her first warning concerned the Sirens with their divine song. We must beware of them and give their flowery meadow a wide berth, but she instructed me alone to hear their voices. You must bind me very tight, standing me up against the step of the mast and lashed to the mast itself so that I cannot stir from the spot. And if I beg and command you to release me, you must tighten and add to my bonds."

'In this way I explained every detail to my men. In the meantime our good ship, with that friendly breeze to drive her, fast approached the Sirens' isle. But now the wind dropped, some power lulled the waves, and a breathless calm set in. Rising from their seats my men drew in the sail and threw it into the hold, then sat down at the oars and churned the water white with their blades of polished pine. Meanwhile I took a large round of wax, cut it up small with my sharp sword, and worked the pieces with all the strength of my fingers. The wax soon grew warm with my vigorous kneading and with the rays of the Sun-god, Hyperion's son. I took all my men in turn and plugged their ears with it. They then bound me hand and foot, standing me up by the step of the ship's mast and then lashing me to the mast itself. This done, they sat down once more and struck the grey water with their oars.

'We made good progress and had just come within call of the shore when the Sirens became aware that a ship was bearing down upon them, and broke into their high, clear song.

'"Draw near, illustrious Odysseus, man of many tales, great glory of the Achaeans, and bring your ship to rest so that you may hear our voices. No seaman ever sailed his black ship past this spot without listening to the honey-sweet tones that flow from our lips and no one who has listened has not been delighted and gone on his way a wiser man. For we know all that the Argives and Trojans suffered on the broad plain of Troy by the will of the gods, and we know whatever happens on this fruitful earth."

'This was the sweet song the Sirens sang, and my heart was filled with such a longing to listen that I ordered my men to set me free, gesturing with my eyebrows. But they swung forward over their oars and rowed ahead, while Perimedes and Eurylochus jumped up, tightened my ropes and added more. However, when they had rowed past the Sirens and we could no longer hear the sound and the words of their song, my good companions were quick to clear their ears of the wax I had used to stop them, and to free me from the ropes that bound me.

'We had no sooner put this island behind us than I saw a cloud of spume ahead and a raging surf, and heard the thunder of the breakers. My men were so terrified that the oars all dropped from their grasp and fell with a splash on to the sea; and the ship herself, now that the hands that had pulled the smooth blades were idle, was brought to a standstill. I went up and down the ship, stood by each man and encouraged them with soothing words.

'"My friends," I said, "we are men who have met trouble before. And this trouble is no worse than when the Cyclops used his brutal strength to imprison us in his cave. Yet my courage, strategy and intelligence found a way out for us even from there; and I am sure that this too will be a memory for us one day. So now let us all agree to do exactly as I say. Oarsmen, stay at your oars, striking hard with your blades through the deep swell, in the hope that Zeus allows us to escape disaster and come out of this alive. Helmsman, your orders are these. Fix them in your mind, for the good ship's steering-oar is in your control. Give a wide berth to that foaming surf, and hug these cliffs, or before you can stop her the ship may take us over there and we'll be wrecked."

'The crew obeyed me immediately. I did not mention the inescapable horror of Scylla, fearing that in their panic my men might stop rowing and huddle below decks. But now I allowed myself to forget Circe's irksome instruction not to arm myself in any way. I put my famous armour on, seized a couple of long spears, and took my stand on the forecastle deck, hoping from there to get the first view of Scylla, the monster of the rocks, who was preparing disaster for my crew. But I could not catch a glimpse of her anywhere, though I searched the sombre face of the cliff in every part till my eyes were tired.

'Thus we sailed up the straits, wailing in terror, for on the one side we had Scylla, and on the other the awesome Charybdis sucked down the salt water in her dreadful way. When she vomited it up, she was stirred to her depths and seethed over like a cauldron on a blazing fire; and the spray she flung up rained down on the tops of the crags at either side. But when she swallowed the salt water down, the whole interior of her vortex was exposed, the rocks re-echoed to her fearful roar, and the dark blue sands of the sea-bed were exposed.

'My men turned pale with terror; and now, while all eyes were on Charybdis as the quarter from which we looked for disaster, Scylla snatched out of my ship the six strongest and ablest men. Glancing towards my ship, looking for my comrades, I saw their arms and legs dangling high in the air above my head. "Odysseus!" they called out to me in their anguish. But it was the last time they used my name. For like an angler on a jutting point, who casts his bait to lure the little fishes below, dangles his long rod with its line protected by an ox-horn pipe, gets a bite, and whips his struggling catch to land, Scylla had whisked my comrades, struggling, up to the rocks. There she devoured them at her own door, shrieking and stretching out their hands to me in their last desperate throes. In all I have gone through as I explored the pathways of the seas, I have never had to witness a more pitiable sight than that.

'When we had left the Rocks, Scylla, and dread Charybdis behind, we soon reached the Sun-god's lovely isle, where Hyperion kept his splendid broad-browed cattle and his flocks of sturdy sheep. From where I was on board, out at sea, I could hear the lowing of cows as they were stalled for the night, and the bleating of sheep. And there came into my mind the words of Teiresias, the blind Theban prophet, and of Circe of Aeaea, who had each been so insistent in warning me to avoid this

Island of the Sun, the comforter of mankind. So with an aching heart I addressed my men.

'"Comrades in suffering," I said, "listen to me while I tell you what Teiresias and Circe of Aeaea predicted. They warned me insistently to keep clear of the Island of the Sun, the comforter of mankind, for there, they said, our deadliest peril lurks. So drive the ship past the island."

'My men were heart-broken when they heard this, and Eurylochus spoke up at once in a hostile manner. "Odysseus, you are one of those hard men whose spirit never flags and whose body never tires. You must be made of iron through and through to forbid your men, worn out by our efforts and lack of sleep, to set foot on dry land, with the chance of cooking ourselves a tasty supper on this sea-girt isle. Instead, you expect us, just as we are, with night coming on fast, to abandon this island and go wandering off over the foggy sea. It is at night that high winds spring up and wreck ships. What port could we reach to save ourselves from going down if we were hit by a sudden squall from the South or the West? There's nothing like the South Wind or the wicked West for smashing a ship to pieces. And they don't ask leave of our lords the gods! No, let us give in to the evening dusk, and cook our supper by the side of the ship. In the morning we can go on board and put out into the open sea."

'This speech of Eurylochus was greeted by applause from all the rest, and it was brought home to me that some god really had a calamity in store for us. I answered him with words on wings: "Eurylochus, I am one against many, and you force my hand. Very well. But I call on every man of you to give his solemn promise that if we come across a herd of cattle or a large flock of sheep, he will not kill a single ox or sheep in a wanton fit of recklessness. Just sit peacefully and eat the food that the goddess Circe has provided."

'The crew agreed and gave the promise I had asked for. Accordingly, when all had sworn and completed the oath, we brought the good ship to anchor in a sheltered cove, with fresh water at hand, and the men disembarked and proceeded efficiently to prepare their supper. When they had satisfied their hunger and thirst, their thoughts returned to their dear comrades whom Scylla had snatched from the hollow ship and devoured; and they wept till soothing sleep overtook them.

'In the third watch of the night, when the stars had passed their zenith, Zeus the Cloud-gatherer whipped up a gale of incredible violence. He covered land and sea with clouds, and down sped night from heaven. As soon as Dawn came, fresh and rosy-fingered, we beached our ship and dragged her up into a hollow cave, which the Nymphs used as a dancing-ground and meeting-place. I ordered all my men to gather round, and gave them a warning. "My friends," I said, "since we have plenty of food and drink on board, let us keep our hands off these cattle, or we shall come to grief. For the cows and the fine sheep you have seen belong to that formidable god, the Sun, whose eyes and ears miss nothing."

'My strong-willed company accepted this. And now for a whole month the South Wind blew without a pause, and after that we had nothing but the South and the West winds. The men, so long as their bread and red wine lasted, kept their hands off the cattle as they valued their lives. But when the provisions in the ship gave out and the pangs of hunger sent them wandering with barbed hooks in quest of any game, fishes or birds, which might come to hand, I went inland to pray to the gods in the hope that one of them might show me a way of escape. When I had gone far enough across the island to be clear of the rest, I found a place that was sheltered from the wind, washed my hands, and made my supplications to the whole company of gods on Olympus. They then cast me into a pleasant sleep. In the meantime Eurylochus was broaching a wicked scheme to his mates.

'"My comrades in suffering," he said, "listen to what I have to say. To us wretched men all forms of death are abominable, but death by starvation is the most miserable way to meet one's doom. So come, let us round up the best of the Sun's cows and sacrifice them in honour of the immortals who live in the broad sky. If ever we reach our homeland in Ithaca, our first act will be to build Hyperion the Sun-god a magnificent temple and fill it with precious offerings. But if in anger at the loss of his straight-horned herds he chooses to wreck our ship, with the support of the other gods, I would sooner drown instantly in a watery grave than waste away by slow degrees on a desert island."

'His ideas found favour with the rest, and they proceeded at once to round up the pick of the Sun-god's cattle. They had not far to go, for the fine cows with their broad foreheads and twisted horns used to graze in the neighbourhood of our blue-prowed ship. The men gathered round the cattle and made their prayers to the gods, using for the ceremony some fresh leaves they stripped from a tall oak-tree, since they had no white barley on the ship. Their prayers done, they slit the cows' throats and flayed them, then cut out slices from the thighs, wrapped them in folds of fat and laid raw meat above them. And since they had no wine to pour over the burning sacrifice, they made libations with water as they roasted all the entrails. When the thighs were burnt up and they had tasted the inner parts, they carved the rest into small pieces and spitted them on skewers.

'Then it was that I suddenly awoke from my deep sleep, and started on my way back to the vessel and the coast. Directly I came near my curved ship the sweet smell of roasting meat was wafted all about me. I exclaimed in horror and called out to the immortal gods. "Father Zeus and you other blessed gods who live for ever! So it was to ruin me that you lulled me into that cruel sleep, while left to themselves my men planned this awful crime!"

'A swift messenger, Lampetie herself, Lampetie of the trailing robes, ran to the Sun-god Hyperion with news that we had killed his cattle; and in a fury he cried out to the immortals: "Father Zeus and you other blessed gods who live for ever, take vengeance on the followers of Odysseus son of Laertes. They have criminally killed my cattle, the cattle that gave me such joy every day as I climbed the starry sky and as I dropped down from heaven and sank once more to earth. If they do not repay me in full for my slaughtered cows, I will go down to the realm of Hades and shine among the dead."

' "Sun," the Cloud-gatherer answered him, "shine on for the immortals and for mortal men on the fruitful earth. As for the culprits, I will soon strike their ship with a blinding bolt out on the wine-dark sea and smash it to pieces."

'This part of the tale I had from Calypso of the beautiful hair, who told me that she herself had heard it from Hermes the Messenger.

'When I had come down to the sea and reached the ship, I confronted my men one after the other and rebuked them. But we could find no way of mending matters: the cows were dead. And the gods soon began to show my crew ominous portents. The hides began to crawl about; the meat, roast and raw, bellowed on the spits; and a sound as of lowing cattle could be heard.

'For six days my men feasted on the pick of the Sun's cattle they had rounded up. But when Zeus brought the seventh day, the fury of the gale abated, and we quickly embarked and put out into the open sea after stepping the mast and hauling up the white sail.

'When we had left the island astern and no other land, or anything but sky and water, was to be seen, Zeus brought a sombre cloud to rest above the hollow ship so that the sea was darkened by its shadow. Before she had run very far, a howling wind suddenly sprang up from the West and hit us with hurricane force. The squall snapped both forestays simultaneously. As the mast toppled, all the rigging tumbled into the hold, and the mast itself, reaching the stern, struck the helmsman on the head and smashed in all the bones of his skull. He plunged like a diver from the deck, and his brave soul left his body. Then at one and the same moment Zeus thundered and struck the vessel with lightning. The whole ship reeled from the blow of his bolt and was filled with the smell of sulphur. My men were flung overboard and round the black hull they floated like sea-gulls on the waves. There was no homecoming for them: the god saw to that.

'Meanwhile I kept shifting from one part of the ship to another, till a great wave tore her sides from her keel, which the sea then swept along denuded of its ribs. It snapped the mast off close to the keel, but as the backstay, which was a leather rope, had fallen across the mast, I used it to lash mast and keel together, and astride these two timbers I became the sport of the furious winds.

'The storm that had blown up from the West subsided soon enough, but was quickly followed by more wind from the South, to my great distress, for this meant that I should have once more to retrace my course to the dread Charybdis. All through the night I was swept along, and at sunrise found myself back at Scylla's rock and that appalling whirlpool. Charybdis was beginning to suck the salt water down. But as she did so, I swung myself up to the great fig-tree, on which I got a tight grip and clung like a bat. I could find no foothold to support me, or any means of climbing into the tree, for its roots were far away below, and the great long branches that overshadowed Charybdis stretched high above my head.

'However, I clung grimly on until she spewed up my mast and keel once more. I longed for them to reappear, and in the end they did, at the time of day when a judge with a long list of disputes to settle between obstinate litigants rises from court for his evening meal. Then at last the timbers reappeared on the surface. I let go, and dropped with sprawling hands and feet, to splash into the water clear of the great logs. I clambered on to them, and paddled along with my hands. And thanks to the Father of men and gods Scylla did not catch sight of me. Otherwise nothing could have saved me from certain death.

'Nine days of drifting followed; but in the night of the tenth the gods washed me up on the island of Ogygia, the home of Calypso of the braided tresses, that formidable goddess with a woman's voice; and she received me kindly and looked after me. But why go again through all this? Only yesterday I told you and your noble wife the whole story here in your home, and it is tedious for me to repeat a tale already plainly told.'

# 13
# ODYSSEUS LANDS IN ITHACA

Odysseus' tale was finished. Held in the spell of his words they all remained still and silent throughout the shadowy hall, till at last Alcinous turned to his guest and said: 'Odysseus, now that you have set foot on the bronze floor of my great house I feel assured that you will reach your home without any further wanderings from your course, though you have suffered much. But now, friends, this is my wish – let it stand as an order to every one of you who comes to my palace to drink the sparkling wine of the elders and enjoy the minstrel's song. The clothing, gold ornaments and other presents that our counsellors brought here are already packed for our guest in a polished strong-box. I now suggest that in addition we each give him a large tripod and a cauldron. Later we will recoup ourselves by a collection from the people, since it would be hard on us singly to show such generosity with no return.'

Alcinous' proposal was approved and all went home to their beds. As soon as Dawn came, fresh and rosy-fingered, they came bustling down to the ship with their welcome bronze-ware gifts, and the great Alcinous himself went up and down the vessel, stowing them carefully under the benches, so that they would not hamper any of the crew as they pulled on the oars. This done, they returned for a banquet to Alcinous' palace, and great Alcinous slew an ox for them to sacrifice to Zeus of the Black Cloud, the son of Cronos, who is lord of all. They burnt the thighs and settled down to enjoy the splendid feast, while in their midst the people's favourite, Demodocus, that divine bard, sang to the music of his lyre.

But Odysseus kept turning his face to the blazing Sun,

impatient for it to set, as he was longing to be on his way. He was like a ploughman who yearns for his supper after his two brown oxen have pulled the ploughshare up and down the field all day; the sunset is welcome to him, and his legs are weary as he plods homeward. Like him Odysseus welcomed the setting of the Sun that day. No sooner was it set than he appealed to the Phaeacians, those lovers of the oar, and to Alcinous in particular:

'Lord Alcinous, my most worshipful prince, make your drink-offerings now and see me safely off. And farewell to you all! For now my dearest wishes have been fulfilled: I have your escort home and I have your welcome gifts. May the gods in heaven bless them, and may I find my wife and loved ones safe and sound on my return home. As for you whom I leave behind, may you all bring happiness to your good wives and to your children; and may the gods prosper you in every way and keep your people from harm!'

This speech of Odysseus won the approval of the whole company. They felt he had spoken in the right way and so now gave instructions that their guest should be sent on his way. Mighty Alcinous called to his squire. 'Pontonous,' he said, 'mix a bowl of wine and serve everyone in the hall so that we can make a drink-offering to Father Zeus before seeing our visitor off to the land of his birth.' Pontonous mixed the mellow wine, went his rounds and served each of the guests, who, from their seats, then made libations to the blessed gods that lived in the far-flung heavens. Then the gallant Odysseus rose from his chair and put his two-handled cup in Arete's hands. He spoke, and his words were winged: 'My Queen, here's fortune all your life, until man's common lot, old age and death, comes to you! I take my leave of you now. Here in your home may you be happy in your children, your people, and Alcinous your King!'

With this the noble Odysseus stepped across the threshold. Mighty Alcinous ordered a squire to accompany him and lead him to the good ship and the sea-shore. Arete sent with him a party of serving-women, one with a clean cloak and tunic, another in charge of his strong-box, and a third carried bread and red wine.

When they had come down to the ship and the sea, the young nobles who were to escort him took charge of his baggage, including all the food and drink, and stowed it in the polished ship. For Odysseus himself they spread a rug and sheet on the ship's deck, well aft, so that he might enjoy unbroken sleep. Then he too climbed on board and quietly lay down, while the crew took their seats at the oars in order, and untied the cable from the pierced stone that held it. No sooner had they swung back and churned the water with their blades than sweet oblivion sealed Odysseus' eyes in sleep, delicious and profound, the very counterfeit of death.

And now, like a team of four stallions on the plain who start as one at the touch of the whip, leaping forward to make short work of the course, so the stern of the ship leaped forward, and a great dark wave of the surrounding sea surged in her wake. With unfaltering speed she forged ahead, and not even the wheeling falcon, the fastest creature that flies, could have kept her company. Thus she sped lightly on, cutting her way through the waves and carrying a man wise as the gods are wise, who in long years of war on land and wandering across the cruel seas had suffered many agonies of spirit but was now lapped in peaceful sleep, forgetting all he had endured.

When the brightest of all stars came up, the star which often ushers in the tender light of early Dawn, the ship's voyage was done and she drew near to Ithaca. Now in that island is a cove named after Phorcys, the Old Man of the Sea, with two projecting headlands sheer to seaward but sloping down on the side towards the harbour. They protect it from the heavy swell raised by rough weather in the open and allow large ships to ride inside without tying up, once they are within mooring distance of the shore. At the head of the cove grows a long-leaved olive-tree and nearby is a pleasant, hazy cavern sacred to the Nymphs whom we call Naiads. This cave contains a number of stone basins and two-handled jars, which are used by bees as their hives; also great looms of stone where the Nymphs weave marvellous fabrics of sea-purple; and there are springs whose water never fails. The cave has two mouths. The one that looks north is the way down for men. The other, facing south, is for the gods; and as immortals come in by this way men do not trespass there.

It was here that the Phaeacians put in, knowing the place; and such was the headway of the ship, rowed by those able hands, that a full half of her keel's length mounted the beach. They rose from the benches, jumped out, and made it their first task to lift Odysseus, sheet, glossy rug and all, out of the hollow ship and deposit him on the sand still fast asleep. Next they took out all the treasures which, at the prompting of the great-hearted Athene, their noble countrymen had given him when he left for home. These they stacked in a pile by the trunk of the olive-tree, well away from the path, in case some passer-by should find them before he awoke and rob him. This done, they set out for home.

And now the Lord of the Earthquake, who had by no means forgotten the threats he had once uttered against the noble Odysseus, asked Zeus what he intended. 'Father Zeus, the immortal gods will lose respect for me, now that these mortals fail to respect me, these Phaeacians, I mean, who after all are my descendants. I said that Odysseus would suffer much before he reached his home, though I never put a final ban on his return, once you had promised it and nodded your assent. But now these people have brought him over the sea in their good ship and landed him asleep in Ithaca, after showering gifts upon him, countless gifts of bronze, gold and woven stuffs; far more than he could ever have won for himself from Troy, even if he had come back unhurt with his fair share of the spoils.'

'Really!' replied Zeus, the Gatherer of the Clouds. 'How can you, the great and mighty Earthshaker, say such a thing? It is not true that the gods don't respect you. It would indeed be a serious matter if they made disrespectful remarks about the eldest and best of their company. As for mankind, if anyone in the pride of his power treats you with disrespect, you have all the future in which to take your revenge. You are free to please yourself: act as your heart directs.'

'Lord of the Black Cloud,' Poseidon answered him, 'I should indeed like to do as you say, but I have always respected your anger and try to avoid it. Now, however, I propose to wreck that fine ship of the Phaeacians on the misty seas as she comes back from her mission, to teach them once and for all to give up this habit of escorting travellers. And I will also fence their town with a ring of high mountains.'

'Dear brother,' said the Gatherer of the Clouds, 'this is what I think best. When all eyes in the city are fixed on the ship's approach turn her into a rock looking like a ship off-shore. Everyone will be astounded. Then there's no need to throw a circle of high mountains round their city.'

When he heard this answer from Zeus, Poseidon made for Scherie, where the Phaeacians live; and there he waited till the approaching ship, making good headway, came close to the land. The Earthshaker then drew near to her and with one blow from the flat of his hand turned her into stone and rooted her to the sea-bottom. Then he went away.

The Phaeacian spectators, oarsmen themselves and seamen of repute, looked at each other and cried out in words that flew: 'Who in heaven's name has stopped our swift ship out at sea as she was making port? Only a moment ago she was in full view.' They might well ask, for they had no inkling of what had happened till Alcinous explained.

'Alas!' he cried. 'My father's prophecy of long ago comes back to me! He used to maintain that Poseidon resented our giving safe-conduct to all and sundry, and he foretold that one day he would wreck one of our fine ships on the high seas as she was returning from such a mission, and would overshadow our city with a ring of high mountains. That is what the old man used to say, and now it's all coming true.[1] But listen and accept what I say. For the future give up your custom of seeing home any traveller who comes to our city; and for the present let us sacrifice twelve picked bulls to Poseidon. He may take pity on us and refrain from hemming in our town with a long mountain range.' In great trepidation they at once prepared the bulls for sacrifice. So the chieftains and counsellors of the

1. In the harbour of Corcyra (Corfu) is a rock which the locals call 'the ship of Odysseus', proof, they say, that Phaeacia was Corcyra.

Phaeacian people gathered round the altar and interceded with the Lord Poseidon.

The good Odysseus now awoke from sleep on his native soil. After so long an absence, he failed to recognize it, because the goddess, Pallas Athene, Daughter of Zeus, had thrown a mist over the place. Her intention was to make Odysseus unrecognizable, to tell him precisely how things stood, and to prevent his being recognized by his wife and friends or the people of the town before the Suitors had paid for all their transgressions. As a result everything in Ithaca, the long hill-paths, the welcoming bays, the beetling rocks and the leafy trees, seemed unfamiliar to its King. He leapt to his feet and stood staring at his native land. Then he groaned, and slapping his thighs with his hands he cried out in dismay:

'Oh no! Whose country have I come to this time? Are they some brutal tribe of uncivilized savages, or a kindly and god-fearing people? Where shall I put all these goods of mine, and where on earth am I myself to go? If only I had stayed there with the Phaeacians! Then I could have gone on to some other powerful prince, who would have received me well and seen me on my way home. As it is, I don't know where to hide them, and I certainly can't leave them here, or someone else will steal them. And what a blow to find that those Phaeacian lords and chieftains were not exactly wise and honest men! They said they would put me down in my own sunny Ithaca, and then they carry me off to this outlandish place. A broken promise – for which I pray they may be punished by Zeus, the god of suppliants, who watches all mankind and punishes offenders. But now I had better count my belongings and make sure that the crew have not robbed me and gone off with anything in their hollow ship.'

With that he checked his fine tripods and cauldrons, his gold and his splendid woven fabrics, and found not a single item missing. So his thoughts turned to his native land, and, homesick and grieving, he dragged himself along the shore of the sounding sea.

Athene now appeared, disguised as a young shepherd, with

all the delicate beauty that marks the sons of kings. A handsome cloak was folded back across her shoulders, she had sandals on her glistening feet and she carried a javelin in her hand. She was a welcome sight to Odysseus, who came forward at once and spoke winged words.

'Good-day to you, friend. Since you are the first person I have met in this place, do not be hostile, but save these treasures and save me; so I pray to you as I would to a god and kneel at your feet. But tell me exactly where I am. What part of the world is this? What is the country called and who live here? Is it one of the sunny islands or is this fertile slope running down to the sea part of the mainland?'

'Sir,' said the goddess of the gleaming eyes, 'you must be a simpleton or have travelled very far from your home to ask me what this country is. It has a name by no means inglorious. In fact it is known to thousands, to all the peoples who live in the direction of dawn and sunrise and all who live in the opposite direction, towards the twilight West. True, it is rugged and unfit for driving horses, and though not extensive it is very far from poor. Corn grows well and there is wine too. Rain and fresh dew are never lacking; and it has excellent pasture for goats and cattle, timber of all kinds, and watering-places that never fail. And so, my friend, the name of Ithaca has travelled even as far as Troy; and that, they say, is a good long way from Achaea.'

Odysseus' patient heart leapt up as Pallas Athene, Daughter of aegis-bearing Zeus, told him its name, and he revelled in the knowledge that he was on his native soil. He addressed her with words on wings, but not with the truth. True as ever to his own interests, he held back the words that were on his lips.

'Of course,' he said, 'I heard tell of Ithaca even over there across the sea in the spacious land of Crete. And now I have come here myself with all this booty, leaving the other half of my fortune to my children. For I am an exile. I had killed Idomeneus' son, the great runner Orsilochus, who was faster on his feet than any living man in the whole island of Crete. He tried to fleece me of all the booty I had won at Troy, my reward for the long-drawn agonies of war and all the miseries of voyages by sea, merely because I refused to obey his father and serve under him at Troy and preferred to lead my own command. So with a friend at my side I laid an ambush for him at the side of the road, and struck him with my bronze spear as he was coming in from the country. There was a pitch-black sky that night covering the heavens and not a soul saw us; so no one knew that it was I who'd killed him.

'However, with the man's blood fresh on my hands, I hastily sought out a Phoenician ship, and threw myself on the mercy of its honest crew. I made them a suitable payment from my booty and told them to take me on board and set me down in Pylos or the good land of Elis, where the Epeians rule. But the wind was too strong and drove them off their course, much to their distress, for they had no wish to cheat me. Driven back from there we reached this island during the night and made the harbour by dint of rowing. And though we badly needed food not a man among us thought of his supper; we all tumbled out of the ship and lay down just as we were. I was so exhausted that I fell sound asleep. Meanwhile the crew fetched my belongings out of the good ship and put them down on the sand where I lay. After which they embarked once more and set sail for their own fine city of Sidon, leaving me and my troubles behind.'

That was Odysseus' story. The bright-eyed goddess smiled at him and caressed him with her hand. She now wore the appearance of a woman, tall, beautiful and accomplished. Then she spoke, and her words winged their way to him.

'Anyone who met you, even a god, would have to be a consummate trickster to surpass you in subterfuge. You were always an obstinate, cunning and irrepressible intriguer. So you don't propose, even in your own country, to drop the tricks and lying tales you love so much! But no more of this. We both know how to get our own way: in the world of men you have no rival in judgement and argument, while I am pre-eminent among the gods for ingenuity and ability to get what I want.

'And yet you did not recognize Pallas Athene, Daughter of Zeus, who always stands by your side and guards you through all your adventures. It was I who made all the Phaeacians take to you so kindly. And here I am once more, to contrive a cunning scheme with you, to hide the treasures that the Phaeacian nobles, prompted by me, gave you when you left for home, and to warn you of all the trials you will have to undergo within your palace. Bear these with patience, for bear them you must. Tell not a single person, man or woman, that you are back from your wanderings; but endure all aggravation in silence and submit yourself to the indignities that will be put upon you.'

'Goddess,' the nimble-witted Odysseus replied, 'it is hard for a man to recognize you at sight, however expert he may be, for you are always changing your disguise. But this I know well, that you were gracious to me in the old days so long as we Achaeans were campaigning at Troy. Yet when we had sacked Priam's lofty citadel and gone on board our ships, and a god had scattered the Achaean fleet, I did not notice you then, Daughter of Zeus, nor see you set foot on my ship to save me from any of my ordeals. No; I was left to wander through the world with a stricken heart, till the gods put an end to my sufferings and the day came, in the rich land of the Phaeacians, when you comforted me with your talk and yourself guided me to their city. But now I beseech you in your Father's name – since I cannot believe that I have come to my bright Ithaca but feel that I must be wandering in some foreign country and that you spoke as you did in a spirit of provocation to lead me astray – tell me, am I really back in my own beloved land?'

'That shows how your mind always works!' said Athene, goddess of the flashing eyes. 'And that is why I cannot desert you in your misfortunes: you are so persuasive, so quick-witted, so self-possessed. Any other man on returning from his travels would have rushed home in high spirits to see his children and his wife. You, on the contrary, are in no hurry even to ask questions and to learn the news. No; with your own eyes you must first make sure of your wife – who, by the way, does nothing but sit at home with her eyes never free from tears as the slow nights and days pass sorrowfully by.

'As for your home-coming, I myself was never in any doubt: I knew in my heart that you would get back, though with the loss of all your men. But you must understand that I was not prepared to oppose my uncle Poseidon, who was incensed when you blinded his own son, and has nursed his grudge against you.

And now, to convince you, let me show you the Ithacan scene. Here is the harbour of Phorcys, the Old Man of the Sea; and there at the head of the harbour is the long-leaved olive-tree, and near by the pleasant, hazy cave that is sacred to the Nymphs whom men call Naiads. This is the broad vaulted cavern where you made many potent sacrifices to the Nymphs. The forest-clad slopes behind are those of Mount Neriton.'

As she spoke the goddess dispersed the mist, and the country-side stood plain to view. Joy came at last to the noble, long-suffering Odysseus. Overjoyed at the sight of his own land, he kissed the fertile soil, then with uplifted hands invoked the Nymphs: 'I had thought, you Nymphs of the Springs, you Daughters of Zeus, that I should never set eyes on you again! Accept my greetings and my loving prayers. I will give gifts too as in days gone by, if this warrior Daughter of Zeus allows me to live and see my son grow up.'

'Be bold,' said Athene of the flashing eyes, 'and dismiss all such worries from your heart. Our immediate task is to hide your goods in some corner of this sacred cave where they may lie in safety. After that we must decide on our best course for the future.'

The goddess now plunged into the gloom of the cavern to explore it for a hiding-place, while Odysseus set about bringing in all his belongings, the gold, the indestructible bronze and the fine fabrics the Phaeacians had given him. After he had stowed them carefully away, Pallas Athene, Daughter of Zeus, closed the entrance with a stone.

The two of them then sat down by the trunk of the sacred olive-tree to scheme the downfall of the presumptuous Suitors. The bright-eyed goddess was the first to speak. 'Odysseus, favourite of Zeus, son of Laertes, master of ingenuity, consider now how you will come to grips with these shameless Suitors who for three whole years have been lording it in your palace, paying court to your incomparable wife and offering her marriage-gifts. All this time she has pined for your home-coming, and though she has given them all some grounds for hope and made promises in private messages to each, her real wishes are very different.'

'Great Heavens!' cried Odysseus of the nimble wits. 'I would certainly have come to the same miserable end as King Agamemnon directly I set foot in my home, if you, goddess, had not made all this clear to me. But come, devise some ingenious scheme to punish these miscreants. And take your stand at my side, filling me with the spirit that dares all, as you did on the day when we pulled down Troy's shining diadem of towers. Ah, Lady of the Bright Eyes, if only you would aid me with such eagerness as you did then, I could fight against three hundred, with you beside me, gracious goddess, with your whole-hearted support to count on.'

'I will indeed stand at your side,' Athene the bright-eyed goddess answered. 'I shall not forget you when the time comes for this task of ours. As for those Suitors who are wasting your fortune, I can already see them staining your broad floors with their blood and brains. But now to work! I am going to change you beyond recognition. I shall wither the smooth skin on your supple limbs and rob your head of its dark locks; I shall clothe you in rags that one would loathe to see on a human being and I shall dim your bright eyes till you are repulsive to the whole gang of Suitors and even your wife and the son you left at home.

'And now for your part – you must first of all go to the swineherd in charge of your pigs. His heart is as loyal to you as ever, and he is devoted to your son and your wise Queen Penelope. You will find him watching over his swine out at their pastures by the Raven's Crag and at the Spring of Arethusa, where they find the right fodder to make them fat and healthy, feeding on their favourite acorns and drinking water from deep pools. Stay there, sit down with him, and question him about whatever you want to know. Meanwhile I will go to Sparta, the city of fair women, to summon Telemachus, your own son, Odysseus, who has travelled to the broad vale of Lacedaemon and visited Menelaus in the hope of hearing news of you, whether you are still alive.'

Resourceful Odysseus replied: 'But why, in your omniscience, did you not tell him that I am? Do you want him too to roam the barren seas in misery while strangers eat him out of house and home?'

'You need not be alarmed for him,' the bright-eyed goddess answered. 'I myself was his escort, so that he would win fame from his journey there. He is in no difficulties, but is sitting quite at ease in Menelaus' palace, in the lap of luxury. It is true that those young men in their black ship are determined to kill him before he can reach home. But I have an idea that they will not succeed. No; sooner than that, the earth will close over some of these Suitors who are wasting your wealth.'

Athene touched him now with her wand. She withered the smooth skin on his supple limbs, robbed his head of its dark locks, covered his whole body with an old man's wrinkles, and dimmed the brightness of his fine eyes. And she changed his clothing into a shabby cloak and tunic, filthy rags grimy with smoke. Over his back she threw a large and well-worn hide of a nimble stag; and finally she gave him a staff and a poor, shabby knapsack with a shoulder-strap.

Their plans prepared, the two parted company, and Athene went on her way to the sacred land of Lacedaemon to fetch Odysseus' son.

# 14
# IN EUMAEUS' HUT

Odysseus turned his back on the harbour and followed a rough track leading through the woods and up to the hills towards the place where Athene had told him he would meet the worthy swineherd, who of all the servants Odysseus had acquired had shown himself to be the most faithful steward of his property.

He found him sitting in the porch of his hut in the farmyard, whose high walls, perched on an eminence and protected by a clearing, enclosed a fine and spacious courtyard. The herdsman had made it himself for his absent master's swine, without help from his mistress or the aged Laertes, building the wall of quarried stone with a hedge of wild pear on top. Outside he had fenced the whole length on both sides with a closely set stockade made of split oak which he had taken from the dark heart of the logs. Inside the yard, to house the pigs at night, he had made twelve sties, all near to one another, in each of which fifty brood sows were penned, and slept on the ground. The boars slept outside the yard; and of these there were far fewer, since their numbers were constantly reduced by the frequent banquets of the courting noblemen, for whom the swineherd used at regular intervals to send down the pick of his fatted hogs. There were three hundred and sixty of them. They were guarded every night by four dogs, as savage as wild beasts, trained by the master swineherd.

He himself was busy shaping a pair of sandals to his feet, cutting them out of a piece of good brown leather. Three of his men had gone in various directions with the pigs to their pastures. He had been obliged to send the fourth to town with a hog for the arrogant Suitors to slaughter and feed on the flesh.

Suddenly the baying dogs caught sight of Odysseus and flew at him, barking loudly. He had the sense to sit down and drop his staff. Even so he would have suffered ignominious injuries then and there, at his own farm, had not the swineherd, letting the leather fall from his fingers, dashed through the gateway, shouted at the dogs and sent them scurrying off in all directions with a shower of stones.

Then he addressed his master. 'Old man, that was a narrow escape! The dogs would have almost torn you to pieces in a moment, and you would have given me the rough side of your tongue. As though the gods hadn't already given me enough pain and grief! Here I sit, yearning and mourning for the best of masters and fattening his hogs for others to eat, while he himself, starving as like as not, is lost in foreign lands and tramping through strange towns – if indeed he is still alive and can see the light of day. But follow me, old man, let's go to my hut. When you have had all the bread and wine you want, you shall tell me where you come from and what your troubles are.'

The good swineherd led the way to his hut, ushered Odysseus in and invited him to sit down on some brushwood that he piled up for him and covered with the shaggy skin of a wild goat, large and thick, which served as his own mattress. Odysseus was delighted by this welcome and thanked him, saying: 'My good host, may Zeus and the other gods grant you your dearest wish for receiving me so kindly.'

And you, Eumaeus,[1] the swineherd, said in reply, 'Stranger, it is not right for me to turn away any stranger, even one in a worse state than you are, for strangers and beggars all come in Zeus' name, and a gift from folk like us is none the less welcome for being small. Servants cannot make larger gifts when they are always in fear of their overbearing masters. I mean these new ones; as for my old master, the gods have set their faces against his return. *He* would have looked after me properly and given

1. Homer really loved Eumaeus, this character he had created, and here, instead of writing *about* him, he felt impelled to speak *to* him directly as if reminding him of the story.

me possessions, a cottage and a bit of land, and a wife that any man would be glad to have, as a kind master does for a servant who has worked hard for him and whose work heaven has prospered, as it prospers the job I toil at here. Yes, the King would have rewarded me well for this, had he grown old in Ithaca. But he is dead and gone. And I wish I could say the same of Helen and all her breed, for she has been the death of many a good man. My master, you see, was one of those who went to Ilium, the land of horses, to fight the Trojans in Agamemnon's cause.'

The swineherd broke off, hitched up his tunic under his belt, and went out to the sties where the young porkers were penned in batches. He selected two, carried them in, and slaughtered them both. Next he singed them, chopped them up, and skewered the meat. When he had roasted it all, he served it up piping hot on the spits, set it in front of Odysseus, and sprinkled it with white barley-meal. He then mixed some mellow wine in an olive-wood bowl, took a seat facing his guest, and encouraged him to eat.

'Stranger,' he said, 'do have some sucking pig, which is all we servants can offer you. For our fatted hogs are eaten up by the Suitors, who have no fear of the wrath to come and no pity in their hearts. Yet the blessed gods don't like wicked acts. Justice and fair play are what they respect in men. Even bloodthirsty pirates, when they've raided a foreign coast and been allowed by Zeus to carry off some loot, are haunted by the fear of retribution as they make for home with their ships full of plunder. So these Suitors must have somehow discovered, maybe through some heaven-sent rumour, that my master has come to a disastrous end – which explains why they will neither pay court to his widow in the regular way nor go home and mind their own business, but sit there instead at their ease and eat up all his livelihood in this high-handed style – no scrimping or saving for *them*. For I tell you they slaughter beasts every single day and night that Zeus sends, never just one or even two at a time, and they draw and swill wine like water.

'My master, you see, was enormously rich; there wasn't a lord on the fertile mainland or in Ithaca itself to touch him. He's worth more than twenty others rolled into one. Let me give you some idea. On the mainland, twelve herds of cattle, as many flocks of sheep, as many droves of pigs and as many scattered herds of goats, all tended by hired labour or his own herdsmen; while here in Ithaca eleven herds of goats graze up and down the coast with reliable men to look after them. And every one of these men has day by day to choose the best of his fatted goats and drive it in for the Suitors; I too, who tend and keep these pigs, carefully pick out the best and send it down to them.'

While Eumaeus was talking, Odysseus eagerly ate the meat and drank the wine, avidly and in silence, but his brain was teeming with thoughts of what he would do to the Suitors. When he had finished supper and felt satisfied, he filled the bowl he had been using and handed it to his host brim-full with wine. Eumaeus accepted with pleasure and Odysseus now said to him with winged words:

'Tell me, my friend, who was the man who bought you with his wealth, this lord whom you describe as so exceedingly rich and powerful? You said he had lost his life in Agamemnon's cause. Tell me his name, describe him – I may find that I know him. Heaven knows whether I can tell you I've met him; but I've certainly roved all over the world.'

'Old friend,' answered the master swineherd, 'no wanderer who comes here and claims to bring news of Odysseus could convince his wife and son. Beggars in need of creature comforts find lying easy, and to tell a true tale is the last thing they want to do. Whenever a tramp comes to Ithaca he goes straight to my mistress and tells a pack of lies. She welcomes him graciously and asks him every detail, point by point, while tears of distress stream down her cheeks, as is natural for a woman whose husband has met his end abroad. Even you yourself, old friend, would be quick enough to invent a tale if someone gave you a cloak and tunic to put on!

'As for my master, he is dead and gone: the dogs and the birds of the air must by now have torn the flesh from his bones; or the fish have eaten him in the sea, and his bones lie there on the shore with the sand piled high above them. Yes, that is how he met his end, and his death has meant nothing but grief for his friends, and for myself above all. For I shall never find so kind a master again wherever I may go, not even if I return to my parents' house, where I was born and bred. And much as I grieve for them and long to be back in my own country and set eyes on them again, it is for the lost Odysseus that my heart aches and yearns. Even in his absence I can hardly bring myself to mention his name. He cared for me and loved me dearly. But even though he is far away, I still call him my beloved master.'

'Friend,' said the patient, good Odysseus in reply, 'since you won't accept what I say, and since you have so little faith that you cannot believe he will ever return, I will not merely state that Odysseus is coming back, I will swear to it. Directly he comes and sets foot in his own house I will claim the reward for the good news and you can dress me in a fine new cloak and tunic. But till that moment, destitute as I am, I will accept nothing; for I loathe like the Gates of Hades the man who is driven by poverty to lie. I swear now by Zeus before all other gods, and by the board of hospitality, and by the good Odysseus' hearth, which I am approaching, that everything will happen as I say. This very month Odysseus will be here. Between the waning of the old moon and the waxing of the new, he will come back to his home and will punish all who dishonour his wife and his noble son.'

And you, Eumaeus, the swineherd, said in reply, 'Old friend, that reward I will never have to pay, nor will Odysseus ever come home again. Drink in peace and let us turn to other matters. Don't remind me of my troubles, for I tell you my heart is wrung when anyone reminds me of my dear King. As for your oath, let us forget it. And may Odysseus still come home, as I pray he will, and as Penelope does, and old Laertes and godlike Telemachus. Ah, there's another cruel anxiety for me – Odysseus' son Telemachus. The gods made him grow like a young sapling, and I had thought he would become as good a man in the world as his father, a fine-looking man, when suddenly some god or perhaps man deprived him of his wits – and off he went to holy Pylos on his father's trail. And now those lordly Suitors are lying in ambush for him on his way home, hoping that godlike Arceisius' line may be wiped out of Ithaca and the very name be forgotten. Well, we must leave him to his fate, whether they catch him, or whether Zeus stretches out his hand to save him.

'But now, old friend, you must tell me about your own troubles. Tell me the truth; I want to know everything. Who are you and where do you come from? What is your city? Who are your family? And since you certainly can't have come on foot, what kind of vessel brought you here? How did its crew come to land you in Ithaca; and who did they claim to be?'

The inventive Odysseus launched into his story. 'I will give you a true account of all you ask. If only you and I had an endless supply of food and wine, here in the hut, and so could eat in peace while the rest got on with the work! I would find it easy to talk to you for a whole year without coming to the end of my sorrows and all the hardships that the gods have made me endure.

'I am a native of the broad lands of Crete, and the son of a rich man. He had a number of other sons who were born and brought up in the house; but they were the lawful issue of his wife, whereas my mother was a concubine he had bought. In spite of this difference my father, Castor son of Hylax, put me on an equal footing with his legitimate sons. The Cretans of his day respected and honoured him like a god for his good fortune, his riches, and his splendid children, but his time came and Death bore him off to Hades' Halls. His high-handed sons then split up the estate and cast lots for the shares, assigning to me a meagre pittance and a house to match. However, I won a wife for myself from a rich land-owning family on my own merits, for I was neither a fool nor a coward. Now it has all gone, yet I think you will still be able to see by the stubble what the harvest was like.

'Since then I have been overwhelmed by troubles, but in the old days Ares and Athene had endowed me generously with the daring that breaks the battle-line; and when it came to planning an attack against the enemy and I had picked my men for an ambush, my proud heart never had a foreboding of death, and I would leap out before all the rest and kill with my spear any enemy who was slower on his feet than I. That was the kind of man I was in battle. But I did not like work on the land, nor the domestic pursuits that make for a fine family of children. What I always loved was ships with oars, and fighting, and polished javelins and arrows – terrible things, which make other people shudder. I suppose that my inclinations were all implanted in me by the gods, for different men find satisfaction in very different ways of earning a living. Anyhow, before the Achaean expedition ever set foot on the coasts of Troy, I had nine times had my own command and led a well-found fleet against a foreign land. As a result, large quantities of loot fell into my hands. From this I used to select what I liked, and a great deal more came my way by lot. In this way my estate increased rapidly and my fellow-countrymen soon learned both to fear and to respect me.

'The time came, however, when all-seeing Zeus devised the dreadful adventure which laid so many men low; and they pressed me and the famous Idomeneus to lead our ships to Ilium. There was no way of avoiding it: public opinion was too much for us. So for nine years we Achaeans campaigned at Troy; and after sacking Priam's city in the tenth we sailed for home and our fleet was scattered by a god. But for my unhappy self the inventive brain of Zeus was hatching more mischief. I had spent only a month in the delights of home life with my children, my wife and my possessions, when the spirit moved me to fit out some ships and sail for Egypt with heroic companions. I got nine vessels ready and the crews were soon mustered.

'For six days my good men gave themselves up to festivity and I provided beasts in plenty for their sacrifices and for their own table. On the seventh we embarked, said goodbye to the broad fields of Crete and sailed off with a fresh and favourable wind from the North, which made our going as easy as though we were sailing with the current. Not a single one of my ships came to harm: we sat there safe and well while the wind and the steersman kept them on their course. On the fifth day we reached the great River of Egypt, and there in the Nile I anchored my curved ships. Then I ordered my good men to stay by the ships on guard while I sent out some scouts to reconnoitre from the heights. But, carried away by their own violence they went on a rampage, and immediately began to plunder some of the fine Egyptian farms, carrying off the women and children and killing the men. The hue and cry soon reached the city, and the townsfolk, roused by the alarm, poured out at dawn. The whole place was filled with infantry and chariots and the glint of arms. Zeus the Thunderer struck abject panic into my party. Not a man had the spirit to stand and face the enemy, for we were threatened on all sides. They ended by cutting down a large part of my force with their sharp weapons and carrying off the survivors to work for them as slaves.

'As for myself, a sudden inspiration saved me – though I still wish I had faced my destiny and fallen there in Egypt, for trouble was in store for me. I quickly took off my fine helmet, let the shield drop from my shoulder, and threw away my spear. Then I ran up to the King's chariot and clasped and kissed his knees. Moved to pity, he spared my life, gave me a seat beside him, and so drove his weeping captive home. Many of his people, of course, were lusting for my blood and lunged at me with their ash-wood spears, for they were thoroughly roused; but he kept them away, for fear of offending Zeus, the Strangers' god, whose wrath is aroused by deeds of cruelty.

'I passed several years in the country and made a fortune among the Egyptians, who were generous to me, one and all. But in the course of the eighth, I fell in with a rascally Phoenician, a thieving rogue who had already done a deal of mischief in the world. I was persuaded by his plausible talk to join him in a voyage to Phoenicia, where he had a house and estate; and there I stayed with him for a whole year. But when the days and months had mounted up, and a second year began its round of seasons, he put me on board a ship bound for Libya, on the pretext of wanting my help with the cargo he was carrying, but really to sell me for a handsome sum when he got there. Full of suspicions but having no choice, I followed him on board.

'With a good stiff breeze from the North the ship took the central route south of Crete. But Zeus had planned their destruction. When we had passed Crete, and no other land nor anything but sky and water was to be seen, he brought a dark cloud to rest above the ship. The sea below it was blackened, Zeus thundered and in the same moment struck the vessel with lightning. The whole ship reeled to the blow of his bolt and was filled with the smell of sulphur. The men were all flung overboard; and round the black hull they floated like sea-gulls on the waves. There was no homecoming for them; the god saw to that. But in this hour of my affliction Zeus himself thrust into my arms the great mast of the blue-prowed ship, to allow me once again to avoid disaster. I coiled myself round it and became the sport of the accursed winds. For nine days I drifted, and on the tenth night, in pitch darkness, a great roller washed me up on the coast of Thesprotia, where Lord Pheidon, King of the Thesprotians, gave me hospitality, asking for nothing in return. His own son found me fainting from exposure and exhaustion, pulled me up by the hand, and took me home with him to his father's palace, where he gave me a cloak and tunic to wear.

'It was there that I heard of Odysseus. The King told me that he had entertained and befriended him on his homeward way and showed me what a fortune in copper, gold and wrought iron Odysseus had amassed. The amount of treasure stored up for him there in the King's house would keep a man and his heirs to the tenth generation! He added that Odysseus had gone to Dodona[1] to learn the will of Zeus from the great oak-tree that is sacred to the god, and to discover how he ought to approach his own rich island of Ithaca after so long an absence, openly or in disguise. Moreover, he swore in my presence over a drink-offering in his own house that a ship was waiting on the beach with a crew standing by to convey Odysseus to his own country. But he sent me off before him because a Thesprotian ship happened to be starting for the corn island of Dulichium. He told its crew to treat me well, and take me to Acastus, the King.

'The crew, however, saw fit to hatch a wicked plot against me, to plunge me deeper still into misery. When the ship on her journey had left land far behind, they set about their scheme to reduce me to slavery. They stripped me of my own cloak and

1. The seat of an ancient oracle of Zeus, who communicated his messages by means of the rustling of the leaves of the oak-tree.

tunic and replaced them with a filthy set of clothes, the very rags, in fact, which you see before you now.

'They arrived in Ithaca when the fields lay under a clear evening sky. They lashed me down tightly under the ship's benches with a strong rope, disembarked, and hastily took their supper on the beach. But the gods found no difficulty in untying my knots for me. I wrapped my rags round my head, slipped down the smooth landing-plank, quietly breasted the water, and struck out with both hands. Very soon I was out of the sea and beyond their reach. I then made my way inland to a thicket of flowering shrubs and crouched down in hiding. They searched around for me with a great deal of shouting, but soon decided that nothing was to be gained by prolonging their search, and so climbed on board their ship once more. The gods made it quite easy for me to remain unseen, and ended by guiding my steps to the home of a man of understanding. So then, I am not yet meant to die.'

And you, Eumaeus, the swineherd, said in reply: 'My poor friend! You have certainly touched my heart with the story of your hardships and wanderings. It is when you come to Odysseus that you go wrong, to my way of thinking; you won't get me to believe that. What call is there for a man like you to tell such pointless lies? As though *I* didn't know all about my master's disappearance, and how the gods showed their utter hatred of him by allowing him neither to fall in battle against the Trojans nor to die in his friends' arms when all the fighting was over. Had he done so, the whole Achaean nation would have joined in building him a mound, and he would have left a great name for his son to inherit. But there was to be no glorious end for him: the Storm-Fiends have spirited him away.

'As for myself, I am a hermit here with my pigs, and never go to the town, except perhaps when news has arrived from somewhere and the wise Penelope invites me. On such occasions everyone gathers round the newcomer and plies him with questions, whether they are those who are pining for their long-lost King or those who have the satisfaction of eating for nothing at his expense. But I personally have lost all interest in such probing and questioning since the day when a fellow from Aetolia deceived me with his tale. He had killed a man, and after being pursued all over the world found his way to my door. I received him kindly and he told me that he had seen Odysseus with Idomeneus in Crete, repairing the damage his fleet had suffered in a gale. He said Odysseus would be back, either in the summer or by autumn, bringing back a fortune and his gallant company. Now a god has brought *you* to my door, my long-suffering friend, but don't *you* try to gratify or soothe my heart with any falsehoods. It is not for that reason that I shall respect and entertain you, but because I fear Zeus, the patron of strangers, and pity you.'

But the cunning Odysseus persisted. 'You certainly have a very suspicious nature,' he said, 'if not even my oath can bring you round and convince you of the truth. Come, let us make a bargain – with the gods of Olympus as witnesses to us both. If your master comes back to this house, you shall give me a cloak and tunic to wear and send me on to Dulichium, where I want to go. If on the other hand your master does not return as I say he will, you shall tell your men to throw me over a precipice, just to teach the next beggar not to tell lies.'

'Yes,' cried the honest swineherd, 'and what fame and fortune I would win for myself in the world, once and for all, if after taking you into my hut and showing you hospitality I was to rob you of your precious life! I would be a willing party to a crime against Zeus, son of Cronos, if I did that. However, it's supper-time, and I hope my men will be in before long, so that we can prepare a tasty meal in the hut.'

As they were speaking the herdsmen came up with their pigs. The men drove the animals in batches into their sties to sleep and the air was filled with the grunting of pigs settling down for the night. The worthy swineherd called out to his men. 'Bring your best hog. I want to slaughter it for a guest I have here from abroad. And we'll enjoy ourselves, after all we've put up with looking after the white-tusked boars all this time, while other people live for nothing off our work.'

He then chopped some firewood with his sharp axe, and his men dragged in a fatted five-year-old hog and held it by the hearth. The swineherd, who was a good and virtuous man, did not forget the immortals, but began the ritual by throwing a tuft of hair from the white-tusked victim into the fire and praying to all the gods that the wise Odysseus might come back to his home. Then he drew himself up and struck the animal with a piece of oak which he had left unsplit. The hog fell stunned. They slit its throat, singed its bristles, and deftly cut the carcass up. The swineherd cut pieces from all the limbs as a first offering to the gods, placed them with raw fat on the thigh bones, sprinkled them with barley-meal and threw them all on to the flames. Then they chopped up the rest of the meat, pierced it with spits, roasted it thoroughly, and after drawing it off the spits heaped it up on platters. The swineherd, with his characteristic fairness, stood up to divide it into helpings. He carved and sorted it all out into seven portions, one of which he set aside, with a prayer, for the Nymphs and for Hermes, Maia's son, and distributed the rest to the company. But he gave Odysseus the portion of honour, the hog's long chine.

This courtesy warmed the heart of his master, who turned to him and said: 'Eumaeus, I hope Father Zeus will look on you as kindly as I do for picking out the best portion for "a man like me".'

And you, Eumaeus the swineherd, said in reply: 'Do start, my strange guest, and enjoy such food as we can offer. The god will give and the god will take away, according to his will, for he can do everything.' Then he made a burnt offering to the immortal gods of the piece he had set aside and, after making a libation of sparkling wine, handed the cup to Odysseus, the sacker of cities, and sat down to his own portion. They were served with bread by Mesaulius, a servant whom Eumaeus had procured for himself during his master's absence, acting without help from his mistress or the old Laertes and buying the man from the Taphians with his own resources. All began to eat the good food spread before them, and when they had satisfied their hunger and thirst Mesaulius cleared away the food. Sated by now with bread and meat they began to prepare for bed.

Night came on, bringing foul weather. There was no moon, rain from Zeus set in for the night, and the wet West Wind blew hard. Odysseus now spoke to them, intending to put the swineherd to the test and see whether out of his obvious concern for his guest he would take off his cloak and lend it to him, or persuade one of his men to do so. 'Listen to me,' he said, 'Eumaeus and all of you. I am going to boast and tell you a story. This is the effect of wine – it makes people do crazy things; it sets the wisest man singing and giggling stupidly; it lures him on to dance and it makes him blurt out what's better left unsaid. However, since I've opened my mouth I might as well go on.

'Ah, I wish I were still as young and strong as I was when we led that surprise attack against Troy! Odysseus and Menelaus, son of Atreus, were the leaders, and at their request I went in with them as third in command. When we came up to the frowning city walls we lay down, crouching under our armour in the dense undergrowth of marshland reeds. The North Wind dropped and a cruel frosty night set in. From overhead the snow came down like hoar-frost, bitterly cold, and the ice formed thick on our shields. All the rest had cloaks and tunics and they slept in comfort with their shields drawn up over their shoulders. But when I started out I had foolishly left my cloak with my men, thinking I wouldn't be cold; and so I joined the party with nothing but my shield and a bright waistband.

'In the third watch of the night, when the stars had passed their zenith, I had a word with Odysseus, who was my neighbour. I nudged him with my elbow. He was all attention. "Son of Laertes, favourite of Zeus, inventive Odysseus," I said, "I shall be a dead man soon. This cold is killing me, because I've got no cloak. A god tricked me into coming with nothing but a tunic. And now there's no way out of my plight." When I put this to him, Odysseus turned it over in his mind and, like the schemer and soldier that he was, he had an idea, as you will see. "Quiet!" he whispered in my ear. "Don't let any of the others hear you." Then he raised his head on his elbow and called to the rest: "Wake up, my friends. The gods have sent me a dream in my sleep. We have come too far from the ships, and I want someone to take a message to Agamemnon, the commander-in-chief, to ask if he will send us reinforcements from the base." A man called Thoas, Andraimon's son, immediately jumped up, threw off his purple cloak, and ran off towards the ships – leaving me to snuggle down in his cloak with a grateful heart till Dawn appeared on her golden throne. Ah, I wish I were still as young and strong as I was then!'[1]

And then you, Eumaeus the swineherd, said in reply: 'Old friend, that is an excellent story you have told us. Not a word was ill-judged – or lost on us! Tonight you shan't go without clothing or anything else that an unfortunate outcast has the right to expect from those he approaches. But in the morning you'll have to wrap up in your own rags once more. We have no stock of cloaks here or change of tunics: each man has to manage with a single cloak. But when Odysseus' dear son arrives, *he* will give you a cloak and tunic to wear, and send you wherever you have set your heart on going.'

The swineherd jumped up, placed a bed for him by the fire and spread on it the skins of sheep and goats. Odysseus lay down and Eumaeus covered him with a great thick cloak, which he kept as a spare garment for exceptionally cold spells.

So there Odysseus slept, with the young farmhands beside him. But the swineherd was unwilling to sleep there away from his boars. He got himself ready for a night outside, and Odysseus was delighted to see his diligent concern for his absent master's property. He began by slinging a sharp sword from his sturdy shoulders. He then wrapped himself in a good thick cloak to keep out the wind, picked up the fleece of a big full-grown goat, and finally took a sharp javelin with which to ward off dogs and men. And so he went off to pass the night where the white-tusked boars slept, under an overhanging rock sheltered from the northerly winds.

1. Lines 504–506 have been omitted as considered not authentic.

# 15
# TELEMACHUS RETURNS

Pallas Athene now went to the broad vale of Lacedaemon to remind great-hearted Odysseus' noble son that it was time for him to return, and to hasten his departure. She found Telemachus and Prince Peisistratus lying in great Menelaus' portico. Nestor's son was sound asleep; but sweet sleep had deserted Telemachus, for anxiety on his father's behalf kept him wakeful all through the ambrosial night.

The bright-eyed goddess stood near him and said: 'Telemachus, it is wrong of you to linger abroad and leave your property unguarded with such a rabble in your house. They might well share out and eat up all you have, and so make your journey futile. Urge your host, Menelaus of the loud war-cry, to let you go at once, if you wish to find your noble mother still in the palace. For her father and brothers are already pressing her to marry Eurymachus, who outdoes all the rest of her Suitors in his gifts to her and keeps offering larger and larger marriage settlements. There is also the danger that she might carry off some of your own things from the house without your permission. You know what a woman's disposition is. She likes to bring riches to the house of the man who is marrying her, but never remembers or asks about the dead husband she once loved or the children she bore him. So when you reach home hand over everything to whichever woman-servant you trust most, until the gods send you a wife worthy of your rank.

'And here's another matter for you to bear in mind. The ringleaders among the Suitors are lying in ambush in the straits between Ithaca and the rugged coast of Samos, intent on murdering you before you can reach home. Not that I think they will succeed. No; sooner than that, the earth will close over some of those Suitors who are consuming your livelihood. However, steer your ship well clear of the islands, and sail on through the night; your guardian god will send you a following breeze. Land in Ithaca at the first point you reach and send the ship and the whole ship's company round to the harbour, but before you yourself do anything else, visit the swineherd in charge of your pigs, who is loyal to you in spite of everything. Stay there for the night and send him to the city to give your wise mother, Penelope, the news that you are back from Pylos and safe.'

Her message delivered, Athene left for the heights of Olympus. Telemachus roused Nestor's son from his sweet sleep with a kick and said: 'Wake up, Peisistratus. Harness the horses to the chariot, and let's be on our way.'

'Telemachus,' his friend replied, 'however eager we may be to start, we cannot possibly drive in complete darkness. It'll soon be dawn. Wait and give the famous spearman Menelaus the chance of putting some presents for us in the chariot and sending us off with a friendly farewell. All his life a guest remembers the host who has treated him kindly.'

Soon Dawn mounted her golden throne and Menelaus of the loud war-cry rose from sleep beside Helen of the lovely hair and made his way towards them. When Odysseus' heroic son saw him coming he hastily drew his shining tunic on, threw his great cloak across his sturdy shoulders, and went out to Menelaus and greeted him. 'Menelaus, son of Atreus, favourite of the gods, sovereign of your people. Please let me return to my own country; I'm longing to be home.'

'Telemachus,' Menelaus of the war-cry replied, 'I will not keep you here long if you wish to get back. I disapprove of any host who is either too kind or not kind enough. There should be moderation in all things, and it is equally offensive to speed a guest who would like to stay and to detain one who is anxious to leave. Treat a man well while he's with you, but let him go when he wishes.

'However, do give me time to bring you some presents and pack them in your chariot – they will be fine ones, as you will see for yourself. And let me tell the women to get a meal ready in the hall; there's plenty of food in the store. It is a glorious privilege to travel far and wide in the world, but you must have a meal first. Perhaps you would like to make a tour through Hellas and the Argive country,[1] in which case I would provide the chariot and horses and serve as your guide to the various cities? Nobody will send us away empty-handed: we can count on each of our hosts for at least one gift, a bronze tripod or a cauldron, a pair of mules or a golden cup.'

'Menelaus, son of Atreus, favourite of the gods, sovereign of your people,' the sensible Telemachus answered, 'I really am anxious to return at once to my own home. For when I set out I left no one in charge of my property. In the search for my godlike father I don't want to lose my life, nor do I want to lose any valuable heirlooms from my house.'

When Menelaus of the loud war-cry heard this, he at once told his wife and the servants to prepare a meal in the hall from the plentiful supplies in the palace. At this moment, Boethus' son Eteoneus, who lived nearby and had just got up, arrived and was told by Menelaus to light the fire and roast some meat. Eteoneus obeyed his instructions, while Menelaus, in company with Helen and Megapenthes, went down to the aromatic store-room. When they had reached the place where the treasures were kept, Menelaus picked out a two-handled cup and told his son Megapenthes to collect a silver mixing-bowl. Helen, meanwhile, went to the chests which contained her elaborately woven dresses, the work of her own hands, and from them, great lady that she was, she lifted out the longest and most richly decorated robe, which had lain underneath all the rest, and now glittered like a star. They then made their way through the house and found Telemachus.

'It is my earnest hope, Telemachus,' said auburn-haired Menelaus, 'that Zeus the Thunderer and husband of Hera will make your home-coming all that you desire. By way of presents you shall have the most beautiful and most precious of the treasures that my palace holds. I am giving you a mixing-bowl

1. 'Hellas' seems to refer to northern Greece, 'Argive country' to southern Greece, the Peloponnese.

of wrought metal. It is solid silver, with a rim of gold, and was made by Hephaestus himself. I had it from the King of Sidon, the Lord Phaedimus, when I stayed with him on my journey home. And now I wish it to be yours.'

The hero Menelaus then handed him the two-handled cup, while his valiant son Megapenthes brought forward the shining silver bowl he had been carrying and set it before him. Helen of the lovely cheeks stood by with the robe in her hands and said, 'Look, dear child, I too have a gift for you here, a keepsake from Helen, made by her own hands. It is for your bride to wear when the longed-for day of your wedding arrives. Till then let it be kept in your mother's room. And now I wish you a joyful return to your own country and your fine house.'

With that, Helen handed the robe to Telemachus, who accepted it joyfully. The heroic Peisistratus took charge of the gifts and admired them as he stowed them in a basket in the chariot. Auburn-haired Menelaus then led the way into the house and they sat down on chairs and seats. A maid brought water in a fine golden jug and poured it out over a silver basin for them to rinse their hands. Next she drew a polished table to their side, and the faithful housekeeper brought some bread and set it by them with a choice of delicacies, helping them liberally to all she could offer. Eteoneus was there to carve and serve the meat, while the great Menelaus' son poured out their wine. And so they helped themselves to the food spread before them.

When they had satisfied their hunger and thirst, Telemachus and Nestor's noble son yoked their horses, mounted their gaily painted chariot, and drove out by the gateway and its echoing portico. Auburn-haired Menelaus, Atreus' son, followed them out with a golden cup of mellow wine in his right hand, to enable his guests to make a drink-offering before they left. He went up to their chariot and raised the cup to them.

'Goodbye, my young friends,' he said; 'and give King Nestor, shepherd of his people, my respects. He was like a kind father to me when we were fighting at Troy.'

'Menelaus, favourite of Zeus,' the thoughtful Telemachus replied, 'we will certainly give him your message when we arrive. I only wish I could find Odysseus at home when I reach Ithaca, and tell him how I have met with nothing but kindness at your hands during my stay and have come away laden with precious gifts.'

As he spoke, a bird came flying from the right. It was an eagle, carrying in its talons a great white goose, a tame bird from the yard. Some men and women were giving chase with shrill cries, and when the eagle reached the chariot it sheered off again towards the right in front of the horses, to the delight of the whole party, whose spirits rose at the sight. Nestor's son Peisistratus was the first to speak. 'Menelaus, favourite of Zeus, ruler of the people, what do you think? Did heaven send this omen for us two or for you?'

Menelaus, dear to Ares, considered carefully how to pronounce correctly on the matter, but his long-robed wife forestalled him. 'Listen,' she said, 'while with the gods' inspiration I explain this omen and what I feel sure it portends. Just as this eagle came down from his native mountains and pounced on our home-fed goose, so shall Odysseus, after many hardships and many wanderings, reach his home and have his revenge. Or he is already there and planning trouble for the whole pack of Suitors!'

'May Zeus the Thunderer and husband of Hera,' cried thoughtful Telemachus, 'make what you say come true; then in my distant home I will worship you as a goddess.'

Then he gave the horses a touch of his whip. They set off briskly and pressed forward through the town towards the open country, and all day long the yoke rose and fell on their necks.

The sun set, and all the ways grew dark. They had reached Pherae, where they drove up to the house of Diocles, son of Ortilochus, whose father was Alpheius. There they stayed the night and were hospitably entertained. As soon as Dawn appeared, fresh and rosy-fingered, they were harnessing their horses once again and mounting the gaily coloured chariot. Out past the echoing portico and through the gates they drove. A flick of the whip to make the horses go, and the pair flew on with such a will that before very long they reached the high citadel of Pylos.

At this point Telemachus turned to Nestor's son and said:

'Peisistratus, I want you, if you can, to do something for me. We may well claim that our fathers' friendship makes a lasting bond between us. Besides which, we are of the same age and this journey will have served to bring us even closer together. So I beg you, favourite of Zeus, not to take me past my ship, but to put me down there and so save me from being kept at the palace against my will by your old father's passion for hospitality. I must get home quicker than that.'

Nestor's son turned the problem over in his mind. How could he manage this successfully? After some hesitation he made up his mind. Turning his horses, he drove down to the ship on the sea-shore, and took out and stowed Menelaus' fine presents of clothing and gold in the ship's stern. He then urged Telemachus on with words that flew.

'Embark at once,' he said, 'and order all your men on board before I reach home and tell my aged father. For I know only too well that he is far too obstinate to let you go, but will come down here himself to fetch you – and I do not see him going back alone. He'll anyway be very angry.'

With these words Peisistratus left him and drove his shiny-coated horses back to the city of Pylos, where he soon reached his home. Meanwhile Telemachus spurred on his crew. 'Men,' he called to them, 'get that tackle properly stowed away, and let's embark and be off.'

The crew leapt to his orders, climbed on board, and took their places at the oars. Telemachus had just supervised their embarkation and was praying and sacrificing to Athene by the ship's stern when he was approached by a stranger from a distant land. This man, who had fled from Argos after killing a man, was a seer descended from Melampus.[1] Melampus had at one time lived in Pylos, the land of sheep, and been known among his fellow-citizens as a wealthy man with a magnificent house. But a time came when he had to flee the country and go abroad to escape from the great King, Neleus the Magnificent. The King seized his rich estate and kept it for a whole year. All

1. The background to the story that follows is given at 11.291.

this time Melampus was a wretched prisoner in the castle of Phylacus, suffering untold miseries, for Neleus' daughter's sake, from the fit of madness into which the Avenging Furies cast him. However, he escaped alive and managed to drive the lowing cattle from Phylace to Pylos, where he had his revenge on King Neleus for the injustice done to him and secured the hand of Neleus' daughter for his brother. As for himself, he went to live abroad, in Argos, the land of thoroughbreds, where he was destined to make his home and establish his rule over a large section of the people.

There he married, built himself a splendid palace, and had two sturdy sons, Antiphates and Mantius. Antiphates became the father of the bold Oicles, and Oicles, in his turn, of that great leader Amphiaraus, a man whom aegis-bearing Zeus and Apollo loved and blessed with every mark of their favour. Even so he never trod the path of old age, but fell at Thebes, the victim of a woman's avarice,[1] leaving two sons, Alcmaeon and Amphilochus. His brother Mantius was the father of Polypheides and Cleitus – Cleitus, who was such a beautiful youth that Dawn of the golden throne carried him off to live with the immortals, and the great-hearted Polypheides, who was made a seer by Apollo, and after Amphiaraus' death succeeded him as the most famous prophet of his age. A quarrel with his father led him to migrate to Hyperesia, where he settled and prophesied to all.

It was his son, Theoclymenus by name, who now appeared and came up to Telemachus, whom he found engaged in libations and prayers by his black ship. 'Friend,' he said to him with winged words, 'since I find you sacrificing here, I beg you by your sacrifice and the god you are honouring, and again by your own life and the lives of these companions who are with you, to be open with me and tell me the truth. Who are you? Where do you come from? What is your town and who are your people?'

'Stranger,' answered the sensible Telemachus, 'I will tell you honestly. Ithaca is my native place, and my father is Odysseus, or was Odysseus, if ever he existed. But he has long since met

1. See note on 11.327.

with some unhappy end. That is what brings me here with my ship and crew. I am trying to find out what has happened to my long-lost father.'

'Like you,' said the noble Theoclymenus, 'I have left my country. I killed a man of my own blood, and the plains of Argos are full of his brothers and kinsmen, who form the most powerful family in the land. It was to avoid death and dark fate at their hands that I ran away. It is my destiny to be a wanderer on the face of the earth. Please take me on board – I seek sanctuary with you – don't let them kill me – I think they are on my track.'

'I shall certainly not bar you from my good ship, if you wish to sail with us,' said the thoughtful Telemachus. 'Come along then; and in Ithaca you shall be welcome to such hospitality as we can offer.'

With these words he took Theoclymenus' bronze spear and laid it on the curved ship's deck. Then he stepped on board the sea-going vessel himself, sat down in the stern, and gave Theoclymenus a place beside him. The hawsers were cast off and Telemachus called to the crew to rig the ship. They obeyed with a will, hauled up the pine mast, stepped it in its hollow box, made it fast with forestays, and hoisted the white sail with plaited leather ropes. And Athene of the gleaming eyes sent a following wind through a clear sky to speed them from astern, so that their ship might most speedily complete her journey across the salt sea. Thus they sailed past Crouni and Chalcis with its lovely streams. The sun set, and all the ways grew dark. They made for Pheae, still wafted on by a wind from Zeus, and then sailed past the good land of Elis where the Epeians rule. After which Telemachus set a course for the Pointed Isles, wondering whether he would get through alive or be caught.

In the hut Odysseus and the honest swineherd, with the farm-hands for company, were having their supper. When they had eaten and drunk their fill, Odysseus sounded Eumaeus out to discover whether he would continue his hospitality and invite him to stay at the farm, or send him to the city.

'Listen to me,' he said, 'Eumaeus and all of you. I intend to leave you in the morning and go to the town to beg, so as not to be a burden to you and your men. But give me advice and the company of a trustworthy guide to show me the way. Once there, necessity will force me to wander about the town on my own in the hope that someone will give me a cup of water and a crust of bread. I would also like to go to godlike Odysseus' palace and deliver my news to his wise Queen, Penelope, and mingle with those high and mighty Suitors you speak of. They have such an abundance of good things that they might well spare me a meal. I should be ready to make a good job of whatever work they wanted done. For I tell you – and mark my words – that by favour of Hermes the Messenger, who gives grace and dignity to every kind of common labour, there's not a man to touch me at servants' work, at laying a fire properly, at splitting dry logs, as a carver, a cook, a wine-steward, in short at anything that humble folk do by way of serving their betters.'

And then you, Eumaeus the swineherd,[1] were most indignant and said, 'Oh no, my friend! What on earth put such a scheme into your head? You will simply be courting sudden death, if you insist on becoming involved with a set of men whose aggressiveness and violence reach as high as the iron heavens. *Their* servants are not at all your kind; they are young fellows with smart tunics and cloaks, their hair and handsome faces always gleaming with oil. That is the kind that wait on them – at polished tables, groaning under their load of bread and meat and wine. No, stay with me, where nobody finds you a nuisance. I certainly don't, nor do any of my men here. And when Odysseus' son arrives, he'll fit you out in a cloak and tunic and send you on wherever you would like to go.'

'Eumaeus,' replied the patient, good Odysseus, 'may Father Zeus look on you as kindly as I do for putting an end to the pain and misery of wandering. Surely to be a vagrant is the worst possible fate, yet men will bear such miseries because of their wretched stomachs. However, since you press me to stay and wait for the prince's arrival, tell me about godlike Odysseus'

1. See note on 14.55.

mother, and his father, whom he left on the threshold of old age when he went abroad. Are they still in the land of the living? Or are they dead by now and in the Halls of Hades?'

'My friend,' said the master swineherd, 'I will tell you all. Laertes is still alive, but every day he prays to Zeus that death may visit his house and release the spirit from his flesh. For he grieves inconsolably for his lost son and for that wise and gentle lady, his wife, whose death was the heaviest blow he has suffered, and left him an old man before his time. As for her, it was pining for her glorious son that brought her to the grave – a tragic death. I hope no one whom I love or who has been kind to me here in Ithaca meets such an end. As long as the unhappy lady was still alive, I always liked to ask after her and hear the news, for it was she who brought me up, together with her daughter, the lovely Ctimene, her youngest child. Yes, we were brought up together and her mother treated me almost as her daughter's equal.

'But when we two young things had reached our youthful prime, that happy time, they married her off to someone in Same – and what a price he paid them! As for me, her mother fitted me out in a fine cloak and tunic, with a new pair of sandals for my feet, and sent me off to work on the farm. But she always kept a tender place for me in her heart. Ah, I have long missed kindness such as hers! The blessed gods have prospered the work which is my livelihood and brings me in enough to eat and drink and allows me to give to the deserving. But from my mistress the wise Penelope there's never a gentle word to be had, nor a kind deed either, ever since the house fell on evil days with the coming of these vicious men. Yet servants do miss it dreadfully when they can't talk face to face with their mistress, and find out all the news, and have some food and a drink, and take back a little something to the farm as well. That is the sort of thing that always warms a servant's heart.'

'You surprise me,' said Odysseus. 'You must have been quite a little fellow, Eumaeus, when you were exiled all that way from your parents and your home! Won't you tell me what happened? Was it sacked, the city of broad streets where your mother and father lived; or did some band of raiders capture you as you tended your sheep and cattle alone and bring you by ship to the palace here and get a good price from your master?'

'My friend,' replied that prince among swineherds, 'you have asked for my story. Very well, listen quietly and enjoy the tale as you sit there and drink your wine. These nights are very long. They give one time to listen and be entertained as well as time to sleep. Nor is there any need for you to go early to bed. Too much sleep is a bad thing. But any of the others, if the spirit moves them, can go and sleep. For at the first sign of Dawn they must have breakfast and go out with our master's pigs. Meanwhile let us two have the satisfaction of sharing our unhappy memories over our food and wine here in the hut. For a man who has been through bitter experiences and travelled far enjoys even his sufferings after a time.

'You were asking me about my story. Let me tell you. There is an island called Syrie – you may have heard the name – out beyond Ortygie, where the Sun turns in his course. It's not so very thickly populated, though the rich land is excellent for cattle and sheep and yields fine crops of grapes and grain. Famine is unknown there and no dreadful diseases plague the people, but as the men and women of each generation grow old in their homes, Apollo of the Silver Bow or Artemis comes and strikes them with kindly arrows and ends their life. There are two cities there, each owning half the island. My father, Ctesius son of Ormenus, a man like a god, was king of both.

'One day the island was visited by a party of Phoenicians – famous sailors, but greedy rogues – with a whole cargo of trinkets in their black ship. Now there happened to be a woman of their race in my father's house, a tall, handsome woman, and clever too with her hands. But the cunning Phoenicians soon turned her head. One of them began it by making approaches to her when she was washing clothes, and seducing her by the ship's hull – and there's nothing like love to lead a woman astray, even a virtuous one. He asked her who she was and where she came from. She replied by pointing out to him the high roof of my father's house, and said: "I come from Sidon, where they deal in bronze. I am the daughter of Arybas, a very rich man. But some Taphian pirates carried me off as I was coming in from the country, brought me here to this man's house and sold me. He gave a good price for me, too!"

'"And how would you like," said her seducer, "to come home again with us and to see the high roof of your *own* house, and your parents in it? For I tell you they are still alive and are known to be well-to-do."

'"I would jump at the chance," said the woman, "if you sailors would swear to bring me safe and sound to my home."

'They swore to do what she asked, and solemnly took their oaths. But the woman went on, "Keep your mouths shut, and don't let any of your party say a word to me if you meet me in the street or at the well. Someone might go to the house and tell the old man, who would lock me up if his suspicions were roused, and do his best to kill you all. No; keep the idea to yourselves, and collect your homeward cargo as fast as you can. When all the stores are on board the ship, quickly send word to me up at the house. I will bring away some gold with me – all I can lay my hands on. And there's something else I would gladly give you in payment for my passage. I am nurse there in the house to my noble master's child – a clever little chap, who trots along at my side when we go out. I'm quite ready to bring him on board with me, and he'd fetch you a fortune in any foreign port where you sold him." With this the woman left them and returned to our fine palace.

'The traders stayed with us for a whole year, during which they had acquired by barter a vast store of goods. When the hollow ship was full and ready to sail, they sent up a messenger to pass the word to the woman. The cunning rascal came to my father's house with a golden necklace strung with amber beads. While my mother and the women-servants in the house were handling the necklace and agreeing a price and all eyes were fixed upon it, he quickly nodded to my nurse, and, after this signal, slipped away to the ship. The woman took me by the hand and led me out through the door, and there in the entrance-hall she noticed the wine-cups and tables that had been used for a banquet given to my father's counsellors. The guests themselves had gone out to attend a public debate in the meeting-place. So she quickly hid three goblets in her bosom and carried them off, and in my childish innocence I followed her.

'The sun set, and all the ways grew dark. We ran down to the great harbour where the fast Phoenician ship was lying. They put us on board at once, climbed in themselves and made for the open sea, with a following wind sent by Zeus. For six days and nights we sailed steadily on, but when Zeus brought the seventh day Artemis the Archeress struck the woman and she crashed headlong into the hold like a gannet diving into the sea. They threw her corpse overboard as carrion for the seals and fishes, and I was left alone in my misery. In due course the winds and currents drove us to Ithaca, where Laertes parted with some of his wealth to buy me. That is how I first came to set eyes on this land.'

'Eumaeus,' said Odysseus, the favourite of Zeus, 'the story of all your miseries has touched me deeply. But Zeus certainly sent you some good luck too, to set off against the bad, since after all these misadventures you came to the house of a kind master, who has obviously been careful to see that you have plenty to eat and drink; so that the life you live is a good one, whereas I have tramped through cities all over the world before arriving here.'

In this way they talked together, then went to sleep – but not for long, just a little while, for soon Dawn appeared, seated on her beautiful throne.

Now Telemachus had reached the coast of Ithaca, and his men were striking sail. Down came the mast, and they rowed the ship into the harbour, where they dropped anchor and made the hawsers fast. Then they jumped out on to the beach, prepared a meal, and mixed the sparkling wine. When they had finished eating and drinking, the sensible Telemachus gave them their instructions. 'Take the ship round to the city,' he said, 'while I pay a visit to the farms and the herdsman. This evening, when I've looked round my estate, I will come down to the city. And tomorrow morning I propose to reward you for coming on the voyage with a sumptuous feast of meat with sweet wine.'

'And where am I to go, dear child?' asked his godlike passenger, Theoclymenus. 'Which of your chieftains' homes shall I make for in this rugged land of yours? Or shall I go straight to your mother's and your own house?'

'In other circumstances,' answered the prudent Telemachus, 'I would invite you to go to our house, where there is no lack of hospitality. But that wouldn't be much help to you as things are, because you won't have me at your side and my mother wouldn't see you. She seldom shows herself to her Suitors in the hall, but keeps away from them and works at the loom in her room upstairs. However, there is a man you *could* go to, and I'll give you his name – Eurymachus, the distinguished son of a wise father, Polybus, who at the moment is my countrymen's idol. He is certainly the leading man there, as well as the keenest bidder for my mother's hand and for my father's rights. But as to that, Olympian Zeus in his heaven is the only one who knows whether or not he will bring the day of doom on them before it comes to weddings!'

As he spoke a bird flew by on his right. It was a hawk, Apollo's winged herald, holding a dove in its talons, from which it plucked out feathers that fluttered down to earth half-way between the ship and Telemachus himself. Theoclymenus beckoned him away from his men, seized his hand, and said: 'Telemachus, it was by a god's will that this bird flew past on your right. Directly I set eyes on it I knew it for a bird of omen. In all Ithaca there is no more royal house than yours. Yours is the power for all time.'

'My friend,' said thoughtful Telemachus, 'may what you say prove true! If it does, you will soon receive from me such friendship and generosity that anyone who meets you will call you a fortunate man.' Then he turned to his loyal friend Peiraeus and said: 'Peiraeus, son of Clytius, of all who joined me on this journey to Pylos you have always been the most ready to fall in with my wishes. Will you now take charge of this guest of ours and treat him with every kindness and attention in your own house till I come back?'

'Yes,' the great spearman Peiraeus replied. 'Even if you stay here a long time, Telemachus, I will look after him. He shall not lack hospitality.'

Peiraeus then went on board the ship and ordered the rest to embark and cast off the hawsers. They quickly got in and took their seats by the oars. Meanwhile Telemachus fastened his elegant sandals on his feet and picked up his powerful bronze-pointed spear from the ship's deck. The men untied the cables, thrust her off, and rowed for the city, as ordered by Telemachus, the dear son of godlike Odysseus. But Telemachus set out on foot and walked at a good pace till he reached the yard where his large droves of pigs were kept and where the swineherd slept among them, loyal heart, faithful servant of his masters.

# 16
# ODYSSEUS MEETS HIS SON

In the hut Odysseus and the worthy swineherd were now preparing their breakfast in the dawn light, after stirring up the fire, and sending the herdsmen off with the pigs to the pastures. As Telemachus approached the hut the baying dogs began wagging their tails, but they did not bark. Odysseus noticed them wagging their tails, and the sound of footsteps also came to his ears. He turned to Eumaeus with winged words: 'Eumaeus, you have a visitor: He must be a friend of yours or someone familiar here, for the dogs are fawning instead of barking. And I can hear his footsteps.'

The last words were not yet out of his mouth when his own son appeared in the doorway. Eumaeus jumped up in amazement and the bowls in which he had been busy mixing the sparkling wine tumbled out of his grasp. Running forward to meet his master, he kissed his forehead, his fine eyes, and both his hands, while the tears streamed down his cheeks. Like a fond father welcoming back his son after nine years abroad, his only son, the apple of his eye for whom he has sacrificed much, the admirable swineherd threw his arms round Telemachus the godlike youth and showered kisses on him as though he had just escaped from death.

'So you are back, Telemachus, light of my eyes!' he said in tears, and his words flew. 'And I thought I would never see you again, once you had sailed for Pylos! Come in, come in, dear child, and let me feast my eyes on the wanderer just home. We herdsmen see little of you here on the farm: you are always in the town. It seems as though you found it amusing to watch that pernicious gang of Suitors!'

'Just as you say, old friend,' said Telemachus. 'I came here because of you. I wanted to see you myself and find out from you whether my mother is still in the palace or whether she has married again and Odysseus' bed is empty and hung with dusty cobwebs.'

'Certainly she is still at home,' said the prince among swineherds. 'She has a patient heart, though her eyes are never free from tears as the slow nights and days pass sorrowfully by.'

As he spoke he took his bronze spear from him, and Telemachus crossed the stone threshold into the hut. At his entrance, Odysseus his father rose to give him his seat. But Telemachus from the other side of the room checked him with a gesture and said: 'Don't get up, stranger. Somewhere in our farm we'll find something to sit on; and here is the man to arrange it.'

So Odysseus sat down again, and the swineherd made a pile of green brushwood for Telemachus, with a fleece spread on top, and there Odysseus' dear son sat down. Eumaeus then put beside them platters of roast meat that had been left over from their meal of the previous day, and with eager hospitality piled baskets high with bread and mixed them some sweet wine in an olive-wood bowl. This done, he himself sat down opposite the godlike Odysseus, and they helped themselves to the good food in front of them. When they had satisfied their hunger and thirst, Telemachus turned to the worthy swineherd and said: 'Old friend, where does this guest of yours come from? Some ship's crew must have brought him here. How did it happen and who did they claim they were? I am quite sure he didn't walk to Ithaca.'

Then you, Eumaeus the swineherd, said in reply, 'My child, you shall have nothing but the truth from me. He claims to be a native of the large island of Crete and says he has tramped as an outcast through half the towns in the world – that seems to be his destiny. But quite recently he managed to escape from a Thesprotian ship and came to my farm here. I will hand him over to you, to deal with as you like, for he has decided to throw himself on your mercy.'

'Eumaeus, this is very mortifying to me,' the thoughtful

Telemachus replied. 'How can I possibly receive the stranger in my house? In the first place I myself am young and I do not yet have the physical strength to cope with anyone who might care to pick a quarrel with me. Then again my mother is in two minds whether to stay at home and keep house for me, out of respect for her husband's bed and public opinion, or whether to go away with that one of her Suitors who is most distinguished and most lavish with wedding presents. However, as the stranger has sought refuge in your home, I will give him a good cloak and tunic, a two-edged sword and sandals for his feet, and send him wherever he wishes to go. But if you want to, keep him here at the farm and look after him. I'll send you the clothes and all the food he'll need, so that he shan't be a burden to you and your men. But I should not like to permit him to come down there and meet the Suitors. Their reckless violence goes beyond all bounds, and if they insulted him, as I fear is likely, that would distress me deeply. But it is difficult for a man to do anything single-handed against a crowd, however strong he may be. They have an overwhelming advantage.'

'I feel sure, my friend,' the steadfast good Odysseus put in, 'that you will allow me to join in your discussion. My indignation has been deeply stirred by what I have learnt from you both of the outrageous conduct of these Suitors, which you, such a fine person, have had to endure. Tell me, do you take this lying down; or have the local people been turned into enemies of yours through hearing an oracle from the gods? Or have you been let down by your brothers, whom a man can normally rely on in a feud, however deadly it becomes? Ah, I wish I were as young as you or as young as I feel; or that I were the noble Odysseus' son, or Odysseus himself, back from his travels. I would be ready here and now to let anyone cut my head off, if I didn't go straight down to the palace of Laertes' heir Odysseus and kill the lot of them. And if they did overwhelm me by numbers, single-handed as I would be, I would rather die by the sword in my own house than witness the perpetual repetition of these outrages, the brutal treatment of visitors, men hauling the maids about for their foul purposes in that lovely house, wine running like water, and those villains gorging themselves, just for the sport of the thing, on and on, and not likely to get anywhere.'

'My friend,' said the thoughtful Telemachus, 'I will tell you the truth of the matter. The people as a whole have no grievance and no hostility towards me. Nor have I been let down by my brothers, whom a man can normally rely on in a feud, however deadly it becomes. For Zeus has made only sons the rule in our family. Laertes was the only son of Arceisius, and Odysseus of Laertes, while I was the only son who had been born to Odysseus when he left his home – and little joy he had of me. As a result, the house is infested by our enemies. Of all the island chieftains in Dulichium, in Same, and in wooded Zacynthus, and of all the princes here in rocky Ithaca, there is not one that isn't courting my mother and plundering my house. As for her, she cannot bring herself to the final step of rejecting all the Suitors or accepting one of them, though she hates the idea of remarrying. Meanwhile they are eating me out of house and home. And they'll soon destroy *me*. However, this is all in the lap of the gods.

'And now, old friend, will you go quickly down and tell my wise mother, Penelope, that she has me safely back from Pylos. I will wait here till you return after delivering your message – which is for her ears alone. Let none of the others hear it. There are plenty of them plotting to harm me.'

Then you, Eumaeus the swineherd, said in reply: 'Agreed; understood . . . A word to the wise! But give me clear instructions on this point – shall I make one journey of it and tell Laertes the news too? The poor man, for all his great grief for Odysseus, used till lately to keep an eye on the farm and eat and drink with the farmhands when the spirit moved him. But ever since you sailed for Pylos, they say that he has not so much as taken a bite or a drink, nor cast an eye over the work on the farm, but sits there moaning and groaning in his misery, with the flesh withering on his bones.'

'That can't be helped,' replied the prudent Telemachus. 'I'm sorry, but we can't do anything for my grandfather just now. If men could have anything for the asking my first wish would be for my *father*'s return. However, deliver your message and come straight back. Don't go wandering about the countryside after Laertes, but ask my mother to send her housekeeper, quickly and secretly. *She* could tell the old man.'

His words spurred on the swineherd, who picked up his sandals, bound them on his feet and set off for the town. His departure from the farm was not unobserved by Athene, who now approached in the guise of a tall, beautiful and accomplished woman, and, halting just outside the door of the hut, made herself visible to Odysseus, though Telemachus did not see her or become aware of her presence; it is by no means to everyone that the gods grant a clear sight of themselves. Only Odysseus and the dogs saw her, and the dogs did not bark but ran whimpering in panic to the other side of the farm. Athene gestured with her eyebrows; Odysseus saw this, and leaving the house went through the walled yard and presented himself before her. Athene spoke: 'Son of Laertes, favourite of Zeus, Odysseus of the nimble wits, speak now to Telemachus and hide nothing so that the pair of you can plot the downfall and death of the Suitors, and then make your way to the great town. I will not leave you alone for long: I am eager for the fight.'

As she spoke, Athene touched him with her golden wand. First she clothed him in a fresh cloak and tunic, then restored his stature and his youthful vigour. His bronze tan returned; his jaw filled out; and the beard grew dark on his chin. Her work done, Athene disappeared, and Odysseus went back into the hut. His son gave him a look of amazement, then withdrew his eyes for fear that he might be a god, and said with words that were winged: 'Stranger, you are not the same now as before. Your clothes are different; your complexion is changed. Surely you are one of the gods who live in the broad sky. Be gracious to us, and we will make you pleasing sacrifices and offerings of wrought gold. Have mercy on us.'

'I am no god,' said the patient, good Odysseus. 'Why do you take me for an immortal? But I *am* your father, on whose account you have endured so much sorrow and trouble and suffered persecution at men's hands.'

With that he kissed his son and the tears ran down his cheeks to the ground; till then he had kept a firm control on his feelings.

But Telemachus could not yet accept that it was his father, and said, 'You are not my father, you are not Odysseus; some divine power is playing me a trick to make my grief all the more bitter. No mortal man could do such a thing by design, though I know that any god who wished could easily make a man young or old. Only a moment ago you were an old man in shabby clothes, and now you look like one of the gods who live in the wide heavens.'

'Telemachus,' replied the resourceful Odysseus, 'you ought not to feel any excessive surprise at your father's home-coming, or be so taken aback. Be quite certain of this, no second Odysseus will return. No, I am the man, just as you see me, back in my own country in the twentieth year of misfortune and wandering. As for these changes in me, they are the work of the warrior goddess Athene, who can do anything, and make me look as she wishes, at one moment like a beggar and at the next like a young man finely dressed. It is easy for the gods in heaven to glorify or debase a man.'

Odysseus sat down, and Telemachus flung his arms round his noble father's neck and burst into tears. And now a passionate longing for tears arose in them both and they cried aloud piercingly and more convulsively than birds of prey, vultures or crooked-clawed eagles, bereaved when villagers have robbed the nest of their unfledged young. So did these two let the piteous tears run streaming from their eyes. And sunset would have found them still weeping, if Telemachus had not suddenly asked his father a question. 'But, my dear father,' he said, 'what ship can have brought you to Ithaca at this time, and who were the men on board? It is obvious that you did not come on foot.'

'My son,' said the patient, noble Odysseus, 'I will tell you exactly how it was. The Phaeacians brought me here, those renowned sailors who provide any stranger who lands on their coasts with his passage home. Well, they brought me across the sea on one of their fast ships and landed me in Ithaca – I was asleep the whole time. They gave me splendid presents too, bronze and vast quantities of gold and woven cloth, all of which, with help from the gods, lie hidden in a cave. Finally, I came up here at Athene's prompting so that we could plan the destruction of our enemies. Now count and list them for me one by one, so that I may know exactly who and how many they are. Then I will turn my mind to deciding whether we two could take them on by ourselves or whether we should seek help.'

'Father,' the prudent Telemachus replied, 'I have always heard of your great reputation as a fighter in combat and tactician in counsel. But this time you speak of the impossible. I am overwhelmed! Two men could not possibly take on so many determined fighters. There are not just ten Suitors, or twenty, but many times more than that. I can tell you their strength here and now. From Dulichium there are fifty-two, the pick of its young men, with six serving-men. From Same there are twenty-four, and from Zacynthus twenty noblemen; from Ithaca itself a dozen of its best, and with them Medon the herald, and an inspired minstrel, besides two servants, expert carvers. If we meet them inside the palace in full force, I am afraid it may be you who pay a cruel and terrible price for the outrages you have come to avenge. So think hard about any ally you can find, who will fight heart and soul on our side.'

'I will tell you,' said the steadfast Odysseus. 'Listen carefully; and ask yourself whether Athene with Father Zeus will be help enough, or must I find some other ally.'

'The champions you mention are a powerful couple,' said the circumspect Telemachus. 'They may sit up there in the clouds, but they rule the whole world of men and gods.'

'And so,' said the patient, good Odysseus, 'when the scene is set in the palace for ordeal by battle between us and the Suitors, it will not be long before those two are in the thick of the fight. However, at the first sight of Dawn, you go home and rejoin these arrogant Suitors. Later, the swineherd will bring me down to the city disguised as a wretched old beggar. If I meet with insults in the house, you must steel your heart to my maltreatment, and even if they haul me out of the place by the feet or throw things at me, you will have to look on and bear it. Talk to them soothingly and ask them to give up their wild behaviour. They won't listen to you of course, but their day of judgement is at hand.

'And here is something else; remember it. When that clever

strategist, Athene, prompts me, I shall give you a nod. Directly you see the signal gather up the weapons of war that are in the hall and stow them away in a corner of a room upstairs – all of them – and when the Suitors miss them and question you, you must lull their suspicions with some plausible tale. You can say: "I rescued them from the smoke, since they look quite different from when Odysseus left them and sailed for Troy. The fire had got at them and damaged them badly. There's another reason too, a more serious one, which Zeus put in my mind – that you might start quarrelling after drinking too much and wound each other, thus spoiling your festivities and disgracing yourselves as Suitors. There's a force in iron that lures men on." But just for us two, leave a couple of swords and spears and two leather shields ready to hand, where we can make a dash and pick them up. Pallas Athene and Zeus the Wise Counsellor will lull the Suitors when the time comes.

'One more word; pay close attention. If you really are my son and have my blood in your veins, see that not a soul hears that Odysseus is back. Tell neither Laertes, nor the swineherd, nor any of the household staff, nor Penelope herself. You and I alone will discover what the attitude of the women is. And we might also sound out one or two of the men-servants, to find out which are loyal and respect us, and which have no concern for us and look down on you as you now are.'

'Father,' his noble son replied, 'you will come to know in due course what I'm made of, and I am certainly not stupid. But I feel that we would gain nothing by acting as you suggest and I urge you to think once more. You will waste a lot of time going round the various farms and sounding out the men one by one, while the Suitors are in our house blithely eating up our stores in their insolent way, stinting themselves of nothing. I certainly think you ought to find out which of the women-servants are guilty or innocent of disloyalty towards you; but, as to the men, I am against going round the farms to sound them out, and would like to postpone that till later, if it is really true that you have had some intimation of the will of Zeus who bears the aegis.'

*

So father and son discussed the situation, and the good ship that had brought Telemachus and his men from Pylos began to approach the harbour of Ithaca. When they reached its deep water they dragged her up on to the beach. Their eager squires carried off their equipment and removed the valuable gifts to Clytius' house. They then dispatched a messenger to Odysseus' palace to tell the wise Penelope that Telemachus had gone to the country and had ordered them to sail round to the city, so that the good Queen might not take alarm and start weeping. As it happened, this messenger and the worthy swineherd, conveying the same news to the lady, met on the way. But when they reached the royal palace, the messenger blurted out his news among all the women-servants: 'Your son is back, my Queen!' The swineherd, however, sought Penelope's own ear and told her everything her son had instructed him to say. His message faithfully delivered, he turned his back on the palace and its precincts and returned to his pigs.

To the Suitors the news came as a shock that cast a gloom over their spirits. They streamed out of the hall through the high-walled courtyard, and there in front of the gates they held a meeting. Eurymachus, son of Polybus, was the first to speak.

'My friends,' he said, 'Telemachus, in his arrogance, has certainly scored a success by safely bringing off this expedition that we swore would come to nothing. But come, let us launch the best available ship, collect a crew of oarsmen, and quickly send word to our friends out there that they must come home at once.'

He was still speaking when Amphinomus, turning round, caught sight of their ship from where he sat. She was riding in the deep harbour and he could see some men taking down the sails, others preparing to row her in. He gave a gleeful laugh and called out to the rest: 'No need to send a message now! They're back. Some god must have sent them word, or they themselves saw Telemachus' ship slip by and couldn't catch her.'

At this the whole company rose and went down to the beach. The crew made haste to drag the black ship up on to land, and eager squires carried their equipment off. The Suitors then went in a body to the place of assembly, where they allowed no one else, young or old, to join them. And there Antinous, Eupeithes' son, addressed them.

'Damnation take it! The gods have saved Telemachus from certain death. All day long we had a succession of scouts posted along the windy heights. We never slept ashore at night, but as soon as the sun set we went on board and stayed at sea till dawn in the hope of catching Telemachus and finishing him off. Meanwhile some god brought him home. Telemachus must not slip through our fingers, but here and now we must think of some way of destroying him. I feel sure that while he lives we shall never bring this business of ours to a satisfactory end. He knows how to think and scheme and the people no longer look on us with any favour at all. I suggest action, before he can call a general Assembly.

'Mark my words, he won't relax his efforts one bit, and it will be an angry man who rises up to denounce us and tell them all how we plotted his murder and then failed to catch him. They certainly won't applaud his recital of our misdeeds. In fact they may do us considerable harm and send us into exile among the foreigners abroad. We must forestall such a move and catch him either in the country well away from the town or on the road. We should then have his property and estates, which we would divide fairly between us, though we might let his mother and her new husband keep the house. But if you disapprove of my suggestion and would rather see him alive and in possession of all his inheritance, I suggest that we no longer meet here, living in luxury at his expense, but that each of us must court the Queen and make his bridal offers from his own house. She could then marry the man who offers the richest gifts and is her destined husband.'

A dead silence followed this speech. It was broken at last by Amphinomus, the famous son of Lord Nisus and grandson of Aretias. He was the leading spirit among the Suitors from the corn and grass lands of Dulichium. Penelope found his conversation especially agreeable, because he was a man of principle. He now began speaking, with their best interests at heart.

'My friends,' he said, '*I* am not willing to put Telemachus to death; it is a dreadful thing to spill the blood of princes. Before all else, let us learn the gods' will. If the oracles of almighty Zeus approve the deed, I will be his executioner myself and urge on the rest of you. But if the gods say no I advise you to hold your hand.' They agreed with what Amphinomus said, and rose straight away, went to Odysseus' palace and sat down on their polished chairs.

It was at this moment that a sudden idea came to Penelope – to confront her Suitors in all their brutal pride. She knew well enough that her son's murder had been plotted in the palace, for Medon the herald had heard of the plot and warned her. So now she gathered her ladies round her and went down to the hall. When she came near her Suitors the great lady drew a fold of her shining veil across her cheeks, took her stand by a pillar of the massive roof, and, turning on Antinous, lashed him with her tongue:

'Antinous, you're an arrogant and evil schemer – and they say that in judgement and eloquence you're the best man among your contemporaries in Ithaca! Now I know you're not. You covetous fool, how dare you plot against Telemachus' life, showing no compassion to suppliants, even though they are under Zeus' eye. It's sacrilege for someone who has received mercy to plot against someone in need of mercy. Or do you not know that your father once sought refuge here from the fury of the mob, when their blood was up because he had joined the Taphian pirates on a raid on the Thesprotians, who were at peace with us? They would have killed him, and had his heart out, and helped themselves to his fortune too, had not Odysseus come to his rescue and controlled their violence – Odysseus, at whose expense you are living free, whose wife you are courting, and whose son you propose to kill. You are causing me great anguish. I command you now to put an end to all this and make the rest obey you.'

Eurymachus, son of Polybus, answered the Queen. 'Penelope,' he said, 'wise daughter of Icarius, have no fear. Dismiss these terrors from your mind. The man does not exist, will not exist, and will never be born, who will lay violent hands on Telemachus your son, so long as I live and am on earth to see the light of day. I assure you, and time will prove it – such a man's black blood would soon be gushing round my spear. Didn't Odysseus, the sacker of cities, befriend me too and often take me on his knees to put a piece of roast meat in my fingers and lift the red wine to my mouth? That makes Telemachus my dearest friend on earth, and I assure him he need have no fear of death at the Suitors' hands. But there is no escape from what the gods decree.'

These encouraging words were on his lips, but death for Telemachus was in his heart. Penelope withdrew to her splendid apartment on the upper floor, and there she wept for Odysseus her beloved husband till bright-eyed Athene closed her eyes in sweet sleep.

That same evening the good swineherd returned to Odysseus and his son. They had killed a yearling pig and were preparing it for supper. Athene had come up to Odysseus, Laertes' son, and touched him with her wand, changing him once more into an old man in filthy clothes. She was afraid that the swineherd would recognize him if he saw him undisguised, and being unable to keep the secret would run down to tell Penelope the news.

It was Telemachus who greeted him: 'So here you are, my good Eumaeus! What news in the town? Are those proud Suitors back from their ambush? Or are they still out there watching for me on my way home?'

And you, Eumaeus the swineherd, said in reply: 'It wasn't my business to go down to the town and make inquiries about that; I was in too much of a hurry to deliver my message and get back here, and I had been joined on my way by a messenger whom your crew had sent running off to the palace. He was the first to give the news to your mother. But there's something that I *do* know, for I saw it with my own eyes. On my way back I had climbed up above the town as far as Hermes' Hill when I saw a ship coming into our harbour. She had a crowd of men on board and a whole armoury of shields and two-edged spears. I took it to be them, but I cannot say for certain.' When the great Telemachus heard this he glanced at his father with a smile which he was careful to hide from the swineherd.

They had now finished preparing the meal, so they sat down and thoroughly enjoyed their supper together. When their thirst and hunger were satisfied they thought of their beds and accepted the gift of sleep.

# 17

# ODYSSEUS GOES TO THE TOWN

As soon as Dawn appeared, fresh and rosy-fingered, noble Odysseus' dear son Telemachus was eager to set out for the city. He bound his elegant sandals on his feet, picked up his strong spear that so well fitted his grasp, and as he set out for the city, said to his swineherd, 'Old friend, I am going to the town now to show myself to my mother; I am sure she won't stop her dismal weeping and lamenting till she sees me in the flesh. So here are my instructions for you. Take our unfortunate visitor to the city and let him beg there for his meals. Anyone who wants to will give him a crust and a cup of water. I myself cannot possibly look after all and sundry: I have too many troubles on my mind. And if he is annoyed by this, so much the worse for him. I believe in plain speaking.'

'Friend,' the quick-witted Odysseus here put in, 'I myself have no wish to be left behind. A town is a better place than the country for a man to beg for food; people who want to will give to me. I am unsuited by my age to live on a farm at a master's beck and call. So go on your way; and presently this man will bring me along as you have told him to, when I have warmed myself at the fire and the sun gets hot. For these clothes of mine are terribly thin and I am afraid the morning frost might be too much for me. It's a long walk to the town, as you have told me.'

Telemachus now went off through the farm with rapid strides, planning vengeance on the Suitors. When he reached the stately palace he leant his spear against one of the tall pillars, then crossed the stone threshold and went in.

The first to see him was the nurse Eurycleia, who was busy spreading rugs over the ornate chairs. With tears in her eyes she ran up to meet him, and soon all the maids of the brave Odysseus were pressing round him and showering affectionate kisses on his head and shoulders. And now the wise Penelope came out from her room, looking like Artemis or golden Aphrodite, and dissolved in tears as she threw her arms round her son's neck and kissed his forehead and his fine eyes. 'You're back, Telemachus, light of my eyes!' she said between her sobs. 'And I thought I would never see you again after you had sailed for Pylos to find out about your dear father – so secretly, so much against my wishes. Come, tell me whether you saw him.'

'Mother,' the thoughtful Telemachus replied, 'do not bring me to tears or stir my emotions when I have just escaped from a violent death. But go upstairs to your room with your ladies, and when you have washed and changed into fresh clothes pray to all the gods, promising them the most perfect offerings if Zeus ever grants us a day of reckoning. I myself will go to the assembly-place to fetch a guest who accompanied me on my journey back. I sent him ahead of me to the town with my good crew and told Peiraeus to take him home and treat him with all care and respect till I came.'

To this Penelope made no reply, but went and bathed, changed into fresh clothes, and then vowed to make a perfect offering to all the gods if ever Zeus should grant her house a day of reckoning.

Telemachus strode across the hall and went out, carrying his spear, with two hunting hounds at his heels. Athene endowed him with such supernatural grace that all eyes were turned on him in admiration as he approached. The highborn Suitors gathered round him in a throng, with kindly speeches on their lips and evil brewing in their hearts. But he evaded them as they crowded round, and found a seat with Mentor, Antiphus and Halitherses, old friends of his father. As they were plying him with questions about his voyage, Peiraeus the famous spearman came up with his guest Theoclymenus, whom he had escorted through the streets to the assembly-place.

Telemachus, far from ignoring his guest, immediately rose to meet him, but it was Peiraeus who spoke first: 'Telemachus, do send some women, straightaway, to my house to collect the gifts Menelaus gave you.'

'No, Peiraeus,' the cautious Telemachus said, 'none of us can tell what is going to happen. If my lords the Suitors assassinate me in the palace and divide up my estate, I should like you or one of my friends here to keep and enjoy the treasures. On the other hand, if I succeed in sending the Suitors to their doom, then bring the gifts to my house and make us both happy.'

This settled, he led the way home for his travel-worn guest and brought him to the stately palace, where they threw down their cloaks on settles and chairs, stepped into the polished baths and bathed. When the maid-servants had finished bathing them and rubbing them with oil, they gave them tunics and threw warm cloaks round their shoulders, and the two left the baths and sat down on chairs. A maid came with water in a fine golden jug and poured it out over a silver basin for them to rinse their hands. She drew up a polished table and the faithful housekeeper brought some bread and set it by them, together with a choice of delicacies, helping them liberally to all she could offer.

Telemachus' mother sat opposite them by a pillar of the hall, reclining in an easy-chair and spinning the delicate thread on her distaff, while they helped themselves to the good food laid before them. When they had all satisfied their hunger and thirst the wise Penelope broke the silence, saying, 'Telemachus, I am going upstairs – I am going to lie down on my bed – my bed of sorrows watered by my tears ever since Odysseus went with the sons of Atreus to Ilium – you could not bring yourself to tell me before the proud Suitors come back to the house, whether you have heard anything about your father's return.'

'Very well, mother,' said Telemachus, 'I will tell you the truth. We went to Pylos and there visited King Nestor, the shepherd of his people, who received me in his great palace and showed me every hospitality. He might have been my father, and I his long-lost son just back from my travels, so kindly did he and his royal sons look after me. But of the brave Odysseus, alive or dead, he said he had not heard a single word from anyone on earth. However, he lent me a sturdy chariot and pair to take me on to the famous warrior Menelaus, Atreus' son. And there I saw Helen of Argos, for whose sake the Argives and the Trojans by a god's will suffered so much. Menelaus of the loud war-cry asked what had brought me to this pleasant land of Lacedaemon, and when I had explained the whole matter he cried:

'"How disgraceful! So the cowards want to creep into the brave man's bed? It is just as if a deer had put her two little unweaned fawns to sleep in a mighty lion's den and gone to range the high ridges and the grassy dales for pasture. Back comes the lion to his lair, and the two fawns meet a grisly fate – as will these Suitors at Odysseus' hands! Once, in the pleasant isle of Lesbos, I saw him stand up to Philomeleides in a wrestling-match and bring him down with a mighty throw which delighted all the Achaeans. By Father Zeus, Athene and Apollo, that's the Odysseus I should like to see these Suitors meet! A swift death and a sorry wedding there would be for all! But as to your appeal and the questions you asked me – I have no wish to deceive you or to put you off with evasive answers. On the contrary I shall pass on to you without concealment or reserve every word that I heard myself from the infallible lips of the Old Man of the Sea. He told me that he had seen your father in great distress on an island, in the Nymph Calypso's palace, where she keeps him captive; for without ship or crew to carry him so far across the sea, it is impossible for him to reach his home." That is all I found out from Atreus' son, the famous warrior Menelaus. This accomplished I left him. The immortal gods sent me a favourable wind and brought me quickly back to my beloved Ithaca.'

Penelope was deeply moved by what Telemachus told her. And now the godlike Theoclymenus joined in: 'Honourable lady, wife of Laertes' son Odysseus, Menelaus has no accurate information. But listen to me; I will give you a clear and truthful prophecy. I swear by Zeus before all other gods, and by the board of hospitality, and by the good Odysseus' hearth at which I stand, that Odysseus is actually in his own country at this moment, at rest or on the move, gathering information about these crimes, and scheming revenge on the Suitors – witness the omen which I saw as I sat on our good ship and revealed to Telemachus.'

'Sir,' said the prudent Penelope, 'may what you say prove true! If it does, you will soon receive from me such friendship and generosity that anyone who meets you will call you a fortunate man.'

While they were talking together inside Odysseus' palace, the Suitors, in their high and mighty way, were amusing themselves outside with throwing the discus and javelin in their usual place, the levelled terrace in front of Odysseus' palace. When supper-time arrived and the sheep returned from the fields round about in the charge of the usual drovers, Medon, who was their favourite herald and always attended their meals, came to summon them.

'Now that you young men have enjoyed your sports,' he said, 'come inside, so that we may get supper ready. There's much to be said for a meal at the right time.' The Suitors did as he requested, left their games and flocked into the stately palace, where they threw down their cloaks on the seats and chairs and prepared for a banquet by slaughtering some full-grown sheep and goats as well as several fatted hogs and a heifer from the herd.

Odysseus and the loyal swineherd were now preparing to come in from the country to the town. It was the master-herdsman who spoke first. 'Friend,' he said, 'I see you are still determined to go to the town today, as my master said you should. I myself would rather leave you here to look after the farm. But I respect and fear him. He might scold me later, and a rebuke from one's master can be very unpleasant. So now let us be on our way. The best part of the day is gone and you may well find it chilly towards evening.'

'Understood and agreed,' said Odysseus. 'A word to the wise! Let's make a start; and you must lead all the way. But do give me a staff to lean on, if you have one cut and ready; you say the path is very slippery.'

As he spoke he threw the strap of his poor, shabby knapsack over his shoulders, and Eumaeus gave him a staff to his liking.

Then the pair set out, leaving the dogs and herdsmen behind to look after the farm. In this way Eumaeus brought his master to the city, hobbling along with his staff and looking like a wretched old beggar in the miserable clothes he was wearing.

They walked on down a rocky path till they were near the city and there came to a solidly built clear-flowing fountain where the people of the town drew their water. It had been built by Ithacus, Neritus and Polyctor. A group of black poplars, flourishing on the moisture, encircled the spot. The cool stream came tumbling down from the rock overhead, and above the fountain an altar had been erected to the Nymphs, where all travellers made their offerings. Here they came across Melanthius son of Dolius, who with two drovers to help him was driving down some goats for the Suitors' table, the pick of all his herds. This man no sooner set eyes on them than he burst into a torrent of vulgar abuse, which roused Odysseus to anger.

'Ha!' the fellow cried. 'One villain leading another – a case of birds of a feather! Tell me, you miserable swineherd, where are you taking this dirty pig of yours, this nauseating beggar and plate-licker at the feast? Just the sort to stand scratching his back against the door-posts, begging for scraps, but never asking for swords and cauldrons.[1] Give him to me, to look after the folds, to muck out the pens and carry fodder to the kids, and he might thrive on whey and put some muscles on his thighs. But the fellow has got into bad ways, and work on the farm is the last thing he's looking for. He'd much rather fill his gluttonous belly by grovelling and begging round the town. You mark my words, and time will prove me right. If he goes to noble Odysseus' palace, a shower of footstools shied at his head by the men there will break in pieces on his ribs.'

With that he passed by, and as he did so the fool landed a kick on Odysseus' hip, failing, however, to push him off the path, so firm was his stance. Odysseus debated whether to leap at the fellow and kill him with his staff or to lift him by his middle and smash his head on the ground. In the end he managed

1. The traditional gifts that reputable visitors might ask for and expect to receive.

to control himself. It was the swineherd who looked Melanthius full in the face and rebuked him.

'Nymphs of the Fountain, Daughters of Zeus,' he cried, raising his hands in earnest prayer, 'if ever Odysseus made you a burnt-offering of the thighs of rams or kids wrapped up in their rich fat, grant me my wish that he himself may be brought back to us by some god. He'd soon cure you, Melanthius, of all the swaggering ways you have picked up since you took to loafing round the town while incompetent herdsmen ruin your flocks.'

'Well I'll be – ! What a lot of snarling from a vicious mongrel!' retorted the goatherd Melanthius. 'One of these days I'll pack him off from Ithaca in a black ship and sell him for a fortune. As for Telemachus, may Apollo with his silver bow shoot him down in the palace this very day, or the Suitors crush him, as surely as Odysseus' chance of returning home from abroad has gone for ever!'

With that he left them to pursue their way, while he himself went ahead and was soon at the King's house, where he went straight in and joined the Suitors, taking a seat opposite Eurymachus, who had a liking for him. The servants helped him to the roast, and the trusty housekeeper brought him some bread.

Odysseus and the good swineherd now arrived. They paused outside and the notes from a polished lyre came to their ears. For Phemius was just tuning up for a song. 'Eumaeus,' said Odysseus, taking the swineherd by the arm, 'this must surely be Odysseus' palace: it would be easy to pick it out at a glance from any number of houses. There are buildings beyond buildings; the courtyard wall with its coping is a fine piece of work and those folding doors are true defences. No one could storm it. I gather too that a large company is there for dinner: one can smell the roast, and someone is playing the lyre. The gods made music and banquets to go together.'

'All that must be obvious,' said Eumaeus, 'to someone as shrewd as you. But now let's consider our next move. Either you go into the palace first and approach the Suitors while I stay where I am; or, if you prefer it, you wait here and let me be the first to go in. But in that case don't be long, or they may see you here outside and throw something at you or drive you away. Do think about this.'

'Right. Agreed,' said the noble, long-suffering Odysseus. 'A word to the wise! You shall go in first while I stay here; for I am quite used to blows and missiles. I have been toughened by what I have suffered on the waves and on the battlefield. After all that, a bit more makes no difference. But if there is anything that a man can't conceal it is the craving of an accursed belly, the cause of so much trouble to men. It even prompts them to fit out great ships and sail the barren seas, bringing death and destruction to their enemies.'

As they stood talking, a dog lying there lifted his head and pricked up his ears. Argus was his name. Patient Odysseus himself had owned and bred him, though he had sailed for holy Ilium before he could reap the benefit. In years gone by the young huntsmen had often taken him out after wild goats, deer and hares. But now, in his owner's absence, he lay abandoned on the heaps of dung from the mules and cattle which lay in profusion at the gate, awaiting removal by Odysseus' servants as manure for his great estate. There, full of vermin, lay Argus the hound. But directly he became aware of Odysseus' presence, he wagged his tail and dropped his ears, though he lacked the strength now to come nearer to his master. Odysseus turned his eyes away, and, making sure Eumaeus did not notice, brushed away a tear, and said:

'Eumaeus, it is extraordinary to see a hound like this lying in the dung. He's a beauty, though I cannot really tell whether his looks were matched by his speed or whether he was just one of those dogs whom their masters feed at table and keep for show.'

Then you, Eumaeus the swineherd, said in reply: 'This dog did have a master, but it's all too plain that he died abroad. If he was now what he was in the heyday of his looks and form, as Odysseus left him when he sailed for Troy, you'd be astonished at his speed and power. No game that he gave chase to could escape him in the deepest depth of the forest. He was a marvel too at picking up the scent. But now he's in a bad way; his master has died far away from home and the women are too thoughtless to look after him. Servants, when their masters are no longer there to order them about, have little will to do their duties as they should. All-seeing Zeus takes half the good out of a man on the day he becomes a slave.'

With this Eumaeus left him, and, entering the stately palace, passed straight into the hall where the haughty Suitors were assembled. As for Argus, the black hand of Death descended on him the moment he caught sight of Odysseus – after twenty years.

The godlike Telemachus was the first to observe the swineherd coming through the palace, and beckoned to him at once to join him. Eumaeus looked about him and picked up a stool which stood there for the carver to sit on when carving meat for the Suitors at their banquets in the hall. This he brought and placed at Telemachus' table, opposite him, and sat down. A steward fetched a portion of meat, which he set before him, and helped him to bread from a basket.

Close on his heels Odysseus entered the buildings. He looked like some wretched old beggar leaning on a stick, his body covered with filthy rags. He sat down on the ash-wood threshold just inside the door, with his back against a pillar of cypress smoothed by some carpenter long ago and expertly trued to the line. Telemachus beckoned the swineherd to his side, and, selecting a whole loaf from the beautiful bowl of bread and as much meat as his cupped hands would hold, he said:

'Take this food and give it to the stranger. And tell him to go the rounds himself and beg from each of the Suitors in turn. For diffidence doesn't suit a person in need.' As instructed, the swineherd went up to Odysseus and spoke these winged words: 'Stranger, Telemachus gives you this and tells you to go the rounds and beg from each of the Suitors in turn. He says that diffidence doesn't suit a beggar.'

Resourceful Odysseus responded with these words: 'I pray to you, Lord Zeus, to make Telemachus a happy man and grant him all the wishes of his heart.' He then stretched out both hands to take the food, put it down in front of his feet on his shabby bag, and ate his meal while the minstrel sang in the hall. He had finished his supper just as the divine bard was coming to an end, and then the company began to fill the hall with uproar. Athene now appeared before Odysseus, Laertes' son, and urged him to go round collecting scraps from the Suitors and so learn to distinguish the good from the bad, though this did not mean that in the end she was to save a single one from destruction.

So Odysseus set off and began to beg from them one after the other, working from left to right and stretching out his hand to each like a man who has been a beggar all his life. They gave him food out of pity, and, surprised at his appearance, asked each other who he was and where he had come from. At this point the goatherd Melanthius called out: 'Suitors of our noble Queen, listen to what I can tell you about this stranger. I've seen him before. It was when the swineherd was bringing him down here. But I really don't know who he is and where he comes from.'

At once Antinous rounded on Eumaeus. 'How typical of our distinguished swineherd!' he cried. 'Why did you bring this fellow to town? Haven't we vagabonds enough already, loathsome beggars, plate-lickers at our feasts? Are you so dissatisfied with the numbers collected here to eat your master's food that you must ask this fellow as well?'

Then you, Eumaeus the swineherd, replied: 'Antinous, you may be nobly born but there's nothing noble in your speech. Who would of his own accord approach and invite a wandering stranger in unless he were a craftsman who worked for the whole community, a prophet, a physician, a carpenter, or even a divine minstrel who can give pleasure with his songs? For all the world over such guests as those are welcomed, whereas nobody would call a beggar in to eat up his food. But of all the Suitors you are always the hardest on Odysseus' servants, and especially on me. However, I care little for that as long as thoughtful Penelope and the godlike Telemachus are alive in the palace.'

'Enough now!' prudent Telemachus interposed. 'Don't bandy words with Antinous. It's always his way to rouse a man's passion with his evil tongue and egg the others on as well.' Then he rounded on Antinous with words that flew. 'Antinous, I appreciate your fatherly concern on my behalf when you tell me to order the stranger harshly out of the house. God forbid such a thing! Give him something yourself. I don't grudge it you; indeed I wish you would. Have no fear, either, of offending my mother or any of my noble father's servants by your charity. But there's no such idea in your head. You'd far sooner eat the food yourself than give it away!'

'What a speech, Telemachus!' retorted Antinous, 'and what a temper! If all the Suitors were to treat him as I shall, the house would not see him for three months.' As he spoke, he seized the stool that supported his smooth feet during meals, and brought it into view from under the table where it lay. All the rest gave something and filled the bag with bread and meat. It looked as if Odysseus might now regain his seat on the threshold without having to pay for his experiment with the Suitors. But he paused beside Antinous and addressed him directly.

'Give me something, my friend,' he said. 'You don't seem the meanest of these lords but the noblest here, since you look every inch a king. Good reason why you should give me a better portion than the rest – and I'd sing your praises the wide world over. Time was when I too was one of the lucky ones with a rich house to live in, and I have often given to such a vagrant as myself, no matter who he was or what his needs were. I had hundreds of servants and plenty of all that one needs to live in luxury and to be known as a rich man.

'But Zeus, son of Cronos – it must have been his will – wrecked my life when he sent me to Egypt with roving pirates, a long journey, to destroy me. I anchored my curved ships in the Nile. There I ordered my good men to stay by the ships on guard, while I sent out some scouts to reconnoitre from the heights. But these ran amuck and, carried away by their own violence, began to plunder some of the fine Egyptian farms, carrying off the women and children and killing the men. The hue and cry soon reached the city, and the townsfolk, roused by the alarm, poured out at dawn. The whole plain was filled with infantry and chariots and the glint of arms. Zeus the Thunderer struck abject panic into my party. Not a man had the spirit to stand and face the enemy, for we were threatened on all sides.

They ended by cutting down a large part of my force and carrying off the survivors to work for them as slaves. As for me, they handed me over to a friend they met to take me to Cyprus, a man called Dmetor son of Iasus, who rules the island by force. And it's from Cyprus that I came here in great distress, as you see.'

'What god,' exclaimed Antinous, 'has inflicted this plague on us to spoil our dinner? Stand out there in the middle and keep clear of my table, or you'll end up in the sort of Egypt and Cyprus you won't relish! The audacity and impudence of the beggar! He has only to pester each man in turn, and they give him food without a thought. They all have plenty before them, and nobody shows restraint or consideration when it comes to being generous with other people's possessions.'

Quick-witted Odysseus drew back and said: 'Well, well! So you haven't the brains to match your looks! You wouldn't give so much as a pinch of salt from your household store to a servant of your own, you who sit here at another man's table and can't bring yourself to take a bit of his bread and give it to me, though there's plenty there.'

This enraged Antinous still more. He gave him a black look and his words flew: 'I fancy you won't leave this hall in one piece after such an insolent speech.' And picking up a stool he threw it and struck Odysseus on the back under the right shoulder. But Odysseus stood firm as a rock and did not reel at the blow. He just shook his head in silence, filled with thoughts of revenge. Then he went back to the threshold, where he sat down, dropped his bulging bag, and addressed the Suitors:

'Listen to me, you lords who are courting the illustrious Queen, while I say what I feel. A knock or two, when a man is fighting for his own property, his oxen or white sheep, is nothing to cry about or resent. But this blow from Antinous was all because of my wretched belly, that cursed thing that is responsible for so many troubles of mankind. If there are any gods and avenging furies for beggars, I hope Antinous will be dead before his wedding day.'

'Sit quietly and eat, stranger,' Antinous, Eupeithes' son retorted, 'or take yourself somewhere else. Otherwise talk like that will end in our young men dragging you through the house by the leg or arm and tearing your skin to ribbons.'

But the rest of them were deeply shocked, and one arrogant youth would say to another: 'Antinous, you did wrong to strike the wretched vagrant. You're a doomed man if he turns out to be some god from heaven. And the gods do disguise themselves as strangers from abroad, and move from town to town in every shape, observing the deeds of the just and the unjust.'

That was the talk among the Suitors, but Antinous took no notice of what they said, and Telemachus, though the blow made him bitterly sorry for his father, let no tear from his eyes fall to the ground, but shook his head in silence, filled with thoughts of revenge. But when the wise Queen Penelope heard of the assault on the stranger in her palace she cried out with her maids around her: 'I hope the Archer Apollo strikes you as you struck him!' And the housekeeper Eurynome chimed in: 'Ah, if we could only have our wishes, there's not a man among them who'd see Dawn on her beautiful throne tomorrow.'

'Nurse dear,' the thoughtful Penelope went on, 'I hate the whole gang for the wicked plots they hatch, but Antinous especially is like a black spirit of destruction. An unfortunate stranger, driven by poverty, came wandering through the house begging. All the rest were generous and filled his bag; but Antinous threw a stool at his back and hit him on the right shoulder.'

While Penelope was speaking to her maids as she sat in her apartment, the noble Odysseus was eating his supper. Penelope now summoned her trusty swineherd and said: 'Go, my good Eumaeus, and ask the stranger to come here. I should like to welcome him and ask whether he has heard anything about my valiant husband or seen him with his own eyes. He has the look of a man who has travelled far.'

Then you, Eumaeus the swineherd, said in reply: 'My Queen, I only wish the young lords would be quiet. With the tales he can tell, the man would hold you spellbound. Three nights I had him, three days I kept him in my hut, for I was the first man he came across on escaping from his ship; but even so he couldn't finish the story of his misfortunes. Sitting in my home he held *me* spellbound. It was like fixing one's eyes on a minstrel who has been taught by the gods to sing words that bring delight to mortals, and everyone longs to hear him when he sings.

'He says he is an old family friend of Odysseus and lives in Crete, the home of the descendants of King Minos. Starting from there, like a rolling stone, and after many painful adventures, he has now arrived here; and he is positive that he has heard of Odysseus, that he's near at hand and alive, in the rich Thesprotian country, and bringing home a fortune.'

'Go now and call him,' said the thoughtful Penelope, 'so that he can tell me his story himself; and let these others sit outside or in the hall below and enjoy themselves, as they're in a cheerful mood. Their own wealth, their bread and mellow wine, lies untouched at home with no one but their servants to consume it, while they spend their whole time in and out of our house. They slaughter our oxen, our sheep and our fatted goats; they feast themselves and drink our sparkling wine, without a second thought. The truth is, much of our wealth is being squandered. There is nobody like Odysseus in charge to purge the house of this blight. Ah, if Odysseus could only come back to his own country! He and his son would soon pay them out for their crimes.'

As she finished, Telemachus gave a loud sneeze, and the startling noise echoed round the house. Penelope laughed, turned to Eumaeus and said in words that flew: 'Go and bring this stranger here to me. Didn't you notice that my son sneezed a blessing on all I had said? May this mean that death is inevitable for all the Suitors! Not a man can escape his doom. One more point, and don't forget it. If, when I hear him tell his own story, I consider he is telling nothing but the truth, I will give him a fine new cloak and tunic.'

With these instructions the swineherd left her, and approaching the stranger spoke these winged words. 'My friend,' he said, 'the wise Penelope, Telemachus' mother, summons you. Sorrow-stricken as she is, she is moved to ask you some questions about her husband. If she considers you are telling nothing but the truth, she will give you a cloak and tunic, which you need more than anything else: and then you can satisfy your stomach by begging for bread in the town, where anyone who wants to will give you food.'

'Eumaeus,' answered the much-enduring Odysseus, 'I should be glad to give Icarius' daughter, the wise Penelope, the whole truth. For I am well informed about Odysseus, whose misfortunes I have shared. But I am frightened of this crowd of hot-tempered Suitors, whose insolence and violent acts reach as high as the iron heavens. Just now when that fellow struck me a painful blow as I was walking harmlessly through the house, neither Telemachus nor anyone else lifted a finger to save me. So ask Penelope to wait in the hall and restrain her impatience till sunset, when she can question me about her husband's homecoming. Then let her give me a seat nearer the fire, for my clothes are mere rags, as you know, since it was you whom I first asked for help.'

When he heard what the other had to say, the swineherd went back. As soon as he crossed the threshold of her room Penelope exclaimed: 'Eumaeus! you haven't brought him? What does the wanderer mean by this? Is he afraid of someone in particular, or is there some other reason why he lingers timidly? A timid beggar is a bad beggar.'

'He talks good sense,' Eumaeus replied. 'Anyone who wanted to avoid being attacked by those insolent men would feel the same. He asks you to wait till sundown. That time would suit you better too, my Queen, as it will allow you to converse with the stranger in private.'

'The stranger is no fool,' the thoughtful Penelope answered, 'however matters turn out. In the whole world I don't believe there's another set of brutal and evil schemers like these.'

His message delivered, the worthy swineherd left her and rejoined the assembled Suitors where he at once sought out Telemachus and, holding his head close, whispered winged words in his ear so that the others could not hear him: 'Dear master, I am leaving presently to look after the pigs and farm, your livelihood and mine. It's for you to see to everything here. Look to your own safety first and take care that you don't come to harm. For plenty of these Achaeans harbour evil thoughts. May Zeus destroy them before they destroy us!'

'Very well, old friend,' said the prudent Telemachus. 'Go when you've had your supper, and in the morning come back with some good beasts for slaughter. I *will* see to everything here, I and the immortal gods.'

The swineherd sat down again on the polished settle and when he had satisfied his appetite and thirst went back to his pigs, leaving the courts and hall full of banqueters who, as the evening drew on, turned to the pleasures of singing and dancing.

# 18
# THE BEGGAR IN THE PALACE

There now appeared a common vagrant who used to beg in the town of Ithaca and was notorious for his insatiable greed and his ability to eat and drink all the time. He was a big fellow, yet in spite of appearances he had no stamina or muscle. Arnaeus was the name his lady mother had given him at his birth, but all the young men nicknamed him Irus,[1] as he ran errands for anyone who asked. This was the man who now came along, intent on chasing Odysseus from his own house. He began to abuse him, and his words flew:

'Get away from the porch, old man, or you'll find yourself dragged off by the foot. Can't you see they're all tipping me the wink to haul you out – though I'm reluctant to? Get up now, or you and I will soon come to blows.'

Odysseus of the nimble wits gave him a black look. 'What's got into you?' he replied, 'I'm not doing or saying anything to hurt you; I don't grudge what anyone may give you, however much it is. This threshold will hold us both and you shouldn't mind if people give me things since, I take it, you are a tramp like myself and we are both dependent on the gods for a living. Think twice before you challenge me; or once you have roused me, old as I am I'll dye your lips and breast with your own blood. That would also give me a quieter day tomorrow, for I don't think that you'd ever come back to this palace of Laertes' son Odysseus.'

At this the beggar Irus lost his temper. 'Well, I'll be – !' he cried. 'How glibly the swine talks, like an old hag at the oven!

1. Iris was the messenger of the gods in the *Iliad*.

But I've a nasty trick in store for him, a right and left that'll smash all the teeth from his jaws on to the ground, like a sow caught eating the crops.[1] Tuck up your clothes, and let all these gentlemen here see how we fight. How can you dare to match yourself against a younger man?'

In this way they lashed each other into a fury, there on the polished threshold in front of the high doors. The great Antinous, hearing them, laughed gleefully and called out to the rest of the Suitors: 'My friends, this beats everything. What a treat some god has laid on for us here in the palace. The stranger and Irus are challenging each other to a fight. Let's make a match of it, quick!'

They all jumped up laughing, and as they crowded round the ragged beggars, Antinous, Eupeithes' son, continued: 'Gentlemen, listen to me, I have a suggestion. We have some goats' paunches roasting there at the fire, which we stuffed with fat and blood and planned to have for supper. Whoever wins and proves himself the better man shall come up and take his pick of them. And not only that, he shall join us regularly at dinner, and we'll allow no other tramp to beg in this company.'

They all approved Antinous' idea, and the wily Odysseus now made a crafty suggestion. 'Friends,' he said, 'there's no way in which an old fellow broken down by hardships can take on a younger man. Yet this mischievous belly of mine eggs me on to take my thrashing. So now I ask you all to take an oath. No one must side with Irus: I don't want to lose to him through an unfair blow from one of you.'

At this they all took the oath he asked of them, and when they had sworn the full oath, the great Telemachus put in his word: 'Stranger, if you have the heart and pluck to match yourself against this man, you need not be afraid of any of these gentlemen. Whoever strikes you will have to face the rest. I am the host here; and the Lords Antinous and Eurymachus, good judges both, support me.'

They all approved his words, so Odysseus tucked up his rags

1. Ancient commentators refer to a law of Cyprus that any landowner who caught a pig damaging his crops was entitled to pull out its teeth.

round his loins and bared his fine massive thighs. His broad shoulders, and his chest and brawny arms were now revealed – Athene herself stood by and filled out the limbs of this shepherd of the people. As a result, all the Suitors were lost in amazement, and significant glances and comments were exchanged:

'Under those rags of his, what a thigh the old fellow has! Irus is going to be un-Irused. He was looking for trouble and he'll find it.'

Irus was badly shaken by these comments. But in spite of that the servants hitched up his clothes and dragged him forcibly to the front, though he was in such a state of panic that the flesh quivered on all his limbs. And now Antinous burst out with a tirade of abuse.

'You great ox! It would be better for you if you were dead or hadn't been born, if you're going to stand quaking there in mortal terror of an old man broken down by the hardships he's endured. I'll tell you this, and it will happen. If this fellow beats you and shows himself the better man, I'll throw you into a black ship and send you over to the mainland to King Echetus the Destroyer, who'll have your nose and ears off with his cruel knife and rip away your privy parts to give them as raw meat to the dogs.'

At these words Irus' limbs trembled all the more. However, they dragged him into the ring, and the pair raised their fists. The patient, good Odysseus considered carefully whether he should fell him with a mortal blow or knock him to the ground with a gentler punch. In the end he decided on the lighter blow, so that the Achaeans would not suspect him. Then they both drew themselves up. Irus aimed a blow at Odysseus' right shoulder, but Odysseus struck Irus' neck below the ear and smashed in the bones so that the red blood gushed up through his mouth and he fell down in the dust with a scream, grimacing and drumming on the earth with his feet. At this the noble Suitors threw up their hands and died of laughing. Odysseus seized Irus by the foot and dragged him out through the entrance across the courtyard to the portico gate. There he propped him against the courtyard wall, put his stick in his hand and said in words that flew: 'Sit there now and scare the pigs and dogs away.

You're a worthless fellow, so don't try to lord it over strangers and beggars, or something worse will happen to you.' Then he slung the strap of his worn and shabby knapsack over his shoulder and, returning to the threshold, sat down again.

The haughty Suitors flocked back into the hall laughing gleefully and congratulated Odysseus. 'Stranger,' they said, 'may Zeus and the other gods grant you your dearest wish and your heart's desire for having stopped that glutton from roaming about the land. Now we'll soon pack him off to the mainland, to King Echetus the Destroyer.'

The noble Odysseus was glad of their unconsciously prophetic word. Antinous now presented him with a large paunch stuffed with fat and blood, and Amphinomus picked out two loaves from a bowl, put them down beside him and drank to him from a golden cup. 'Your health, my ancient friend!' he said. 'You are having a hard time now; but here's to your future happiness!'

'Amphinomus,' the resourceful Odysseus answered him, 'you seem to be sensible, like your father, Nisus of Dulichium – I have heard of his great reputation as a good man and a rich one. You are his son, they say, and seem to be intelligent, so I am going to say something important to you. Listen and take it to heart.

'Of all the creatures that breathe and creep about on Mother Earth there is none so helpless as man. As long as the gods grant him prosperity and health he imagines he will never suffer misfortune in the future. Yet when the blessed gods bring him troubles he has no choice but to endure them with a patient heart. The reason is that the view we mortals take of this earthly life depends on what Zeus, the Father of gods and men, sends us day by day.

'There was a time when I was marked out as successful in my dealings with men, but I abandoned myself to a life of looting and violence, and committed many wicked crimes, under the delusion that my father and brothers would stand by me. Let that be a lesson to every man never to live a lawless life, but quietly to enjoy whatever the gods may give him. Yet what I see here are suitors plotting these outrages, wasting a man's property and treating his wife with disrespect – a man who will not be away much longer from his friends and his own country. In fact he is very near; and I hope that some power may guide you away to your own home and that you will not have to face him on the day he returns to his native land. Once he is under his own roof I have an idea that blood will be spilt before he and the Suitors are parted.'

As he finished, Odysseus made his libation and drank the mellow wine; then returned the cup into the young nobleman's hands. But Amphinomus went back through the hall with a heavy heart, shaking his head; for he was filled with a foreboding of disaster. Not that it saved him from his fate, for Athene had already marked him out to fall to a spear from Telemachus' hand. Meanwhile, he went back and sat down again on the chair he had just left.

It was now that Athene, goddess of the flashing eyes, put it into the head of Icarius' wise daughter Penelope to appear before the Suitors, with the idea of opening their hearts and enhancing her value in the eyes of her husband and her son. So with a forced laugh she said: 'Eurynome, my heart moves me, as it never has before, to show myself to my Suitors – much as I detest them. I should also like to have a word with my son for his own good and warn him not to spend too much time with these unruly Suitors, whose words are friendly but whose intentions are evil.'

'My child,' said the housekeeper Eurynome, 'everything you say is quite right. Go and speak frankly to your son; tell him what is in your mind. But first wash yourself and anoint your cheeks. You mustn't go like this, with your face stained with tears. It's a bad thing to be endlessly weeping, and your son is quite grown-up now – it was always your special prayer to the gods to see him with a beard.'

'Eurynome,' said the sagacious Penelope, 'I know your concern for me, but don't encourage me in this way to wash myself and anoint my cheeks. The gods of Olympus robbed me of my looks on the day my husband took ship and sailed away. However, tell Autonoe and Hippodameia to come here to attend me in the hall. I am not going to face that masculine company alone: modesty forbids.'

So the old woman went off through the house to take this message to the maids and send them to their mistress. The bright-eyed goddess Athene now had another idea. She shed sweet drowsiness on Penelope so that her whole body relaxed and she leant back and fell asleep on the couch where she was sitting. The great goddess then endowed her with immortal gifts to make the Achaeans marvel at her beauty. First she cleansed her fair cheeks with a divine ointment used by Aphrodite when she puts on her lovely crown to join the Graces in their charming dance. Then she made her taller and fuller in appearance, and her skin whiter than newly sawn ivory. When her work was done the goddess withdrew, and the white-armed maids came up from another part of the house, chattering. Penelope woke up, rubbed her cheeks with her hands and exclaimed: 'What a wonderful sleep, in spite of all my troubles! I wish holy Artemis would grant me a death as gentle as that this very moment, and save me from wasting my life in anguish and longing for my dear husband, who had all the virtues, and was the finest man in all Achaea.'

Then she left her bright room and went downstairs, not by herself, but with the two waiting-women. When she came near to her Suitors the great lady drew a fold of her shining veil across her cheeks and took her stand by a pillar of the massive roof, with a faithful maid on either side.

The Suitors went weak at the knees. Their hearts melted with desire, and every man among them voiced a prayer that he might sleep with her. But Penelope turned to her dear son. 'Telemachus,' she said, 'your sense and judgement aren't what they were. As a boy you used to have much greater shrewdness, but now that you are grown-up and have entered on manhood, and anyone from the outside world, seeing how tall and handsome you are, would take you for a rich man's son, you no longer show the same sense and judgement. Look what has just happened in this hall, how you allowed this visitor of ours to be so shamefully treated. What if our guest sitting quietly in our home were to suffer serious harm from such rough handling? It is on you that people would lay the blame and the disgrace.'

'Mother,' the sensible Telemachus replied, 'I don't resent your indignation at what happened. But I do note and understand everything they do, the good and the bad – I am not the child I was. But it is impossible for me always to take the sensible line. I am being harassed by these mischief-makers who surround me here: and there's no one to support me. However, this fight between the stranger and Irus did not go as the Suitors wished, and the stranger won. Ah, Father Zeus, Athene and Apollo, how I should love, this very day in our palace, to see these Suitors beaten men, scattered about in the courtyard and in our halls with their heads lolling on their shoulders and the strength knocked out of all their limbs, just like Irus sitting out there at the courtyard gate, his head lolling like a drunkard's and unable to stand up on his feet and find his way home to his own place – a broken man!'

These were the words that passed between them. Then Eurymachus said to Penelope: 'Daughter of Icarius, wise Penelope, if all the Achaeans in Ionian Argos could set eyes on you, even more Suitors would be feasting in your halls tomorrow, for in loveliness of face and form, and in wisdom, you are supreme among women.'

'Ah, Eurymachus,' the prudent Penelope replied, 'the gods destroyed my loveliness of face and form and my pre-eminence when the Argives embarked for Ilium and my husband Odysseus went with them. If he could return and devote himself to me, my good name would indeed be embellished and enhanced. But I am left to my misery: a power above has heaped so many troubles on my head. When he left this land of his, he gently took me by the wrist of my right hand and said: "Wife, I do not think all the Achaean soldiers will return from Troy unhurt. For they say the Trojans are good fighters too, both with javelin and bow, and as charioteers, who can tip the scales in an evenly matched battle more quickly than anything. So I cannot say whether the gods will let me come back or whether I shall fall there on Trojan soil. But I leave everything here in your charge. Look after my father and mother in the house as you do now, or with even greater care when I am gone. And when you see a beard on our boy's chin, marry whom you want to and leave your home." That is what he said; and now it is all coming true.

I see approaching me the night when I must accept a detestable union. It will be the end of me; Zeus has destroyed my happiness.

'Meanwhile here is something that is causing me the utmost distress. Yours is by no means the right and time-honoured way for rivals to conduct their suit for a lady of good family and a rich man's daughter! Such suitors bring in their own cattle and sheep to make a banquet for the lady's friends, and also give her valuable presents. They do not enjoy free meals at her expense.'

The noble, patient Odysseus was delighted at her words, because she was extorting gifts from her suitors and bewitching them by her persuasive words, while all the time her heart was set on something quite different.

It was Antinous, Eupeithes' son, who answered her. 'Daughter of Icarius, wise Penelope,' he said, 'by all means accept every gift that any of us may wish to bring you. It would be ungracious not to give, but we will not return to our own estates nor go anywhere else till you marry the best man among us.'

The others agreed and each sent off his squire to fetch a gift. For Antinous they brought a long embroidered robe of the most beautiful material on which were fixed a dozen golden brooches, each fitted with a pin with a curved sheath; and for Eurymachus a golden chain of exquisite workmanship strung with amber beads that gleamed like the sun. For Eurydamas his two squires brought a pair of ear-rings, with clusters of three drops glowing with beauty; and from the house of Prince Peisander, Polyctor's son, there came a squire with a necklace – a lovely piece of jewellery. Thus each of the young lords contributed his own valuable gift, and presently the great lady Penelope withdrew to her upper apartment escorted by her waiting-women, carrying the magnificent presents.

From then till dusk the Suitors gave themselves up to the pleasures of dancing and the delights of song. Darkness found them still revelling. They set up three braziers in the hall to give them light, heaped them with dry fire wood thoroughly seasoned and newly split, and thrust some burning brands into each pile. The maids of the long-suffering Odysseus took it in turns to feed the flames. But it was Odysseus himself, the favourite of Zeus, the master-strategist, who now spoke to them.

'Maids of Odysseus, your long-absent master, go to the room where your mistress the Queen is, sit with her and cheer her spirits, spinning wool with her or carding it with your fingers. Meanwhile, I will provide light for the company, and even if they wish to carry on till Dawn arrives on her throne they won't exhaust me. I don't tire easily.'

The girls laughed and exchanged glances. But Melantho of the pretty cheeks jeered at him outrageously. She was a daughter of Dolius, whom Penelope had reared and looked after as tenderly as her own child, giving her all the toys she could desire. But in spite of this the girl had no sympathy for Penelope's woes; she was in love with Eurymachus and had become his mistress. It was she who now spoke insultingly to Odysseus.

'You still here? You must be soft in the head not to go for your night's lodging to the smithy or some other doss-house, instead of coming here and airing your views so boldly and disrespectfully before all these gentlemen. The wine has fuddled your wits, or perhaps you talk such rubbish only because you are always like this. Has the beating you gave the beggar Irus gone to your head? Look out, or before long a better man than Irus will stand up to punch your head in with his great fists and send you packing covered in blood.'

'You bitch!' retorted the ready-witted Odysseus, giving her a black look. 'I shall go straight over and tell Telemachus what you said, so he can hack you to pieces on the spot.'

His words sent the women scuttling through the house, their knees trembling beneath them in alarm, for they were convinced he meant it. But Odysseus took his stand by the burning braziers, tending the lights and keeping an eye on them all, though his thoughts were busy elsewhere with schemes that were not doomed to come to nothing.

Athene meanwhile had no intention of allowing the insolent Suitors to abandon their caustic insults; she wished the anguish to bite deeper yet into the heart of Odysseus, Laertes' son. Eurymachus was the first to taunt the stranger and raise a laugh among his friends. 'Listen, fellow Suitors of our noble Queen!' he cried. 'Something in me prompts me to speak. This fellow's coming to Odysseus' palace is a godsend. At any rate it seems to me that the torchlight comes from the man's head; there's not the slightest vestige of hair on it.'

He then turned to Odysseus, the sacker of cities. 'Stranger,' he said, 'I wonder how you'd like to work for me if I hired you, at a proper wage of course, choosing stones for building walls and planting trees for timber on an outlying farm of mine? I would see that you had regular food and provide you with clothing and sandals. But you've got into bad ways, and work on a farm is the last thing you're looking for. You'd much rather fill your gluttonous belly by grovelling and begging round the town.'

'I only wish, Eurymachus,' replied the ready-witted Odysseus, 'that you and I could compete as labourers in the spring when the days are drawing out, in a hayfield, I with a curved reaping-hook and you with another, so that we could test each other at work, with nothing to eat till well after dusk and plenty of grass to cut. Or we might have a pair of oxen to drive, tawny great thoroughbreds, bursting with fodder, matched in age and strength, and champing with power, in a four-acre field with loam that yielded nicely to the ploughshare. You'd see then whether I could cut a furrow straight! Or I wish that Zeus would this very day stir up a war from somewhere, and that I had a shield and a couple of spears and a bronze helmet fitting round my temples. It would be out in the front line that you'd find me then, and you'd have no more quips to make at this paunch of mine. But you're just a braggart with the heart of a bully, who take yourself for a big man and a hero only because the people you meet are so few, and so undistinguished. Ah, if Odysseus could only return to his native land and come here, you'd soon find that doorway there, wide though it is, too narrow for you in your hurry to run away.'

Eurymachus' wrath boiled over. With a black look he rounded on Odysseus. 'You miserable creature,' he cried, 'I'll soon make you pay for talking with such barefaced impudence in front of this company. The wine must have got at your wits, or perhaps you talk such rubbish only because you are always like this. Has the beating you gave that beggar Irus gone to your head?' And as he spoke he seized a stool. But Odysseus, fearing his attack, ducked down at the knees of Amphinomus of Dulichium, and Eurymachus' missile struck the wine-steward on the right hand so that his jug dropped with a clang on the floor and he himself with a cry fell backwards in the dust.

The shadowy hall was at once filled with uproar. The Suitors looked at each other, saying, 'If only the vagabond had died somewhere else before he came here! Then he would never have caused such a commotion. Here we are, at blows about beggars, and our pleasure in this fine feast is going to be spoiled by this outburst of hooliganism.'

But now the great Telemachus spoke out: 'What's got into you? You are out of your senses. It is obvious you can't hold your food and wine. Some god must be stirring you up. Come now, you have dined well; I suggest you go home to bed when you are ready, though of course I am hustling no one out.'

At this they could only bite their lips and wonder that Telemachus should have the nerve to address them so. At last Amphinomus, the famous son of Aretias' son Lord Nisus, spoke up. 'My friends,' he said, 'when the right thing has been said, carping criticism and resentment are out of place. Let nobody maltreat this stranger or any of the servants of the noble Odysseus' household. Come, let a wine-steward fill each man's cup so that we can make offerings and go home to bed, leaving our visitor here in the palace to Telemachus' care. For after all it is to his house that he has come.'

Everyone welcomed his suggestions. Mulius, a squire from Dulichium in Amphinomus' retinue, mixed them a bowl of wine and then went the rounds and served them all. They poured out their offerings to the blessed gods before drinking up the mellow wine, and when they had made their libations and drunk all they wanted they dispersed for the night, each to his own home.

# 19
# EURYCLEIA RECOGNIZES ODYSSEUS

So noble Odysseus was left in the hall plotting the destruction of the Suitors with Athene's aid. Straightaway he spoke to Telemachus, and his words were winged.

'Telemachus, we must hide every single weapon and piece of armour. When the Suitors miss them and question you, you must lull their suspicions with some plausible tale. You can say: "I have rescued them from the smoke, since they look quite different from when Odysseus left them and sailed for Troy. The fire has got at them and damaged them badly. There's another reason too, a more serious one, which a god put in my mind – you might start quarrelling in your cups and wound each other, thus spoiling your festivities and disgracing yourselves as Suitors: there's a force in iron that lures men on." '

Acting on his father's orders, Telemachus called the nurse Eurycleia to his side and said: 'Nurse dear, I want you to keep the women shut up in their quarters till I have stowed away my father's fine arms in the store-room. In my father's absence I have allowed them to lie about, uncared for, tarnished by the smoke. I was still a child when he went away, but now I want to store them where the heat from the fire won't reach them.'

'My child,' his dear old nurse replied, 'I wish one day you *would* take the trouble to look after your house and protect all your possessions! But tell me, who is to go along with you and carry a light? The maids would have done it, but you won't allow them to come out.'

'This stranger will,' the thoughtful Telemachus replied. 'I keep no man idle who has eaten my bread, however far he may have journeyed.'

Without saying a word in reply, the old woman locked the doors leading from the fine hall. Odysseus and his splendid son now sprang up and began stowing away the helmets, the bossed shields and the pointed spears. Pallas Athene herself went in front, carrying a golden lamp, which shed a beautiful light. At this, Telemachus suddenly exclaimed, 'Father! This is a great marvel to behold! The walls of the hall, the beautiful alcoves, the pine-wood beams and the soaring pillars all seem to my eyes to be lit up by a blazing fire. One of the gods who inhabit the wide heaven must be present here.'

'Hush!' said the resourceful Odysseus. 'Keep your thoughts to yourself and ask no questions. This is the way of the gods who live on Olympus. Go to your bed now and leave me here to stir up the maids a little more, and your mother also. In her distress she is sure to question me about everything.'

So Telemachus went off through the hall to find his way by torchlight to the bedroom where he always slept. There he settled down to sleep till the coming of divine Dawn. The good Odysseus was left once more in the hall, plotting the destruction of the Suitors with Athene's help.

The wise Penelope now came down from her apartment, looking like Artemis or golden Aphrodite; and they drew up a chair for her in her usual place by the fire. It was adorned with curling inlays of ivory and silver, and was the work of a craftsman called Icmalius. To the framework itself he had attached a foot-rest, over which a large fleece was spread. Wise Penelope took her seat, and the white-armed maids, issuing from their quarters, began to clear away the remains of the meal, and the tables and cups from which the arrogant men had drunk. They also raked out the fire from the braziers on to the floor and heaped them high with more wood for light and warmth.

Melantho now renewed her abuse of Odysseus. 'Ha! Still here,' she cried, 'to plague us all night long, prowling around the house and ogling the women! Off with you, wretch, and be glad of the supper you had, or you'll find yourself pelted out of the house with lighted brands.'

Odysseus of the nimble wits turned on her with a black look.

'What's got into you, woman?' he said. 'Why attack me with such spite? Is it because I'm dirty and dressed in rags and go round the country begging? But I have no choice; this is how it is for all beggars and vagrants. There was a time when I too was one of the lucky ones with a rich house to live in, and I've often given alms to such a vagrant as myself, no matter who he was or what his needs were. I had hundreds of servants and plenty of all one needs to live in luxury and be counted rich. But Zeus – it must have been his will – wrecked my life. So be careful, my girl, or one day you may lose the fine position that puts you above the other maids. Your mistress may turn against you in anger or Odysseus may come back. There's still a chance of that; and, if he's really dead and gone for ever, he has a son by the grace of Apollo as good as himself; he's of an age when no bad behaviour in the palace of any of you women escapes his notice.'

Wise Penelope, who had listened, rounded on the maid with a rebuke. 'You may be sure, you bold creature, you shameless bitch, that I am not unaware of your disgraceful behaviour and you shall pay dearly for it. For you knew perfectly well – you heard me say so myself – that in my ever-present distress I meant to question this stranger here in my house for any news he might have of my husband.' And turning to Eurynome, the housekeeper, she said: 'Bring a chair here, with a rug on it, for my guest to sit on, so that he and I can talk to one another. There are questions I want to ask him.'

Eurynome hurried off and came back with a polished chair on which she spread a rug. Here the noble and stalwart Odysseus sat down, and thoughtful Penelope spoke first. 'Stranger, the first question I will ask you is: who are you and where do you come from? What is your city and who are your parents?'

'My lady[1],' answered the resourceful Odysseus, 'there is not a man in the wide world who could find fault with you. For your fame has reached broad heaven itself, like that of some illustrious king, ruling a populous and mighty country with the fear of the gods in his heart, and upholding justice. As a result

1. The Greek word *gyne* can mean 'wife' or 'lady'.

of his good leadership the dark soil yields its wheat and barley, the trees are laden with ripe fruit, the sheep never fail to bear their lambs, nor the sea to provide its fish; and his people prosper under him. So now that you have me in your house, ask me any other questions, but do not inquire about my ancestry and my country, or you will bring fresh sorrow to my heart by making me recall the past. For I am a man of many sorrows. Yet there is no necessity for me to sit sobbing and sighing in someone else's house. Unremitting grief is tiresome and I'm afraid some of your maids here or you yourself might lose patience with me and conclude that it was the wine that had gone to my head and released this flood of tears.'

'Sir,' said Penelope, 'my loveliness of face and form and my pre-eminence the gods destroyed when the Argives embarked for Ilium and my husband Odysseus went with them. If he could return and devote himself to me, my good name might indeed be embellished and enhanced. But I am left to my misery: the powers above have heaped so many troubles on my head. For of all the island chieftains who rule in Dulichium, in Same and in wooded Zacynthus, or who live here in our own sunny Ithaca, there is not one who is not forcing his unwelcome suit upon me and plundering my house. As a result I neglect my guests, I neglect the suppliants at my door, and even the messengers that come on public business. I eat my heart out in longing for Odysseus. Meanwhile they are pressing me to name my wedding-day and I have to devise tricks to deceive them.

'First a god gave me the inspiration to set up a great web on my loom here and begin weaving a large and delicate piece of work, saying to my suitors: "My lords, my Suitors, now that noble Odysseus is dead, restrain your ardour, do not urge on this marriage till I have done this work, so that the threads I have spun may not be altogether wasted. It is a shroud for Lord Laertes. When he succumbs to the dread hand of remorseless Death that stretches all men out at last, I must not risk the scandal there would be among my countrywomen here if one who had amassed such wealth were laid to rest without a shroud."

'That is what I said, and they magnanimously consented. So

by day I used to weave the great web, but every night I had torches set beside it and undid the work. For three years I took them in by this stratagem. A fourth began and the seasons were slipping by, when through the connivance of my shameless and irresponsible maids they caught me at my task. They reproached me angrily, and I was forced reluctantly to finish the work. And now I can neither evade marriage with one of them nor think of any means of escape. My parents are pressing me to marry and my son is exasperated at the drain on our estate. He realizes what is happening, being a man by now and well able to look after the house – the sort of man on whom Zeus showers glory. But do give me an account of your family, for you certainly did not spring from a tree or a rock like the one in tales of long ago.'

'Honoured wife of Laertes' son Odysseus,' answered the inventive Odysseus, 'will you never stop asking me about my ancestry? Very well, I will tell you. Yet you will be making me more miserable than I already am – as is only to be expected when a man has spent as long a time as I have away from home, wandering through the world from town to town – a miserable existence. However, here is my tale and an answer to all your questions.

'Out in the wine-dark sea there lies a land called Crete, a rich and lovely sea-girt land, densely peopled, with ninety cities and several different languages. First there are the Achaeans; then the genuine Cretans, proud of their native stock; next the Cydonians; the Dorians, with their three clans; and finally the noble Pelasgians. One of the ninety towns is a great city called Cnossus, and there King Minos ruled and every nine years conversed with mighty Zeus. He was the father of my father, the great Deucalion, who had two sons, myself and Prince Idomeneus. Now Idomeneus had gone in his beaked ships to Ilium with the sons of Atreus; so it fell to me, the younger son, Aethon by name, and not so good a man as my elder brother, to meet Odysseus and exchange the gifts of friendship. He had been driven to Crete by a gale which had blown him off his course at Cape Malea when bound for Troy. He put in at Amnisus, where the cave of Eileithyie is – a difficult harbour to make – only just escaping from the storm.

'The first thing he did was to go up to the town and ask for Idomeneus, whom he described as a dear and honoured friend. But nine or ten days had already gone by since Idomeneus had sailed for Ilium in his beaked ships. So I took Odysseus to the palace and made him warmly welcome. Our wealth enabled me to entertain him lavishly; and as for his comrades who were with him, by drawing on the public store I provided them with grain and sparkling wine and all the cattle to slaughter they could want. These fine Achaeans stayed with me for twelve days, cooped up by that northerly gale stirred up by some hostile god, and so strong that even on land it was not possible to keep one's feet. But on the thirteenth the wind dropped and they put out to sea.'

He made all these lies sound so convincing that, as she listened, the tears poured from Penelope's eyes and drenched her cheeks. As the snow that the West Wind has brought melts on the mountain-tops when the East Wind thaws it, and, melting, makes the rivers run in spate, so did the tears she shed drench her fair cheeks as she wept for the husband who was sitting at her side. But though Odysseus' heart was wrung by his wife's distress, his eyes, as if made of horn or iron, remained steady between their lids, so guilefully did he repress his tears.

When Penelope had wept to her heart's content she said in answer, 'Now, stranger, I mean to test you and find out whether you really entertained my husband and his godlike company in your palace as you say. Tell me what sort of clothes he was wearing and what he looked like; and describe the men who were with him.'

'My lady,' replied the resourceful Odysseus, 'it is difficult for me to speak after parting so long ago; and it is twenty years since he left my country. However, I'll give you the picture of him that I have in my mind's eye. Noble Odysseus wore a thick, double, purple cloak, displaying a golden brooch with a pair of sheaths into which the pins fitted. There was a device on the face of it: a hound holding down a dappled fawn in his forepaws and ripping it as it scrabbled. Everyone admired the workmanship, the hound ripping and throttling the fawn, the fawn scrabbling with his feet in his efforts to escape – and the whole thing done in gold. I noticed his tunic too. It gleamed on his body like the skin of a dried onion, it was so smooth; and it shone like the Sun. I tell you, all the women were fascinated by it.

'I cannot say whether Odysseus wore these clothes at home, or whether they had been given him by one of his friends when he embarked, or by some acquaintance he visited. For Odysseus had friends everywhere; few Achaeans were like him. I myself gave him a bronze sword, a fine purple mantle, and a tunic with a fringe, and I saw him off with all honours in his well-found ship. And here's another thing. He had a squire in his retinue who was a little older than himself. I'll tell you what he looked like too. He was round in the shoulders and had a dark complexion and curly hair. Eurybates was his name, and Odysseus thought more of him than of anyone else in his company, for the squire saw eye to eye with his leader.'

Odysseus' descriptions made Penelope even more disposed to weep, recognizing, as she did, the infallible signs that he had disclosed. She found relief in tears once more, then turned to him and said: 'Friend, I pitied you before; but now you shall be a dear and honoured guest in my house. For it was I who gave him those clothes, just as you describe them; I who took them from our store-room; I who folded them and pinned on the bright brooch as an ornament for him. And now I shall never welcome him home to the land he loved so well. It was an evil day when Odysseus sailed in his hollow ship to that city, evil Ilium, which I loathe to name.'

'My lady, honoured wife of Laertes' son Odysseus,' replied the subtle Odysseus, 'do not ravage those fair cheeks any more nor wring your heart by weeping for your husband. Not that I would blame you. Any woman mourns when she loses her husband with whom she makes love and whose children she has borne, even though he is a lesser man than Odysseus, whom people speak about as if he were a god. But dry your tears now and hear what I have to say. I am speaking the truth and am holding nothing back when I tell you that I have news of Odysseus' return, that he's alive and near, in the rich land of Thesprotia, and that he's bringing home a large fortune which he has solicited from the people there. But he has lost all his faithful companions and his hollow ship on the high seas. On his way from the island of Thrinacie, Zeus and the Sun-god were at odds with Odysseus because his men had killed the cattle of the Sun; and his whole crew were drowned in the tempestuous sea.

'But he himself clung to the keel of his ship and was thrown up on shore by the waves in the country of the Phaeacians, who are close to the gods. These people in the goodness of their hearts paid him divine honours, showered gifts upon him, and were anxious to see him safely home themselves. Indeed Odysseus would have been here long ago, had he not thought it the more profitable course to travel about in the pursuit of wealth – at accumulating wealth he is unsurpassed; in fact not a man alive can rival him. I had all this from Pheidon, the Thesprotian King, who moreover swore in my presence over a drink-offering in his palace that a ship with a crew standing by was waiting on the beach to convey Odysseus to his own country. But Pheidon sent me off before him as a Thesprotian ship happened to be starting for the corn island of Dulichium. He even showed me what wealth Odysseus had amassed. The amount of treasure stored up for your lord there in the King's house would keep a man and his heirs to the tenth generation.

'Odysseus himself, Pheidon said, had gone to Dodona to find out the will of Zeus from the great oak-tree that is sacred to the god, how he should approach his own native land after so long an absence, openly or in disguise. So he is safe and will soon be back. Indeed, he is very close. His exile from his friends and country will be ended soon; and you shall have my oath as well. I swear first by Zeus, the best and greatest of the gods, and then by the great Odysseus' hearth which I have come to, that everything will happen as I foretell. This very month Odysseus will be here, between the waning of the old moon and the waxing of the new.'

'Friend,' the wise Penelope replied to this, 'may what you say prove true! If it does, you will soon receive from me such friendship and generosity that anyone who meets you will call you a fortunate man. But what my heart forebodes is this, and this is how it will be. Odysseus will not come home nor will you secure your passage from here; for we have no leaders of men like Odysseus (if ever there was such a man), to receive strangers with proper respect and send them on their way.

'But come, my maids, wash our guest and spread a bed for him, with mattress, blankets and glossy rugs, so that he may sleep warm till Dawn appears on her golden throne; and first thing in the morning you must give him a bath and rub him with oil so that he may feel ready to take his place beside Telemachus at breakfast in the hall. And if any one of those men plagues our guest out of spite, so much the worse for him. His chances of achieving his object here will vanish: he can rage and fume as he will. For how are you, stranger, to find out whether I really am more intelligent and resourceful than other women, if I leave you to sit down to meals ragged and dirty in my house? Man's life is short enough. The whole world prays that a heartless man who behaves heartlessly will suffer misfortune in his life, and derides him after his death; whereas when a man behaves kindly because his heart is kind, his reputation is spread far and wide by the guests he befriends, and he has no lack of people to sing his praises.'

'Honoured wife of Laertes' son Odysseus,' replied the astute Odysseus, 'I have a dislike of blankets and gleaming rugs ever since I sailed off in my long-oared ship and said farewell to the snow-capped hills of Crete. So I will lie just as I have often lain through sleepless nights in the past. For many's the night I've spent in some wretched place, waiting for Dawn on her bright throne. Nor does the prospect of having my feet washed appeal to me. Nor shall any of your maidservants here touch my feet, unless there is some old and trusty woman whose heart has suffered as much as mine. If there is such a one, I should not object to her touching my feet.'

To this the wise Penelope replied, 'My dear friend – as I cannot help calling the most understanding guest this house has ever welcomed from abroad, for you put everything so well and you talk with such understanding – I have just such a maid, an old woman of great discretion who faithfully nursed my unhappy husband and brought him up and took him in her arms the moment he was born. She will wash your feet, although she is rather frail. Come, my dear kind Eurycleia, get up and wash the feet of someone who is of the same age as your master. No doubt Odysseus' hands and feet are like our guest's by now, for people age quickly in misfortune.'

At this the old woman, covering her face with her hands, shed warm tears and gave voice to her grief: 'Alas, my child, how helpless I am to do anything for you! Zeus must indeed have hated you above all men, god-fearing though you were. For no one ever burnt for the Thunderer so many fat pieces from the thigh and such choice sacrifices as you used to offer him when you prayed that you might reach a comfortable old age and bring up a splendid son. Yet you are the only one to whom Zeus has denied a home-coming. Perhaps the women in a foreign land have mocked my master when he called at some great house, just as you, sir, have been mocked by all these bitches here. It was to avoid their insults and sneers that you refused to let them wash your feet. Well, my wise Penelope, daughter of Icarius, has given me the task, and I am most willing. I will bathe your feet, both for Penelope's sake and for your own, since your unhappiness has touched my heart. But hear me out: there's something else I want to say. We have had plenty of travel-weary strangers here before, but not one that I have seen has reminded me so strongly of Odysseus – your looks and your voice and your very feet – as you.'

'Old woman,' said the quick-witted Odysseus, 'that is what everyone says who has set eyes on us both, that we are remarkably alike, as you yourself so shrewdly observe.'

The old woman fetched the gleaming basin which she always used for washing the feet of guests, poured in plenty of cold water and added warm. Odysseus was sitting by the fire, but now he swung abruptly round to face the dark, for it had struck him suddenly that in touching him she might notice a certain scar he had, and his secret would be out. Eurycleia then came up to her master and began to wash him. At once she recognized the scar, the one Odysseus had received years before from the white tusk of a boar when on a visit to Autolycus and his sons. This nobleman, his mother's father, was the most accomplished thief and manipulator of oaths of his day. He owed his pre-eminence to the god Hermes himself, whose favour he sought by sacrificing lambs and kids in his honour, and in whom he secured a willing accomplice. He once went over to the rich island of Ithaca, where he found that his daughter had just given birth to a son. Eurycleia put the baby on its grandfather's knees as he finished supper, and said: 'Autolycus, think of a name to give your daughter's son: he has been much prayed for.'

By way of answer, Autolycus said: 'My son-in-law, my daughter, I will give you a name for him. I have been at odds with many men and women up and down this bounteous earth, so let his name, Odysseus, signify this. And when he has grown up and comes to his mother's old home at Parnassus, where I keep my worldly goods, I will give him a share of them and send him back a happy man.'

This led in due course to a visit from Odysseus, who went over to receive his grandfather's generous gifts. Autolycus and his sons greeted him with open arms and welcoming words, and his grandmother, Amphithee, threw her arms round his neck and kissed his forehead and both his fine eyes. Autolycus told his splendid young sons to make preparations for a banquet, and they readily obeyed. They quickly brought in a five-year-old bull, which they flayed and prepared by cutting up the carcass and deftly chopping it into small pieces. These they pierced with spits, and carefully roasted, and served out helpings. And so they banqueted for the rest of the day till sunset, all sharing alike and all contented with their share. When the Sun sank and darkness fell, they went to their beds to accept the gift of sleep.

As soon as Dawn appeared, fresh and rosy-fingered, Autolycus' sons, accompanied by the good Odysseus, set out for the chase with a pack of hounds. Climbing the steep and wooded heights of Parnassus, they soon reached the windswept glens of the mountain; and it was just as the Sun, fresh from the smooth-flowing, deep-running stream of Ocean, was touching the plough-lands with his first beams that the beaters reached a certain wooded hollow. Ahead of them ran the hounds, hot on a scent. Behind came Autolycus' sons, and with them the good Odysseus, close up on the pack and brandishing his long spear.

It was in this spot that a mighty boar had his lair, in a thicket so dense that when the winds blew moist not a breath could penetrate, the Sun's rays never entered, the rain never soaked right through, and the ground was deep in dead leaves.

As the hunters came near, urging on the hounds, the sound of the feet of men and hounds reached the boar. He emerged from his lair and with bristling back and eyes aflame faced the hunt. Odysseus was the first to act. Poising his long spear in his great hand, he rushed forward, eager to strike. But the boar was too quick and caught him above the knee, where he gave him a long flesh-wound with a cross lunge of his tusk, but failed to reach the bone. Odysseus' thrust went home as well. He struck him on the right shoulder, and the point of his bright spear transfixed the boar, who sank to earth with a grunt and there gave up his life. Autolycus' sons took charge of the carcass. They also skilfully bandaged the handsome, godlike Odysseus' wound, staunching the dark blood with an incantation; and before long they were back at their father's palace.

Under the care of Autolycus and his sons, Odysseus recovered from his wound and in due course, loaded with presents, was given a happy send-off to his own home in Ithaca. His father and his gentle mother were delighted to see him back. They asked him all about his adventures, and how he had come by his scar, and Odysseus gave them a full account of how in the course of the chase he had been gashed by a boar's tusk on the expedition to Parnassus with Autolycus' sons.

It was this scar that the old woman felt and recognized as her hand passed over it. Abruptly she let go of her master's foot, which made the metal ring as it dropped against the basin, upsetting it and spilling all the water on the floor. Delight and anguish swept through her heart together; her eyes were filled with tears; her voice stuck in her throat. She lifted her hand to Odysseus' chin and said, 'Of course! You are Odysseus, my dear child. And I never knew till my hands passed all over my master!'

With this she turned her eyes in Penelope's direction, wishing to let her know that her own husband was in the room. But Penelope was not able to meet her glance or pay any attention because Athene had distracted her. In the meantime Odysseus' right hand sought and gripped the old woman's throat, while with the other he pulled her closer to him.

'Nurse,' he said, 'do you want to ruin me, you who suckled me at your own breast? I am indeed home after twenty years of grief and trouble. But, since a god has revealed it to you, keep your mouth shut and let not a soul in the house learn the truth. Otherwise I tell you plainly – and you know I make no idle threats – that if the gods deliver these fine Suitors into my hands I won't spare you, though you're my own nurse, on the day when I put the rest of the maids in my palace to death.'

'My child,' the sensible Eurycleia replied, 'what a thing to say! You know well enough how staunch and unyielding my spirit is. I'll keep silent as a block of stone or iron. Remember this too, that if a god delivers these fine Suitors into your hands, I will go through all the women and pick out the disloyal from the innocent.'

'Why mention that?' said the resourceful Odysseus. 'There's no need. On my own account I will take note of each and mark them down. Meanwhile keep all this to yourself and leave the issue to the gods.'

At this the old woman went out of the hall to fetch water for his feet, as the whole basinful was spilt. When she had washed and rubbed them with olive-oil, Odysseus drew his stool up to the fire once more to get warm, and covered the scar with his rags.

It was wise Penelope who reopened their talk. 'My friend,' she said, 'I have one more thing to ask you – just a small matter, as it will soon be time for sweet sleep – at least for those whose grief allows them such a peaceful repose. But in my own case, heaven seems to have set no limit to my misery. By day my one relief is to weep and sigh as I go about my tasks and supervise the work of the maids in the house; but when night falls and brings sleep to everyone else, I lie on my bed, and anxious cares come thronging into my restless, grieving heart and give me no peace.

'You know how Pandareus' daughter, the tawny nightingale, perched in the dense foliage of the trees, makes her sweet music when the spring is young, and with many turns and trills pours out her full-throated song in sorrow for Itylus her beloved son, King Zethus' child, whom mistakenly she killed with her own hand. In the same way my inclination wavers this way and that. Am I to stay with my son and keep everything intact, my belongings, my servants, and this great high-roofed house of ours, in loyalty to my husband's bed and deference to public opinion? Or shall I go away now with the one of my Suitors here in the palace who is the most distinguished and the most generous with wedding presents? While my son was young and dependent it was out of the question for me to leave my husband's house and marry again. But now that he has grown up and entered on manhood, he implores me to leave the house, so concerned is he for his estate, which he sees the Achaean lords squandering.

'But enough. Listen to this dream of mine and interpret it. I keep a flock of twenty geese here. They come in from the pond to pick up their grain and I delight in watching them. In my dream I saw a great eagle with a crooked beak swoop down from the hills and break their necks, killing them all. There they lay in a heap on the floor while he soared up into the open sky. I wept and cried aloud, still in my dream, and beautifully dressed Achaean ladies gathering about me found me sobbing my heart out because the eagle had slaughtered my geese. But the bird came back. He perched on a jutting beam of the roof, and breaking into human speech he checked my tears. "Take heart," he said, "daughter of the far-famed Icarius. This is not a dream but a happy reality which you shall see fulfilled. The geese were your Suitors, and I that was the eagle am now your husband, home again and ready to inflict a gruesome fate on every man among them." At this point I awoke. I looked around me and there I saw the geese in the yard pecking their grain at the trough in their usual place.'

'Lady,' replied the subtle Odysseus, 'it's not possible to interpret this dream in any other way; you have learnt from Odysseus himself how he will make it come true. Clearly, the Suitors are all of them doomed: there is not one who will escape his destined death.'

'Dreams, my friend,' said the thoughtful Penelope, 'are

awkward and confusing things: not all that people see in them comes true. For there are two gates through which these insubstantial visions reach us; one is of horn and the other of ivory. Those that come through the carved ivory gate cheat us with empty promises that never see fulfilment; whereas those that issue from the gate of burnished horn inform the dreamer what will really happen. But I fear it was not from this source that my own strange dream came, much as I and my son would rejoice if it proved so.

'However, there is something else I want to tell you that will give you matter for thought. The hateful day is drawing very near which is to tear me from Odysseus' house. For I intend to propose a test using the very axes which he sometimes set up here at home, twelve in a row like the props under a new keel. Standing a good way off, he could shoot an arrow through them all.[1] And now I am going to make the Suitors compete in the same test of skill. Whoever proves the handiest at stringing the bow and shoots an arrow through each of the twelve axes, with that man I will go, bidding goodbye to this house that welcomed me as a bride, this lovely house so full of all good things, this home which even in my dreams I never shall forget.'

'Honoured wife of Laertes' son Odysseus,' the resourceful Odysseus answered, 'do not delay this contest in the palace, for the resourceful Odysseus himself will be here long before those fellows have finished their fumbling attempts to string the polished bow and shoot an arrow through the iron axes.'

'Ah, my friend,' said the wise Penelope, 'if you would only sit here at my side in the hall and give me the pleasure of your company my eyes would never close in drowsiness. But no one can do without sleep for ever. The gods have given it its allotted place in our daily lives, like everything else on this bounteous earth. So now I shall go upstairs to lie down on what has always been for me a bed of sorrows, watered by my perpetual tears,

1. It was long supposed that the metal axe-heads were partly buried in the ground and the test was to shoot through the holes where the handles went. But to do this the archer would have had to lie on the ground. It is now generally agreed that the targets were the rings on the end of the wooden handles by which the axes usually hung on the walls, as ornaments.

since the day when Odysseus sailed away to that city, evil Ilium, which I loathe to name. There I will lie down. And as for you, lie down somewhere in the house – spread bedding on the floor or let them make you a proper bed.'

So Penelope went up to her bright room, not alone but escorted by her ladies. But as soon as they were all upstairs, she wept for Odysseus, her beloved husband, till Athene shed sweet sleep on her eyelids.

# 20
# PRELUDE TO THE CRISIS

The good Odysseus now lay down to sleep in the portico. He spread an untanned oxhide on the floor and piled it up with plenty of fleeces, from sheep that the Suitors slaughtered daily; and Eurynome put a blanket over him when he had settled down. As he lay there wide awake brewing trouble for his rivals, a group of women, the Suitors' regular mistresses, came trooping out of the house giggling and joking among themselves. Odysseus' anger rose in him. For a long time he debated in his mind and heart what to do. Should he leap up and put them all to death; or should he let them spend this one last night in the arms of the arrogant Suitors? His heart growled within him as a bitch growls standing guard over her helpless pups, ready to fight when she sees a stranger. In the same way he growled inside himself in outrage at their wickedness. But, striking his chest, he called his heart to order and said: 'Patience, my heart! You had something far more ignominious than this to endure when the invincible Cyclops devoured your brave comrades. And yet you managed to hold out, till your cunning notion got you clear of the cave where you had thought your end had come.'

But though Odysseus was able by such self-rebuke to quell all mutiny in his heart and steel it to endure steadily, nevertheless he could not help twisting and turning just as a paunch stuffed with fat and blood is turned this way and that in the blaze of the roaring fire by a man who wants to get it quickly roasted. Twisting and turning, he pondered how, single-handed against such odds, he could get his hands on the shameless Suitors, when Athene descended from heaven and approached him in the form of a woman. She stood above his head and spoke to him: 'Sleepless again, Odysseus, most ill-fated of mortals? And why? This house is your home, your wife is inside, and so is your son, a youth whom any man might wish to have for a son.'

'Goddess,' replied Odysseus, the master-schemer, 'all that you say is true. And yet my heart is in some perplexity. How am I to get my hands on these shameless Suitors? I am alone, whereas they are always together in a crowd when they are here. And there's another and still more perplexing matter on my mind. If by Zeus' will and yours I kill them, where could I go to escape vengeance? I ask you to consider these problems.'

'You really are incorrigible!' exclaimed the bright-eyed goddess. 'Most people are content to put their trust in far inferior allies, mere mortals entirely devoid of cunning such as mine. But I who have never ceased to watch over you in all your adventures am a goddess. I will make my meaning plain: you and I could be surrounded by fifty companies of men-at-arms, all thirsting for our blood, but you would still drive away their cows and sheep. Come now, go to sleep. It is wearying to lie awake and keep watch the whole night through; and presently you'll rise above your troubles.' With which the lady goddess closed his eyes in sleep and returned to Olympus.

But no sooner had sleep come to Odysseus, resolving all his cares as it relaxed his limbs, than his faithful wife awoke, and sitting up in her soft bed gave way to tears; then, tired of weeping, she made a special prayer to Artemis: 'Artemis, Lady Goddess, Daughter of Zeus, O for an arrow from your bow to pierce my heart and take away my spirit in this very hour! Or let the Storm-wind snatch me up and carry me down the misty ways to drop me where the stream of Ocean circles back on itself, just as the daughters of Pandareus were carried away by the Demons of the Storm! The gods had killed their parents and left them orphaned in their home; but the divine Aphrodite nourished them on cheese, sweet honey and mellow wine; Hera made them beautiful and wise beyond all other women; chaste Artemis made them tall; and Athene taught them the skills to make beautiful things. But there came a day when the divine Aphrodite went to high Olympus to ask Zeus the Thunderer, who knows everything that is destined or not destined for mankind, to grant these girls a happy marriage, and on that very day the Storm-Fiends snatched them up and handed them over to the tender mercies of the Avenging Furies, the dreaded Erinyes. Gods of Olympus, annihilate me like that; or strike me dead, Artemis of the beautiful hair, so that I may sink underneath the hateful earth with Odysseus' image in my heart, rather than delight the heart of a lesser man.

'Grief is endurable when one weeps with an ache in the heart during the day but can at least sleep at night and forget everything, good and bad, once one's eyelids close. But all that a god sends me are bad dreams. This very night again I thought I saw Odysseus by me in bed, looking exactly as he looked when he sailed away with his army, and my heart leapt up, because I took it for no dream but reality.'

Close on her words golden-throned Dawn appeared. The noble Odysseus caught the sound of her weeping, and as he mused about it he imagined he could see her beside him with the light of recognition in her eyes. He took the blanket and sheepskins from his bed and put them on a chair, carried the oxhide out and laid it down, then lifted up his hands in prayer: 'O Father Zeus, if it is true that after all your persecution you gods willed to bring me home over dry land and sea to my own country, let someone in the palace where they are waking now utter a word of good omen for me and let some other sign outside the palace be given.'

That was his prayer. Far above the clouds Zeus the Counsellor heard it and thundered in the clear sky. Noble Odysseus rejoiced; and close upon this, from within the palace, there came the words he wanted, from a female slave in a building nearby, where the King's hand-mills stood. Twelve women had to toil away at these mills, grinding barley and wheat for nourishing bread. At the moment they had all ground their share and gone off to sleep, all except one not so vigorous as the rest, who had not yet finished her task. This woman stopped her mill now and uttered the words of omen for her master: 'Zeus, lord of gods and men, how loudly you thundered from a starry sky! And never a cloud in sight! You must have meant it as a sign for someone. Listen to poor me too, and let my wish come true. Let today's be the very last of the Suitors' sumptuous feasts in Odysseus' palace. My knees have grown weak from the heart-breaking drudgery of grinding corn for the Suitors. May this be their last dinner, say I.'

The woman's words of omen combined with the clap of thunder to make Odysseus a happy man. He felt that a crushing[1] revenge on the sinners was assured.

By this time the other maids were stirring in Odysseus' fine palace and making up the fire which never quite died down on the hearth. Telemachus got up from his bed looking like a young god, and put on his clothes. He slung his sharp sword from his shoulder, bound a beautiful pair of sandals on his glistening feet, picked up his great bronze-pointed spear, and made his way to the threshold of the hall, where he spoke to Eurycleia.

'Nurse dear,' he said, 'did you women attend properly to our visitor here, in the matter of food and bedding? Or did he sleep as best he could? That would be just like my mother, who for all her wisdom is far too ready to make much of a lesser man and send a better man packing.'

'Come, my child,' said the level-headed Eurycleia. 'I wish you wouldn't blame your mother when there is no cause. The man sat and drank as long as he wanted; as for food, he said he had no appetite for more. Your mother asked him; and when the time came to think of sleep, she told the servants to make him a proper bed. But like a poor fellow utterly down on his luck, he refused to sleep between blankets on a bed, and lay down instead on an undressed hide and some sheepskins in the portico. It was we who spread a blanket over him.'

That was her account. Telemachus set out from the hall, spear in hand, escorted by two hunting-dogs, and made his way to the assembly-place to join his fellow-countrymen. Meanwhile the daughter of Ops, Peisenor's son, the excellent Eurycleia, issued her orders to the maids.

'To work!' she called. 'You there, sweep and sprinkle the

1. This is an attempt to reproduce Homer's play on words between 'sinners' and 'grinding' or 'crushing'.

floors. Look sharp about it, and spread the purple coverings on those special chairs. And you, sponge all the tables down, and wash the wine-bowls and those precious two-handled cups. And you others, run off to the well and fetch us some water as quick as you can. We shall soon have the Suitors in the hall. They're coming early: today's a festival.'

The girls heard and obeyed. Twenty went off to draw water from the dark waters of the well, while the rest got on efficiently with the work indoors. The haughty men-servants next appeared, and chopped up the firewood in a neat and business-like manner. The maids soon came back from the well, and after them came the swineherd, who drove up three fatted hogs, the pick of all his beasts. He left the animals to root around for food in the spacious courtyard, and came up to Odysseus, whom he greeted affably: 'Well, friend, are the Suitors behaving better towards you, or do they still treat you like dirt?'

'Ah, Eumaeus,' answered the resourceful Odysseus, 'how I hope that the gods may some day pay the villains out for their insults and outrageous behaviour in another man's house! They don't feel a spark of shame.'

While the two were talking together, up came Melanthius the goatherd, driving in the choice goats from his flocks for the Suitors' table. There were two other herdsmen with him. They tethered the goats under the echoing portico, and Melanthius began baiting Odysseus once more: 'What, you still here? Still set on begging from the gentlemen and upsetting the whole house, rather than pack yourself off? I fancy that you and I will have to sample each other's fists before we say goodbye. I don't like your way of begging. And anyhow this house is not the only one where people dine.' To this crafty Odysseus made no reply. He merely shook his head in silence, though his heart brooded on revenge.

A third new arrival was the master-cowherd Philoetius, who was driving in a heifer and some fatted goats for the Suitors. These beasts had been brought over from the mainland by the ferrymen who take across any travellers who arrive. Philoetius carefully tethered his animals under the echoing portico, and came up to the swineherd and asked: 'Who is this stranger that has just come to our house? Who does he say his people are? Where is his family, and what is his native land? He seems down on his luck, and yet he has the bearing of a king. But even kings are allotted misery in their lives – as for mere wandering beggars, the gods completely submerge them.'

With this, he went up to Odysseus, proffered his hand and greeted him with winged words. 'A welcome to you, old friend! You are in deep trouble now; but here's to your future happiness! Father Zeus, you are the cruellest of gods. You have no compunction about dealing out misfortunes, misery and suffering to us men; yet it was you who caused us to be born. My friend, when I caught sight of you just now, the sweat broke out on me and my eyes are still filled with tears, because you bring Odysseus to my mind; for I reckon that he too, in just such rags as you have on, must be a wanderer on the face of the earth, if indeed he is alive and can see the sunshine still.

'If not, if he is dead and gone to Hades' Halls, then here's a sigh for Odysseus, that marvellous man who put me in charge of his cattle in the Cephallenian country when I was only a youth. And now those broad-browed herds of mine are too many to count, like ears of ripening corn; never could any mere mortal man's cattle breed better. But now these outsiders order me to bring them in, just for themselves to eat, not caring for his son's presence in the house or fearing the wrath of a god. Indeed the King has been away so long that nothing will content them now but to share out his goods. And what a quandary for me! I keep turning it over and over in my mind. With a son of his alive, it seems quite wrong for me to take myself and all my herds to foreign parts and strange people. Yet it's more difficult still to stay here and live a life of hardship tending cattle that have passed to other hands. I'd have run away long ago and found some great prince to protect me, since things have come to such a pass that I can't bear it; but I still have hopes of my unhappy master; I still think he may turn up from somewhere and drive these Suitors headlong through the palace.'

'Cowherd,' replied the quick-witted Odysseus, 'you are clearly an honourable and thoughtful man, and I can tell you are a man who can be trusted. So here's a piece of news for you which I vouch for with my solemn oath. I swear by Zeus before all other gods and by the hospitable table and hearth of the good Odysseus which I have reached, that before you leave Ithaca Odysseus will be back, and if you wish, you shall see with your own eyes the killing of these Suitors who play the part of master here.'

'Stranger,' said the cowherd in reply, 'may Zeus grant that all you say may happen! You'd soon know my mettle and what I can do with my right arm!' And Eumaeus added a prayer to all the gods that the wise Odysseus might come back home again.

While they were talking the Suitors were once again devising schemes for Telemachus' murder, when a bird of omen appeared on their left, a soaring eagle with a trembling dove in its talons. Amphinomus rose and said, 'Friends, our plot to kill Telemachus won't succeed. Let's think about the feast.' His suggestion pleased them and they adjourned to the noble Odysseus' palace, where they threw down their cloaks on seats and chairs and proceeded to slaughter the large sheep, the fatted goats and pigs, and a cow from the herd. They roasted and served the inner parts and mixed the wine in the bowls; the swineherd laid a cup for each man; the master-herdsman Philoetius served them with bread in fine dishes; Melanthius went round with the wine; and they helped themselves to the good food spread before them.

Telemachus with clever calculation chose for Odysseus a place by the stone threshold, just within the great hall, where he placed a battered stool for him and a diminutive table. He helped him to the entrails, poured him some wine in a golden cup, and said: 'Now sit and drink with the company. I will protect you from any insolence or blows from them. This is not an inn but the palace of Odysseus, which I inherited from him. And you Suitors, refrain from all provocation and violence, so that we may have no brawls or wrangling here.'

It amazed them that Telemachus should have the audacity to address them in this style. They all bit their lips, and the only comment came from Antinous, Eupeithes' son, who said: 'Well, sirs, offensive as it is, I suppose we must put up with this demand from Telemachus: his tone was certainly menacing. Zeus has obviously frustrated us, otherwise we would have silenced him here, shrill and vociferous though he is.' Antinous had his say. But Telemachus took not the slightest notice of him.

Meanwhile, in the town, the beasts destined for sacrifice on this holy day were being led by heralds through the streets; and the long-haired Achaean townsfolk were congregating in the shady grove of Apollo the Archer. But the party in the palace, after the outer flesh had been roasted, taken off the spits, and carved up, devoted themselves to the pleasures of the table. The serving-men gave Odysseus his fair share, which was the same as they got themselves, in accordance with the instructions of his son Telemachus. But Athene had no intention of letting the arrogant Suitors abandon their caustic insults: she wished the anguish to bite deeper yet into the heart of Laertes' son Odysseus.

They had among them a man with no sense of right and wrong, whose name was Ctesippus. He lived in Same, and he too, confident in his fabulous wealth, was courting the wife of the long-absent King. He now addressed the high and mighty Suitors: 'My noble lords, listen to me; I have something to say. Our guest has already been served with a fair share, as is only proper, for it would be neither good manners nor common decency to stint any friends of Telemachus who come to the house. But look! I am going to make him a present worthy of a guest, so that he may have something valuable to pass on to the bath attendant or one of the other servants in the palace of the good Odysseus.'

With this, he laid his great hand on a cow's hoof that was in the bowl and hurled it at him. But Odysseus avoided it by tilting his head slightly to one side, and the only sign of his anger, as the missile struck the solid wall, was a grim sardonic smile. Telemachus rounded on Ctesippus at once: 'It was lucky for you, Ctesippus, that my guest dodged and you didn't hit him. For if you had, I'd have run you through with my spear, and your father would have held a funeral here instead of a wedding. Understand, I won't have this disgraceful behaviour from anyone in my house. I have learnt to use my brains by now and to know right from wrong: my childhood is a thing of the past. And although I must, and do, put up with the sight of all this, the slaughtered sheep, the wine and bread consumed, since I could hardly stop you all single-handed, refrain from these wicked and malicious acts against me. But if you are all set now to murder me, well, I should prefer it so and think it a far better thing to die than day after day to look on while disgraceful things like this are done, my guests are maltreated, and my maids are hauled about this lovely house for your foul purposes.'

No one moved; a long silence followed Telemachus' outburst. It was broken at last by Agelaus, son of Damastor.

'My friends,' he remarked, 'when the right thing has been said, carping criticism and resentment are out of place. Let nobody maltreat this stranger or any of the noble Odysseus' household. And now I have a friendly suggestion to make to Telemachus and his mother, in the hope that both will accept it. As long, Telemachus, as you and your mother could still cherish the hope that the noble Odysseus would one day come home, no one could be angry with you for holding back and keeping the Suitors waiting. It was in your interest – had Odysseus really succeeded in finding his way back. But it is obvious by now that he is not destined to do so. So go and sit by your mother and tell her to marry the man among us who is most distinguished and most generous with wedding presents: and then you will enjoy your inheritance at ease, with plenty to eat and drink, while she looks after her new husband's house.'

'I swear to you, Agelaus,' the thoughtful Telemachus replied, 'I swear by Zeus and by the sufferings of my father, who I suppose is a long way from Ithaca, and either dead or lost, that I am certainly not delaying my mother's marriage, that I am urging her to make her choice and marry again, and that I promise her a most generous settlement. But I'd feel ashamed to drive her from the house against her will. May the gods save me from that!'

Pallas Athene had fuddled the Suitors' wits to such effect that they greeted Telemachus' reply with peal after peal of uncontrollable laughter. But before long their laughing faces took on a strained and alien look. Blood was spattered on the food they ate. Their eyes were filled with tears, their hearts with forebodings of grief.

And now the voice of the godlike prophet Theoclymenus was heard. 'Unhappy men,' he cried, 'what horror is this that has descended on you? Your heads, your faces and your knees are veiled in night. The air is ablaze with lamentation; cheeks are streaming with tears. The walls and lovely alcoves are splashed with blood. The porch is filled with ghosts. So is the court – ghosts hurrying down to darkness and to the Underworld. The sun is blotted out from heaven and a foul mist has crept upon the world.'

They laughed at him. They laughed delightedly, with one accord; and Polybus' son, Eurymachus, got up and shouted: 'Our new friend from abroad is out of his mind. Quick, you fellows, show him out and direct him to the assembly-place: he imagines it is night in here.'

'Eurymachus,' the godlike Theoclymenus retorted, 'I want no help from you to find my way. I have eyes and ears and two feet of my own, and a sound enough head on my shoulders – quite enough to get me through those doors, where I am going now. For I see advancing on you all a catastrophe which you cannot hope to survive or shun, no, not a single one of you with your brutal acts and reckless plots here in the home of godlike Odysseus.' And with that he strode from the splendid palace and sought out Peiraeus, who gave him a warm welcome.

But the Suitors, after exchanging glances, all began to bait Telemachus by holding up his guests to ridicule. 'Telemachus,' said one young man, and his sneer was typical of the rest, 'there never was a man so unfortunate with his guests. First you drag in this grubby tramp. All he wants is food and drink. He has never heard of a hard day's work; in fact he is just a burden on the earth. And now up jumps another to play the prophet. You'd much better take my advice: let's clap these friends of yours on board a fast ship to Sicily, where you could sell them for a profit.'

Telemachus ignored these comments. He kept his mouth shut and his eyes fixed on his father, watching for the moment when Odysseus would be ready to attack the shameless Suitors.

The prudent Penelope, Icarius' daughter, had placed her beautiful chair where she was able to hear every word spoken by the men in the hall. They had slaughtered cattle freely, and amid shouts of laughter had prepared a delicious and appetizing midday meal. But as for their supper, nothing less palatable could be imagined than the fare which a goddess and a strong man were soon to spread before them; but it was their villainy that had started it all.

# 21
# THE GREAT BOW

Athene, goddess of the flashing eyes, now prompted the wise Penelope, Icarius' daughter, to confront the Suitors in the palace with the bow and the axes of grey iron that were to be a test of their skill and the instruments of their destruction. She went upstairs to her room and with her strong hand picked up a well-made bronze key with an ivory handle. She then made her way with her ladies to a store-room in a distant corner of the palace where her lord's treasure was kept – bronze, gold and wrought iron. Here too was the supple bow and quiver full of deadly arrows which had been given to him by his friend the godlike Iphitus, Eurytus' son, when they met in Lacedaemon.

The two came across each other at the house of the shrewd Ortilochus in Messene. Odysseus had come over to recover a public debt, some Messenians having stolen three hundred sheep from Ithaca, and their shepherds too, and carried them off in their many-oared ships. This was the business that brought Odysseus so far afield, though a mere boy at the time. His father and the other elders had entrusted him with the mission. Iphitus, for his part, had come in search of a dozen mares he had lost, with their sturdy little mules at foot. In the event these horses led to his death in a fatal encounter with Heracles, the lion-hearted Son of Zeus and hero of the mighty Labours. For Heracles killed him in his own house, though he was Iphitus' host, caring no more in that cruel heart of his for the vengeful eye of the gods than for the hospitality he had given him – feasted the man first, then killed him, and appropriated the large-hooved mares, keeping them in his own palace stables.

It was on his quest for these animals that Iphitus met Odysseus and gave him the bow, which in years gone by the great Eurytus, his father, had carried and at his death bequeathed to him in his lofty palace. In return, Odysseus gave Iphitus a sharp sword and a strong spear as a token of a warm friendship. But before the two could meet as host and guest, the son of Zeus had killed the heroic Iphitus, the giver of the bow. This bow Odysseus never took on to his black ships with him when he sailed to the war, but laid it up at home in memory of a treasured friend, though he used it on his own estate.

The great lady reached the store-room and set foot on the oaken threshold – the work of some carpenter of bygone days, who had smoothed it well and trued it to the line, fixed the door-posts in their sockets and hung the polished doors on them. She quickly undid the thong attached to the hook, passed the key through the hole, and with an accurate thrust shot back the bolt. With a groan like the roar of a bull at grass in a meadow, the doors flew open before her, and she stepped on to the raised floor-boards. Here stood the chests where clothing was laid in scented herbs. Reaching up, Penelope lifted the bow in the shining case off its peg. And there she sat down with the case on her knees and burst into tears and wept aloud as she drew out her husband's bow. But when the torrent of tears had brought its own relief, she set out for the hall to face the proud Suitors, carrying the supple bow and the quiver with its deadly load of arrows in her hands, and her women followed with a box full of the iron and bronze axes that their master had won as prizes. When she drew near to the Suitors the great lady drew a fold of her shining veil across her cheeks and took her stand by a pillar of the massive roof, with a faithful maid on either side. Then she issued her challenge to the Suitors:

'Listen, proud Suitors. You have exploited this house, in the long absence of its master, as the scene of your endless eating and drinking, and you could offer no better pretext for your conduct than your wish to win my hand in marriage. Come forward now, my gallant lords: the prize stands before you. I shall now place the great bow of godlike Odysseus in front of you. Whoever strings the bow most easily and shoots an arrow through every one of these twelve axes, with that man I will go, bidding goodbye to this house which welcomed me as a bride, this lovely house so full of all good things, this home that even in my dreams I never shall forget.'

She then turned to the good swineherd Eumaeus and told him to hand over the bow and the iron axes to the Suitors. As he took them from her and set them down, Eumaeus burst into tears, and the cowman beyond him also began sobbing when he saw his master's bow. Antinous turned on them with abuse. 'You snivelling peasants,' he exclaimed, 'who can't see further than your noses! You miserable pair, what are you standing there for, snivelling and upsetting your mistress, as though the loss of her beloved husband weren't painful enough? Sit down and eat your food in silence; or else clear out of here and cry outside. But leave the bow where it is, the bow that will seal our fate. I don't think that polished bow will prove easy to string! There's not a man in this whole company like Odysseus. I saw him myself; I remember it well, though I was only a child at the time.'

In spite of what he said, Antinous nursed a secret hope that he himself might string the bow and shoot through all the iron rings. In fact he was to be the first to sample an arrow from the hands of the peerless Odysseus whom, sitting there in the palace, he was insulting, and encouraging all his friends to do the same.

But the great Telemachus broke in: 'Extraordinary! Zeus seems to have taken away my wits. My dear mother, in her wisdom, says she will leave this house to marry again, and here I am, smiling and chuckling to myself like a witless idiot. Well, gentlemen, step forward. Here is your prize – a lady whose like you will not find today in all Achaea, no, not in sacred Pylos, nor in Argos, nor Mycene, nor in Ithaca itself, nor on the dark mainland. But you know this well enough. What need for me to sing my mother's praises? So come along! No false excuses or long delays! String the bow and then we'll see. I shouldn't mind trying myself. And if I string the bow and shoot an arrow through the axes, I won't be too upset if my mother says goodbye to this house and goes away with another man leaving me here, as I'll know that at last I'm capable of winning the fine prizes my father won.'

As he finished speaking Telemachus leapt from his seat, thrust the purple cloak off his shoulder and removed the sword hanging there. He proceeded to dig a single long trench for all the axes; then he planted them in it, getting them exactly in line, and stamped down the earth around them. The men watching could not help admiring the neat way in which he set them up, though he had never seen it done before. Then he took his stance on the threshold and tried the bow. Three times he made it quiver in his efforts to bend it; three times his strength failed, though he still hoped to succeed in stringing it and shooting through the iron rings. And the fourth time he put such pressure on the bow that he might well have strung it yet, if Odysseus had not put an end to his attempts with a shake of the head.

'Dammit!' the great Telemachus exclaimed. 'I suppose I shall always be a coward and a weakling. Or perhaps I'm too young, not sure enough yet of my own strength to defend myself against anyone who may care to pick a quarrel with me. Well, sirs, it is now up to you, who are stronger men than I; let's get the contest settled.'

With this he put the bow down on the ground, propping the tip against the polished woodwork of the door with the arrow resting against the beautiful door-handle. Then he resumed his seat. Antinous, Eupeithes' son, called out: 'Come forward, friends, one by one, from left to right, beginning from where the wine is poured.' This was agreed, with the result that the first man to get up was Leodes, son of Oenops, who used to officiate at their sacrifices and always sat by the great wine-bowl in the far corner. Unlike the rest, he abhorred the Suitors' recklessness, and their conduct filled him with indignation. Rising now to take the first turn, he picked up the bow and arrow, took his stand on the threshold and tried the bow. But long before he could string it, the effort of bending it tired out his delicate, unhardened hands.

He turned to the Suitors. 'My friends,' he said, 'I cannot string it; let the next man try. Believe me, this bow will break the heart and spirit of many a champion here. Yet it is far better to die than to live on without ever winning the prize that lures us all here every day and keeps us always hoping. As it is some of you are hoping and longing to marry Odysseus' wife Penelope. Let them try the bow and see! They'll soon be courting and laying their gifts at the feet of some other long-robed Achaean woman. And so Penelope will be able to marry the man who offers most and is her destined husband.'

Leodes relinquished the bow, propping the tip against the polished woodwork of the door with the arrow leaning against the beautiful door-handle, and so resumed his seat. But Antinous took him to task with asperity: 'Leodes! What a preposterous speech! It's a monstrous suggestion, which I strongly resent, that this bow will "break the heart and spirit of many a champion here" – just because you cannot string it yourself. It's clear that your good mother didn't bring you into the world to string bows and shoot arrows. However, there are others in this noble company who will string it soon enough.' Then he turned to Melanthius the goatherd. 'Look sharp, Melanthius,' he ordered, 'and make a fire in the hall, draw up a big stool with a fleece on it, and bring a large round of tallow from the stores, so that we young men can warm and grease the bow before we try it and settle the match.'

Melanthius quickly made up the fire, which was still glowing, drew up a stool, on which he spread a fleece, and fetched a large round of tallow from the store. The young men greased the bow with the hot tallow, tried their best, but failed to string it; they were not nearly strong enough. Antinous, however, and Eurymachus of the godlike looks, held back for the time being, though they were the leaders of the party and by far the best men in it.

Meanwhile the cowman and the swineherd of the noble Odysseus had joined forces and slipped out of the house. Odysseus himself followed them out, and when they had passed through the door and the courtyard, he called out, 'Cowman! Swineherd!' and then proceeded tactfully to sound them out: 'Shall I speak out, or shall I hold my tongue? No, I feel I must speak. If it came to fighting for Odysseus, what line would you men take – supposing he were to turn up from somewhere, suddenly, brought back by some god? Would you be on the Suitors' side or his? Tell me which way your real feelings lie.'

'Father Zeus,' the cowman said, 'hear my prayer. May some power lead him home! You'd soon know my strength and the power of my right arm.' And Eumaeus added a prayer to all the gods that the wise Odysseus might see his home again.

Odysseus, thus assured of their genuine feelings, said: 'Well, here I am! Yes, I myself, home again in my own country in the twentieth year after much suffering. I know that you are the only two of all my men who will be glad to see me back, for I have not heard a single one of the others put up a prayer for my return. So I'm going to tell you two exactly what the future holds for you. If the powers above let me overthrow these arrogant Suitors, I'll find you each a wife, give you possessions and build you houses near to mine; and from that day I shall regard you both as Telemachus' friends and brothers. I will now show you something as positive proof so that you can be absolutely sure in your hearts who I am – it is this scar, where I was struck by a boar's tusk when I went to Parnassus with Autolycus' sons.'

As he spoke, he drew his rags aside and exposed the long scar. The two men looked, and examined it carefully. Then, weeping, they flung their arms round wise Odysseus' neck, and showered kisses on his head and shoulders. Odysseus in turn kissed their heads and hands: and the sun would have gone down on their weeping had not Odysseus himself checked them: 'Stop crying,' he said, 'or someone coming from the hall may see us and tell the people indoors. Go in now, one after the other, not together. I shall go first; and you must follow. And here's your cue. The others, those fine Suitors, will refuse to let me have the bow and quiver. When that happens, good Eumaeus, bring the bow down the hall and put it in my hands. Also, tell the women to lock that tight-fitting door which leads to their rooms, and say that if they hear groans or any other noise from the men's part of the palace, they are not to stir from their quarters but to stay quietly where they are and get on with their work. The job of bolting and barring the courtyard gate I give to you, good Philoetius. Fasten it tight!' When he had given them these instructions Odysseus went back into the stately palace and sat down on the stool he had recently left. The two servants of the godlike Odysseus followed him in.

By now the bow had come into the hands of Eurymachus, who was turning it round and round in front of the glowing fire to warm it. But he failed to string it for all that, and he groaned from the depth of his proud heart. 'Damnation take the thing!' he cried in his rage. 'I feel this bitterly, not for myself alone but for us all. I'm not upset so much about the marriage, though that is a bitter blow – there are plenty of women left in sea-girt Ithaca and in other towns. What does grieve me is the thought that our failure with his bow proves us such weaklings compared with the godlike Odysseus. The disgrace will stick to our names for ever.'

But Antinous, Eupeithes' son, protested: 'Eurymachus, it won't be like that, and you know it. Today is a public holiday in honour of the god. Is that a time for bending bows? Put the thing down and forget it. And why not leave the axes standing where they are? I'm sure nobody's going to break into the palace of Laertes' son and steal them. Come, let the wine-steward go round and pour a little into each cup. We'll make our libations and give archery a rest. And tomorrow tell the goatherd Melanthius to bring in the very best goats from all his flocks, so that we can sacrifice thigh-bones to the great Archer, Apollo, and then try the bow and see who wins.'

This was very much to their liking. Accordingly their squires came and sprinkled their hands with water and the pages filled the mixing bowls to the brim with drink, and then, after first pouring a little into each man's cup, served them all with wine. When they had made their libations and satisfied their thirst, the crafty Odysseus came out with a wily suggestion.

'Listen to me, Suitors of our famous Queen, and let me tell you what I feel I must. And my plea is particularly directed to Eurymachus, and godlike Antinous, who spoke so sensibly. Lay aside the bow for the moment and leave the issue to the gods. Tomorrow the Archer god will grant his favourite the strength to win. Meanwhile just pass me the polished bow, so that while you watch I can test the strength of my hands and find out whether there's any power left in these limbs that were once so supple, or whether the privations of a roving life have robbed me of it all by now.'

His request enraged them beyond measure, for they really feared he might string the bow; and Antinous turned on him in a fury: 'Miserable intruder, you're quite out of your mind. Can't you be content to dine in peace with your betters, to get your share of every dish and to listen to our talk, which no other visitor or tramp is privileged to hear? This mellow wine has got to you. It's the downfall of any man who gulps it down instead of drinking in moderation. Remember Eurytion the famous Centaur! It was the wine that stupefied him in brave Peirithous' palace, during his visit to the Lapithae. Stupefied with drink he perpetrated that outrage[1] in Peirithous' very home. His hosts leaped up in anger, dragged him to the porch and threw him out of doors; but not before they had ruthlessly sliced his ears and nose off with a knife. He staggered away stupefied, carrying the burden of his folly in his darkened mind. That was the beginning of the feud between Centaurs and men. But he was the first to suffer, and he brought his troubles on himself by getting drunk. And you, I warn you, will come to grief in much the same way, if you string this bow. You will be given no sympathy in our part of the country. We'll pack you off in a black ship to King Echetus the Destroyer; and nothing will get you out of his clutches! So drink in peace, and don't attempt to compete with men younger than yourself.'

But here the prudent Penelope intervened: 'Antinous, it is neither good manners nor common decency to show such meanness to people who come to this house as Telemachus' guests. Do you imagine that if this stranger has enough faith in his own strength and bends the great bow of Odysseus he is going to carry me home with him and make me his wife? I don't believe he ever thought of such a thing himself. So do not let that spoil anyone's dinner here. That is out of the question.'

It was Eurymachus, Polybus' son, who answered her:

1. Eurytion got drunk at the wedding of Peirithous and Hippodameia and tried to rape the bride.

'Daughter of Icarius, wise Penelope, we do not imagine that this man will win your hand. That is out of the question. What we shrink from is what men and women will say. We don't want the common people to be saying: "A poor lot, these; not up to the fine man whose wife they want to marry! They can't string his bow! But in comes some casual tramp, strings the bow with the greatest ease, and shoots through the iron rings!" That is the sort of comment they will make and that would bring disgrace on us.'

'Eurymachus,' wise Penelope retorted, 'no men who desecrate and destroy a great man's household can anyhow have a high reputation among the people, so why would that comment bring disgrace on you? Our guest here is a very big and well-built man, who also claims to be of noble birth. So give him the bow now and let us see what happens. I promise – and these are no idle words – that if Apollo answers his prayer and he succeeds in stringing it I shall give him a fine new cloak and tunic, a sharp javelin to keep off dogs and men, and a two-edged sword, as well as sandals for his feet, and I shall see him safely to wherever he wants to go.'

'As for the bow, mother,' shrewd Telemachus interposed, 'there is not a single Achaean who has a better right than I to give it or refuse it as I wish. And that applies to every chieftain here in rugged Ithaca or in the isles off Elis where the horses graze. There is not one of them who will override my decision, even if I make up my mind to give this bow to my guest once and for all and let him take it away. So go to your quarters now and attend to your own work, the loom and the spindle, and see that the servants get on with theirs. The bow is the men's concern, and mine above all; for I am master in this house.'

Penelope was taken aback, but retired to her own room, for she took her son's sensible decision to heart. Attended by her maids she went upstairs to her bedroom, where she gave way to tears for Odysseus, her beloved husband, till bright-eyed Athene closed her eyes in sweet sleep.

Meanwhile the worthy swineherd had picked up the curved bow and was taking it along, when protests rang out from all the Suitors in the hall. One of the insolent youths, expressing the general feeling, yelled: 'Where are you taking that bow, you wretched swineherd, you vagabond? If Apollo and the other immortal gods favour us, the very dogs you've bred will tear you to pieces, out there among your pigs away from everybody.'

Eumaeus, cowed by the angry cries in the hall, then and there put down the bow. But now Telemachus' voice came loud and menacing from the other side. 'Come on, bring the bow, old fellow! You'll soon find that you can't obey us all. Take care I don't chase you up the fields with a shower of stones. I may be young, but I am more powerful than you. If only I had the same advantage in muscle over all the Suitors in the place, I'd soon send them packing back where they belong and out of this house of mine where they hatch their ugly plots.'

The Suitors greeted this speech with roars of hilarious laughter, which took the edge off their resentment against Telemachus. The swineherd picked up the bow, carried it down the hall to wise Odysseus and put it in his hands. He then called the nurse Eurycleia from her quarters and said: 'Eurycleia, you're sensible. Telemachus' orders are for you to lock those close-fitting doors to the women's rooms. And if anyone hears groans or any other noise from the men's part of the house, they are not to stir from their quarters, but must stay quietly where they are and get on with their work.'

Without a word Eurycleia went and locked the doors leading out of the great hall. At the same time Philoetius slipped quietly out and barred the door leading into the courtyard, which he made fast with a ship's hawser of reeds that was lying under the colonnade. This done, he went in and sat down on the stool he had left, with his eyes fixed on Odysseus.

Odysseus now had the bow in his hands and was twisting it about and bending it at both ends, in case worms had eaten into the horn in the long absence of its owner. The Suitors glanced at one another and one said: 'Ha! Quite the expert, with a critic's eye for bows! No doubt he collects them at home or wants to make one, judging by the way he twists it about. The old vagabond is up to no good.' Another arrogant youth said: 'I hope he has as much luck at that as he has chance of ever stringing the bow!'

While they were talking Odysseus, master of stratagems, had picked up the great bow and checked it all over. As a minstrel skilled at the lyre and in song easily stretches a string round a new leather strap,[1] fixing the twisted sheep-gut at both ends, so he strung the great bow without effort or haste. Then with his right hand he tested the string, and it sang as he plucked it with a sound like a swallow's note. The Suitors were utterly mortified; the colour faded from their cheeks; and to mark the moment there came a thunderclap from Zeus, and Odysseus' long-suffering heart leapt up for joy at this sign of favour from the Son of Cronos of the devious ways.

One arrow lay loose on the table beside him; the rest, which the Achaean lords were soon to experience, were still inside their hollow quiver. He picked up this shaft, set it against the bridge of the bow, drew back the grooved end and the string together, all without rising from his stool, and, with a straight aim, shot. Not a single axe did he miss. From the first handle-ring, right through them all and out at the last the arrow sped with its burden of bronze.

Odysseus turned to his son. 'Telemachus,' he said, 'the stranger sitting in your hall has not disgraced you. I did not miss the target, or make hard work of stringing the bow. My powers are unimpaired, and the Suitors did me an injustice when they disparaged me. But the time has come now to get their supper ready, while it is light, and after that to pass on to the further pleasures of music and dancing, which add to the delights of a banquet.'

As he finished, he gave a nod. Whereupon noble Odysseus' son, Telemachus, slung on his sharp-edged sword and gripping his spear took his stand by the chair at his father's side, armed with resplendent bronze.

1. Pegs did not exist. The string was tied round a leather strap at the bar end; one tuned the lyre by moving or twisting that.

# 22
# THE BATTLE IN THE HALL

Throwing off his rags, the resourceful Odysseus leaped on to the great threshold with his bow and his full quiver, and poured out the swift arrows at his feet.

'The match that was to seal your fate is over,' he called out to the Suitors. 'Now for another target which no man has yet hit – if I can hit it and Apollo grants my prayer.' And with that he levelled a deadly shaft straight at Antinous.

Antinous had just reached for his fine cup to take a draught of wine, and the golden, two-handled beaker was balanced in his hands. No thought of bloodshed entered his head. For who could guess, there in that festive company, that one man, however powerful he might be, would bring evil death and black doom on him against such odds? Odysseus took aim and shot him in the neck. The point passed clean through his tender throat. The cup dropped from his hand as he was hit and he lurched over to one side. His life-blood gushed from his nostrils in a turbid jet. His foot lashed out and kicked the table from him; his food was scattered on the ground, and bread and meat lay there in the dirt.

When the Suitors saw the man collapse, there was uproar in the hall. They sprang from their chairs and rushed in confusion about the room, searching the solid walls on every side. But not a shield or sturdy spear was there to lay hands on. They rounded in fury on Odysseus: 'Stranger, men make a dangerous target; you have played your last match. Now you shall surely die. You have killed the greatest nobleman in Ithaca: for that the vultures shall eat you.' Each of them laboured under the delusion that he had killed the man by accident. It had not dawned upon the fools that the fate of all of them was sealed.

The master-strategist Odysseus gave them a black look. 'You dogs!' he cried. 'You never thought to see me back from Troy. So you fleeced my household; you raped my maids; you courted my wife behind my back though I was alive – with no more fear of the gods in heaven than of the human vengeance that might come. One and all, your fate is sealed.'

Fear drained the colour from their cheeks and each man cast round to find some sanctuary from sudden death. Eurymachus alone found his tongue: 'If you really are Odysseus of Ithaca home again, then what you say of all the unforgivable outrages the Achaeans have committed, here in your house and on your lands, is justified. But the man who was responsible for everything lies dead already, Antinous there, the prime mover in these misdeeds, inspired not so much by any wish or need to marry as by a very different aim, in which Zeus Son of Cronos has thwarted him. And that was to make himself King of the fair city and land of Ithaca, after ambushing your son and murdering him. But he has got his deserts now and been killed. So spare us, who are your own people. And afterwards we will make amends to you by a public levy for all the food and drink that has been consumed in your house. We will each bring a contribution to the value of twenty oxen, and repay you in bronze and gold, till your heart softens. Meanwhile, no one could blame you for your anger.'

The shrewd Odysseus gave him a black look and said: 'Eurymachus, not if you made over all your patrimony to me, everything you possess, and anything else that may come your way, would I keep my hands from killing until you Suitors had paid for all your transgressions. The choice now lies before you, either to face me and fight, or else to run and see if you can escape death and doom, though I do not think any of you will get away alive.'

When they heard this, their hearts quaked and their knees shook underneath them. But once again Eurymachus spoke up. 'My friends,' he said, 'this man will not refrain from using his unconquerable hands. He has got the polished bow and the quiver and will shoot from the threshold floor till he has killed us all. Let's stand and fight! Draw your swords; hold up the tables to keep off his murderous shots, and advance on him all together. That way we may drive him from the threshold and the door, retreat through the town, and quickly raise the alarm. This man would soon find out that his shooting days were over.'

As he spoke, he drew his sharp two-edged sword of bronze, and leapt at Odysseus with a blood-curdling shout. But at the same moment the good Odysseus let an arrow fly, which struck him on the breast by the nipple with such force that it pierced his liver. The sword dropped from his hand. He doubled up and fell sprawling over the table, hurling the food and wine-cup to the floor. In his agony he beat his forehead on the ground; his feet lashed out and rocked the chair, and mist closed over his eyes.

Amphinomus was the next to attack the illustrious Odysseus, making straight at him, sword in hand, to force him somehow from the doors. But before he could close, Telemachus hit him from behind, midway between the shoulders, with a spear that pierced his breast. He fell with a crash and struck the ground with his forehead. Telemachus leapt back, leaving the long spear planted in Amphinomus' body, because he was terrified that one of the enemy might dash in and strike him with a sword as he pulled at the long shaft or stooped above the corpse. So he ran off quickly to rejoin Odysseus and, standing at his side, spoke words that flew: 'Listen, father, I am going to fetch you a shield now and a couple of spears and a bronze helmet to fit round your temples. I shall arm myself too when I come back, and do the same for the swineherd and the cowherd. It would be better to be armed.'

'Run,' said the resourceful Odysseus, 'and bring the arms while I have arrows left for my defence, or they may drive me from the doorway while I'm alone.'

Telemachus obeyed his father and hurried off to the storeroom where they kept their weapons. There he picked out four shields, eight spears, and four bronze helmets topped with horsehair plumes, and carrying these made all haste to his father's side, where he at once proceeded to arm himself. The two servants did the same and took their stand by the masterly, resourceful Odysseus.

As long as he had arrows to fight with, Odysseus kept shooting the Suitors one by one in the hall till the dead lay in piles. Eventually the archer had used up all the arrows. He then propped his bow between one of the door-posts of the great hall and the burnished side of the porch, slung a shield of fourfold hide over his shoulder, put a strong helmet on his heroic head, with the horsehair plume nodding menacingly above, and finally picked up two stout spears tipped with gleaming bronze.

Now let into the solid masonry of the wall there was a side door, on the same level as the raised threshold of the hall, that gave access to a passage. It was usually kept firmly shut with close-fitting doors. Odysseus told the swineherd to stand on guard by this side door, to which there was only one approach. But Agelaus shouted out for all to hear: 'Friends, can't somebody climb to the side door and tell the people and quickly raise the alarm? We could have help in no time and our friend here would soon find his shooting days were over!'

'Impossible, my lord Agelaus,' answered the goatherd Melanthius. 'The big door into the courtyard is alarmingly near, and the mouth of the passage is dangerously narrow: one strong man could keep us all back single-handed. But let me fetch you some armour to put on from the store-room. I have an idea that Odysseus and his famous son have hidden the arms in the house and nowhere else.'

So Melanthius the goatherd went up by devious ways through the palace to Odysseus' store-room, where he helped himself to a dozen shields and spears and a dozen bronze helmets topped with horsehair plumes. He returned at once and had soon handed them over to the Suitors. When Odysseus saw them putting on armour and brandishing great spears in their hands, his knees quaked and his heart failed him. He realized the peril of the situation. He spoke to Telemachus with words that flew: 'Telemachus, I am certain that one of the household women here is responsible for this dangerous turn in the battle. Or else it's Melanthius' work.'

'Father,' the sensible Telemachus admitted, 'the mistake was mine, and no one else is to blame. I left the tightly fitting door of the strong-room open and they kept a sharper lookout than we did. Quick, good Eumaeus, go and shut the store-room door and see whether it's one of the women who is doing this, or Melanthius, Dolius' son, as I suspect.'

As they were talking, Melanthius the goatherd set out once more for the store-room to fetch more fine armour. But the worthy swineherd spied him and at once said to Odysseus, who was close at hand: 'Heaven-born son of Laertes, resourceful Odysseus, that same scoundrel we suspected is off to the store-room again. What are your orders? If I can overpower him, shall I kill him or shall I bring him to you here to pay for all his crimes in your palace?'

To this shrewd Odysseus replied: 'Telemachus and I will keep these arrogant Suitors penned up in the hall, however hard they fight. The two of you must bind Melanthius' hands and feet behind his back, throw him into the store-room, strap him to a plank, tie a rope round his body and hoist him up a pillar to the roof, to torture him for a while.'

His words fell on willing ears, and they set out at once for the store-room. Melanthius was already there but did not see them come, as he was hunting around for arms in a corner of the room. The two men stood by the door-posts on either side and waited. The goatherd came out across the threshold with a fine helmet in one hand and in the other a large and ancient shield spotted with mildew. It had belonged to the heroic Laertes in his prime, but had been lying there for some time with the seams of its straps rotted. The two men pounced upon him, dragged him in by the hair and threw him, terrified, on the floor, where they tied his hands and feet together with agonizing knots, relentlessly forcing the limbs till they met behind him, as Laertes' son, the long-suffering good Odysseus, had ordered. Finally, they tied a rope round his body and hauled him aloft up a pillar right up to the rafters. Then you, Eumaeus the swineherd, jeered at him.

'A long, long watch for you, Melanthius, reclining all night on the soft bed that you deserve. And you'll be sure to see the young Dawn ascending her golden throne from Ocean's Stream, about the time when you usually drive in the goats for the Suitors' table in the palace.' And there Melanthius was left, racked in the grip of those murderous cords, while the pair put their armour back on, closed the polished door, and returned to Odysseus, their shrewd and capable master.

It was at this point, when the two parties were breathing defiance at each other, the four on the threshold facing the large and formidable body in the hall, that Zeus' daughter Athene, assuming Mentor's voice and appearance, approached them. Odysseus hailed her with joy. 'Help us, Mentor, or all is lost!' he cried. 'Remember your old friend and the good things I've done for you in the past. You and I grew up together!'

He had a shrewd idea, when he said this, that he was addressing the warrior goddess, Athene. The Suitors opposite greeted her with a chorus of abuse. Agelaus, son of Damastor, was the first to react, calling out with a menacing voice: 'Mentor, don't let Odysseus talk you round and make you fight for him against the Suitors. I'll tell you just how *we* intend to finish this affair. When we have killed both father and son, you too shall die for what you are so eager to do. With your own life you shall pay the price. And when our swords have repelled the violent assaults of you all, we shall combine all you possess – your house and lands – with Odysseus' estate. We shan't allow sons of yours to live in your house, and your daughters and good wife won't dare to show themselves in the streets of Ithaca.'

These threats infuriated Athene, who rounded on Odysseus and rebuked him scathingly: 'Where is your spirit, Odysseus? Where has your prowess gone? You are not the man you were when for nine relentless years you fought the Trojans for royal Helen of the white arms, killed your man in the bitter struggle time and time again, and planned the stratagem that captured Priam's town with its broad streets. So how can it be that now, when you are in your very own home, and amongst your own possessions, you whine about your lack of courage in face of the Suitors? Come, my old friend, stand by my side and watch me in action, to learn how Mentor son of Alcimus the Courageous repays past kindness in the thick of battle.'

In spite of these words Athene did not yet grant him decisive victory, but continued to put the strength and courage of both Odysseus and his noble son to the test, but she herself, taking the shape of a swallow, darted aloft to perch on the smoky main beam of the hall.

The Suitors were now rallied by Agelaus son of Damastor, Euronymus, Amphimedon, Demoptolemus, Peisander son of Polyctor, and the able Polybus, who stood out as the bravest among those surviving to fight for their lives, many having already succumbed to the arrows that had showered on them from the bow. It was Agelaus who took command and called out to them all: 'Comrades, this man's unconquerable hands are weakening at last! See how Mentor deserted him after his idle boast, and the four of them are left alone in front of the doors. Don't cast your long spears all together, but let us six throw first in the hope that Zeus will allow us to hit Odysseus and cover ourselves with glory. The others won't count, once he has fallen.'

The six did as he ordered and threw with all their might. But Athene made the whole volley miss. One man hit the door-post of the great hall, another the solid door, and the massive bronze point of the ash-wood spear of a third struck the wall. Unscathed by this volley from the Suitors, patient Odysseus' men now heard him say: 'My friends, I will now give the word for us to aim into the thick of the Suitors, who are adding to their other crimes by this attempt to butcher us.'

They all took careful aim and four sharp lances left their hands. Odysseus killed Demoptolemus; Telemachus killed Euryades; the swineherd Elatus; and the cowherd Peisander. Four men had bitten the dust of the wide floor together. The Suitors retreated to the far corner of the hall, and Odysseus' party dashed in and withdrew their weapons from the bodies.

Once more the Suitors threw their sharp spears with all their might, but Athene made the whole volley miss. One man hit the door-post of the great hall, another the solid door, and the massive bronze point of the ash-wood spear of a third struck the wall. But Amphimedon succeeded in catching Telemachus on the wrist – a glancing blow, the bronze just grazed the skin.

And a long spear from Ctesippus, flying over Eumaeus' shield, scratched his shoulder before it passed beyond and fell to the ground. Again the men under Odysseus' shrewd and capable command hurled their spears into the thick of the enemy. This time Eurydamas fell to Odysseus, sacker of cities, Amphimedon to Telemachus, Polybus to the swineherd, and finally the cowherd struck Ctesippus in the breast and exulted over his foe: 'You foul-mouthed son of that braggart Polytherses! Now control your fatuous tongue and don't talk so big, but entrust your speaking to the gods, who are far stronger than you. Take that in return for the cow's hoof you gave godlike Odysseus when he begged in the hall.' So spoke the herdsman of the cows with the twisted horns.

Next, Odysseus stabbed Agelaus with his great spear at close range, and Telemachus struck Euenor's son Leocritus right in the flank with a spear, driving the point clean through the man, who fell face down and struck the ground full with his forehead. And now, high in the roof above their heads, Athene raised her deadly aegis. The Suitors were scared out of their senses. They scattered through the hall like a herd of cattle that a darting gadfly has attacked and stampeded, in the spring-time when the long days come in. But the others swooped down on them just as vultures from the hills, with curving claws and crooked beaks, swoop down upon the smaller birds, who though they shun the upper air and hug the ground find no help there and no escape. The vultures pounce on them and kill, and men enjoy the hunting. So did Odysseus' party chase the Suitors headlong through the hall and hack them down. Ghastly screams rose up as men's heads were smashed in, and the whole floor ran with blood.

Leodes now rushed forward, clasped Odysseus' knees and appealed to him with words that flew: 'I am at your knees, Odysseus. Respect your suppliant, have mercy on me. I swear to you that never, by word or deed, have I done wrong to any woman in the house. I even did my best to stop other Suitors from behaving like that. But they wouldn't listen when I told them to keep their hands from mischief, and their own outrageous behaviour has brought them to this hideous fate. But I was only their priest; I did nothing. And now I am to share their fate! This is all the thanks one gets for good deeds.'

Shrewd Odysseus looked at him with a scowl. 'You say you were their priest,' he answered. 'How often, then, you must have prayed in this hall that the happy day of my return might be long delayed and that my dear wife might follow you and bear your children. For that, nothing shall save you from the bitterness of death.' And with his great hand he picked up the sword dropped on the ground by Agelaus as he died, and with it struck Leodes full in the neck, so that his head fell in the dust even before he had stopped speaking.

The minstrel Phemius, Terpius' son, who served unwillingly as their bard, was still hoping to escape the black hand of death. He stood now close to the side door, the tuneful lyre in his hands, debating in his mind whether to slip out of the hall and seat himself at the massive altar of mighty Zeus, Protector of the Court, on which Laertes and Odysseus had made so many burnt offerings, or to run forward and clasp Odysseus' knees in supplication. He weighed the two courses and decided to clasp the knees of Laertes' son, Odysseus. So he laid the hollow instrument on the ground half-way between the mixing-bowl and the silver-studded chair, ran up to Odysseus, clasped him by the knees and appealed to him with words that flew.

'I am at your knees, Odysseus. Respect your suppliant and have mercy. You will repent it later if you kill a minstrel like me, who sings for gods and men. I had no teacher but myself. The god has implanted in my heart all manner of songs; and I am worthy to sing for you as for a god. Therefore, in your fury do not cut my throat. Besides, your own son Telemachus could tell you that I never came to your house of my own free will or by choice to sing at the Suitors' banquets, but only because brute force and numbers dragged me there.'

The great Telemachus said to his father next to him: 'Wait! The man is innocent. Don't kill him. And Medon the herald, who always looked after me at home when I was a boy, is another we must spare, unless indeed he has already been killed by Philoetius or the swineherd, or met you as you stormed through the hall.'

His words reached the herald's ears. For Medon, that sensible man, had wrapped himself up in the newly flayed hide of an ox and lay cowering under a chair, trying to escape black death. He promptly emerged from this refuge and, throwing off the hide, made a dash for Telemachus, whom he clasped by the knees and appealed to him with words that flew: 'My dear lad, here I am. Spare me, and speak for me to your father. Don't let him kill me with that cruel sword, irresistible as he is and maddened by these Suitors who fleeced his home and hadn't even the sense to treat you with respect.'

The shrewd Odysseus smiled at the man and said: 'Dismiss your fears. My son has saved you so that you may know in your heart – and tell others – that doing right is a much better policy than doing wrong. Now leave the hall, you and the songful minstrel. Go into the courtyard away from this carnage, and sit there till I've done the work I have to do indoors.'

The two made off at once out of the hall and seated themselves at the altar of mighty Zeus, peering about on every side and expecting to be killed at any moment. Odysseus looked round his house to see whether any survivors were hiding to escape black Death. But he found the whole company lying in heaps in the blood and dust, like fish that the fishermen have dragged out of the grey surf in the meshes of their net on to a curving beach, to lie in masses on the sand longing for the salt water, till the bright sun ends their lives. So there the Suitors lay in heaps, one upon another.

'Telemachus,' said the shrewd Odysseus to his son, 'call the nurse Eurycleia here, so that I can tell her what I want.'

Telemachus obediently went off, rattled the door of the women's quarters and called out to Eurycleia. 'Get up, old woman, and come here. You're in charge of the serving-women of the household. My father is calling for you. He has something to say.' Eurycleia made no reply, but immediately opened the door of the apartments, came out and hurried along behind Telemachus. She found Odysseus among the corpses of the dead, spattered with blood and gore, like a lion when he comes from feeding on some farmer's bullock, with the blood dripping from his breast and jaws on either side, a fearsome spectacle.

That was how Odysseus looked, with the gore spattered on his legs and arms. But when Eurycleia saw the dead men and the sea of blood she felt like crying out in triumph at the mighty achievement that confronted her. Odysseus, however, checked her exuberance with a sharp rebuke.

'Restrain yourself old woman, and gloat in silence. I'll have no cries of triumph here. It is an impious thing to exult over the slain. These men fell victims to the will of the gods and their own infamy. They paid respect to no one on earth who came near them – good or bad. And now their own transgressions have brought them to this ignominious death. But what of the women-servants in the house? Tell me which have been disloyal to me and which are innocent.'

'My child,' his fond old nurse Eurycleia replied, 'I'll tell you the truth. You have fifty women serving in your palace, whom we have trained in household duties like carding wool and to be willing servants. Of these there are twelve all told who behaved shamelessly and snapped their fingers at me and Penelope herself. Telemachus has only just grown up and his mother would not allow him to order the maids about. But let me go upstairs now to your wife's bright room and give her the news. Some god has sent her to sleep.'

'Don't wake her yet,' said the subtle Odysseus. 'But tell the women who have behaved disgracefully to come here.'

The old woman left the hall to tell the women and hurry them along, while Odysseus called Telemachus, the cowherd and the swineherd to his side and gave them orders in words that flew: 'Start carrying out the dead and make the women help you. Then clean the tables and our fine chairs here with sponges soaked in water. When the whole palace is restored to order take the women out of the hall between the round-house and the great wall of the courtyard, and set on them with your long swords till you have executed them all and they have forgotten their secret love-making in the arms of the Suitors.'

Wailing bitterly, with the tears streaming down their cheeks, the women all came in together. First they removed the bodies of the dead, which they laid under the portico of the walled courtyard, propping them one against the other. Odysseus himself took charge and urged them on: unwillingly they carried the bodies out.

Next they washed down the tables and the beautiful chairs with sponges and water, after which Telemachus and the two herdsmen scraped the floor of the great hall with spades, while the maids removed the scrapings and got rid of them outside. Finally, when the whole hall had been set in order, they took the women out of the building, and herded them between the round-house and the great courtyard wall in a narrow space from which there was no escape. Then the thoughtful Telemachus spoke.

'I swear I will not give a decent death to women who have heaped insults on my head and on my mother's, and slept with the Suitors.'

With that he took a cable which had seen service on a blue-bowed ship, made one end fast to a high column in the portico, and threw the other over the round-house, high up, so that their feet would not touch the ground. As when long-winged thrushes or doves get entangled in a snare, which has been set in a thicket – they are on their way to roost, but find a grim reception – so the women's heads were held fast in a row, with nooses round their necks, to bring them to the most pitiable end. For a little while their feet twitched but not for very long.

Next they dragged Melanthius out through the hall entrance and across the court. There with a pitiless knife they sliced his nose and ears off; they ripped away his genitals as raw meat for the dogs, and in their fury they lopped off his hands and feet. Then, after washing their own hands and feet, they went back indoors to Odysseus and the business was finished.

Odysseus turned now to his fond nurse. 'Eurycleia,' he said, 'bring some sulphur to clean the pollution, and make a fire so that I can purify the house. Then ask Penelope to come here with her ladies-in-waiting and tell all the maids to come through into the hall.'

'My child,' said the fond nurse, Eurycleia, 'all that you have said is right and proper. But let me bring you a cloak and tunic to put on, and don't stand about like that in the house with only rags over your broad shoulders, or people will be shocked.'

'The first thing I want,' the calculating Odysseus replied, 'is a fire in this hall.' The fond nurse Eurycleia did not disobey him. She brought fire and sulphur, with which Odysseus thoroughly purified the hall, the house and the courtyard outside.

Meanwhile the old woman went off through the royal palace to give the other women the news and tell them to come. Flocking out of their quarters torch in hand they embraced Odysseus in welcome, and took and kissed his shoulders, head and hands. A sweet longing came on him to weep and sob, as he remembered them every one.

# 23
# ODYSSEUS AND PENELOPE

Chuckling as she went, the old woman bustled upstairs to tell her mistress that her beloved husband was in the house. Her legs moved so fast that she almost tripped over her feet. She stood at the bedside and said: 'Wake up, Penelope, dear child, and see with your very own eyes what you've longed for all these days. Odysseus has come and is *home* after all these years. And he's killed the arrogant Suitors who turned his whole house inside out, ate up his wealth, and bullied his son.'

'My dear nurse,' the sensible Penelope said, 'the gods have driven you crazy. They can, after all, rob the wisest of their wits and make stupid people wise. And now they've deranged *you*, who used to be so sensible. Why do you make fun of my distress by waking me when I had closed my eyes, and was deep in a happy sleep, only to tell me this nonsense? Never have I slept like this since Odysseus sailed away to that city, evil Ilium, which I loathe to name. Now go downstairs and back to your own room! If any of the other maids had come and woken me up to listen to such a message, I'd soon have sent her packing to the servants' quarters in tears. Your age can at least save you from that.'

But the dear nurse, Eurycleia, persisted. 'I am not making fun of you, dear child,' she said, 'Odysseus really has come and is home, just as I told you. He's the stranger whom they all insulted in the hall. Telemachus has known for some time that he was back, but had the sense to keep his father's plans a secret till he'd made those upstarts pay for their crimes.'

Penelope's heart leapt up. She sprang from the bed and clung to the old woman, with the tears streaming from her eyes, and spoke winged words. 'Dear nurse, I beg you for the truth! If he is really home, as you say, how on earth did he single-handed overcome those shameless Suitors who were always hanging about the house in a pack?'

'I didn't *see* anything and wasn't *told* anything,' said the dear nurse Eurycleia, 'but I heard the groans of dying men. We sat petrified in a corner of our quarters, with the doors shut tightly on us, till your son Telemachus shouted to me to come out. His father had sent him to fetch me. And then I found Odysseus standing among the bodies of the dead. They lay round him in heaps all over the hard floor. It would have gladdened your heart to see him, spattered with blood and gore like a lion. By now all the corpses have been gathered in a pile at the courtyard gate, while he has had a big fire made and is purifying the palace. He sent me to call you to him. So come with me now, so that you two may begin a time of happiness together after all your sufferings. The wish you cherished so long has today come true. Odysseus has come back to his own hearth alive; he has found both you and his son at home, and in his own palace he has had his revenge on every one of the Suitors who wronged him.'

'Dear nurse, do not laugh and exult so soon,' said prudent Penelope. 'You know how everyone here would welcome the sight of him, and nobody more than myself and the son we brought into the world. But this tale of yours does not ring true. One of the immortal gods has killed the young lords, enraged by their sickening insolence and wickedness. For they respected nobody they met – good men and bad were all the same to them. And now their offences have brought them to disaster. Meanwhile Odysseus in some distant land far from Ithaca has lost his chance of ever returning, and with it lost his life.'

'My child,' her dear nurse Eurycleia exclaimed, 'how can you say such things! Here is your husband at his own fireside, and you declare he never will get home. You never trust anyone. But let me tell you something else as positive proof. The scar he had where he was wounded long ago by the white tusk of a boar – I saw that very scar when I was washing him, and would have told you of it, if Odysseus, for his own crafty purposes, hadn't clapped his hand over my mouth and prevented me. Come with me now. I'll stake my life upon it. If I'm misleading you then kill me in the cruellest way you can.'

'Dear nurse,' the sensible Penelope replied, 'you are a very wise old woman, but even you cannot probe into the minds of the everlasting gods. However, let us go to my son, so that I can see the Suitors dead, and the man who killed them.'

As she spoke she left her room and made her way downstairs, a prey to indecision. Should she remain aloof as she questioned her husband, or go straight up to him and kiss his head and hands? When she had crossed the stone threshold into the hall, she sat down in the firelight by the wall, on the opposite side to Odysseus. He was sitting by one of the great columns with his eyes on the ground, waiting to see whether his good wife would say anything to him when she set eyes on him. For a long while Penelope sat there without a word, with bewilderment in her heart. As she gazed into his face, at times she saw a likeness to Odysseus, at others she failed to recognize him because of the vile clothes he was wearing. Then Telemachus spoke out and rebuked her.

'Mother,' he said, 'my hard-hearted, unmotherly mother, why do you keep your distance from my father like this? Why aren't you sitting at his side, talking and asking questions? No other woman would have had the perversity to hold out like this against a husband who had just returned to her in his native land after twenty wearisome years. But then your heart was always harder than flint.'

'My child, the shock has numbed it,' she said. 'I cannot find a word to say to him; I cannot ask him anything at all; I cannot even look him in the face. But if it really is Odysseus home again, we two shall soon know each other more certainly; for there are signs hidden from others which only we two know.'

Patient, good Odysseus smiled, and spoke winged words. 'Telemachus, leave your mother to put me to the proof here in our home. She will soon come to look at me in a different light. At the moment, because I'm dirty and in rags, she undervalues me and won't admit that I'm Odysseus. But you and I must consider what is best to be done. In any community, when a man kills someone, even someone who has no friends at all to avenge him, he still goes into exile, abandoning his family and native land. But we have killed the best of Ithaca's young men, the mainstay of our state. Do consider this.'

'It's for you to consider it, dear father,' the shrewd Telemachus rejoined. 'You are held to be the best man in the world for stratagems; no one else can compare with you. We will follow your lead wholeheartedly, and whatever our strength may be, our courage will not be lacking.'

'Very well,' Odysseus the great strategist replied, 'I'll tell you what I think is the best plan. First wash yourselves, put on your tunics, and tell the maids in the house to put on fresh clothes. Then let our divine minstrel strike up lively dance music for us with his clear-toned lyre so that, if the music is heard outside by anyone passing in the road or by one of our neighbours, they may imagine there is a wedding-feast. That will prevent the news of the Suitors' death from spreading through the town before we have visited our farm among the orchards. Once there, we shall weigh up whatever opportunity the Olympian sends us.'

They carried out his instructions. The men washed themselves and put on their tunics, and the women decked themselves out. The divine bard took up his hollow lyre and soon aroused their desire for sweet music and the pleasures of dance. The great hall echoed to the sound of the dancing feet of the men and the elegantly gowned women. 'Ah!' said the passers-by as the sounds reached their ears. 'Somebody has married our much-courted Queen. The heartless creature! Not strong-willed enough to keep watch over the great house till her lawful husband comes back!' That was what they said. They little knew what had really happened.

Meanwhile the lion-hearted Odysseus, in his own home again, was bathed and rubbed with oil by the housekeeper Eurynome, and clothed by her in a beautiful cloak and tunic. Then Athene enhanced his comeliness from head to foot. She made him look taller and sturdier, and she caused the bushy locks to hang from his head thick as the petals of a hyacinth in bloom. Just as a craftsman trained by Hephaestus and herself in the secrets of his art takes pains to put a graceful finish to his work by overlaying silver-ware with gold, she endowed his head and shoulders with an added beauty. He came out from the bath looking like one of the everlasting gods, and went and sat down once more in the chair opposite his wife.

'What a strange woman you are!' he exclaimed. 'The gods of Olympus gave you a harder heart than any other woman. No other wife could have steeled herself to keep so long out of the arms of a husband who had just returned to her in his native land after twenty wearisome years. Well, nurse, make a bed for me to sleep in alone. For my wife's heart is as hard as iron.'

'What a strange man *you* are,' said the cautious Penelope. 'I am not being haughty or contemptuous of you, though I'm not surprised that you think I am. But I have too clear a picture of you in my mind as you were when you sailed from Ithaca in your long-oared ship. Come, Eurycleia, move the great bed outside the bedroom that he himself built and make it up with fleeces and blankets and brightly coloured rugs.'

This was her way of putting her husband to the test. But Odysseus flared up at once and rounded on his loyal wife. 'Lady,' he cried, 'your words are a knife in my heart! Who has moved my bed? That would be hard even for a skilled workman, though for a god who took it into his head to come and move it somewhere else it would be quite easy. No man alive, not even one in his prime, would find it easy to shift. A great secret went into the making of that complicated bed; and it was my work and mine alone. Inside the court there was a long-leaved olive-tree, which had grown to full height with a trunk as thick as a pillar. Round this I built my room of compact stonework, and when that was finished, I roofed it over carefully, and put in a solid, neatly fitted, double door. Next I lopped all the branches off the olive, trimmed the trunk from the root up, rounded it smoothly and carefully with my adze and trued it to the line, to be my bedpost. I drilled holes in it, and using it as the first bedpost I constructed the rest of the bed. Then I finished it off with an inlay of gold, silver and ivory, and fixed a set of gleaming purple straps across the frame. So I have shown you the secret. What I don't know, lady, is whether my bedstead stands where it did, or whether someone has cut the tree-trunk through and moved it.'

At his words her knees began to tremble and her heart melted as she realized that he had given her infallible proof. Bursting into tears she ran up to Odysseus, threw her arms round his neck and kissed his head. 'Odysseus,' she cried, 'do not be angry with me, you who were always the most understanding of men. All our unhappiness is due to the gods, who couldn't bear to see us share the joys of youth and reach the threshold of old age together. But don't be cross with me now, or hurt because I did not give you this loving welcome the moment I first saw you. For I had always had the cold fear in my heart that somebody might come here and deceive me with his talk. There are many who think up wicked selfish schemes. Helen of Argos, born of Zeus, would never have slept in her foreign lover's arms had she known that her countrymen would go to war to fetch her back to Argos. It was the god who drove her to do this shameful deed, though not until that moment had her heart contemplated that fatal madness, the madness which was the cause of her woes and ours. But now you have faithfully described the secret of our bed, which no one ever saw but you and I and one maid, Actoris, who was my father's gift when first I came to you, and was the keeper of our bedroom door. You have convinced my unbelieving heart.'

Her words stirred a great longing for tears in Odysseus' heart, and he wept as he held his dear and loyal wife in his arms. It was like the moment when the blissful land is seen by struggling sailors, whose fine ship Poseidon has battered with wind and wave and smashed on the high seas. A few swim safely to the mainland out of the foaming surf, their bodies caked with brine; and blissfully they tread on solid land, saved from disaster. It was bliss like that for Penelope to see her husband once again. Her white arms round his neck never quite let go. Rosy-fingered Dawn would have found them still weeping, had not Athene of the flashing eyes had other ideas. She held the night lingering at the western horizon and in the East at Ocean's Stream she kept golden-throned Dawn waiting and would not let her yoke the nimble steeds who bring us light, Lampus and Phaethon, the colts that draw the chariot of Day.

At last the shrewd Odysseus said to his wife, 'Dear wife, we have not yet come to the end of our trials. There lies before me still a great and hazardous adventure, which I must see through to the very end. That was what Teiresias' soul predicted for me when I went down to the House of Hades to find a way home for my followers and myself. So come to bed now, dear wife, and let us at last enjoy a sweet sleep in each other's arms.'

Thoughtful Penelope answered: 'Your bed shall be ready the moment you wish, now that the gods have brought you back to your own country and your lovely home. But since you have mentioned it – since a god put it in your heart – tell me all about this new ordeal; I suppose I shall hear about it sooner or later, so I might as well learn about it at once.'

'What a strange woman you are!' said the quick-witted Odysseus. 'Why press me so insistently? However, I will tell you all, holding nothing back. Not that you will find it to your liking, any more than I do! Teiresias told me to carry a well-balanced oar and wander on from city to city, till I came to a people who know nothing of the sea, and never use salt with their food, so that crimson-painted ships and the long oars that serve those ships as wings are quite beyond their experience. He gave me this infallible sign (which I now reveal to you) – when I met some other traveller who referred to the oar I was carrying on my shoulder as a "winnowing-fan", then, he said, the time would have come for me to plant my oar in the earth and offer the Lord Poseidon the rich sacrifice of a ram, a bull and a breeding boar. After that I was to go back home and make ceremonial sacrifices to the everlasting gods who live in the far-flung heavens, to all of them this time, in due precedence. As for my end, he said that Death would come to me away from the sea, and that I would die peacefully in old age, surrounded by a prosperous people. He assured me that all this would come true.'

'If the gods make your old age a happier time,' the sagacious Penelope replied, 'there is a hope of an end to your troubles.'

While they were talking, Eurynome and the nurse, by the light of torches, were putting soft bedclothes on their bed. When the work was done and the bed comfortably made, the old woman went back to her own quarters for the night, and the housekeeper Eurynome, with a torch in her hands, lit them on their way to bed, taking her leave when she had brought them to their room. And blissfully they lay down on their own familiar bed.[1]

As for Telemachus, the cowman, and the swineherd, they brought their dancing feet to rest, dismissed the women and lay down for the night in the shadowy hall.

But Odysseus and Penelope, after they had enjoyed the pleasure of love, turned to the pleasure of talk. The noble Queen told him all she had endured in his home, watching that destructive gang of Suitors at their work, of all the cattle and fat sheep that they had slaughtered in pursuit of her, of all the jars they had emptied of wine. And in his turn Odysseus, favourite of Zeus, told her of all the discomfiture he had inflicted on others and all the miseries which he himself had undergone. She listened entranced, and her eyelids never closed in sleep till the whole tale was finished.

He began with his victory over the Cicones and his visit to the fertile land where the Lotus-eaters live. He spoke of what the Cyclops did, and the price he had made him pay for the fine men he ruthlessly devoured. He told her of his stay with Aeolus, who gave him a friendly welcome and saw him on his way; and how the gale, since it was not his destiny to reach his home so soon, had caught him once more and driven him, sick at heart, over the teeming seas, Next he told how he came to Telepylus, where the Laestrygonians destroyed his fleet and all his fighting men, the black ship that carried him being the only one to get away. He told about Circe and her complex arts; of how he sailed across the seas in his great ship to the dank Halls of Hades

1. Two famous ancient critics held that this was the 'end' of the Odyssey, and that the remainder was by some later and lesser hands. Some modern critics agree, instancing 'un-Homeric language', and inconsistencies in the narrative. Others disagree, holding that on the whole the writing is typical and worthy of Homer, and that several important themes are satisfactorily rounded off.

to consult the soul of Theban Teiresias, and saw all his former comrades and the mother who had borne him and nursed him as a child.

He told her how he had listened to the sweet song of the Sirens; how he had sailed by the Wandering Rocks, by dread Charybdis, and by Scylla, whom no sailors pass unscathed; how his men had killed the cattle of the Sun; how Zeus the Thunderer had struck his fast ship with a flaming bolt, and all his fine company had been killed at one fell swoop, though he himself escaped their dreadful fate. He described his arrival at the Isle of Ogygia and his reception by the Nymph Calypso, who had longed to marry him and kept him in her vaulted cavern, a pampered guest, offering immortality and ageless youth, but never won him round. Finally how he arrived, after a disastrous voyage, at Scherie, where the Phaeacians honoured him in their hearts like a god and sent him home by ship with generous gifts of bronze and gold and clothes. He had just finished this last tale when sleep came suddenly upon him, relaxing all his limbs and banishing his cares.

And now Athene of the flashing eyes had another idea. When she was satisfied that he had had his fill of love and sleep in his wife's arms, she roused fresh golden-throned Dawn to leave Ocean's Stream and bring daylight to the world. Odysseus too rose from his soft bed and told Penelope what he wanted her to do. 'Dear wife,' he said, 'the pair of us have had our share of trials, you here in tears because of my distressing absence from home, and I yearning to get back to Ithaca but harassed and kept in exile by Zeus and all the gods. But now we have returned to the bed we both longed for, I leave the house and my belongings in your care. As for the ravages the insolent Suitors have made among my flocks, I shall repair the greater part by raiding on my own, and the people of Ithaca must contribute too, till they have filled up all my folds again. But now I am going to our orchard farm, to see my good father, who has suffered so much on my account. And this, my dear, is what I wish you to do, though you are too wise to need telling. Since it will be common knowledge, as soon as the sun is up, that I have killed the Suitors in the palace, go with your ladies-in-waiting to your room upstairs and stay quietly there, see nobody, and ask no questions.'

Odysseus fixed his splendid armour round his shoulders, woke up Telemachus, the cowman and the swineherd, and told them all to pick up their arms. They carried out his orders and put on their bronze armour. Then they opened the doors and went out with Odysseus leading. It was already broad daylight over the land, but Athene hid them in darkness and soon led them clear of the town.

# 24
# THE FEUD IS ENDED

And now Cyllenian Hermes began to summon the souls of the Suitors from the palace, holding in his hand the splendid golden wand that he can use at will to cast a spell on men's eyes or wake them from sleep. He marshalled and led them with this, and they obeyed his summons, squeaking as bats squeak when they flutter around after one of them falls from the cluster in which they hang upside down from the rocky roof in the depth of some mysterious cave. With such squeaking the ghosts journeyed on together, following Hermes the Deliverer down the dark paths of decay. Past Ocean's Stream, past the White Rock, past the Gates of the Sun and the region of dreams they went, and before long they reached the meadow of asphodel, which is the dwelling-place of souls, the disembodied wraiths of men.

Here they encountered the souls of Peleus' son Achilles, of Patroclus, of the handsome Antilochus, and of Ajax, who in stature and in manly grace was second to none of the Danaans except the peerless son of Peleus. These were gathered round Achilles' soul. And now there came near them the soul of Agamemnon, Atreus' son, who came to them plunged in grief and surrounded by the souls of all that met their doom and died with him in Aegisthus' house. Achilles' soul addressed him first. 'Agamemnon, we used to think of you, among all our princes, as the lifelong favourite of Zeus the Thunder-lover, because of the size and bravery of the army you commanded in the land of Troy when we Achaeans suffered so much. But you too were to be visited in your prime by that deadly Fate which no man born can evade. How I wish you could have met your doom and died at Troy in the full enjoyment of the honour due to you as our leader. For then the whole nation would have joined in building you a mound and you would have left a great name for your son to inherit. But instead you were doomed to die a pitiable death.'

'Son of Peleus, godlike Achilles,' the soul of Atreus' son replied, 'happy man, to have died in the land of Troy far away from Argos. There the flower of the Trojan and Achaean forces fell around you in the battle for your body. Mighty you lay in a swirl of dust, a mighty corpse, all your horsemanship forgotten. And the whole day long we fought. Indeed we never would have ceased had Zeus not stopped us with a storm. Then we carried you off from the battlefield to the ships, cleansed your fair flesh with warm water and unguents, and laid you on a bed. Your countrymen gathered round you, shedding hot tears and cutting their hair.

'Your mother, when she heard the tidings, came up from the sea with the immortal Sea-Nymphs, and a mysterious cry came over the waters. All the Achaeans were seized by panic and would have leaped up and fled on to the ships, but for one man, Nestor, rich in ancient wisdom. It was not for the first time that his wise counsels had prevailed. With their best interests at heart he addressed them, calling out: "Halt, Argives! Achaeans, stand your ground! This is Achilles' mother who has come out of the sea with her immortal Sea-Nymphs to be with her dead son." At this the brave Achaeans checked their flight. The daughters of the Old Sea-god stood round you with bitter lamentations, and wrapped your body in an imperishable shroud. The Nine Muses chanted your dirge in sweet antiphony and you would not have seen a single Argive without tears in his eyes, such was the clear-voiced Muses' song.

'For seventeen days and seventeen nights we mourned for you, immortal gods and mortal men alike; and on the eighteenth day we committed you to the flames, with a rich sacrifice of fatted sheep and crooked-horned cattle round you. You were burnt in the clothing of the gods, with lavish unguents and sweet honey; and Achaean heroes in full armour, infantry and charioteers, moved in procession round the pyre where your body was burning and filled the air with sound. When the

Hephaestean flames had consumed your body, we gathered your white bones at dawn, Achilles, and steeped them in unmixed wine and oil. Your mother gave us a golden urn, a gift, she said, from Dionysus, made by the great Hephaestus. In this your white bones lie, my illustrious Achilles, and mingled with them the bones of Menoetius' son Patroclus, dead before you, but separate from those of Antilochus, who next to Patroclus was your closest friend. Over their bones we soldiers of the mighty Argive force built up a great and glorious mound, on a foreland jutting out over the broad waters of the Hellespont, so that it might be seen far out at sea by the men of today and future ages.

'Then, in the middle of the arena where the Achaean champions were to test their skill, your mother placed the magnificent prizes she had asked the gods to give. You have attended the funerals of many heroes, when the young men strip and make ready for the games in honour of their dead king, but if you had seen the splendid prizes offered in your honour by the divine silver-footed Thetis you would have marvelled at them as the most wonderful you had ever seen. For the gods loved you very dearly. So even death, Achilles, did not destroy your name, and your great glory will last for ever among all mankind. But after I had brought the war to a close, what satisfaction was there for me? For on my journey home Zeus planned a miserable end for me at the hands of Aegisthus and my accursed wife.'

So they talked together and Hermes the Giant-killer approached, ushering into the world below the ghosts of the Suitors whom Odysseus had killed. Astonished at the sight, the pair moved quickly towards them and the soul of Agamemnon, Atreus' son, recognized the famous Amphimedon, Melaneus' son, who had entertained him in his home in Ithaca. The soul of Atreus' son was the first to speak. 'Amphimedon,' he said, 'what catastrophe has brought you all down into the land of darkness, all chosen men and all of the same age? Someone choosing a city's best would have selected men like these. Did Poseidon raise tempestuous winds and surging waves, and overwhelm you and your ships? Or did enemies strike you down as you were rounding up their cattle and their flocks, or as they were defending their town and women? Tell me, for you and I have been host and guest. Don't you remember the time when I came over to your house in Ithaca with godlike Menelaus to persuade Odysseus to join forces with me and sail against Ilium? It was a full month before we completed our voyage over the wide sea, so hard was it to win over Odysseus, Sacker of Cities.'

'Most noble son of Atreus, Agamemnon, lord of men,' the soul of Amphimedon replied, 'I well remember all that you speak of, favourite of Zeus, and will give you a full and honest account of our tragic end and the manner of our death.

'In the prolonged absence of Odysseus we began to court his wife. She refused to give an absolute "No" or an absolute "Yes" to a marriage which was so distasteful to her, but scheming instead to bring about our downfall and our death she devised this trick. On her loom in her house she set up a great web and began weaving a large and delicate piece of work. And she said to us: "My lords, my Suitors, now that noble Odysseus is dead, restrain your ardour, do not urge on this marriage till I have done this work, so that the threads I have spun may not be altogether wasted. It is a shroud for Lord Laertes. When he succumbs to the dread hand of remorseless Death that stretches all men out at last, I must not risk the scandal there would be among my countrywomen here if one who had amassed such wealth were laid to rest without a shroud."

'That is what she said, and we magnanimously consented, so by day she used to weave at the great web, but every night had torches set beside it and undid the work. For three years she took us in by this stratagem. A fourth began, and the seasons were slipping by, when one of her women, who knew all about it, gave her mistress away. We caught her unravelling her beautiful work, and she was forced reluctantly to complete it. But no sooner had she woven the great web, laundered the robe and shown it to us gleaming like the sun or moon, than some evil god landed Odysseus out of the blue in a distant corner of his estate where the swineherd had his hut. Noble Odysseus' son, just back from sandy Pylos in his black ship, made for the same place. The two of them plotted our assassination, and made their way to the famous city of Ithaca, or, rather, Telemachus went first and Odysseus followed later. The swineherd brought him down disguised in rags, and looking like a wretched old beggar as he hobbled along with his staff. In the miserable clothes he was wearing none of us, not even the older members, realized that this was Odysseus when he suddenly appeared among us. In fact we abused and insulted him and threw things at his head. For the moment he put up patiently with the abuse and blows in his own palace.

'But when the will of Zeus, Lord of the Aegis, stirred him, with Telemachus' help he removed the excellent weapons they possessed and stowed them in the store-room and bolted the doors. Then, in his cunning, he persuaded his wife to set out in front of the doomed Suitors a bow and some grey iron axes, to be a test of our prowess and the instruments of our death. Not one of us could string the mighty weapon; we were far too weak. But when it came to handing the great bow to Odysseus, we all protested loudly that he should not have it, however much he argued. Telemachus was the only one who encouraged him and told him to take it. And so the patient good Odysseus got his hands on the bow, which he strung without effort, and shot through the iron rings. Then he leapt on to the threshold and with murder in his eyes tipped out his swift arrows, and shot Lord Antinous; after which, aiming carefully, he shot at the rest of us with his deadly shafts. We fell thick and fast; and it was obvious that some god was on their side. For in their fury they charged through the hall and hacked us down right and left. As heads were smashed ghastly screams filled the hall and the whole floor ran with blood.

'That, Agamemnon, is how we were destroyed. And our corpses still lie uncared-for in Odysseus' palace, as the news has not yet reached our homes and brought our friends to wash the dark blood from our wounds, to lay our bodies out and mourn for us, as is a dead man's right.'

'Son of Laertes, shrewd Odysseus!' the soul of Agamemnon, son of Atreus, cried. 'You are a fortunate man to have won a wife of such pre-eminent virtue! How faithful was your flawless Penelope, Icarius' daughter! How loyally she kept the memory of the husband of her youth! The glory of her virtue will not fade with the years, but the deathless gods themselves will make a beautiful song for mortal ears in honour of the constant Penelope. What a contrast with Clytaemnestra, the daughter of Tyndareus, and the infamy she sank to when she killed me, the husband of her youth. The song men will sing of her will be one of detestation. She has destroyed the reputation of her whole sex, virtuous women and all.'

Those were the words that passed between them as they stood in Hades' Halls, under the secret places of the earth.

Odysseus and his party left the town behind, and before long had reached the rich and well-run farmlands of Laertes, which he had reclaimed from their natural state by his own exertions long ago. Here was his cottage, surrounded by outbuildings where the serfs that laboured for him had their meals and sat and slept. An old Sicilian woman lived in the cottage, devoting all her care to the old man's comfort on his farm, far from the town.

When they reached the place, Odysseus said to his son and his servants: 'Go into the main building now and straight away kill the best pig you can find for our midday meal. Meanwhile I shall test my father, to find out whether he will know me when he sees me, or fail to recognize me after so long an absence.'

As he spoke, he handed his armour to the servants, who then went straight into the house, and Odysseus moved off towards the luxuriant vineyard on his quest. As he made his way down into the great orchard, he did not see Dolius or any of the serfs or Dolius' sons, who had all gone with the old man at their head to gather stones for the vineyard wall. He found his father alone on the vineyard terrace hoeing round a tree. He was wearing a filthy, patched and shabby tunic, a pair of stitched cowhide leggings strapped round his shins to protect them from scratches, and gloves to save his hands from the brambles. There he stood, with a hat of goatskin on his head to emphasize his grief.

When the patient good Odysseus saw how old and worn his father looked and realized the depth of his misery, he halted under a tall pear-tree and the tears came into his eyes. He deliberated in his heart and mind whether to hug and kiss his father, and tell him the whole story of his own return home to his native land, or first to question him and thoroughly test him. Upon reflection he thought it better to start by testing him with words that would rouse him. With this purpose in mind the good Odysseus went straight up to his father.

Laertes was still hoeing round the tree with his head down, as his illustrious son came up and spoke to him.

'Old man, you keep everything so well tended here that I can see there is little about gardening that you do not know. There is nothing, not a green thing in the whole enclosure, not a fig, olive, vine, pear or bed that is not carefully looked after. But I cannot help remarking – and please don't take offence – that you don't look after *yourself* very well; in fact, what with your unkempt appearance and your shabby clothes old age has hit you very hard. Yet it can't be on account of any laziness that your master fails to look after you, nor is there anything in your build and size to suggest the slave. You look more like a man of royal blood, the sort of person who sleeps on a soft bed when he has had his bath and dined; this is how the old should be treated. However, tell me the truth. Whose serf are you and whose is this garden you look after? And tell me honestly – I need to be sure – am I really in Ithaca? A fellow I met on my way up here just now assured me that I was. But he was not very obliging; he couldn't be bothered to answer me properly or listen to what I said, when I mentioned a friend of mine and asked him whether he was still in the land of the living or dead and gone to Hades' Halls.

'Listen, and I'll tell you about him. Some time ago in my own country I was host to a man who arrived at our house and proved the most attractive visitor I have ever entertained from abroad. He said he was an Ithacan, and that Arceisius' son Laertes was his father. I took him in, made him thoroughly welcome and gave him every comfort that my rich house could offer, including presents worthy of his rank. Seven talents of wrought gold he had from me, a solid silver wine-bowl with a floral design, twelve single-fold cloaks, twelve rugs, twelve splendid robes and twelve tunics, and besides all this, four women skilled in fine handicraft and good-looking. I let him choose them himself.'

'Sir,' said his father, with tears on his cheeks, 'Yes, you have come to the land you're seeking; but it's in the hands of violent and evil men. The gifts you lavished on your friend were given in vain, though had you found him alive in Ithaca he would have sent you on your way with an ample return in presents and hospitality, as is right when such an example has been set. But please tell me exactly how long ago it was that you were host to that unfortunate man, my unhappy son – if I ever had one – who far from friends and home has been devoured by fishes in the sea or fallen a prey, maybe, to the wild beasts and birds on land. His mother and I, we two who brought him into the world, had no chance to wrap his body up and lament over him, nor had his richly dowered wife, constant Penelope, the chance to close his eyes and mourn him on his deathbed – the tributes due to the dead.

'But tell me about yourself – I'm curious. Who are you, sir, and where do you come from? What is your native town and who are your parents? And where is she moored, the good ship that brought you here with your gallant crew? Or were you travelling as a passenger on someone else's ship, which landed you and sailed away?'

'I will tell you all you wish to know,' said the subtle Odysseus. 'I come from Alybas. My home is the palace there, for my father is King Apheidas, Polypemon's son. My own name is Eperitus. I sailed from Sicania, but some god drove me here against my will; and my ship is anchored opposite open country some way from the town. As for Odysseus, it is five years since he bade me farewell and left my country, ill-fated man. And yet the omens when he left were good – birds on the right, which pleased me as I said goodbye, and pleased him as he started out. We both had every hope that we should meet again as host and guest and give each other splendid gifts.'

When Laertes heard this, a black cloud of misery enveloped him. Groaning heavily, he picked the black dust up in both his hands and poured it over his grey head. Odysseus' heart was touched, and suddenly, as he watched his dear father, a sharp spasm of pain shot through his nostrils. He rushed forward, flung his arms round his neck, and kissed him. 'Father,' he cried, 'here I am, the very man you asked about, home in my own land after twenty years. But no more tears and lamentation, for I have news to tell you, and there is need for haste. I have killed that gang of Suitors in our palace. I have taken revenge for their bitter insults and all their crimes.'

Laertes answered him: 'If you who have come here really are my son Odysseus, home again, give me some definite proof to convince me.'

'To begin with,' the quick-witted Odysseus said, 'look at this scar, where I was wounded by the white tusk of a boar when I went to Parnassus. You and my mother had sent me to my grandfather Autolycus, to fetch the gifts he solemnly promised me when he came to visit us. Then again, I can tell you all the trees you gave me one day on this terraced garden. I was only a little boy at the time, trotting after you through the orchard, asking about this and that, and as we wound our way through these very trees you told me all their names. You gave me thirteen pear-trees, ten apple-trees, and forty fig-trees, and at the same time you pointed out the fifty rows of vines that were to be mine. Each ripened at a different time, so that the bunches on them were at various stages of ripeness as the seasons of Zeus weighed down their branches.'[1]

At these words Laertes' knees gave way and his heart melted, for he recognized the positive proof given by Odysseus. He flung his arms round the neck of his beloved son, and patient good Odysseus clasped him fainting to his breast. When his breath came back and he returned to consciousness he said to his son, 'By Father Zeus, you gods are still there on high Olympus if those Suitors have really paid the price for their outrageous insolence! But in my heart I have a horrible fear now that all the people of Ithaca will soon be on us here, and that they will send urgent messages for help to every town in Cephallenia.'

1. We have here the old King carefully tending his orchard, vineyard and vegetable beds. And forty-five years previously he was knowledgeably conducting his young son Odysseus round the estate. King Alcinous and Circe also had luscious gardens. Yet we never hear of the heroes eating fruit and vegetables in the palaces of kings or herdsmen, or beggars doing so in the hut of a swineherd.

'Have no fear,' said his resourceful son, 'and do not feel anxious about that; but come with me to the farmhouse here by the orchard. I sent Telemachus ahead with the cowman and swineherd to prepare a meal as quickly as they could.'

When they had finished talking the two set out, and in the pleasant well-built farmhouse they found Telemachus and the two herdsmen carving lavish portions of meat and mixing the sparkling wine. His Sicilian maid-servant bathed the great-hearted Laertes in his room and rubbed him with oil and put a cloak around him. Athene came and filled out the limbs of this shepherd of his people, making him seem taller and sturdier than before, so that as he stepped out of the bath his own son was amazed to see him looking like an immortal god.

'Father,' he exclaimed, and his words were winged, 'I'm sure one of the immortal gods has made you handsomer and taller than ever!'

To which the thoughtful Laertes replied: 'By Father Zeus, Athene and Apollo, if only I could have been the man I was when as King of the Cephallenians I took the stronghold of Nericus on the mainland cape, and like that have stood by you yesterday in our palace, with armour on my shoulders, and beaten off those Suitors! I'd have laid many of them low in the halls and delighted your heart!'

So they talked together, and the others finished their task of preparing the meal. They took their places on seats and chairs, and were helping themselves to food, when the old man Dolius came in with his sons, weary after their work. They had been called in by their mother, the old Sicilian woman, who looked after them and lovingly cared for their old father now that his years sat heavily upon him. When they set eyes on Odysseus and realized who he was, they stopped short in amazement. Odysseus joked pleasantly with them as he greeted them. 'Old man,' he said, 'sit down to your lunch. And all of you, stop looking so amazed. We have been longing to get our hands on the food in here, waiting all this time and expecting you every minute.'

Dolius ran up with outstretched arms, seized Odysseus by the hand, and kissed him on the wrist. 'So you have come back to us, my dear master,' he said, with words that had wings, 'and fulfilled our dearest wishes! We had given up hope, but the gods have led you back. Greetings and welcome home, and may the gods shower their blessings on you! But tell me this, for I am anxious – has the wise Penelope heard of your arrival here, or shall we send someone to tell her?'

'She knows already, my old friend,' resourceful Odysseus answered, 'Why must you concern yourself with that?' Dolius sat down again on his polished stool, and now it was his sons' turn to gather round the famous Odysseus, welcome him and clasp his hand. Then they all took their seats by Dolius their father.

So they busied themselves with their meal in the farmhouse. But Rumour the messenger flew rapidly through the town, with the fateful news of the Suitors' hideous death. When the people heard it, with one accord they gathered from all sides in front of Odysseus' palace, with wailing and lamentation. They carried out the corpses and each group buried their dead; the corpses from other towns were put on ships and sent home in the care of the crews. Grieving, they made their way in a body to the meeting-place, and there, when they were all duly gathered, Eupeithes rose to address them. His heart was heavy with inconsolable grief for his son, Antinous, the first of the great Odysseus' victims.

'Friends,' he began, weeping for his son, 'What terrible harm this man has done to us Achaeans! He sailed away taking many of our fine young men in his hollow ships, but he lost his ships, he lost his men, and now on his return he has killed the best of the Cephallenians. Quick, now! Before he can escape to Pylos or to sacred Elis where the Epeians rule, let us make a move, or our shame will last for ever. We shall be disgraced even in the eyes of generations yet unborn if we do not avenge ourselves on the murderers of our sons and brothers. I, for one, should find no further pleasure in living, but should prefer to die and join the dead. Let us make a move or they may be across the seas before we can stop them.'

His tears and his words stirred all his countrymen to pity. But at this moment Medon and the divine minstrel appeared. On waking they had come straight from the palace, and now took their stand in the centre of the assembly. Everyone was amazed, but the wise Medon spoke out. 'Listen, fellow-Ithacans, it was not against the will of the deathless gods that Odysseus carried out his plans. With my own eyes I saw an immortal, who looked exactly like Mentor, standing at his side. And this immortal was at one moment ahead of Odysseus, cheering him on, and at the next storming through the hall, striking terror into the Suitors; they fell in heaps.'

At these words the blood drained from their cheeks; and now the hero, old Halitherses, Mastor's son, the only man there who could look into the future as well as into the past, rose up to give them some well-meant advice. 'Ithacans,' he cried, 'Listen to what I have to say. Your own stupidity, my friends, is to blame for what has happened. You would not listen to me or to Mentor, the shepherd of the people, when we urged you to check your sons in their career of folly. They were guilty of a great wrong, because they wickedly abandoned all standards of civilized behaviour, plundering the estate and insulting the wife of our greatest man, whom they counted on never seeing here again. Be persuaded by me. Let us *not* make a move; or I fear that some of you may bring doom on your heads.'

At the end of this speech, some of them remained where they were, but more than half leaped to their feet with loud war-cries, rejecting his advice and following that of Eupeithes, the great persuader. They rushed to arms, equipped themselves in their gleaming bronze and mustered outside the spacious town. Eupeithes in his folly took command. He saw himself avenging his son's death, though he was never to come back alive but was to meet his fate in that very place.

It was now that Athene said to Zeus: 'Father of ours, Son of Cronos, King of Kings, answer my question and say what thoughts are hidden in your heart. Will you further this strife with its horrors and turmoil or establish peace between the two sides?'

To this Zeus the Cloud-gatherer replied: 'My child, why come to me with such questions? Was it not your own idea that Odysseus should return and avenge himself on his enemies? Act as you please, but I will tell you the best way. Since the noble Odysseus has had his revenge on the Suitors, let them make a treaty of peace to establish him as King in perpetuity, and let us wipe from their minds the memory of the slaughter of sons and brothers. Let them be friends as before and let peace and plenty prevail.' With this encouragement from Zeus, Athene, who had already set her heart on action, flashed down at once from the peaks of Olympus.

In the farmhouse, after they had enjoyed a satisfying meal, the patient good Odysseus said: 'Will one of you go and see whether they aren't close to us already!' At his bidding, one of Dolius' sons jumped up and went to the threshold. Standing there, he saw them all quite close and called to Odysseus with words that flew: 'They are on us, quick! To arms!' Whereupon they leaped up and put on their armour – Odysseus and the three with him, and Dolius' six sons. Laertes and Dolius, grey-headed though they were, also armed themselves, warriors by necessity. When all were clad in gleaming bronze they opened the gates and went out, Odysseus leading.

They were now joined by Athene, Daughter of Zeus, who had assumed Mentor's appearance and voice. The patient, good Odysseus was overjoyed to see her. He turned at once to his dear son and said: 'Telemachus, when you find yourself in the thick of battle, where the best men prove their mettle, you will soon learn how not to disgrace your father's house. In all the world there has been none like ours for courage and manliness.'

And the thoughtful Telemachus replied: 'If you care to, father, you will see me in my present mood by no means disgracing my father's house, as you put it.'

Laertes was delighted. 'Dear gods!' he exclaimed. 'What a day this is to warm my heart! My son and grandson competing in valour!'

Athene of the flashing eyes came up to him now and said: 'Laertes, son of Arceisius, dearest of all my friends, pray to the Lady of the flashing eyes and to Father Zeus; then quickly poise your long spear and throw it.'

As she spoke Pallas Athene breathed vigour into him, and he immediately poised his long spear with a prayer to the Daughter of great Zeus, and threw it. He struck Eupeithes on the bronze cheek-guard of his helmet. The helmet failed to stop the spear; the bronze point pierced clean through and with a clang of armour Eupeithes crashed to the ground. Then Odysseus and his illustrious son attacked the front rank of the enemy and struck them with their swords and double-pointed spears. They would have destroyed them all and seen that none went home alive, if Athene, Daughter of aegis-bearing Zeus, had not raised a great cry and checked the whole throng: 'Ithacans, stop this disastrous fight and separate at once before blood[1] is shed.'

At Athene's cry the colour drained from their cheeks. In terror at the sound of her voice they let their weapons drop from their hands on to the ground. Then they turned and made for the city for dear life. The much-enduring good Odysseus raised a terrifying war-cry, gathered himself together and pounced on them like a swooping eagle. But at this moment Zeus flung a flaming thunderbolt which fell in front of the bright-eyed Daughter of that formidable Sire. Athene called out to Odysseus: 'Odysseus, favourite of Zeus, resourceful son of Laertes, hold your hand! Stop fighting your countrymen, in case you incur the wrath of Zeus the Thunderer.'

Odysseus obeyed her, and his heart rejoiced. Then Pallas Athene, Daughter of aegis-bearing Zeus, still using Mentor's form and voice for her disguise, established peace between the two sides.

1. One would expect 'more blood'. This, and the fact that Athene, advised by Zeus to make peace, urges on the battle and then tells the combatants to stop, are particularly glaring examples of inconsistencies in the narrative. See note on 23.296.

# Index and Glossary

This index contains only the proper names that occur in the *Odyssey*, with the exception of an entry under SUITORS. There is also an entry for 'the gods' under ZEUS. 'Etc.' indicates that where a term occurs frequently not all occurrences have been listed. Selective detail only is given for important people or places, which are indexed in capitals; in these cases, not all instances of the name are referenced.

The term *xenia* means 'welcoming and entertaining an outsider'.

Asopus, Boeotian river and river god, father of Antiope 11.260

Asphalion, attendant of Menelaus 4.216

Asteris, small island off Ithaca where the suitors planned to ambush Telemachus 4.846

ATHENE, goddess of female arts, intelligence and war, daughter of Zeus, patroness of Odysseus: and Ajax and the arms of Achilles 11.546–8; bestows strength/grace on Telemachus (2.12, 17.63–4), Laertes (24.367–74, 520–21), Odysseus (6.229–37, 8.19, 18.71, 23.155–62), Penelope (18.192–6); closeness to Odysseus 13.221–348; destroys Greeks on way home from Troy 3.135, 5.108–9; departs like a bird 1.320, 3.371–2, 22.239; disguised, as herald (8.8), a man (8.194), Mentes (1.105), Mentor (2.401, 22.205, 24.503, 548), water-carrier (7.20), shepherd (13.222), woman (13.288, 20.30–31); disguises Ithaca (13.190), Odysseus (13.396–438); grove in Phaeacia 6.291, 322; guides and inspires Telemachus 1.89–95, 272–96, 320–24, 2.380, 3.75–8, 13.470–74, 15.1–43; prompts/inspires Odysseus (13.393–6, 16.167–71, 17.360, 19.33, 20.47–51), Penelope (18.158, 188, 19.479, 21.1–4), Eurymachus (18.346), Ctesippus (20.284), suitors (20.345–6); rebukes Odysseus 22.226–35; respects Poseidon, so does not help Odysseus 6.328–31, 13.341–3; sends dream to Penelope (4.796), Nausicaa (6.29–46); tests Odysseus and Telemachus 22.237–8: waves aegis 22.297; works on behalf of Odysseus 1.45–62, 3.218–22, 5.382–7, 427, 437, 492, 6.112, 139–40, 7.14, 8.9, 193, 13.121, 302, 22.256, 273, 23.242, 344, 24.472, 530–48

Athens, city in Attica 3.278, 307, 7.80, 11.323

Atlas, Titan, father of Calypso 1.52, 7.245

Atreus, father of Agamemnon and Menelaus 1.35, etc.

Atrytone, unique title for Athene, meaning unknown: 4.762, 6.324

AUTOLYCUS, father of Anticleia, grandfather of Odysseus 11.85; names Odysseus 19.399–412; trickster and confidant of Hermes 19.394–8; 21.220, 24.334

Autonoe, maidservant of Penelope 18.182

Boethus, father of Menelaus' attendant Eteoneus, 4.31

Bootes, 'the Bear', a constellation 5.272

Cadmeians, people of Cadmus 11.276

Cadmus, a founder of Thebes (*see* Amphion (1) ), father of Ino 5.333

Dmetor, son of Iasus (2), King of Cyprus 17.443
Dodona, site of an oracle of Zeus in north-western Greece 14.327, 19.296
DOLIUS, old servant of Penelope 4.735; father of Melanthius (17.212, 22.159) and Melantho (18.322); works on Laertes' estate 24.222–498
Dorians, a people located by Odysseus on Crete 19.177
Dulichium, a large island in Odysseus' domain near Ithaca, whence fifty-two suitors come 1.246, 16.247 etc.
Dymas, a Phaeacian 6.22

Earth, mother of Tityus 7.324, 11.576
Echeneus, a Phaeacian elder 7.155, 11.342
Echephron, son of Nestor 3.413, 439
Echetus, a cruel Greek King 18.85, 116, 21.308
Egypt, the country 3.300, 4.43–581, 14.246–75, 17.426–48
Eidothee, sea-goddess, daughter of Proteus 4.366
Eileithyie, goddess of childbirth 19.188
Elatreus, 'Paddler', a Phaeacian 8.111, 129
Elatus, a suitor 22.267
Elis, district of north-western Peloponnese 4.635, 13.275, 15.298, 21.347, 24.431
Elpenor, companion of Odysseus, killed by falling off a roof 10.552, 11.51–7, 12.10
Elysian fields, home of the blessed, where Menelaus will go after death 4.563
Enipeus, river and river-god in Thessaly 11.238–40
Epeians, people from Elis 13.275, 15.298, 24.431
Epeius, maker of the Wooden Horse 8.493, 11.523
Eperitus, fictional name of Odysseus 24.306
Ephialtes, brother of Otus, giants killed by Apollo 11.308
Ephyre, unknown town somewhere in western Greece 1.259, 2.328
Epicaste (better known as Jocasta, the name Sophocles gives her in his play *Oedipus the King*, in which Oedipus also blinds himself and abandons the throne), wife and mother of Oedipus 11.271
Erebus, the underworld 10.528
Erechtheus, legendary hero-king of Athens 7.81
Erembians, people met by Menelaus on his travels 4.84
Eretmeus, 'Oarsman', a Phaeacian 8.112
Erinyes, *see* Furies
Eriphyle, wife of Amphiaraus, was bribed by Polyneices, son of Oedipus, to persuade her husband to join the war against Thebes, where he was fated to be killed 11.326
Erymanthus, mountain in north-western Peloponnese 6.103
Eteoneus, attendant of Menelaus 4.22, 31, 15.95

Ethiopia, a distant eastern land visited by Poseidon 1.22, 23, 4.84, 5.282, 287
Euanthes, father of Maron 9.197
Euboea, large island east of central Greece 3.174, 7.321
Euenor, father of Leocritus 2.242, 22.294
EUMAEUS, Odysseus' swineherd: care for Odysseus' property 14.524–33; cries 21.82, 223; disbelieves rumours 14.122–5, 363–4, 378–89; entertains Odysseus 14.45 ff.; grief at loss of Odysseus 14.40–44, 144–7, 169–70; grief at loss of Telemachus 14.174–82, 16.23–5; helps execute maidservants and mutilate Melanthius 22.454–76; hut 14.5–13; jeers at Melanthius 22.195–9; loves Telemachus like a father a son 16.14–22; no longer goes to the city 14.372–89, 15.374–9; pessimistic about Odysseus 14.61–71, 132–8, 365–71, 17.318–19; and pigs 14.14–22; plous 14.83–42, 420–48; prays for Odysseus to return 17.240–43, 20.238–9, 21.203–4; in prosperity 17.591–606; reunion with Odysseus 21.205–25; respect for masters 14.59–61, 17.187–9; story of life 15.403–84; takes bow to Odysseus 21.359–79; takes message to Penelope 16.154–452; trust in Telemachus and Penelope 17.389–91; understands *xenia* 14.57–9, 388–9; wants beggar-Odysseus to stay 15.334–6, 17.186–7
Eumelus, husband of Iphthime, Penelope's sister 4.798
Eupeithes, father of Antinous 1.383, 24.422–523, etc.
Euryades, a suitor 22.267
Euryalus, a Phaeacian who insulted Odysseus 8.115–58, 396–400
Eurybates, an attendant who went with Odysseus to Troy 19.247
EURYCLEIA, Odysseus' and Telemachus' nurse: bars doors of palace 21.387; bought by Laertes 1.429–33; complicity with Telemachus admitted 4.744–57; fears suitors 2.367–8; guards store-room 2.344–7; hopeful about Odysseus' return 4.754–7; informs on the faithless servants 22.423–7; loves Telemachus 1.434–5; naming ceremony for Odysseus 19.401–4; passionately greets Telemachus 17.315; pessimistic about Odysseus' return 2.365–6; protects Penelope 20.135–43; self-control 19.493–4; taken into confidence by Telemachus 2.337–76; tells Penelope of death of suitors 23.1–84; tended baby Odysseus 19.353–6, 482–3; triumph checked 22.407–12
Eurydamas, a suitor 18.297, 22.283
Eurydice, wife of Nestor 3.452

hide beggar's identity 16.300–304, 476–7, 23.30; mutilates Melanthius 22.473–6; need for Odysseus, 1.114–17, 2.58–61, 3.164–7; orders suitors out 1.368–80, 2.40–79, 138–45, 18.405–9; Orestes' parallel 1.298–307, 2.196–200, 3.195–7, 306–17; pessimism about Odysseus 1.166, 215–20, 231–43, 354, 3.208, 240–41, 15.268–9; praises Penelope 21.106–10; prays to Athene 2.262–6; rebukes Eumaeus (21.368–75), Penelope (1.346–59, 17.45–56, 20.129–33, 21.344–53, 23.97–103); rejects Antinous' hand 2.310–22; resembles Odysseus 1.207–12, 2.270–80, 3.120–25, 218–24, 4.140–54, 611, 14.175–7, 16.300, 24.512; reunion with Odysseus 16.172–221; sarcastic to suitors 17.392–408; stays in the palace 16.25–9; urges marriage on Penelope 20.341–2; visits Nestor 3.1 ff.; visits Menelaus 4.1 ff. (returns from Menelaus 15.1 ff.)

Telemus, prophet to the Cyclops 9.509

Telephus, father of Eurypylus 11.519

Telepylus, citadel of Lamus in Laestrygonian territory 10.82, 23.318

Temese, place in Cyprus invented (?) by Athene 1.184

Tenedos, small island near Troy 3.159

Terpius, father of Phemius 22.330

Thebes (1), city in Egypt 4.127

Thebes (2), city in Boeotia 10.492 etc.

Themis, goddess of law and order 2.68

THEOCLYMENUS, prophet from Argos: his story 15.222–55; lodged with Peiraeus, gives a favourable prophecy 15.508–46; prophesies to Penelope 17.151–65; vision of suitors' impending doom 20.345–72; welcomed aboard by Telemachus 15.256–86; welcomed into Odysseus' palace 17.71–84

Theseus, hero of Athens 11.322, 631

Thesprotians, people from north-western Greece 14.315–35, 16.65, 427, 17.526, 19.271–92

Thetis, goddess, mother by Peleus of Achilles 24.92

Thoas, Greek hero at Troy, son of Andraemon 14.499

Thon, Egyptian met by Menelaus 4.228

Thoon, 'Goahead', a Phaeacian 8.113

Thoosa, mother of Cyclops by Poseidon 1.71

Thrace, area of northern Greece 8.361

Thrasymedes, a son of Nestor 3.39, 414, 442, 448

Thrinacie, island of the Sun-god, where he kept his forbidden cattle 11.107, 12.127–35, 19.275

# PENGUIN CLASSICS

## *The Classics Publisher*

'Penguin Classics, one of the world's greatest series' JOHN KEEGAN

'I have never been disappointed with the Penguin Classics. All I have read is a model of academic seriousness and provides the essential information to fully enjoy the master works that appear in its catalogue' MARIO VARGAS LLOSA

'Penguin and Classics are words that go together like horse and carriage or Mercedes and Benz. When I was a university teacher I always prescribed Penguin editions of classic novels for my courses: they have the best introductions, the most reliable notes, and the most carefully edited texts' DAVID LODGE

'Growing up in Bombay, expensive hardback books were beyond my means, but I could indulge my passion for reading at the roadside bookstalls that were well stocked with all the Penguin paperbacks . . . Sometimes I would choose a book just because I was attracted by the cover, but so reliable was the Penguin imprimatur that I was never once disappointed by the contents.

Such access certainly broadened the scope of my reading, and perhaps it's no coincidence that so many Merchant Ivory films have been adapted from great novels, or that those novels are published by Penguin' ISMAIL MERCHANT

'You can't write, read, or live fully in the present without knowing the literature of the past. Penguin Classics opens the door to a treasure house of pure pleasure, books that have never been bettered, which are read again and again with increased delight' JOHN MORTIMER

# READ MORE IN PENGUIN

HOMER

# The Iliad

*'Look at me. I am the son of a great man. A goddess was my mother. Yet death and inexorable destiny are waiting for me'*

One of the foremost achievements in Western literature, Homer's *Iliad* tells the story of the darkest episode in the Trojan War. At its centre is Achilles, the greatest warrior-champion of the Greeks, and his refusal to fight after being humiliated by his leader Agamemnon. But when the Trojan Hector kills Achilles' close friend Patroclus, he storms back into battle to take revenge – although he knows this will ensure his own early death. Interwoven with this tragic sequence of events are powerfully moving descriptions of the ebb and flow of battle, of the domestic world inside Troy's besieged city of Ilium and of the conflicts between the gods on Olympus as they argue over the fate of mortals.

E. V. Rieu's acclaimed translation of *The Iliad* was one of the first titles published in Penguin Classics, and now has classic status itself. For this edition, Rieu's text has been revised, and a new introduction and notes by Peter Jones complement the original introduction.

*Translated by* E. V. RIEU
*Revised and updated by* PETER JONES *with* D. C. H. RIEU
*Edited with an introduction and notes by* PETER JONES